JUST FOR KICKS

A MILWAUKEE GROWLERS NOVEL

TRACY SOLHEIM

Sun Home Productions

This one is for Greg.
Thanks for making my dreams come true.

ACKNOWLEDGMENTS

As always, a big thank you to the home team for their unending support—and the wine! Many thanks to Laura Cifelli for your editing expertise. Also, thanks go to Anna Doll and Mary Mullenbach for helping to catch all those last-minute mistakes. Kudos for the perfect cover go to Lee Hyat. To my pal, Jeannie Moon, thanks for answering my panicked texts and phone calls. Your support means the world. Shout out to Ann Chandler, one of my fans on Facebook, who suggested the name Shear Envy for the salon. And to all the readers and bloggers who wrote asking for more football, this one is for you!

ONE

ACCORDING TO DEX Fletcher, the single best reason for wearing his clan's plaid was the easy access the kilt provided for a woman's soft, wandering fingers. Unfortunately, the hand currently creeping up the back of his thigh belonged to none other than his Milwaukee Growler's teammate, Kane Palmer. Executing a move that looked more at home in a mixed-martial arts ring than a professional football team's locker room, Dex pinned the annoying rookie to the floor before his fingers could do any more walking.

"Keep yer girlish paws off my arse, Palmer." Dex allowed his Scottish brogue to slip its normally tight leash as he snarled into the punter's ear. "If you want to palm some balls, I suggest ye hit the practice field and take some snaps so ye willnae let one sail over yer head like ye did last week." Based on the roar of gleeful laughter filling the locker room, his teammates were delighted to hear their place-kicker use his native tongue, so to speak.

The late August morning was sunny and warm, matching the light, relaxed mood at the Growlers' practice facility. With the season opener just ten days away, the league's flagship franchise possessed the swagger and confidence to match its exorbitant payroll. Players in various stages of dress milled around the locker room, filled with optimism as they prepared for practice.

Having just endured a two-hours-too-long photo shoot the team's promotional department had coerced him into, Dex wasn't feeling as jovial as the rest of the guys right now. He leaned an elbow into Palmer's back just to put the rookie in his place. *At least the kid could take a hit well*, he thought. Now all Palmer needed to do was back up his big mouth with his leg so the Growlers would continue to dominate other teams with their kicking game. Dex took great pride in his title as the league's leading scorer. Dubbed the 'Man with the Million Dollar Leg,' he fully intended to own the scoring honors for several more years to come.

Palmer grunted from beneath the weight of Dex's brawny body. "If you don't want to get felt up, stop wearing a skirt to work out in, Fletcher."

"Asshole rookie." Dex jumped to his feet. "It can only be called a skirt if I wear something under it." His smug declaration prompted more laughter from the other players, with a few catcalls and shrill whistles thrown in for good measure.

"You know, Palmer, word around town is Fletcher's balls are too big to fit into a pair of jeans, so he has to wear that damn wrap," Luke Kessler, the team's star wide receiver, called out from across the aisle. "If you don't believe me, check out the size of his cup."

Palmer reached for Dex's locker presumably to do just that, but Dex shoved the rookie's arm away. "What did I tell you about those wandering hands?"

"No need to get testy, old man. I *wouldnae* steal yer codpiece." Palmer's poor attempt at imitating Dex's accent had the players cracking up yet again.

Shaking his head, Dex turned his back on the heckling of his teammates, mooning them all when he unwrapped his kilt from around his waist. A coach's whistle blew, signaling the start of practice. The lingering laughter was drowned out by the sound of cleats tapping against the concrete floor as the players headed down the hall to the waiting field.

"You know the skirt doesn't bother me as much as the knee socks with the little tassels on them." Sitting in a metal folding chair in front of the locker beside his, Trey Van Horn, the Growlers quarterback, jerked his chin toward Dex's stocking clad feet. "You better be careful not to wear those during a game, or the league office will fine you for a uniform violation."

Dex shot his teammate the bird before tugging on his compression shorts, followed by a pair of nylon running shorts. "I stole them from your last girlfriend. Her ma is probably miffed she had to buy a new pair for the lass's school uniform."

Van Horn chuckled. The quarterback had a reputation for liking his arm candy to be fresh-faced socialites. Dex was one of the few people within Van Horn's inner circle who saw through his teammate's act. But since Dex had his own reasons for not pursuing any romantic entanglements, he was content not to cast any stones at his friend's character.

"I'll give you fifty bucks for your mathletes if you wear those girly socks to practice," Kessler said as he passed by Dex's locker on his way to the field. The brash receiver was the main instigator of crazy dares among the Growlers. But Kessler always put his money where his mouth was. For his part, Dex never said no to a contribution to his favorite charity.

"You're on." He pulled his cleats on over the thick wool knee stockings. The shoe on his kicking foot was smaller and tighter than the one on his other foot, but it was just the way he liked it. He yanked a Growlers' T-shirt over his head before he stood, then shrugged into his practice jersey.

Van Horn handed Dex his helmet and turned to the wide receiver. "You should have dared him to wear his kilt to practice, Kessler."

"Nah," their teammate replied as the three men made their way outside. "There are a bunch of pee-wee league kids visiting practice today. No need to scare them with a glimpse of Fletcher's ugly *bullocks*."

Kessler's Scottish accent made Van Horn laugh as he shoved

his helmet on his head. The quarterback slapped Dex on the shoulder and jogged onto the center of the field to take his place as the rightful ruler of this kingdom of jocks.

Grinning broadly, Dex dropped down beside Kessler onto the turf, reveling in the bright sunshine, the brotherhood of his teammates, and the promise of the season ahead. He loved playing this game, playing for this team. Football was his sanctuary. If he had to endure an exile from his beloved Scotland, he couldn't think of a place he'd rather be than on the field with these guys.

The trainers and coaches led the players through a series of stretches and conditioning exercises before they split them up into offensive and defensive units. Dex lined up behind the special teams' offensive line to practice faking field goals and muffed snaps. Then Van Horn held the ball while Dex kicked it through the uprights several times. After that, it was Palmer's turn. He worked on his punting by taking several reps with the Growlers' long-snapper. After six weeks of watching Palmer punt, Dex had to grudgingly admit the team hadn't wasted a seventh-round draft pick on the mouthy kid from Oklahoma.

The scrimmages ended, and the players and coaches dispersed into smaller practices within each specialty. With the rest of the team involved in other drills, he and Palmer made their way toward the locker room. They would emerge an hour later when the team reconvened for thirty minutes of full-contact play.

If Dex enjoyed the camaraderie of his Growler teammates, he loved the quiet solitude of the locker room more. He'd grown up the studious son of a math professor and a primary school headmaster. While always a natural athlete, the muscle he exercised the most growing up was his brain. The idea that he'd one day be the highest-paid professional athlete at his position—playing with the wrong kind of football, no less—never once entered a young Declan Fletcher's imagination.

Until fate intervened.

"Legend has it you grew up in St. Andrews." Palmer took a Big Bertha putter out of his locker and began tapping a golf ball into a plastic cup he'd laid on its side. "The freakin' birthplace of golf." The rookie sighed in reverence as he bent over the ball.

Dex let out his own beleaguered breath before dragging his eyes away from the chess set in his locker. For six seasons, he and Palmer's predecessor had matched wits over a chessboard while the rest of the team duked it out on the practice field. Palmer didn't look like he'd sit still long enough to play a game of tic-tac-toe, much less a game of chess.

Resigned, he grabbed his iPad out of his gym bag and headed for one of the leather sofas scattered around the locker room. If nothing else, he could come up with some math drills for the team of high school students he worked with each week. Unfortunately, the rookie punter hadn't picked up on the fact that Dex liked to brood in peace. Palmer dogged his steps across the room as Dex stretched out on the sofa.

"Don't get me wrong. I love football, but not as much as I love golf," Palmer was saying. "If I play my cards right, I can build my nest egg here in the league and, when I hang up my cleats, I'll join the professional golfers' seniors' tour." The ball smacked against the back of the cup from ten feet out. "Life is good when you can earn a living playing a game, huh, Fletcher?"

I'm gonna earn my keep playing a game, Dex. Ain't that pure dead brilliant?

Memories of another young athlete, as boastful and arrogant as Palmer, suddenly swam in front of Dex's eyes. Niall's cheeky smile and brilliant talent had been the pride of St. Andrews. The familiar tightening began in his chest. He squeezed his eyelids shut to block out the image, but it was no use. There was no way to exorcise the past from his conscience. It—along with the guilt—had burned a hole deep within his soul.

"Hey, Fletcher," one of the trainers called into the locker room. "You've got company in the lobby. A woman."

Palmer let loose a taunting whistle before refocusing on his putting. Dex swung his legs down to the floor, grateful for the distraction from his thoughts of home and the people he'd never be able to face again. Other than reporters, it was highly unusual for someone to visit him at the practice facility. Especially a woman.

His thoughts immediately jumped to the young students he tutored in mathematics each week. They were kids with difficult lives caused by unfortunate circumstances. They were also Dex's outlet, his way to atone for the sins in his earlier life. A pang of unease raced up his spine as Dex wondered if one of them was in trouble.

Another form of dread gripped him as he made his way out of the locker room, and he quickly began to catalog all the women he'd been with the past several months. He'd been up-front with all of them. His commitment level was set firmly at no-strings-attached sex. The seven—or was it eight—women he'd hooked up with had been in complete agreement. Of course, it wouldn't be the first time in history a woman fed him a line just to get at what was beneath his kilt.

Damn it.

Increasing his pace, he navigated the long hallway leading to the lobby. He blew out a breath of relief when he rounded the corner and saw his personal assistant, Marlene, waiting near the reception desk. Then he noticed the normally unflappable older woman wringing her hands. Whatever couldn't wait until he got home was clearly important. His gut seized as he thought of his family in Scotland, many of whom he hadn't seen for nearly ten years.

"What's wrong?" Dex asked once he reached her side.

"I'm sorry to bother you," she whispered, her eyes darting back and forth behind her wire-rimmed glasses. "I didn't know what else to do."

"Tell me," he commanded. "Is it my father? Or my ma?" *Christ, please don't let it be my little sister, Annis.*

Marlene placed a hand over his on the counter. "Oh, no, Dex, your family is fine. It's not that at all."

His relief was palpable. The Fletcher family had endured

enough pain. Whatever the 'trouble' was that had Marlene so distressed, it couldn't be as dire as Dex's greatest mistake.

He reached out and gave Marlene's shoulders a gentle squeeze. "Relax and breathe. Whatever it is, it can be fixed."

She glared over his shoulder. "I'm not so sure about that. This guy says you're in trouble."

"What guy?"

"Perhaps I should explain." A slender man dressed in a navy suit stepped out from behind the display case housing the Growlers championship trophies. He extended his hand before pulling it back when confronted with Dex's fierce glare. "I'm Victor Figueroa. It's an honor to meet you, Dex. Can I call you Dex? I mean, I'm from Chicago, so the Bears are my team and all, but any football fan would be honored to meet you."

Dex narrowed his eyes even more at the guy's rambling. He didn't know what in the hell was going on, but the last thing he needed was a crazy Bears fan trying to sniff his jockstrap. "And how exactly do you fit into this story, Figueroa?"

"Actually, it's Agent Figueroa." He reached inside his suit jacket and pulled out a leather ID holder. "I'm with U.S. Immigration and Customs Enforcement, and I'm here to facilitate your deportation back to Scotland."

IT SEEMED LIKE a good idea at the time. But now that Andi Larsen was sitting in the attorney's office, she was seriously second-guessing her decision to allow sweet Mrs. Hilbert to talk her into meeting with her son. Not because the man was aiming an annoyed glare at both women—there was a glass desk the size of a skating rink separating them, fortunately. But because she wasn't sure she wanted her dirty laundry aired out in public. The embarrassment of her few friends knowing was bad enough, but this man, a man who possessed not only the common sense but the aptitude to survive law school and pass the bar, would also know her shame.

There was no way he wouldn't believe she was gullible, stupid, or worse, reckless.

And she was none of those. Well, except for maybe the reckless part. But only a little bit. And she was working on it. Really, she was.

"Mom, I've told you a hundred times I'm not that kind of a lawyer."

Beside Andi, Mrs. Hilbert squared her shoulders. "Of course, you are a lawyer, Kurt. I paid for you to go to law school." She donned a proud smile and turned to Andi. "Did I tell you he originally went to school to study opera? His voice is divine. It will give you goosebumps. Sing something for her Kurt."

"Mother!"

Andi flinched at his yell. She was definitely sporting goosebumps all right. Although divine wouldn't be the word Andi would choose to define the man right at this moment. Peeved was a more apt description. She glanced sheepishly at the lawyer. His face was pink with frustration. A sudden image of him donning a Viking helmet complete with horns and yellow braids while belting out a song in some indistinguishable language on stage flashed before her eyes. Stocky and tall, he would make an intimidating Norseman. He was certainly doing a good job of intimidating Andi.

His mother? Not so much. The woman had more than four decades of practice ignoring her son's antics. She simply arched an eyebrow at him. With an anguished sigh, he ran his fingers over his bald head as though trying to summon some sort of follicle that would rid him of both women. Andi was about to oblige him when Mrs. Hilbert's hand on her arm stayed her in the chair. For such a petite lady, she had the grip of a python.

"Kurt." Mrs. Hilbert attempted to soothe him. "Andi needs our help. It doesn't matter what kind of lawyer you are. I raised you to be kind to others."

Andi had to hand it to the older woman; she employed guilt with as much precision as a chef at a Benihana wielded a knife. Her son caved instantly.

"Okay." He blew out a resigned sigh. "Let's hear your story, Annie, and I'll see if I can make some calls to an attorney who will best fit your case."

"Andi," both she and Mrs. Hilbert said at the same time.

"My name is Andi. Andi Larsen," she repeated.

"Apologies." He studied her speculatively. "Just how do you two know each other, anyway?"

It was a fair question given the fifty years separating the two women.

"She works at Shear Envy salon, dear."

As if by reflex, Mrs. Hilbert fingered her sleek, ash-blonde bob, reminding Andi that she needed to order more 9v color. She wasn't the stylist who did the older woman's hair, but as the salon's receptionist and office manager, she made a point to ensure every client who walked in the door received top-notch service.

"You're a hairstylist?"

"No. I'm—"

"Andi wants to be an entrepreneur," Mrs. Hilbert interrupted. "She makes the most wonderful soaps using all-natural ingredients. They're luxurious and very pretty. I gave you some for your birthday. Don't you remember? The lemongrass and lavender ones. They're meant to help you relax. I worry about you. He's always very stressed," she confided to Andi.

As if his tight mouth and flushed cheeks hadn't already given that fact away.

"Oh, I know," Mrs. Hilbert continued, excitement making her voice rise a few octaves. "Once we fix Andi's legal issues, maybe you can help her get on *Shark Tank*." She turned to Andi. "My son works with famous people all the time. But when you go on the show, don't let Kevin buy into your company. Hold out for Laurie. She seems nice."

The lawyer groaned in annoyance at his mother's meandering tale.

"I'm a senior at Marquette," Andi explained before he

summoned a security guard to escort her out. "I work in the salon during the day while I earn my business degree at night."

"That's admirable."

"You might want to hold that thought until I finish my story."

The corners of his mouth wobbled as if he were biting back a smile. Or a scowl. It was hard to tell. He excelled at a poker face, which was probably an advantage in his profession.

"Your mom is right. I want to open my own company someday. That's why I've been careful to pay my tuition with grants and scholarships. It's taken a few extra years that way, but at least I won't have any debt when I graduate. My professor says the lack of loan debt will give me a big advantage when I apply for funding with a venture capital firm to kick-start my business."

That had been the plan, anyway.

"Why do I sense a 'but' coming?"

"Because her ex is a butt," Mrs. Hilbert interjected. Then the woman laughed. "That's kind of *punny*, isn't it?"

Her son ignored her, keeping his focus on Andi. He nodded for her to go on, but her throat tightened up with embarrassment. It was bad enough she'd been duped so easily that no venture capitalist would even look at lending her a dime. Saying it out loud in front of a perfect stranger somehow seemed to make it even more real.

"Tell him," Mrs. Hilbert coaxed. "He can't help unless you tell him the whole story."

She sincerely doubted the man in front of her would be able to help her, but she'd taken an hour off work to come here. Nothing ventured, nothing gained.

"Kenny, my ex-boyfriend, somehow figured out how to access my financial aid account. He took out multiple public and private student loans in my name and kept the money for himself."

"How much?"

These words were harder to get past her thick throat. The enormity of what she now owed both angered and frightened her. "Seventy thousand dollars."

He whistled in surprise. "You don't need a lawyer. You need a cop."

"I've been to the police. They took my statement, but since Kenny left the state with the money, they told me my case isn't a priority." That was after making her feel naive and like she deserved to be conned. Her jaw clenched at the memory of leaving the police station feeling mortified.

The lawyer's face grew hard. "They should have referred you to someone else who could help you. Where did this Kenny guy go?"

"Las Vegas." She felt her cheeks begin to grow warm. "He bragged to a friend he was invited to sit in on a high-stakes poker tournament. He conned his way in using my money, figuring he'd be rich by now. But Kenny has never won at anything."

"Well, that's a life lesson they can't teach you in business school."

Mrs. Hilbert patted Andi's hand. The gesture of reassurance made her feel even more humiliated. Her son had drawn the same conclusion as the police, that she didn't have the bandwidth to know when someone is taking advantage of her.

Except she had known better.

She just chose to ignore her head, instead basking in Kenny's charm and the idea that someone finally wanted to have her in their life. Both were survivors of the foster care system, except his transition into adulthood was a bit bumpier than hers. False bravado and charisma could only carry a person so far. Andi assumed the role of parent and provider while he began to brood and act out like a child. Still, he was all she had, and she refused to give up hope that with a little love and guidance, he could succeed. Together they would show everyone who labeled them as cast-offs that pedigree didn't matter. It didn't take long for her to realize while Kenny wanted to rise above his past, he didn't really want to put in the work to achieve success. Feeling sorry for him, she let him hang around and mooch off her for too long.

And now she was paying the price.

"Do you have any family that can help you out?" the lawyer asked.

"No. It's just me."

And she was more determined than ever to keep it that way. *People always let you down.* She'd had that lesson drilled into her for her entire life. When the foster care system had cast her off, turning her out into the "real world" at eighteen with whatever she could squeeze into a state-issued duffel bag and nothing more, she'd made a vow never to have to rely on anyone ever again. She'd slipped up with Kenny. There wouldn't be a second time. From here on out, she was a one-woman show.

Mrs. Hilbert's son scrubbed his face with his hand before speaking. "Okay, here is what we are going to do. First, I'll make some calls to the police to follow up on your complaint. Then I'll ask around to see if I can find you an attorney who'll take your case pro-bono. Does this Kenny dude have a job?"

Andi shook her head. "His only income is from selling vintage shoes on eBay."

The poker face was long gone now. His eyebrows nearly rolled over his bald head at the absurdity of Kenny's profession, if you could call it that.

"Then I'm afraid the likelihood of you recovering your loan debt from him will be nil. I'll have to find an attorney who can deal with the bureaucracy of the Department of Education. Then we'll follow up with the police to get him prosecuted for identity theft."

She'd already resigned herself not to expect to see a red cent from Kenny. Still, she was grateful the man in front of her was willing to help her clear her name as well as her credit score. Her name was all she had left.

"Why can't you handle her case?" Mrs. Hilbert demanded.

"Because those famous people you're so fond of telling everyone I know are my clients. I'm a sports agent, Mother. Not a trial attorney!"

"It's fine," Andi interjected before the other lady spoiled it for her. "I'm grateful for anything you can do for me." It was her turn to pat Mrs. Hilbert's hand. "Really."

He picked up his pen. "How do I get in touch—"

"You can't go in there," a voice shouted just before the office door was nearly ripped off its hinges.

Ignoring the warning, a man stormed in, his hands balled in fists.

"Oh, my," Mrs. Hilbert exclaimed.

'Oh, my' was right. The man making his way into the room was compact and rugged, with broad shoulders, and a swagger that might have been cocky were he not so distressed. His thick, dark hair had been finger-combed until it practically stood on end. But it was what he was wearing that made her mouth gape. The interloper was dressed in an actual kilt showcasing a pair of well-sculpted legs beneath its hem. A disheveled dress shirt was hastily tucked in above it. He resembled an untamed Highlander from centuries past—one with a very wild edge that seemed to be a siren's call to parts of her body if the fluttering deep within her belly was any indication

The attorney shot out of his chair. "Declan? Is everything all right?"

"Hell, no," the other man shouted. "I'm being bloody deported!"

A lick of desire danced down Andi's spine at the sound of his craggy voice before his words registered. And she thought she had problems. Clearly, his case was more urgent. Not only that, but the fewer people who learned of her embarrassing predicament, the better. She began to stand so the attorney could focus on the other man.

"Sit," Mrs. Hilbert commanded while jutting up her chin. "We were here first."

The Highlander jerked to a stop at the sound of the old woman's voice. Obviously, he was so consumed with his own dilemma, he didn't realize there were others present. Andi's breath hitched when his gaze landed on her. Pale, dove-gray eyes framed by thick dark lashes quickly assessed her from head to toe and back up again. The look she saw within them startled her more than his intimate appraisal. Fiery desperation burned in their depth, but there was something else, too. Something Andi recognized instantly. She saw the same expression every time she looked in a mirror: loneliness. The deep, isolated lonesomeness Andi felt even in a crowded room.

Mrs. Hilbert wiggled her fingers at him. "Nice to see . . . so much of you again, Declan."

"Deported? What are you talking about?" The attorney's question had the Highlander breaking his gaze and refocusing his attention to the matter at hand.

"An ICE agent showed up at the practice facility." He waved a bunch of papers in front of the lawyer's face. "He came to give me my final deportation notice in person. My bloody renewal paperwork for my visa was never filed. The notices weren't ever delivered to me. Damn it. I pay you handsomely to take care of that for me, Kurt. Now I have three days to clean up this mess or I'll be sent home to Scotland. For *six whole months!*"

The attorney was frantically punching keys on his laptop. "This can't be. The paperwork was completed two months ago. I handed it off to Nicole to file with ICE."

The Highlander gripped the back of his neck while releasing a string of angry words in a language Andi didn't understand.

"Oh, for crying out loud, Dex." The attorney glared at him. "Don't tell me you're the one behind Nicole's emotional breakdown that caused her to quit."

"Hey! I made it clear up front there was never going to be anything more than one night!"

Mrs. Hilbert tittered. Her son groaned. Andi felt her cheeks flush. Her thoughts immediately conjured up carnal images of the sexy man before her slowly unwrapping his kilt and strutting toward her in all his muscled glory. She sucked in a ragged breath, just barely resisting the urge to fan herself. She really needed to stop watching that *Magic Mike* movie on cable.

For his part, the Highlander looked sheepish, dragging his fingers through his hair. "Now what do I do? The season starts in a week and a half."

The attorney sighed. "Let me make some calls. There's got to be some way to get around this."

"Of course there is," Mrs. Hilbert chimed in. "It's simple, really."

Both men turned to stare at her expectantly.

"Dex needs to get married." She beamed in triumph before turning to Andi. "And aren't we lucky we have the perfect bride right here."

TWO

DEX RECOILED AT THE SUGGESTION.

Married.

The very word gave him the bloody shakes. A loving companion, a family, happiness. Those weren't in the cards for him. Not after he'd taken all that away from Niall.

Too bad his agent's wacky mother didn't know that.

"Problem solved." Mrs. Hilbert punctuated her declaration with a saucy wink.

Her companion, on the other hand, remained wide-eyed and mute. Blue eyes, the color of the cornflowers in his gran's window boxes, studied him overtly. Potent arousal flickered within their depths before she quickly doused it. Not surprising. He was used to that look from women.

What did surprise him was the swift crackle of awareness that traveled up his spine when their gazes clashed. This woman was so far from his type it was almost laughable. Slim and petite, with a slender chin and pixie-like ears to go with her doe eyes, she was more like one of those wee highland fairies his little sister was always searching for in the garden, right down to the pink hair pulled back in a loose ponytail.

"Actually," Kurt was saying. "That's not a bad idea. It could work."

Dex opened his mouth to object, but the fairy beat him to it.

"Whoa, hold on just one minute." She jumped from her seat. "I came in here for legal advice." Those blue eyes grew even wider as her gaze frantically darted around the room. "Sure, my situation may be a little dire, but not dire enough to marry some dude who's aged out of a boy band."

Not dire enough to marry who? What the bloody hell did she mean by that? Someone needed to inform the little pixie that women had actually proposed to *him*, thank you very much. And what was this bullshit behind her 'boy band' insult?

"What did you just call me?" he demanded.

She gestured to his plaid. "Halloween is two months away, Jamie Fraser. If you're not in a boy band, what's up with the skirt?" Her eyebrows went up a fraction. "Unless you work at one of those strip clubs. In that case, no way am I marrying a man who spends more time getting waxed than I do."

A low growl escaped the back of his throat as he took a step closer to her. "How many times do I have to tell you Sassenachs? It's *not a bloody skirt!*"

"Fireworks already." Mrs. Hilbert clapped her hands together with glee. "This is going to be one passionate marriage."

Kurt stepped between him and the fairy. "That's enough, Mother." He pointed to a chair. "Sit," he ordered. "Both of you."

Dex locked eyes with the annoying pink-haired woman. She notched up her chin but took her seat as directed. Reluctantly, he sank down into the chair Kurt indicated.

"Dex," Kurt said. "This is Annie Larsen."

"Andi," she snapped. "My name is Andi. A. N. D. I."

Kurt rubbed his head. "Sorry, *Andi* Larsen. Andi is a friend of my mother, and she is in a bit of a financial bind right now."

The revelation had her shoulders sinking a notch.

"Andi," Kurt continued. "This is my client, Declan Fletcher. Dex is the placekicker for the Milwaukee Growlers football team. Fortunately for you, he needs a wife temporarily, and he's got the funds to solve your dilemma."

Dex braced himself for the requisite fawning, but she remained stoic. He couldn't decide if he was irritated or relieved that she didn't seem to care he was famous and wealthy.

"So, to clarify, he's not a stripper," she commented. "Just an over-paid professional athlete." She jutted her chin toward his plaid. "Who makes unusual fashion choices, presumably for attention."

Irritation quickly won out.

"He's Scottish, Andi. The kilt is his schtick," Mrs. Hilbert explained with a loud whisper.

He let out another low growl. "For your information, there seems to be a dress code clause in my damn contract." He glared at his agent who had the grace to look chagrined. "It stipulates that I wear my plaid for bloody photoshoots. I don't trot the blasted thing out every day."

Mrs. Hilbert tsked. "Of course not. This is Milwaukee. I imagine . . . *things* could get very cold under there."

The fairy's lips twitched. Kurt groaned. Dex felt like his head was going to explode. He leaped from the chair.

"I have three days to get this situation resolved, Kurt. Can we please find another room where we come up with a solution that doesn't involve me getting handfasted?"

Kurt held up a palm. "Hear me out, Dex. Whatever we come up with is going to take longer than three days. Not to mention involving a lot of favors and publicity. If you want to avoid going home to Scotland, a fake marriage is probably the quickest way. It will just be a formality so you can keep your visa, and we can sort this all out at the end of the season."

"And this is who you pick to be my pretend wife? A tiny fey creature?" Dex gestured to his head. "With pink hair, no less? Do you really think anyone will believe I'm daft enough to marry some pixie fairy?"

Andi rolled her eyes at his description. At least she could take what he dished out. Mrs. Hilbert shot him a horrified look, however.

"It's a matter of being in the right place at the right time," his agent argued. "Andi needs you as much as you need her. All we need to do is draw up a prenup stating the terms, and you two can jet off to Vegas tomorrow, get married, and you'll be back in time for practice on Monday."

"She marries me to get out of debt, but what's to stop her from selling me out the next time she lands in 'a bit of a financial bind'?" Dex asked.

"It wasn't my fault!" she declared fiercely.

"The prenup will state she can't divulge any of this to the media or anyone else, now or in the future," Kurt interrupted her. "Not to mention the fact that she'll be complicit in a federal crime."

"Wait, no one said anything about breaking the law." She shook her head. "Yet another reason why I am so not doing this."

At least she had good judgment. Whatever she'd gotten herself into, it likely wasn't illegal. He felt a small measure of relief at the knowledge.

Kurt stared her down. "I'll give you seventy thousand reasons why you should do it, Andi."

Dex rocked back on his heels. "Seventy thousand dollars! I'd say that's a wee bit more than a financial bind."

Her shoulders slumped again.

"It definitely is," Kurt added. "And getting out from under that kind of debt could take a lifetime for most people, Andi. I'd think very carefully before I said no. I've known Dex for ten years. He's a decent guy. You only have to play the part of a loving couple in public. The rest of the time, you can live your own life."

The room grew quiet as she studied the floor intently.

"How long? How long would we carry out this ridiculous charade?" she murmured after a long moment.

"Six months should do it," Kurt answered. "By then, the season will be over, and we can readdress the situation."

Mrs. Hilbert reached over and patted her hand. "Andi, honey, the law doesn't stipulate that the people entering marriage have to be in love. If that were the case, half the marriages in the world would be illegal at some point. You just need to look at this as a simple business transaction. Nothing more."

Dex had to concede that the older woman made a valid point. If he looked at the situation as simply a means to an end, it could work. Too bad it wasn't in his wheelhouse to ignore all the other probabilities for failure.

"Can Tinkerbell and I have a few minutes alone?" he surprised himself by asking.

She shot him a frosty look, but at least she remained in her chair. He still wasn't sure this was a good idea. But it beat the alternative of returning to Scotland.

That he could never do.

"Come on, Mom." Kurt helped his mother from her chair. "Let's give them the room."

At the sound of the door closing behind him, Dex slid back into the chair he'd vacated and stretched his legs out in front of him.

She sighed wearily. "Surely, there are a bevy of women vying for the title of Mrs. Declan Fletcher within your contact list. I mean, just those legs alone should be incentive enough."

"Aye," he replied. "Sadly, all of them are more interested in the fame and glamour that goes with being the wife of a professional football player. You just want my money."

She snorted. "Don't kid yourself. They want your money, too."

"True." He surprised himself yet again by laughing. "That's twice you've mentioned my legs, lass."

Damn. Now he was flirting with her.

Her nose twitched slightly. "They are your money makers."

She had him there.

"Have you no family to help you?"

She shook her head. "It's just me."

Her eyes dared him to pity her. He doubted she'd allow it. Little Orphan Andi was stronger than she looked. She likely had to be. Perhaps this make-believe marriage could work after all. Given how she sparred with him, there was something more than air between those cute little ears. But then how had she managed to owe seventy thousand dollars? He was about to ask when she stood from her chair.

"Look, I need to get back to work."

He stood, too. "We haven't resolved anything."

Sweat began to bead on the back of his neck. Everything in his being told him not to let her leave. Without her, he'd be sent back home to face his past. Crazy as it sounded, a fake marriage to a pink-haired nymph he barely knew seemed the lesser of two evils.

"Do you really want to do this?"

He was surprised at his body's powerful reaction to her softly uttered question.

"What choice do I have? What choice do you have?" he added, hoping to guilt her into agreeing.

Her eyes darted past him, taking in the panoramic view of Lake Michigan afforded by the exorbitant fees Kurt charged his clients. She was silent for several long heartbeats before responding.

"We'd get married in Las Vegas?"

"I believe that would be the most expedient, yes."

She nodded. "Fine. Have Mrs. Hilbert text me the details."

And with that, his future make-believe bride walked out the door.

"I CAN'T BELIEVE you're going through with this." Clive was still wearing an expression of worry as he looked back at her from the front seat.

His concern was ironic since she'd spent the years they were in foster care looking out for the scrawny kid whose homosexuality ended up getting him picked on more times than not. He'd been Lenny back then before emerging from the system out, proud, and with a new name fit for a genius with scissors, a razor, and hair color. It wasn't long before others recognized his talent and he had a list of clients who traveled from as far as Chicago. When he decided to open his own salon, he sought out financing from a local bank but got more than he bargained for in his partner, Daniel, an investment banker.

"I can believe it," Daniel chimed in from the driver's seat as he took the exit for Mitchell airport. "Have you seen that guy's eyes? They're so gorgeous it's practically a crime. And his legs?" He lifted a hand off the wheel to fan himself. "Damn, that man is sexy."

Andi could relate. When that slow smile broke over Dex's face yesterday, it transformed him from the brooding Highlander to a gorgeous heartthrob. Feeling a traitorous flush begin to warm her body, she'd hightailed it out of the lawyer's office before she did something stupid. Not that agreeing to a fake marriage with him wasn't stupid.

Or reckless.

"Don't worry, Clive. We're not getting married." She'd already violated the terms of the contract—*prenup*—she'd signed this morning by sharing the details with Clive and Daniel. But they were her family, such as it was. And, if she was jetting off to Las Vegas with a total stranger, she at least needed to let them know where to look for her body. "He's probably found someone more suitable by now. Or paid someone off to get his visa renewed."

That was *not* disappointment in her voice. After Google searching her fake-fiancé late last night, she'd confirmed her theory that he had a revolving door of arm candy in his life. Judging by the adoring looks on their faces when they'd been photographed with him, all of them would throw down for the right to be his wife—

pretend or not. Not only that, but any one of them would come with a cheaper price tag than Andi.

"I doubt he'll even be on the flight. But I will. I'm not going to pass up a free ticket to Las Vegas where I can track down that sleazeball Kenny and get him to own up to what he's done."

She didn't miss the look the two men exchanged.

"What?" she demanded.

"Sweetheart, that loser isn't ever going to own up to what he's done." Clive left out the I-told-you-so, but she heard it in his tone nonetheless.

Unlike her, he had seen through Kenny right away. Andi hated to think her inability to pick up the warning signs about her dead-beat ex was due to jealousy over Clive finding his 'family' with Daniel. Had the prospect of being alone again made her tone-deaf to her friend's warnings? Apparently. But that was a mistake she didn't plan on making ever again.

"Kenny committed fraud," she insisted. "One way or another, he's going to pay for what he's done."

Daniel pulled up to the kiss and ride. "Las Vegas is a big place. How will you even find him?"

Sliding across the backseat, she tapped her phone. "He's all over social media boasting about some big poker game tonight. Obviously, he hasn't lost all the money he stole."

Clive pulled open her door for her. "There's no messing with you when you're on a mission. I almost feel sorry for the piece of chicken-shit."

"At least enjoy your wedding night," Daniel teased from the front seat.

She blew him a kiss. "Not gonna be a wedding, Danny-boy."

The nerves she'd been so valiantly trying to hide bubbled up when she turned to face Clive. Her childhood friend saw through her immediately. He pulled her into a fierce hug.

"You don't have to do this," he murmured against her hair. "Daniel is brilliant with money. Let us find a way to help you."

Shaking her head, she pulled out of his embrace. "I can't let you do that. I've been standing up for myself since I was ten. I'm not going to stop now."

He smoothed down the arms of her ice blue Abercrombie blouse. She paired it with dark jeggings and Steve Madden flats she'd found at a consignment store. Her grandmother's silver cross was the only piece of jewelry she wore.

"I wish you'd let me dye your hair back," Clive said. "You'd still have your pretty blonde color were it not for that hair show last week."

"It's fine. Besides, if anyone compliments me, I can tell them it's your work. I even have a Shear Envy T-shirt I can wear in the casino."

He smiled warily. "Just don't do anything too crazy, okay?"

"Promise." She gripped the handle of her borrowed carry-on with a bit more determination than she felt. "I'll text you when I get there."

With another wave to Daniel, she made her way inside and followed the signs to security. The airport was smaller than she'd imagined, and before she had time to change her mind, she'd reached the TSA checkpoint. Her stomach fluttered as she stepped in line only to have it bottom out when a male voice spoke behind her.

"I thought you might chicken out."

She spun on her heel. Declan Fletcher inched up nearer to her in the line. A Milwaukee Brewers baseball cap shoved low on his head, and a pair of wire-framed glasses did nothing to diminish his virility, but she suspected they were his attempt at a disguise. Not that Andi objected. The less she saw of Declan Fletcher's body, the better.

"I didn't recognize you without the . . . kilt."

The corners of his mouth turned up. Whether he was amused or irked, she couldn't tell because he was already stepping ahead of her in line.

"We need to hurry. Our flight boards in ten minutes."

Andi followed the lead of the other passengers as they passed through security, making sure to mimic exactly what they did. The last thing she wanted to do was embarrass herself. She was still slipping on her shoes when his toned legs began to stride toward the gate. Dragging her bag behind her, she had to trot to keep up.

What she should have done was turn around and head right back out to the kiss and ride. She'd been so sure he wouldn't show. That he'd find another solution. And now, here he was, seemingly eager to jet off to Vegas and marry her.

Her conscience nagged her. She couldn't marry him. But she couldn't afford to fly to Vegas to confront Kenny. And now that she had the opportunity, she was reluctant to let it go.

The gate attendant was announcing first-class passengers could board. Dex made his way to the kiosk and scanned the boarding pass on his phone. Andi's hand trembled when she followed suit. Her heart began to hammer wildly as she trailed him down the jetway.

His attempt at a disguise didn't fool the flight attendant who greeted him with a smile that held the promise of extra attention during their trip. Unbidden annoyance flared in Andi's chest, but it was quickly trampled out by dread. The cabin was a lot smaller than she expected. He stopped at the first row, one that would afford him ample leg room, but was awfully close to the door for Andi's comfort.

"Slide in." He indicated the seat next to the window.

She hesitated. Everything about this was a bad idea.

"Hurry, before the rest of the passengers begin boarding and get a good look at us."

Someone greeted the flight attendant behind her. Andi sucked up her courage, handed him her bag to stow, and took her seat. He was beside her in an instant. His muscled body blocked her escape route. Her breath began to saw through her lungs. A stream of passengers filed down the aisle. Dex was careful to avert his face, but that meant he was studying her with those pale eyes of his. Guilt and fear warred within her making her palms sweat.

"I can't," she whispered.

"What do you mean you can't?" His face grew hard. "You signed a contract this morning."

"I can't do this," she repeated.

"Can't? Or won't?"

There was a loud bang on the tarmac and the plane jerked a bit. Andi stifled a shriek, but her body began to shake.

"Jaysus. Don't tell me you're afraid of flying? Why didn't you mention that beforehand?"

"Since this is the first time I've ever been in an airplane," she managed to snap. "It wasn't exactly an issue I was aware of."

The flight attendant began talking about flotation devices and air masks. Thoughts of both made an army of black dots start to swim in front of Andi's eyes.

"Lass, stay with me."

Dex's plea sounded as if it was coming from a long tube. Suddenly, she was being wrapped in a warm blanket. The armrest between their bodies disappeared, and he snaked one arm around her shoulders while he cradled her face with his fingers on his other hand.

"You've got this," he murmured. "You've survived worse. I know you have. I won't let anything happen to you."

At the sound of his reassuring words, her eyes slowly regained their focus. Except now she was becoming lightheaded concentrating on the sensual way his lips moved as they coaxed her to breathe.

"That's it. In through your nose and out through your mouth."

Embarrassed, she tried to pull away, but he had a death grip on her shoulders.

"Relax." The low timbre of his voice sent shockwaves through her belly so that she was far from relaxed.

"We have an audience," he continued.

She peeked through her lashes around the first-class cabin. The flight attendant eyed her curiously from the jump seat across the aisle. The plane began to pick up speed on the runway and so did Andi's heart rate.

Dex nestled her in closer to his chest. "Just keep breathing."

Somehow, she managed to do just that, and before she knew it, they were airborne. A couple of dips and bumps later and the plane settled into a smooth ride. Andi's pulse did the same. Of course, the warm body wrapped around hers didn't hurt.

"I think I'll be okay now," she announced when the flight attendant began to move about the cabin.

His only response was a grunt, but his arm stayed put. She glanced over at him. His eyes were closed and his face was pale. Apparently, she wasn't the only one who didn't like flying. And yet he'd ignored his own discomfort to soothe her. Andi's chest squeezed. What she was doing was so wrong. She needed to tell him she couldn't marry him. He still had two days left to find another solution.

"Dex—"

"Something to drink?" The stewardess leaned in so he had a birds-eye view of her abundant cleavage.

Too bad for her, he didn't bother lifting his lids, but he was quick to pull Andi in closer to his body. "Two glasses of champagne, please."

The other woman pinned Andi with a surprised glance before stepping away.

"We're supposed to be playing it cool, remember?" Andi reminded him, all the while trying but failing to free herself.

"It would look odd if we didn't act as if we were at least a couple."

He had a point. And likely a reputation to keep up. She conceded the inevitable and relaxed against his hard chest, ignoring the little somersault in her belly when she did.

"I guess a weekend in Las Vegas is a pretty common date for you celebrity athletes."

His long lashes snapped open and his gaze locked with hers. This close, she could see the dark rings around his gray pupils. Daniel was right; it was a crime for a man to have such gorgeous eyes.

"I've never taken a woman to Vegas before."

There went her stomach again, doing more backflips than an Olympic gymnast. "Oh."

The flight attendant arrived with their champagne. Dex released her to take both glasses. She immediately felt bereft. *Stop it,* she ordered her traitorous body. Moving a little closer to the window to put some distance between them, she took the glass from him and swallowed a few hefty sips of the champagne.

"Whoa, there, lass."

When she looked over at him, he was wearing a lop-sided grin that had her girl parts quivering. She gulped the remainder of her champagne.

"That's one way to overcome your fear of flying." He took the glass from her hand. "But contrary to what one would think, you have to be sober to get married in Las Vegas."

She closed her eyes. He intended to go through with the wedding. With her as the bride. The champagne sloshed around in her stomach as she tried to work up the courage to tell him she'd never intended to marry him. But when she lifted her lids and her eyes collided with his, her tongue refused to move.

"Tell me about yourself," he urged quietly.

"There's not much to tell."

"You didn't just hatch as a full-grown woman."

"Perhaps I am the pixie fairy you think I am."

His smile was full now, and she nearly moaned in ecstasy at its potent effect. She should look away. Stupid woman that she was, she didn't.

"My parents died when I was young." She deliberately kept the details brief when she spoke of her childhood. The pity people doled out upon hearing her life's story was too often suffocating. She suspected, given his kindness earlier, his reaction would be even more painful. "I lived with my grandmother for a while, but when she passed, I went into foster care. It's not *Oliver Twist*, but it's not like you're growing up in the Tanner household, either."

"And yet, here you are."

The admiration she detected in his words made her chest squeeze.

"When I turned eighteen, I had to leave the family I was with to make way for another foster child."

His eyes grew wide. "Did you have a place to go?"

"I had friends who aged out before me. I lived with them for the first couple of years. Right now, I rent a small garage apartment near the Marquette campus." Luckily, she'd had Clive and a small military survivor benefit account from her mom. "I go to school at night and I work at a salon during the day." She gestured to her hair. "It's temporary. My boss needed a model last week."

"I'm finding myself warming up to that pink hair. It suits you. Not quite fiery, but definitely unique."

She swallowed roughly, surprisingly pleased at the unexpected compliment.

"And what about your family? How will you explain *this—*" She flailed a hand between them. "—to them."

His face suddenly grew hard and his eyes shuttered. "I won't. They must know nothing of you. Of this." He mimicked the gesture she had just made with her hands. "Ever."

A sudden chill seemed to overtake her. She gripped the blanket more tightly around her shoulders. Disappointment snaked through her limbs. Of course he wouldn't want his family knowing he'd married a nobody like Andi Larsen. Why had she expected anything different?

The joke was on him though, because they weren't getting married. She'd just ignore her conscience and wait until they arrived in Las Vegas to break the news to him. When a fan came up and asked Dex for his autograph, she took the opportunity to turn toward the window and feign sleep.

THREE

ANDI PIROUETTED SLOWLY around the center of the cavernous room, stopping in front of the wall of windows overlooking the Las Vegas strip. Sparkling chandeliers, no doubt made of expensive crystal, flickered above her head, their light dancing off the gold fixtures and polished marble surrounding her. *And this is just the bathroom.* A bathroom nearly the size of the small efficiency she rented in Milwaukee. She shook her head in amazement.

"No wonder they call this place Sin City." Her words echoed back to her in the empty room.

It was pretty childish to lock herself in the bathroom of the five-room suite—a suite that came with its own butler, for crying out loud—but Andi was still trying to catch her breath. She told herself the frenetic energy emanating from the city, coupled with the arid heat that threatened to suffocate her the moment she exited the airport, was making her light-headed. But she knew that was a lie. She was still stung by Dex's sudden about-face on the plane, and her emotional response to him made her angry. This was supposed to be pretend. Clearly, he was better at maintaining a game-face than she was.

Not only had Dex remained aloof for the duration of their flight, but once they'd arrived in Las Vegas, he'd stoically led her through the lavish lobby of the Wynn Towers, bypassing the reception desk as if he owned the place. Instead, he'd made a beeline down the mosaic tile walkway lined by tropical foliage, before steering her into a gold-plated elevator. All without uttering a single word. Once they'd arrived in their suite, he'd grunted something about "fetching the parson" and vanished back out the door.

She was relieved to see she'd have her own bedroom and bath. Not that she would be staying on as Declan Fletcher's pretend anything. She was using him as much as he was using her. The fact that she was apparently the only one who felt any guilt about their arrangement was something she needed to ignore. She hadn't come to Las Vegas to marry the brooding Scotsman. And his desertion gave her the perfect opportunity to accomplish her primary goal, which was tracking down Kenny. At least now she didn't have to make up some lame excuse for venturing out on her own.

After swiping on some lip gloss, she grabbed her purse and made her way out into the hallway. She'd almost made it to the double doors when the butler appeared at her side, seeming to vaporize out of nowhere, his presence startling her nearly out of her shoes.

"Is there something I can help you with, miss?"

"Uh, no. No, thank you." She surprised herself by getting the words out without stammering. "I'm just going for a walk."

"Very good," he replied with a stiff nod.

But when he reached for the door handle, Andi suddenly felt anything but 'very good.' Panic lanced through her making her knees wobble. Would he block her exit? Had Dex left instructions to keep her locked up until he returned with the judge?

She was about to lunge for the door when the butler slowly swung it open, his face impassive as he held it for her to walk through.

Andi managed a weak smile for the man while silently rebuking herself for her wild thoughts. Dex may try to appear a bit mercenary, but there was genuine kindness behind his Highlander façade. Too bad it was a kindness he was going to dish out to her sparingly.

The elevator was blessedly empty when its doors slid open. She managed to make it all the way down to the lobby without encountering anyone. Had she not been so afraid of running into Dex, she might have taken a few minutes to explore the beautiful hotel. But she needed to stay on task. She had less than two hours to locate Kenny before his poker game started.

Hurrying out of the hotel, she was prepared for the assault of the heat this time.

"Can I get you a cab, miss?" the bellman asked.

"No, thanks."

As much as she wanted to avoid walking in the brutal temperature, she couldn't afford the fare. Instead, she pulled up a walking map of Las Vegas on her phone and set out toward the Bellagio hotel.

Twenty-five minutes later, she rounded the corner and the famous fountains came into view. After navigating the crowded sidewalks for more than a mile in the desert heat, her blouse was stuck to her skin, and she welcomed the blast of cool air that greeted her when she strolled through the doors of the Bellagio. But that wasn't what took her breath away. Her attention was immediately drawn to the thousands of blown-glass flowers twinkling in the ceiling above her. She'd always envisioned her soaps and lotions packaged in colorful bags and tissue paper resembling the artwork overhead. Transfixed, she was nearly run over by a family of tourists.

You're not here to take in the sights. Admonishing herself, she checked the info in Kenny's Facebook post and made her way to the concierge desk.

"Can you tell me where the poker games are played?"

The man behind the desk eyed her curiously. No doubt, bedraggled, sweaty, and sporting pink hair, she didn't look the part of a high-stakes gambler. Except that this man had probably seen it all. He gestured to the entrance of the casino. "Follow the path to the poker room. It's in the back corner of the casino. Tables fill up fast, though. If you can't get a seat, make sure to put your name on the waiting list."

Andi smiled her thanks, not bothering to tell the man she wasn't interested in sitting in or adding her name to the waitlist. She was there to stake out the room and lie in wait for Kenny. And when she found him, she was going to call him out for the criminal he was.

Thirty minutes and a very expensive bottle of water later, Kenny was a no-show. The concierge was right. The tables filled up quickly with groups seeming to arrive all at once and taking over every seat. But Kenny wasn't among the crowd. Her confidence inched lower when she checked his social media account again. According to his post, the game he boasted about wasn't supposed to start for another half hour. Yet all these people didn't look like they were going to vacate their seats anytime soon.

From where she stood with her back against one of the columns surrounding the tables, she scanned the room one last time, her head snapping left as she realized she'd overlooked two tables roped off in the back. Both were still empty. Buoyed, she weaved her way around the occupied tables only to be stopped by a beefy security guard once she reached the rope.

"Sorry, miss." The guard held up a large hand. Despite having one of those velvety bedroom voices that matched his smooth, dark skin, the guy was no teddy bear. "This area is private. Invite only."

Her pulse began to beat an excited tattoo in her ears, drowning out the chatter of the players and the clinking of the chips. *This has to be where Kenny is headed.*

"Actually, I'm looking for someone who is supposed to be here." She glanced around for a place to wait. "I'll just stand over there." She nodded to another pillar situated beyond the tables.

The security guard shook his head. "Our players don't like it when people loiter around the tables." He indicated a woman leaning against a podium at the front of the room. "You need to put yourself on the waiting list and wait inside the casino until a seat becomes available."

"But—"

"No 'buts,' lady." He motioned for another security guard. "Walter will walk you to the casino."

Walter strolled over and began to herd her toward the entrance.

"Wait! Is there another entrance to this room?" If she waited in the right place, she could get Kenny before he got to the security guard.

The teddy bear got squinty-eyed.

Andi sighed. "I told you, I'm just waiting for someone."

The two guards exchanged a look.

"Ma'am, I think it's best if Walter walks you out to the lobby."

"For Heaven's sake, I'm not some crazy stalker!" The shrill tone she used to deliver her statement would indicate otherwise. She was so close to accomplishing her goal, only to be sent two steps back. It was frustrating.

Walter inched closer.

"Fine. I'll wait in the lobby." With a huff, she turned on her heel and headed out of the poker room. Barney Fife trailed her all the way through the casino and out to the lobby. He spoke into a microphone tucked into his jacket when she positioned herself just outside the casino entrance. Talking into his sleeve, the man looked as ridiculous as she felt. She rolled her eyes when she saw two women in uniform approaching. If they threatened a strip-search, she was hightailing it out of the hotel, Kenny or no Kenny.

Except she didn't have to. Because she suddenly spied him among a group of men walking through the lobby.

"Kenny," she called, startling both of the officers and her prey.

The two women turned their focus to him, and the look on Kenny's face was almost comical. The men he was with wisely hurried on, leaving Kenny stranded in no man's land between her and the two advancing guards.

"Andi, what are you doing here?" he asked sheepishly.

Taking advantage of his shock, she wrapped her fingers around his scrawny biceps and tugged him toward the coffee shop tucked behind the reception desk.

"I thought I'd come to see what all the fuss is about," she replied through clenched teeth.

One of the female officers blocked their path. "Everything okay here?"

Andi squeezed Kenny's arm. He nodded mutely.

"Just a little misunderstanding." Andi pasted on a smile for the benefit of the woman eying them. She shamelessly played to their solidarity as females. "My boyfriend here thinks he can earn the money for an engagement ring in a poker game. I'm fine with a small ring we can afford."

The officers nodded in tacit understanding.

"We'll just leave you two to sort it out," one of them said.

The other woman gave Kenny a stern look. "Gambling's no way to start a marriage."

Walter and his lady friends faded into the crowd, leaving Andi and Kenny in the center of the lobby.

"I offered to marry you once." He shrugged his arm free. "You said no."

"Puh-leaze." She rolled her eyes again. "You just wanted the extra food stamps."

"So?"

She stared at her onetime lover, wondering what she'd ever seen in the man. He looked ragged around the edges. His puddle brown eyes were red-rimmed, his blonde-beard scraggly, and his clothes looked as though they had been slept in. No doubt because they likely had.

He's no Declan Fletcher.

She gave herself a slight shake. Of course he wasn't. But that wasn't the point. She forced her thoughts back to the business at hand.

"So you found me. Now what?" he whined.

"Now I want my money back."

He dragged a hand through his unkempt hair. "Look, the bank wasn't going to just give someone like me a loan. You have a job, a small annuity, and good credit."

"*Had* good credit," she snapped at him. "Until you ruined it."

"It's not ruined until you have to pay it back." He sounded like a petulant toddler. "You have two years after you graduate before you have to start making payments. I'll have plenty of money by then to repay the loans."

And monkeys can fly.

"I don't want to wait until then. I want my money now," she demanded.

He looked as if she'd struck him. "I-I don't have it."

Of course he doesn't.

No matter how much she'd prepared herself to hear his admission, she felt her stomach drop.

"You stole from me, Kenny." She pushed the words out through her suddenly dry mouth. "You do realize you've committed a felony, don't you?"

A sheen of sweat broke out on his forehead. "Jesus, Andi. It's not like that."

Except it was like that, and they both knew it.

"Give me one good reason why I shouldn't call those officers back and have them arrest you."

"Because you're the only one who ever believed in me," he sputtered. "Because you love me."

She slammed her eyes shut, her shoulders sinking beneath his verbal grenades. Guilt warred with anger inside her. She knew what it was like to be alone in the world, to have an uncertain future. But she was doing something about it. Kenny was just a mooch. From the looks of it, he always would be. She needed to be strong.

When she opened her eyes, she was careful at shielding her emotions. He was too adept at reading her. If he sensed even a whiff of pity, he'd run with it for miles. He looked as if he was holding his breath. Or poised for flight, depending on what he saw in her eyes.

"Kenny," she began, but he didn't let her finish.

"I can win it back," he pleaded. "My luck will change now that you're here." He took a step closer. "Please, Andi. Believe in me. Come sit with me at the poker table. You'll see. Give me one night. I'll win everything back."

"You honestly think you can win seventy-thousand dollars in one night?"

He looked sheepish again. "If I get into the high stakes game, I can," he bragged. "I just need to pony up another two K for the ante." His eyes grew wide before he reached for the purse slung over her shoulder. "Hey, you've got a credit card. What kind of limit does it have?"

Flabbergasted, Andi took a giant step back. He narrowed his eyes at her.

"Do you want your money back or not?" he snapped.

The loser was certifiable if he thought he was getting any more money from her. He began to close the gap between them.

"Walter!" Andi yelled.

"What the hell are you doing?"

"What I should have done when I first laid eyes on you. I'm calling security. Walter!" she called again.

The guests milling about the lobby slowed their steps in curiosity, but Walter was nowhere to be found.

"What the fuck?" Kenny had the audacity to look as if *she* had wronged *him*. "You'll never see your money now."

She opened her mouth to call for security again, but he'd already slithered away and disappeared among the crowd.

SHE'D GHOSTED HIM.

Night had fallen over the desert. Dex stood in front of the wall of windows offering him a birds-eye view of the Las Vegas strip in all its glory. The marriage license Kurt had paid a fortune for was still folded up in his back pocket. The judge his agent had somehow coerced into performing a hush-hush ceremony had endured Dex's embarrassed silence for a half-hour before deserting him, too. Dex was alone with his thoughts and a bottle of whiskey. It was a testament to how low he was that he'd cracked it open despite the damn stuff being distilled in bloody Ireland.

He should have known his agent's plan was too good to be true. He'd suspected the little pink-haired fairy was a flight risk from the get-go. Not that the whole idea of a fake marriage didn't make him uneasy. He wasn't built for fraud. He'd just have to trust that Kurt could finagle a way to quickly renew his green card. No way the Growlers would want to lose him, and the team had the money to make this whole mess go away.

Yep. It was for the best that she'd stood him up at the proverbial altar.

So why did he feel so disappointed?

Because he'd effing touched her, that's why! She'd looked at him with those unsettling blue eyes and he'd completely forgotten why he thought he wouldn't be attracted to a woman like her. Forsaking common sense, he'd wrapped his arm around her and pulled her against his body as if she belonged there. And damn it if when she'd snuggled against him, she didn't touch off a firestorm of want and possessiveness that scared the living shit out of him.

Swearing violently beneath his breath, he took a hefty swallow of his drink. He'd gone too long without a woman, that was all. He'd remedy that situation tonight, right after he sent an SOS to Kurt. He was certainly in the right place. What happens in Vegas, stays in Vegas and all that bullshit. Hell, he was a celebrity jock. He'd have his choice of willing bedmates. A leggy blonde or a voluptuous redhead. He didn't need a wisp of a woman with cotton candy hair and fathomless blue eyes.

She would have been too much of a hassle, anyway, he reminded his bruised ego. No doubt she was messy. Or needy. Or both. Obviously, she had multiple bad habits if she owed so much money. He toasted himself for dodging a bullet where Andi Larsen was concerned. She was likely in the casino digging herself into a deeper hole.

His gut clenched at the thought. *Damn it.* Who would look out for her? A desperate woman could get into all sorts of trouble in a casino. Several scenarios ran through his mind, each of them more sinister than the last.

Not my problem.

A woman like that could bring all sorts of trouble to his doorstep. Dex had enough to deal with on his own. He had no business worrying about a waif of a lass he'd known for barely twenty-four hours.

At least that's what he kept telling himself.

A movement in the window caught his attention. His breath hitched. As though his thoughts had conjured her up, Andi stood behind him in the living room. Something that felt an awful lot like relief settled in his gut. He didn't bother turning around to acknowledge her, instead studying her reflection as he sipped from his glass. The cocky boldness she'd hid behind in Kurt's office yesterday was nowhere to be found. Instead, she wore a look of weary desperation. Only when their eyes met in the window did she muster her shoulders up a notch. He almost smiled at her bravado before catching himself.

"I'm sorry."

Her softly uttered words caught him off guard. He turned slowly, anchoring a shoulder against the window so he wouldn't do something foolish like march over to her and hold her as he had on the plane.

She glanced around the room. "The judge?"

"Long gone."

With a heavy sigh, she slumped down onto one of the sofas in the room. "Probably just as well. I wasn't going to marry you anyway."

Dex bit back the animosity that threatened. She'd signed a

bloody contract. But the defeat he heard in her tone cooled his temper. There was something he was missing here.

"I came here under false pretenses."

He responded with a raised eyebrow. "This entire trip is based on false pretenses."

She uttered a forlorn sigh. "I can't take your money. It wouldn't be right to involve you in my messed-up life."

His fingers became numb around the glass he was holding. His gut had been right; she was in more trouble than she'd let on.

"I only agreed because I needed to come to Las Vegas."

Dex wracked his brain to remember any details Kurt had shared about her. Specifically, how she owed seventy-thousand dollars and to whom. But he'd been so consumed with his own problem that he hadn't bothered to ask about hers. And now he had a very bad feeling.

"You don't say?" Could she be a compulsive gambler? "Tired of the casinos up on the Indian reservations?"

"What? No." She shook her head with a snort. "Gambling is for fools."

His chest relaxed at her words. "Actually, gambling is for those with a proper handle on mathematics and probability. The fools are the people who try their hand at it without those particular skills."

A ghost of a smile danced over her lips before she quashed it. She jumped from the sofa and began to pace.

"I came to find Kenny."

"Kenny?" *Who the hell is Kenny?* He was suddenly holding his breath, hoping she'd say 'my brother' and not 'my husband' or 'my son.'

"One of those foolish gamblers who used to be my boyfriend."

He refused to acknowledge how her words "used to be" made him feel.

"If he's such a fool and no longer your boyfriend, why come to find him?"

"Because he's the reason I owe seventy thousand dollars. He's gambling with money he stole using my identity."

Jaysus.

Damn Kurt for leaving that part out. Pulling away from the window, he stalked over to the bar and refilled his drink before pouring some into a glass for her.

"Please tell me Kurt is helping you prosecute this Kenny guy?" He handed her the glass, and they both took seats on opposite sofas.

"It's not that simple." She took a sip of the whiskey. "More like it's not a priority with law enforcement."

"Meanwhile, you get hung out to dry."

"Something like that."

"What were you planning to do if you found this Kenny guy?" Dex suddenly knew what he wanted to do if he found the blighter.

She'd gone from sipping the whiskey to taking a healthy swallow. "In my heart, I naively thought he'd just give the money back to me. Even though my brain knew he'd already lost it all."

Dex sat forward. "Wait? You found him?"

"Yeah. I wasn't kidding about the idiot part. He loves a good social media brag post." She set the glass down on the table between them. "He claimed he was going to pay me back long before the loans come due. Of course, that was right before he asked to borrow another couple of thousand so he could sit in on a high-stakes poker game."

"Tell me you didn't give it to him," he practically growled.

Andi huffed. "Thanks for the vote of confidence. Even if I had that kind of money sitting around, I wouldn't give it to Kenny. I didn't buy his boast that he could win everything back in one night. There is no way he could win seven dollars much less seventy *thousand* at poker in one game. I doubt anyone could."

She was wrong.

He was already calculating the probabilities. It would have to be a game of very high stakes. And superior play. Something her ex obviously couldn't muster. But, lucky for her, he could. And he had the bankroll to make it happen. Such a challenge might be just the thing to get his mind off his impending doom.

"Where exactly is this game?" he asked, ignoring the part of his brain yelling at him to get the hell out of Vegas before he did something stupid.

"The Bellagio." A hollow laugh escaped her throat. "I wanted to go back to look more carefully at the artwork in the lobby, but Kenny ruined even that for me."

Dex pulled out his phone, scrolling through his contacts before shooting off a text. He downed the rest of his whiskey as he got to his feet.

"Come along, lass."

Her eyes were wide as cue balls again. "Wh-where? I told you I can't marry you."

"Relax," he said, despite the fact his ego took a hit every time she said she wouldn't marry him. "We're going back to the Bellagio."

"To do what?" she asked as she got to her feet.

"You're going to look at the artwork. I'm going to play poker."

FOUR

NIGHTFALL HAD COOLED off the city, but Andi was still perspiring. This time with anxiety. On the cab ride back to the Bellagio, she tried to talk Dex out of whatever point he was trying to prove.

"This is ridiculous. You shouldn't be wasting your night playing poker. Not when you need to find a way out of your immigration mess," she pleaded.

He pinned her with a side-eye glare but remained mute.

Guilt flared deep inside her. He had a way out of his immigration mess.

Her.

"I'm serious," she tried again. "What makes you think your luck will be any better than Kenny's? Granted, you have more disposable income to waste, but kicking field goals isn't exactly the same as playing five-card stud."

This time there was an inarticulate growl accompanying his glare.

She gave up with a huff. "Fine. Go try to prove you can

outsmart a bunch of gamblers. What do I care? After this weekend, our paths will never cross again."

Turning to stare out the window, she tried to ignore the disappointment swirling in her stomach. There was no reason for her to feel sad she'd never see Declan Fletcher again.

Never again experience the sensation of his low voice murmuring in her ear.

Never again feel his strong arms wrapped around her.

Never again hear his heart beating against her cheek.

Gah!

What in the living hell was she thinking? They weren't lovers, for crying out loud. Heck, they weren't even friends. Where in the world was her mind going with this? Her cheeks grew warm at her silliness. The only thing she had a right to be disappointed about was the two days of pay she was missing out on by traveling here to seek out Kenny.

"Coming, lass?"

She was so busy fantasizing about her make-believe relationship with Dex, she didn't realize they'd already arrived at the Bellagio. The bellman held the car door open for her while the object of her fantasy stood on the pavement wearing an irritated scowl. His attitude irked her. She was tired and hungry. And the swimming pool-sized bathtub back in the suite was calling to her. She didn't want to spend the evening watching a crazy kilt-loving jock throw his not-so-hard-earned money away playing a game of chance.

Something in her expression must have given her away because, in a flash, he was leaning into the car and gently wrapping his fingers around her wrist.

"I won't force you to live up to your end of our bargain, but the least you could do is carry on with the charade while we are here."

There was that guilt again, churning up the acid in her empty stomach. A corner of his mouth kicked up at the loud growl coming from her midsection.

"Do this for me and you can order whatever you want from the menu. Please, Andi."

It was the first time he'd uttered her name and the sultry sound of it rolling off his lips sent shock waves throughout her body. Somehow, it was more intimate than the preponderance of "lasses" he'd been bandying about since they met. But it was the "please" he'd accompanied it with that had her acquiescing. This wasn't a man who begged, she was sure of that. Whatever he intended to do this evening was important to him for some reason. Just as important as her presence obviously was. She'd come this far. With a nod, she accepted his help from the car.

He released her wrist, but only to move his hand to her lower back so he could steer her possessively through the throng of guests strolling about the lobby. His touch had her nerve endings simmering.

"Fletcher!"

A man dressed in a loud Hawaiian shirt emerged from the crowd. The shirt was obviously a costume of some sort because his pasty white skin and sunken eyes marked him as someone who didn't see the light of day often, much less a sandy beach.

"Hal." Dex extended his free hand to the man. "Thanks for accommodating me."

"Are you kidding? I've been trying to get you to sit in on one of these games for years. I'm just glad you finally took me up on my offer."

Dex glanced over at her. "Well, there are some extenuating circumstances tonight."

A sly grin tugged at the corners of Hal's mouth as he scrutinized Andi. "The things we do for women. Although, you're the last guy I figured to follow the whim of the fairer sex." The man shrugged. "But if it gets you to a poker table, I'm not gonna complain."

Andi's cheeks flamed at the other man's false assumption. "It's not—"

Dex pressed his hand more firmly against her back, presumably to silence her.

"Andi, allow me to introduce Dr. Hal Levin. Hal is a math

professor at UNLV. Hal, this is Andi Larsen. She's only here for the food."

His friend laughed. "I've heard that a time or two."

Before she could object any further, Hal was leading them back through the casino toward the poker room.

"I don't suppose you'd let one of my grad students shadow you?" Hal steered them through the maze of slot machines.

Dex shook his head. "I don't want to call any additional attention to myself. Besides, tonight is not about research. It's about winning."

Hal looked as astounded as Andi felt.

"Research?" she asked.

"Winning?" Hal said at the same time. "You haven't played to win since we needed beer money in grad school. In fact, I remember a vow never to play for money ever again."

"I told you," Dex replied crisply. "The circumstances are different tonight."

She wanted to stop right where they were, in the center of the casino, and demand answers. What exactly were the *circumstances*? Did he think he could play the white knight and somehow teach Kenny a lesson? Her breath hitched at the idea of someone actually caring about her. But as much as she would enjoy that scenario, she felt another tinge of guilt for involving Dex in her screwed-up life. She needed to stop this. Except his hand was still firm against her back, its warmth now permeating the fabric of her blouse. Like a love-struck puppy, she continued to allow him to guide her forward.

Clearly, Hal was a regular in the poker room because Walter's friend waved them in without a second glance—until his eyes landed on Andi. Her step faltered slightly when the teddy bear security guard strode toward them. Dex slid his hand to her shoulder, drawing her in closer to his body. He leveled a look at the security guard that had him backing off. She quickly surveyed the room looking for Kenny, relief and disappointment warring within her when she didn't see him among the other players.

Hal stopped at a table tucked into the back corner of the room. When he leaned down to speak quietly to one of the players, the man's head snapped up and he shot a surprised gaze in their direction.

"Ladies and gentlemen." The man gathered up his chips and stood. "I hope you don't mind if I relinquish my seat. I'm sure you'll enjoy playing with a real-life celebrity. Let's see if he can earn the title of leading scorer at the poker table tonight."

The arm draped over her shoulders stiffened briefly at the introduction, but the haughty look on Dex's face never wavered. Whatever he was up to, he wasn't planning on enjoying it. The knowledge caught her off guard.

"The ante is twenty-five thousand," the man continued. "But I'm sure that's chump change for you."

"Holy hell," she murmured, her heart pounding. The amount was nearly equal to a semester's tuition. Chump change or not, she wasn't comfortable sitting around watching him waste that kind of money. Just the thought made her nauseous.

She turned within the circle of his arm. "Dex—"

But, once again, he seemed able to read her thoughts. "Give me a kiss for luck, lass," he commanded, effectively cutting off her protest with both his words and his lips.

She didn't have time to react. Not that she could if she wanted to. She was too stunned. Or too . . . *something.*

The moment his mouth met hers, a storm of sensations threatened to overwhelm her. The velvety firmness of his lips. The tangy whiskey on his breath. The sparks of awareness created by the brush of his fingers against her skin.

It was all too much.

And yet, not nearly enough.

Her body moved of its own accord, edging close enough that she couldn't tell if it was her heart hammering against her chest or his. She failed to contain the sigh emanating from the back of her throat when his lips coaxed hers apart and his tongue delved into her mouth. The fingers at her nape tightened ever so slightly at the sound before he abruptly released her.

It took a long moment for awareness of her surroundings to return. The ping of the slot machines and the crackle of shuffling cards was followed by the hum of hundreds of conversations taking place within the casino. When she finally regained focus, Dex was still inhabiting the space in front of her, heat and something else unidentifiable radiating off him.

"Well done, lass," he murmured.

Andi's gaze snapped up to meet his. Her stomach sank at his amused expression. *Damn it.* He was playing a role. This whole evening was some sort of play for him. One where she didn't know the lines. She was a fool to think it was anything more.

Taking a step back, she forced her lips up into a smile she didn't feel. Declan Fletcher may be a better gamer than she was, but Andi was nothing if not a quick learner. She'd had to be. So she decided to play along.

Placing both hands on his chest, she stretched up on her toes and pressed her lips to the corner of his. "Try not to lose it all in one sitting," she said loud enough for their audience to overhear.

With a pat to his magnificent pectoral muscles, she left him standing there mute, while she went in search of food. And a large glass of wine.

NORMALLY, DEX LOVED math. He thrived on it, actually. Calculating probability quickly and accurately was a greater skill than kicking a bloody fourteen-ounce leather ball through the uprights. In the past, exercising his agile mind outsmarting his opponents in a card game was an excellent diversion from whatever else was troubling him. He'd thought the same would be true tonight. But not so. He blamed his pink-haired fake fiancé.

If touching her had been a bad idea, kissing her was the mother of all bad ideas. Too bad he was having trouble convincing his body of that. Parts of him were screaming to take her back to their hotel suite and finish what he'd started. She was right; after this weekend, they'd likely never see one another again. Based on her reaction to his kiss, she was more than willing to take things further.

Or was she?

Why did he have the feeling she might be playing him? Probably because she'd scammed both him and Kurt by agreeing to a marriage of convenience in order to secure a free trip to Las Vegas. Hell, her crazy story about a shady ex could be a farce. And he'd fallen for it, using the excuse that he wanted to make things right for her as a reason to while away the night playing poker.

He picked up the cards the dealer doled out, not even bothering to look at them. Instead, his gaze was locked on the little vixen who was currently using her wiles on Hal. His friend already looked smitten, fetching her a plate of food and a glass of champagne. Dex refrained from grinding his teeth. Hal was married with three kids, dammit. Besides, the guy was supposed to be working.

In addition to being a math professor, Hal served as a consultant on the casino's security team. He coordinated a group of graduate students who surveyed the games to look for any individual who might be cheating. Technically, using your own brainpower couldn't be construed as dishonest, but casinos tended to frown on players whose intellect gave them an unfair advantage. Given that Dex held the same PhD from MIT as his friend Hal, he fit squarely into that group. Normally, he avoided gambling as a rule. But tonight, he was making an exception. He just hoped he wasn't making a grave mistake, as well.

"You in?"

At the question posed by the dealer, Dex reined in his ambling thoughts, finally giving his hand of cards the attention they deserved. He flipped several chips into the pile at the center of the table. "I'm in."

It took a few hands, but he eventually settled into a rhythm, focusing on the cards and the play around him. That comfort he sought settled over him, blotting out everything but the game. If the other players believed him to be an egomaniac jock when he sat down, he'd quickly convinced them otherwise.

Six hours in, the game was down to two players. He had already won Andi's money back and then some. But no way was he walking away until he'd won the final hand. He did a quick probability calculation in his head, leading him to conclude the best hand his opponent could have was a straight and even the probability of that was extremely low. Glancing down at his own cards, he decided to end the game here.

He shoved a pile of chips into the center of the table, reserving just enough to cover Andi's debt, and arched an eyebrow at the man across the table. His opponent scrutinized the bet for a tense moment.

"I'll see your bet," he finally said, tossing the matching amount of chips on the pile.

The other players seemed to be holding their collective bets. Dex nodded to his opponent to lay down his cards. Damn if the guy didn't have a bloody straight of spades, ace high. He leaned back in his chair and grinned at Dex in challenge.

Taking his time, Dex laid out his own cards one-by-one. Five cards, each bearing a heart. A flush trumped a straight, making him the winner. The assembled crowd broke out in a smattering of applause and wild cheers.

Hal clapped him on the back. "You haven't lost a step, Professor MacMath. Well played."

Dex rolled his shoulders. "I take it you'll be discussing my strategy in class this week?"

"You know it. I'll have my students dissecting every hand." Hal laughed. "On the other side of campus, some poor kicker will be doing the same with game film. You're quite the enigma, Fletcher."

Dex chuckled at the irony. "Yeah, well, I think this is a one and done, so your students will have to be satisfied with tonight's performance."

"You're definitely a 'one and done' in my hotel." Hal scooped the pile of chips into a deep plastic bowl, then handed it to Dex. "I only allowed you to sit in so that big brain of yours could offer perspective on the other players in the game. You keep winning everyone's money and you're going to have to move to tournament play."

A line of people had begun to form, all of them with phones in their hands in hopes of a selfie. Despite being exhausted and ravenous, he obliged for nearly ten minutes until Hal cut them off. His friend gestured to a row of chairs against the back wall. "You might want to get her out of here."

Jaysus. He'd gotten his wish and become so absorbed in the game that he'd forgotten all about Andi. Not that she'd notice. She was sprawled along the chairs, earbuds in, eyes closed, mouth open. A strand of her hair wafting through the air with each puff from her lips.

"How long has she been out?"

Hal grinned indulgently. "She barely lasted an hour."

A twinge of something pierced his chest. He'd been an asshat. He should have left her in the bloody suite. But his ego insisted she come along. If he was going to save her pretty little ass, she could at least look on adoringly. Except nothing with this woman went as expected.

He crouched down in front of her. Relaxed in sleep, the worry lines gone, she looked so much younger. So much more vulnerable. Not at all like a woman who was playing him. Just a lass who'd had to fight for whatever she wanted out of life. His gut hadn't let him down. He'd done the right thing.

Reaching out a finger, he captured the stray lock of hair. Pink blurred with a sunny blond color on the soft strand. He gently tucked it behind her ear, tracing the curve of her jaw with his finger as he did so. Her lids fluttered opened. Soft blue eyes considered him for a long moment, so earnest and trusting, before recognition dawned. She shot upright, her cheeks pink with embarrassment.

Chuckling, Dex took the seat beside her. "Sorry the entertainment was lacking, lass."

"It—it wasn't. I just . . ." Her voice trailed off.

"Can't handle champagne. I figured as much."

Her head snapped around to argue, but something in his expression made her face soften.

"How much did you lose?" she asked instead.

He arched an eyebrow. "Lass, I never lose."

His words had the desired effect because he detected a slight shiver before she suppressed it. Her eyes darted everywhere but his face, finally settling on the bowl of chips.

"Are those all yours?"

When he didn't answer, she was forced to meet his gaze. He searched her face for any sign of duplicity, but her expression remained dumbfounded. Dex placed the bowl of chips in her lap.

"No, lass. They're yours."

FIVE

ANDI STARED AT him in astonishment. Surely, she hadn't heard him correctly.

"Come, again?"

He nudged the bowl on her lap. "You heard me. No need to worry about getting that Slytherin, Kenny, to pay you back."

She was dreaming. Any moment now, she would wake up. Except she wasn't sure she wanted to wake up. Not when there was a sexy man seated next to her who looked at her as though she was holding a warm plate of cookies just for him.

And, oh my, was he sexy first thing in the morning. Stubble had begun to form on his jaw and his beautiful eyes had dark smudges beneath them making him look more like a pirate than the white knight she'd envisioned earlier. A pirate who'd swooped in to snatch the booty and offer it to her as a prize as if he'd plucked a flower from a meadow and simply handed it to her.

There had to be a catch.

There always was.

Emotion clogged her throat. "How—how much is this worth?"

"By my count, seventy-eight thousand, four hundred and fifty-three dollars," Hal announced.

Dark spots began to form in front of her eyes. "It's too much. I —I . . ."

"Hush." He reached up and gently wrapped her fingers around the bowl. "When someone is being chivalrous, you're supposed to be grateful."

"I can't take your money because I'm not going to marry you!" she blurted out without thinking.

He flinched beside her. Hal let out a low whistle.

"Um, you know what? It's three in the morning," Hal said. "I think I'll head home. I'll text you later, Fletcher."

Dex didn't bother responding. He kept his gaze trained on her. Andi swallowed roughly at the disappointment that flashed briefly in his eyes before it disappeared.

"It's not my money, lass. It's my opponents' money. And now, it's your money. Do with it what you wish. If I'd meant to force you to honor your end of the bargain, I wouldn't be giving it to you, now would I?"

The sharpness of his tone was like a gut punch. She was being ungracious. But she couldn't help it. In her defense, she wasn't used to strangers showing her such kindness. Especially nearly eighty thousand dollars' worth of *kindness*. But she was beginning to realize Declan Fletcher was not your average stranger.

"I duped you about the marriage. Yet you did—" She shook the bowl with such force, several of the chips slipped over the rim and onto the carpet. "—this! Forgive me if I don't believe it's sincere."

He leaned his head back against the wall and closed his eyes. "I'm sorry people have let you down, Andi. But I saw a way to fix your problem and I took it. Believe me when I say there are no strings attached."

Well, he didn't have to sound so definite about that last part.

"I'm sorry. I'm just not used to—"

"Kindness?" he snapped. He swiped a hand down his face. "Now I'm sorry. Forgive me. I'm hungry and I'm tired." Steely eyes bored into her skin. "But know this, Andi Larsen. Everyone deserves kindness. Even you. If it makes you feel uncomfortable, pay it forward someday. Believe me, that can ease a litany of sins."

Her chest squeezed so tightly it nearly cut off her breath. The idea that she'd experienced very little kindness in her life obviously troubled him. And that made her feel something so unexpected, she didn't have a name for it.

With a groan, he got to his feet. "I'm going to find some food before we head back to the suite."

"Wait!" She clamored after him. "What are you going to do about your situation?"

He checked his watch. "It's too early to call Kurt. Although it would serve him right if I ruined his beauty sleep."

"Do you think he'll be able to resolve things before they . . . they—"

"Totally screw up my life and career by deporting me? Jaysus, I hope so." A cocktail waitress shot him a sly smile as she passed by. "Of course, I could always find someone else to fulfill your end of the bargain."

She didn't like the way he checked out the other woman's toned ass. Or the burning feeling bubbling up in her chest.

"You'd just marry a stranger?"

Judging by the look he shot her, she wasn't the only one who thought it was a stupid question.

"Sorry. I'm a little jetlagged, also."

He arched an eyebrow. "Lass, you just took a five-hour nap."

"In a casino. It doesn't count."

One side of his mouth kicked up in another one of those smiles that made her insides quiver. He draped an arm over her shoulder. "Come on. Let's go cash in those chips before you drop them in your exhaustion."

As much as she enjoyed this lighter side of him—not to mention his muscled arm wrapped around her—the guilt still gnawed at her.

"What if Mrs. Hilbert's son can't come up with a quick fix?"

He gave her shoulders a squeeze. "Then I guess I'll just have to marry Mrs. Hilbert. I'm sure she'd go through with it. In fact, she strikes me as the type who'd be a lot of fun." He winked. "She's awfully frisky."

Andi stopped in her tracks. Words deserted her. He couldn't be serious. The idea was beyond ridiculous. He was obviously delirious with exhaustion. But he was correct, Mrs. Hilbert *would* go through with it. She was the type who never passed on a good dare. The problem would be that the marriage would be so preposterous it would never pass muster with the authorities. The fact that her chest was still burning had nothing to do with anything.

"No." Her objection had his arm tensing against her shoulders.

"*No?*"

"I'll do it."

He pulled his arm away and shoved his hands into his pockets. The lightness was gone from his eyes. "You'll do what?"

Now he was just being obtuse. She glanced around to make sure no one was paying too close of attention to them.

"I'll marry you," she mumbled.

He leaned in closer. "I'm sorry. I didn't quite catch that."

She was pretty certain he had. "You don't have to call Kurt. Or his mother. I'll hold up my end of the bargain. I'll marry you."

His silence stretched for so long, she worried she might just drop the bowl full of tokens yet.

"Make up your mind, lass. You said—more than once, mind you--that you *wouldn't* marry me."

His teasing demeanor was long gone. She could almost feel the tension radiating off of him. Gathering up her courage, she jumped in for real this time.

"But that was different. This won't be a contractual arrangement. It will be more like a friend doing a favor for another friend." She hefted the bowl of chips and shook it at him. "You did me a favor with no strings attached. I'll be doing the same. It's like Mrs. Hilbert said, we don't have to be in love to be married. But if we're two people who mutually respect one another, it's okay."

He stepped in closer, so that now, only the bowl of tokens stood between them. His eyes narrowed as he gazed down at her, studying her face carefully. The world seemed to fade away around them as she tried not to squirm under the intense scrutiny. The moment stretched and her heart began to race. After all this, he was going to reject her. Tell her she wasn't good enough. That Mrs. Hilbert was a safer alternative. She'd heard it all before.

Bracing herself for the inevitable, she refused to acknowledge how deeply his answer would wound her. Which was totally ridiculous, because she'd only just met the man. But twice now, he'd shown her compassion for no other reason than it was the appropriate thing to do. Declan Fletcher was an enigma. One that she suspected could do more damage to her psyche—not to mention her heart—if she spent any more time around him. She ought to be relieved he was going to reject her.

"Then we do it now," he shocked her by saying. "Tonight."

"R-right now?"

He snatched the bowl of chips from her fingers. With his free hand, he steered her out of the casino.

"Yes, right now, lass," he said, tersely. "I won't risk you changing your mind again."

Dumbfounded by his swift agreement, Andi let him drag her along, all the way reminding herself that none of this was real.

OF COURSE, THE judge Kurt hired was out of the question at this time of night—*make that morning*. That left them with taking a chance at one of the wedding chapels Las Vegas was famous for. Much to Dex's surprise, however, many of them were too crowded for his liking. Apparently, quickie weddings were a booming business no matter what the hour. But the idea was to keep their marriage on the down low. The only people who needed to know about it were those trying to deport him.

They wandered to the farthest end of the strip, ending up in a small chapel tucked into what looked like a gas-station-turned-pizza-joint-turned-wedding-venue. A young woman manning the reception desk barely looked up from her phone when they entered.

"Can I help you?" she muttered half-heartedly.

"We'd like to get married."

That got him a quick glance from her before she returned to whatever was so captivating on her phone. He wondered what she would do if he asked for a pepperoni pizza, as well. His stomach growled at the thought.

"Do you have an appointment?" she asked.

"Seriously?" Andi raised an eyebrow at the other woman before gesturing to the empty lobby.

The receptionist sighed. "I guess I can make an exception. As long as you have a license."

The tone of her voice indicated she really hoped they didn't have a license. Dex pulled the paper out of his back pocket, snapping it open with authority before laying it on the counter. He resisted the urge to smirk at her.

Barely.

The receptionist gave it a cursory glance before returning to her phone. "Princess, you're up!"

Dex's imagination ran wild as he imagined any number of the Disney princesses his sister Annis used to dress up as. He wasn't sure he could stomach Belle performing his farce of a marriage ceremony. Instead, an older woman emerged from the back of the chapel. She was wearing a Princess Leia costume that was easily two sizes too small for her. Her long grey hair was coiled up in braids on the sides of her head. A light saber dangled from her finger tips. Dex wasn't quick enough hiding his surprise. The woman narrowed her eyes at the chuckle he failed to swallow.

"If you're looking for Elvis," she said with a voice that sounded more Minnie Mouse than intergalactic princess. "You're out of luck. He's off this weekend. We're running a *Star Wars* special that's *out of this world*, though."

He had to admire the woman's pluck. "That sounds perfect."

"That'll be five hundred bucks," the girl at the counter said.

At the sound of Andi's sharp intake of breath, Princess Leia added "That includes photos and a video. Just give us a minute to set up the cameras."

"No pictures."

He realized his mistake too late when his harshly uttered words had the girl ditching her phone and now giving him her undivided attention.

"Just a ceremony and a marriage certificate will be fine," Andi chimed in from beside him, offering a placating smile to both women.

Princess Leia's eyes darted between his and Andi's before she shrugged. "Suit yourself. But the fee is the same no matter what. When you settle up, come on back. Luke Skywalker and Chewbacca will serve as your witnesses."

When neither he nor Andi showed any of the requisite excitement about their witnesses, she muttered something under her breath and disappeared into the back room. Dex withdrew five one-hundred-dollar bills from his wallet and handed it to the girl at the counter. She tucked it in a drawer before sliding a worn three-ringed-binder in his direction.

"Here's our catalog of vows. Pick the ones you want to use."

The back of his neck grew damp with sweat. He hadn't considered this part. Would he have to promise to love Andi? Would it count if he crossed his fingers behind his back? He could certainly promise to respect and protect her, that wouldn't be a lie. But love? *Jaysus,* what had he gotten himself into?

Andi was already leafing through the notebook. "No," she muttered turning the pages. "No. No. No." She huffed in annoyance. "How is the word obey still even in wedding vows these days?"

Dex nearly laughed. He was worried about giving her the wrong idea by pledging to love her until death do they part and the only thing she was growing indignant about was promising to obey.

"Does it really matter?" He tried to convey with his tone that none of this was real. Too bad he was having trouble believing that himself.

Her eyes narrowed for a breath before she nodded in agreement. She pointed to a paragraph listed under the heading 'Short and Sweet Wedding Vows.'

"What about these?"

He scanned the words on the page.

Promise to love you forever.

. . . falling in love a little more every day . . .

Love of my life.

Soul-mate.

Dex slapped the book closed. "Isn't there something generic we can use?"

The girl behind the desk responded with a sly grin. "Of course. Just tell the Princess you want the vows that go with the package."

"Good." Wrapping his fingers around Andi's hand, he drew her into the chapel only to stop short when they crossed the threshold. The room didn't resemble a chapel at all. Instead, it looked like the bridge of Han Solo's Millennium Falcon, of all things.

"I'm kind of bummed you said no pictures," she whispered beside him. "This is too crazy not to document."

Her bright blue eyes bounced around the room taking everything in. The corners of her lips turned up in a bemused smile when she spied the Wookie standing at the altar. "She wasn't kidding about Chewbacca."

Despite being a lifelong fan of *Star Wars*, Dex couldn't quite summon a similar level of excitement. "I can't imagine this is what you anticipated when you dreamed of your wedding."

She lifted her gaze to his. "I never let myself dream of a wedding."

Her matter-of-fact statement rendered him speechless. *What woman doesn't dream of her wedding?*

"No family, remember? No church." She shrugged. "Definitely

no money. In fact, this is much more than a girl like me could hope for. And it will definitely be memorable."

Once again, he was reminded she wasn't like most women of his acquaintance. She hadn't spent long afternoons gabbing with her friends and dreaming of her picture-perfect future. Instead, she'd spent much of her life dodging the curve balls the world had thrown at her, doing what she had to in order to survive.

"Sorry." The single word was wholly inadequate, but, insensitive jerk that he was, he couldn't think of a suitable comeback. Of course, she took his callousness in stride, and that stung even more.

Her lips quirked. "Don't tell me you spent your life dreaming of your marriage. Maybe proudly waiting at the altar wearing your kilt and one of those caps with the pom-poms on top?"

She couldn't have hit him harder if she'd actually thrown a punch. The memory of standing at the altar, dressed exactly as she said, Niall proudly beside him, had the breath catching painfully in his throat. "Men don't dream of their weddings," he managed to grind out.

"Uh, huh. Your face says otherwise."

He opened his mouth to object but she spoke first.

"Save it. This is a temporary arrangement. I don't need to know all your secrets." Still hand in hand, she dragged him up to the front of the chapel. "Come on, Highlander. Let's do this."

She was right. This was a temporary arrangement. No longer a business deal, but more like a pact. *Between friends.* Both of them were going into it with their eyes wide open. He'd just take a page from her book and play along with their absurd situation. Trudging up to the altar, he gave into the moment and felt himself begin to relax.

Right up until a pimply-faced Luke Skywalker opened his mouth. "Do you have rings?"

Dex flinched at the question. He'd insisted to Kurt that he would not wear a ring. Not only would it call attention to this pretend marriage, but it would be dishonest to the principles his parents instilled in him.

"We're getting them tattooed after we're official," Andi quipped, before winking slyly at him.

Her quick reply caught him off guard. The damn woman was actually enjoying this. Her twinkling eyes dared him to do the same. A man could lose himself in those eyes if he wasn't careful. Good thing he was famous for being cautious and methodical. Not to mention, sarcastic.

"Just as long there isn't a nose ring involved."

She smiled at his lame joke and he forgot to breathe. Damn, she was breathtaking when she wasn't riddled with anxiety. A dimple he hadn't noticed before peeked out of her cheek daring him to kiss it. He felt himself leaning in to do just that when Princess Leia spoke up.

"Beings from throughout the galaxies, we are gathered here tonight to eternally unite—" She glanced down at the license. "Declan Edward Fletcher and Andrea Faith Larsen."

Faith. Her middle name was Faith. Dex couldn't imagine a more appropriate name for the slight but steely woman standing beside him.

"This historic union will allow this couple to travel through the galaxy of life and provide them protection against aggressions from the Evil Empire."

Beside him, Andi smothered a chuckle with a cough. Princess Leia eyed her sternly. Andi cleared her throat and nodded for the Princess to continue.

"Declan, do you take Andrea to be your wife?"

"I do."

"Andrea, do you take Declan to be your husband?"

"I do," Andi managed to say between giggles.

Princess Leia was throwing death glares now. "Declan, please turn to face Andrea and take her hands."

Biting back another fit of laughter, Andi pivoted toward him offering both her hands. He took her small fingers in his.

"Declan, do you vow to make Andrea your Queen as you travel the galaxy? Do you pledge to stand with her within the illumination of her love, to comfort her, honor her, respect her, and protect her from the Dark Side from this day forward, until the Death Star do you part?"

A sweat broke out at the base of his neck at the mention of the "L" word. Andi seemed unfazed, however, too busy fighting off hysteria at the irreverence of the ceremony.

He cleared his throat. "I do."

"Andrea, do you take Declan to be your wedded husband? Do you pledge to stand with him within the illumination of his love, to comfort him, honor him, respect him, and protect his offspring from the Dark Side from this day forward, until the Death Star do you part?"

Andi's eyes were shining with mirth. "I do," she choked out.

Princess Leia huffed in annoyance. "Then, by the power vested in me by the Force and the state of Nevada, I pronounce you King and Queen, husband and wife. May your life together be full of happiness and peace and may the force be with you both always." She nodded at Dex. "You may kiss your Queen."

Andi arched an eyebrow at the word 'Queen,' her body beginning to twitch with pent up laughter. He tugged her closer, intending to peck her cheek. But the instant her body made contact with his, it detonated a storm of sensations within in him. Judging by the way her eyes went wide, she felt it, too. *Keep it light*, he told himself. He brushed her mouth with a kiss that was meant to be perfunctory, but at the small sound of pleasure that whispered past her lips, it turned into something else entirely. He mindlessly coaxed her lips apart, plunging deeper to explore the sweetness of her mouth as if it belonged to him. As if *she* belonged to him. She answered by curling her fingers into his shirt, and letting her tongue tangle with his. Suddenly his hands were no longer on her shoulders, but exploring the sweet curve of her ass. His heart was pounding so loudly in his ears, he almost didn't hear the sound of a throat being cleared.

"We charge extra for a hotel room," Princess Leia announced.

At the other woman's words. Andi jumped from his arms as if

she'd been burned. With unfocused eyes and swollen lips, she glanced around the room looking embarrassed.

Jaysus!

How had he lost his composure so quickly? He was renowned for his self-discipline on and off the field. But when he was around this woman it all flew out the window. *That has to end now,* he vowed. Because, while he couldn't promise to love Andi, he could definitely see himself liking her. A lot. And that could turn out to be a very big problem when their fake wedding came to its contracted conclusion.

SIX

"AS YOUR QUEEN, I hereby decree that bacon must be served at every meal." Andi sighed reverently before biting down on a piece of the crispy stuff.

Across the booth from her, Dex shook his head with what sounded like a snort. They'd stopped for breakfast at a twenty-four-hour diner on the way back to their hotel. Food seemed like a good way to help lessen the tension zinging between them following their screwball wedding ceremony.

Not to mention that kiss.

Her nerve endings began to tingle just recalling the way her body responded every time his lips touched hers. Too bad her breakfast companion seemed to be immune. When he looked up from his plate of Eggs Benedict, that game face she was beginning to hate was firmly in place. Not only was he a star football player and a card shark, but apparently an award-winning actor as well. He'd played her again. The kiss in the wedding chapel—just like the one in the casino—was all for show.

If only her body were as blasé.

"Well then, as your king," he drawled. "I have a decree of my own. No more kissing."

She struggled not to choke on her bacon. *Of all the nerve!* As if she'd been the one jumping his bones every time she got close enough. Well, her body certainly got the message now. His declaration might as well have been served up with a bucket of ice water.

"You won't get any complaints from me, your highness. And let the record state, you started it. Both times."

He cocked an arrogant eyebrow at her. "So glad you're keeping count."

"I've got a score card running on social media."

That got his attention.

"The contract explicitly prohibits any mention of our marriage on social media."

Too bad the contract didn't explicitly prohibit kissing. "Gullible much?"

With a scowl, he refocused his attention on his breakfast. Her appetite now gone, Andi pushed her scrambled eggs across the plate with her fork. "How's this going to work, anyway?"

His head snapped up. "The no kissing?"

"For someone who doesn't want to kiss me, you sure do mention it a lot."

"I never said I didn't *want* to kiss you," he snapped before something that looked like remorse shadowed his face.

Huh.

He swore violently as he shoved his plate away. "Look, Andi. I'm exhausted and stressed, and I certainly don't mean to insult you in any way. You're . . . sweet and—" His fumbling for words made her cringe. "And you're attractive. I'm sure most guys . . ." His voice trailed off before he dragged his fingers through his hair. "But this is just pretend, remember?"

Oh, she remembered. She also remembered how her body melted when his tongue invaded her mouth. Right now, though, her stomach was dropping for an entirely different reason. He obviously wasn't "most guys." He'd morphed back into one of those asshole superstars who liked their women leggy, big-bosomed, and empty-headed. In other words, nothing like her.

But she knew there was more to Declan Fletcher than the stereotypical professional athlete. She'd met that Dex on the airplane and in the casino. Fool that she was, she was continuing this charade holding out hope *that* guy would reveal himself again.

"No offense taken," she lied. "I'm not into brawny jocks who double as card sharks anyway."

There went his eyebrow again, disbelief plain as day on his face. She notched her chin up, daring him to contradict her. He tore his eyes away with a heavy sigh.

"Back to my question. How is this going to work?" She gestured between the two of them before lowering her voice. "How is our marriage going to work?"

"We go back to Milwaukee and return to our lives. No one has to know about this except the folks from ICE. I'm sure there will be some forms to fill out and perhaps an interview or something. Kurt will have that all figured out by the time we get back."

She nodded while her stomach sank even further. Rejection was commonplace for her. So why did it hurt so much from a man she barely knew?

He fiddled with his spoon. "I suspect you may have to move in with me for a while."

Just like that, her stomach was back in her throat, choking off her speech. There had been no mention of co-habitation in the contract.

"I have a penthouse right on the lake."

Of course he did.

"It's close to the university and roomy enough for both of us to go days without seeing one another. My assistant will see about getting your things moved in."

"No need."

He jerked forward so that his face was inches from hers. "ICE won't buy this if we don't live together."

She closed her eyes to block out his sexy gray ones that always seemed to make her heart leap. Her throat constricted with embarrassment. "I meant there's no need for your assistant to help me move in. I barely have a couple of boxes' worth of stuff."

When she lifted her lids, his face was still inches from hers. She searched his eyes for the pity sure to be there after her admission, but there was none. Only a flash of something that looked like awe before he slipped behind his game-face once again.

Settling back against the booth, he signaled for the waitress to bring the check.

Andi's palms began to sweat again. "If we're going to live together, how are you going to keep this from your family?"

"My family still lives in Scotland. There's no reason for them to know anything."

"I don't understand. If they live in Scotland, what's the big deal with having to go home to renew your visa? Did you have to flee the country or something? Cheat someone at cards, maybe?"

Her attempt at humor fell drastically flat. His face grew even harder, as if that were possible. She'd been down this road before when she asked about his family while they were on the plane. Why hadn't she learned from his reaction then?

Because she never learned.

You need to think before you speak.

You're too reckless with your opinions.

You're too impetuous for your own good, Andrea.

Why can't you just be like everyone else?

It was the soundtrack of her life. One that always ended up with the refrain: *Then maybe a family will want you.*

But why would anyone distance themselves from their family if they had one? Why avoid returning home? Most likely he was supporting them with the multi-million dollars he earned each year for parading around in his kilt and kicking a ball through the goalpost. That had to be it. Because no one in their right mind would just desert their family. She opened her mouth to apologize, but he spoke first.

"Yeah, you guessed it. I cheated. I cheated someone out of their future."

With that cryptic remark he swiped up the paper tab and headed for the cash register up front.

SEVEN HOURS LATER, Andi was awakened by the shrill sound of her cell phone ringing. Disoriented, it took her several long breaths to remember where she was: smack in the middle of the big comfortable bed in her suite at the Wynn. After their pre-dawn breakfast, they'd returned to the hotel. With a growled good-night, Dex had disappeared into his own room to sleep or brood or whatever it was surly athletes did in their free time.

Ignoring the guilt settling in her belly, she snatched up the phone to see Clive's name on the screen. *Damn.* In all the excite-ment last night, she'd forgotten to send him a text filling him in on what went down with Kenny. The ringing stopped and she let out a sigh of relief. Suddenly, she wasn't sure what she wanted to tell her best friend. How should she explain how she'd gotten the money? And why was she reluctant to reveal that she'd actually gone through with marrying Dex?

Her reprieve was short-lived however, because the ringing began again almost immediately. Panicked that her friend was calling with something urgent and not anything involving her or her crazy, mixed-up life, she answered breathlessly.

"Clive, what's wrong? Is everything okay?"

"What's *wrong*?" Her friend sounded incredulous. "You tell me, *Mrs. Declan Fletcher*. I hope I'm not interrupting your honey-moon, but you did promise to call me before you did anything foolish."

She snapped upright. "How—how did you know I went through with it?"

"Well, you didn't expect to marry one of *People* magazine's "Sexiest Men Alive" and not have anyone find out. It's all over the Internet."

"Princess Leia," she hissed in annoyance.

Clive's chuckle sounded equal parts annoyed and hurt. "Guess that explains the Wookie watching the two of you playing tonsil hockey."

Andi banged her head against the wall. "There's a picture of us *kissing?*"

"Gurrrl, judging by that photo, you two were leading up to a lot more than just a kiss. The image practically melted my phone."

This can't be happening.

"Maybe his agent can get them to take it down," she whispered.

Clive's laugh held little humor. "That genie is already out of the bottle, honey. It's already at over seven hundred thousand views and it hasn't even been up for two hours. Congratulations. You're a viral sensation."

She slammed her eyes shut. This was a disaster. It was hard enough carrying out this charade as it was. Now it seemed they'd be playing at their fake marriage under a media microscope. Not only that, but Dex had to be furious. For some odd reason, he didn't want his family—or anyone else—knowing they'd tied the knot.

"Oh, Clive," she whispered. "What have I done?"

"Tell me he didn't force you into this?" She heard Daniel in the background angrily threatening to skewer Dex.

"No! Nobody forced me to do anything." With a less than steady voice, she recounted the whole story from their arrival in Las Vegas to their wedding earlier that morning. "After everything he did, I couldn't not help him. But no one was supposed to find out."

Her friend's voice softened. "Andi, you do know that 'What happens in Vegas, stays in Vegas' is just a slogan. It's not really true."

"Why can't I ever catch a break?"

"Seems to me you did," Clive replied. "You got the money to pay off what Kenny stole from you. Now you just have to figure out a way to fulfill your end of the bargain while still retaining your dignity."

Easy for him to say. He didn't have to pretend to be married to a man with sexier legs than hers. A man she was also ridiculously attracted to. The same man who'd made it very clear that attraction was not reciprocated.

"Come home, Andi. Daniel and I will figure out a way to make this work for you."

Grateful to have Clive still in her corner, she muttered her thanks and told him she'd call when she landed later tonight. Her friend was right, of course. No matter what happened, she needed to carry out her end of the bargain. She owed it to Dex—the compassionate Dex. Surely there was a way she could survive their fake marriage with her sanity—and her heart—intact.

DEX PACED AROUND THE SUITE, his phone pressed to his ear as he tried to smooth things over with his mother. *Damn that wedding chapel.* He said no bloody pictures. This is exactly what he *didn't* want to happen. His phone began exploding an hour ago, waking him from an X-rated dream featuring a pink-haired temptress naked on a poker table. Teammates, friends, and reporters all wanted the low-down on his sudden marriage. Dex just wanted to see how his dream played out. The first thing he was going to do was have Kurt sue Princess Leia and the rest of the Rebel Force.

Right after he finished this agonizing call from his parents.

As usual, Ma was doing her best to appear unruffled by his sudden marriage even though he knew from the irritated texts his sister had sent him that his parents were crushed.

"I'd always hoped I'd get to meet the woman my son fell in love with *before* he married her. Instead I'm introduced to her via the Internet."

The L word.

"I'm sorry about the timing, Ma." It seemed he was forever apologizing to his mother. "But it couldn't be helped."

"Well, I'm proud of you for doing the right thing by this woman. Most professional athletes aren't as honorable." His mother always tried to paint him in a positive light even when he was constantly disappointing her. He didn't deserve her love. But he was deeply grateful for it nonetheless. "But Declan Edward Fletcher, don't you dare think an ocean is going to keep me and your father from our first grandchild," she added.

He was glad she couldn't see his pained wince. Social media had gone crazy with the theory Andi was pregnant, necessitating their rash wedding. Kurt had texted advising that neither of them should deny that rumor just yet. It would provide them a cover from ICE, his agent reasoned. But in the cold light of day, Dex couldn't add another lie to the major deception he continued to perpetuate over his parents.

"There's no baby, Ma," he told her. "It's not like that at all."

There was a prolonged silence from the other end of the phone. Apparently, his mother was even disappointed that he *hadn't* knocked up Andi. He couldn't kick his way to a win.

"Well, since you're going to keep quiet about the reasons for your hasty marriage to a woman we don't know," she finally said, "then I guess we'll just have to accept that. Just as we do with the rest of your life choices."

Dex sucked in a deep breath laced with guilt. He couldn't tell her the truth. The reason for this farce of a marriage would hurt her even more than he'd been hurting her for the past ten years. He'd avoided returning home for nearly a decade. Avoided facing his greatest mistake and the harm he'd caused. In so doing, he'd missed so many of the special moments and shared milestones with his parents and family. No way could he tell his ma he'd married Andi just so he wouldn't have to come home and face the music. It would break his parents.

Instead, he chose the least painful excuse he could think of. "It was a spur of the moment thing. That's all." It wasn't a lie. Of course, he could only imagine what his mother thought of him now.

She paused again. Dex grimaced. His mother's silence was the most painful weapon in her arsenal. "Well, I'm sure she *is* a wonderful person if you felt the need to wed yourself to her for life."

His head began to pound. Why didn't his mother reach through the bloody phone and rip the flesh right off of him? This was exactly why he didn't want his folks to know about his make-believe marriage. Because to them, it wouldn't be make-believe. To Rose and Douglas Fletcher, marriage was sacred.

And it was forever.

"I guess we will have to settle with getting to know her when you both are in London later in the season. I'm sure we'll all adore her as much as you do."

Her words had him nearly tripping over his own feet. Shit. Shit. *Shit!* He'd completely forgotten the Growlers were playing a game in Wembley this year. His entire family was coming to watch him play. They'd been talking about it since the schedule was announced eighteen months ago. His plan was to avoid most of them, using the excuse that he had to prepare for the game. But his mother could be like a dog with a bone when she wanted something. And no doubt she'd not only want to meet Andi, but to introduce her to the entire stinking Fletcher clan.

"Andi won't be coming to London, Ma," he blurted out. "She's afraid to fly."

A muffled gasp alerted him he was not alone. He glanced across the room to see his pretend bride, leaning against the bar, arms crossed over her chest. Unlike in his dream, she was fully clothed, looking fresh-faced and well rested, yet distinctly peeved. He could practically hear her delicate eyebrow snapping up in annoyance.

"Afraid to fly?" his mother asked. "Then how did you two get to Las Vegas?"

Shit. How could he forget nothing got past the woman? Not

with nineteen years as headmistress of a primary school under her belt.

"She didn't realize it until she got on the plane. But you can meet her when you come visit in the spring." And there was lie number four hundred fifty-two. His family would never meet Andi. By the time the season ended and he was sharing a beach-front villa somewhere with his parents and sister, he'd be single again.

Across the room, Andi shook her head with what looked like disgust before heading to the kitchen. *Damn it.* Now he had two women angry with him. "Look, Ma, can I call you back when we get back to Milwaukee?"

His mother gulped back what sounded like a sob. "Not before you speak to your father."

Dex's gut clenched. This was going far worse than he could have imagined.

"For Chrissake, son, what the hell is going on there?" his normally sanguine father barked into the phone. "You've made your mother into a watering pot and Annis is threatening to dye her hair purple like her new sister-in-law."

"Purple? Why purple? Andie's hair is pink."

"Pink. Purple. Smurf blue. Does it bloody matter?"

Yes, it does matter, he nearly yelled into the phone before getting a grip. What was happening to him? He was arguing with his father over hair color as if it were the most important issue between him and his family. Pinching the bridge of his nose, he went in for one last lie. "Look, Da, we have to catch a plane. I'll call you tomorrow night and we can all talk once the shock has died down."

His father said something unintelligible before abruptly hanging up.

Dex swore violently.

"Please. Not in front of the baby."

He looked up as Andi poured herself a cup of coffee from a carafe on the bar and took a seat at the dining table. Despite her joke, her tone was terse and her movements wooden. He could only imagine her reaction when she had scrolled through social media. At least he was used to the public scrutiny. *Try missing a kick in overtime that could have won the game.*

With the life she'd lived, Andi was no shrinking violet, but finding herself embroiled in a sensational scandal couldn't be easy. Her attempt at humor had to be a good sign, however. He decided to follow her lead.

"Are you sure you should be drinking anything caffeinated in your condition?"

Definitely not his best play. She pierced him with a look that would have a grizzled lineman backing away. He wrapped a hand around the back of his neck.

"I thought we were laughing it off," he hedged.

She didn't respond, instead blowing softly on her coffee.

The erotic image scattered his thoughts back to the dream he'd had of her last night. He mentally kicked himself. *This is pretend.* Real or not, he shouldn't be fantasizing about his fake wife. Not if he wanted to stay sane. If they were going to pull this off, he needed to keep his head—the one housing his brain—in the game.

"Look, in a couple of weeks, when it becomes obvious that you're *not* pregnant, this will all blow over."

Continuing to ignore him, she sipped from her mug.

Great. Another woman who weaponized silence.

"Trust me. They'll move on to something else," he tried again to placate her.

"Says the one who comes out of this still smelling like a rose. While I'm painted as the conniving baby mama." Her fingers formed air quotes around the last two words. "A no-name piece of trash who tricked you into marriage by getting pregnant."

People could be so cruel on social media. "No one believes that."

"Your parents obviously did," she snapped.

The look of anguish that flashed in her eyes nearly took him out at the knees. Behind her brash exterior was a vulnerable woman. One who definitely cared what people thought of her. Cautiously, he slid into the chair opposite hers.

"I'm sorry," she surprised him by saying. "I shouldn't be taking this out on you. Social media never would have gotten wind of any of this if I'd kept up my end of the bargain and we were married by the judge." She swallowed roughly. "Your parents would still be blissfully ignorant of your new wife."

Her apology nearly slayed him. None of this was her fault. Hell, he could have called the judge this morning. But something deep inside him had screamed at him last night not to wait. The same voice that pleaded with him not to let her walk out of Kurt's office the other day. It demanded loudly that he tie himself to her as soon as she proposed the idea so she couldn't slip away again.

"I set them straight. Believe me when I tell you they aren't upset with you. They're disappointed in me."

Again.

Still.

"Because you married a no-name piece of trash woman with pink hair."

She had such a spunky spirit it was easy to miss there was a battle-weary woman inside. One who'd been abandoned repeatedly. One who thought she wasn't good enough for his parents. He reached a hand across the table to reassure her before snatching it back. Touching her was a bad idea. Every time he did, it was harder to let go. He scrubbed his hand down his face instead.

"I may not have much to my name, but up until now, at least I had my name," she murmured. "And no one is going to invest in my startup after this."

"Invest in your startup?" He really should have gotten her life story from Kurt.

Andi glared at him as though he was something she'd scraped off the bottom of her shoe. A hard knot pressed against his ribcage. His phone beeped, saving him from the rest of what had become a very confusing conversation. He punched the speaker button.

"Talk to me, Kurt."

"I was able to book a private jet leaving North Las Vegas Airport in ninety minutes," his agent said. "A car will pick you up at the hotel in an hour. The concierge will take you out a back entrance. I'll leave you booked on the commercial flight leaving out of McCarran right up until the last minute. That should throw off most of the paparazzi. But that might not fool all of them. You're not going to like this, but you're going to have to face the media at some point. It's best to meet them head on. I'm trying to coordinate an interview for tomorrow."

Bloody hell. Dex didn't realize he'd said the words out loud until Kurt replied.

"You're just going to have to overcome your interview phobia this once, Declan."

He didn't have an interview phobia. He just didn't like answering questions about his personal life. With good reason. He tolerated the weekly post-game pressers and that was it. The media knew the score, but that didn't mean they stopped asking. When they did, Kurt politely refused, but only after lecturing Dex about how he was hurting his 'brand.' Dex didn't give a damn about his bloody brand. Just his privacy. And keeping his secrets safe.

Up until now, his strategy had worked. With a heavy sigh he glanced over at his new wife. He'd sworn off marriage at one time, too. It seemed his orderly life was coming down like a house of cards.

"Fine," he said. "Set it up."

"Done." At least his agent had the good grace not to gloat. "But we need to come up with a plausible story you're going to tell first."

Dex locked eyes with Andi. "Start off by telling them there's no baby."

Her chin dropped in surprise.

"But—" Kurt tried to argue.

"No buts. I won't have Andi misrepresented by the media. Not for another minute. She didn't sign up for that. Release a statement immediately, Kurt. The marriage will have to be enough for ICE. We'll see you in a few hours."

SEVEN

A PAIR OF gold eyes tracked Andi as she moved about her spacious suite within Declan's penthouse. His unit took up the entire twelfth floor of the building with floor-to-ceiling windows providing a stunning view of Lake Michigan. The rooms she was given were decorated with sleek, stylish furniture in varying shades of warm grays. Decorative pillows and throw blankets artfully scattered around the space added a few pops of color. Her sitting room housed a small fireplace beneath a stunning landscape of a castle high atop a craggy mountain with gorgeous meadows of thistle below. The place was so elegant, Andi was afraid to touch anything.

"He has a cat."

"A cat?" Clive repeated. "Declan Fletcher doesn't strike me as a cat guy."

Holding her cellphone to her ear, she took a tentative step out onto the balcony that jutted out from the building, giving her a bird's eye view of the lake. She wasn't too fond of heights, and despite the gorgeous view of the night sky, she was uneasy being so close to the railing. Cautiously, she reached for the metal baluster, testing it for soundness.

"Well, he has a big fluffy cat who seems to worship him."

He laughed. "Must be a female."

"Probably. It doesn't seem to like other females poaching on its territory." She glanced back at the feline crouched on the top shelf of one of the bookcases bracketing the fireplace. The only part of the furry, mocha-colored animal that stirred was its eyes as they stalked Andi's every step.

"A cat and a fireplace," Daniel chimed in. "Sounds like you've found a story-book castle to live in."

"Be careful," Clive teased. "Most castles in story-books are spooky, and Declan Fletcher is bound to have a few scorned women haunting him."

She wandered back inside, nearly colliding with Dex's assistant, who was carrying a stack of fluffy white towels into the bathroom.

"He does have a female assistant," Andi murmured into the phone once the other woman disappeared.

"I knew it." Daniel sounded very pleased with himself. "I'm picturing Sandra Bullock from *Two Weeks' Notice*. Is she hot like that?"

Marlene emerged from the bathroom, her gray curls bouncing as she walked. She pushed her wire rim glasses up on her nose and mouthed "good night" before slipping out of the room. The woman made it seem as though the women Dex brought home frequently slept in his guest suite rather than his bed. Then again, Marlene was likely paid well for her discretion.

Still, it was a relief to know there would be a chaperone around. Not that there would be any more toe-curling kisses. Dex had made that very clear. But having a matronly housekeeper living with them would certainly provide an added buffer.

"Umm, I'd put her more in the Mrs. Doubtfire category."

Daniel groaned while Clive laughed. She made her way into the spacious bathroom. It wasn't as large and ostentatious as the one in Las Vegas, but it still made her own bathroom look more like an outhouse in comparison.

"I can't believe his agent already got you an interview with *The Morning Blend*." Clive's attempt to sound surprised didn't fool her. He was a shrewd businessman and she knew what his next comment would be.

"Believe it. Apparently, we are the flavor of Labor Day weekend. And before you ask, I'm sure the name of the salon will come up. If not, I'll make sure I mention it," she promised, beating him to the punch.

She fingered the soap at the sink before bringing it up to her nose. The scent of sulfates and other harsh chemicals tortured her nostrils. With a disappointed sigh, she wiped her fingers on the hand towel. She'd just have to replace the soap with some of hers.

"I'm more concerned about what story you two are going to come up with to make this reporter believe you've been secretly in love without anyone knowing," Clive responded. "Be sure and run the deets by us before the media starts flocking to the salon. That way, we can all get our stories straight."

He wasn't the only one concerned about their supposed love story. Dex and his agent were closeted in a room on the other side of the penthouse, hammering out a script. Mr. Hilbert assured her it would be very brief on details. "Less is more," he had explained. That way the media didn't have anything to question.

Fortunately, by the time their plane had landed in Milwaukee, those posting on social media had stopped speculating about whether or not Andi was pregnant. Whatever Mr. Hilbert had done worked. She smiled appreciatively at her reflection in the mirror just thinking about Dex's intervention. Of course, he had likely done it to appease his parents, but she didn't care. By setting the record straight, he'd ridden to her rescue again.

He'd slept the entire plane ride back, so she hadn't yet had the chance to thank him. But she had a good idea how to do that now. It was her turn to hold up her end of the bargain.

Beginning with tomorrow's interview.

The woman who was going to be introduced to Milwaukee as Mrs. Declan Fletcher would be worthy of the role. Not just for Dex, but for his family, too. Whatever his reasons for avoiding returning home, it was apparent he cared for his family and wanted to protect them. She may never get to meet them, but for the next few months, Andi would finally have relatives, so to speak, and she wasn't about to let them down.

She fingered her hair. "I've got a better idea for coordinating our stories, Clive. Would you be willing to come by and do my hair and makeup before the interview tomorrow?"

"He was afraid you'd never ask," Daniel answered for Clive. "We can even bring your things from your apartment to save you a trip."

More likely it would give Daniel an excuse to tag along, but she wasn't complaining. She needed the comfort of familiar faces right now.

Ten minutes later, she found herself in the luxurious study at the other end of the penthouse. The room afforded a panoramic view of the historic Third Ward of Milwaukee. Lights from the Hoan bridge twinkled in the distance as people strolled the city streets, enjoying the unofficial last weekend of summer.

The décor in this part of the apartment was definitely more masculine. An intimidating chess set dominated a side table while an actual set of bagpipes rested in the corner of the room. The instrument was yet another homage to a homeland Dex was clearly proud of, yet would do anything to avoid. *But why?* She doubted she'd ever get the answer to that question. At least not from the man himself. *It doesn't matter.* She didn't need to know his secrets to carry off this sham. Better to just enjoy this life of luxury while it lasted. She wandered farther into the room.

Bulky leather sofas were strategically situated in front of a big-screen TV, and a bar framed by bookcases showcasing memorabilia from Dex's career took up one wall. Curiosity had her wandering in that direction. Nestled between the awards and footballs were photos of him spanning various years. Many were with what appeared to be teammates, but others looked to be of family. She lifted one of the frames displaying a photo of him with a young redhead whose luminous smile was so open and genuine, it made Andi ache to know her. Judging by the way Dex was gazing tenderly at her, she must be someone special.

"My baby sister, Annis," he drawled from behind her.

Feeling a bit like she'd just been caught snooping, she started slightly. Her heart sped up when she realized how close he was. "She doesn't look like a baby in this picture."

The smell of eucalyptus and freshly showered male teased her senses when he reached around her and plucked the photo from her hands. He gingerly replaced it on the shelf. "She's not but twenty-two."

Andi wondered if he realized how his accent grew more notice-able whenever he spoke to or of his family. Turning on her heel, she all but rolled her eyes at him. "I hope you're not trying to infer that women in their early twenties are immature?"

He had the good grace to look sheepish.

"Not to mention, I'm only three years older than your sister."

"Since I can't change the fact that she's eight years younger than I am, Annis will always be a baby to me."

Envy coursed through her, sharp and hot. How lucky that beautiful woman was to have a brother looking out for her. Even one so apparently over-protective as Declan Fletcher. Burying the pain just as she always did, Andi stepped away from him and cast her gaze at the other photos on the shelves.

"If we are going to pull off this interview, I should probably know how many brothers and sisters you have and their names." Thanks to the Internet, she already knew Annis was his only sibling, but the question allowed her a moment to compose herself.

"It's just me and my sister."

She moseyed around the room, his eyes tracking her the same way his cat had earlier.

"Easy-peasy, then." She traced a finger over the cool, smooth surface of one of the many trophies in the room.

Across the room, he cleared his throat roughly. "My parents are both teachers."

Not surprising given the number of books lining the shelves. According to Wikipedia, both specialized in mathematics, which explained his connection to Professor Hal of the University of Nevada's math department. Other than the names of his sister and parents and their occupations, however, the Internet wasn't exactly a font of information on the rest of Declan Fletcher's private life.

"Given how tight lipped you are about them, I assume we won't be discussing the Fletcher clan during the interview tomorrow."

"Aye."

The word sliced through the room as though he was wielding a sword one of his ancestors likely held at one time. She risked a peek at him. He was leaning a hip against the bar, arms crossed tightly over his broad chest. His face was inscrutable, but his posture looked as if he was ready to pounce. Certainly not on her given his no kissing decree. She wasn't sure whether it was relief she felt, or something else, when his agent strolled into the room.

"For tomorrow's interview, I want you both to kiss," he announced as he took a seat on one of the sofas. "We're going to Keep. It. Simple."

He gestured for both of them to sit. Andi sagged with relief onto the opposite sofa, telling herself she wasn't disappointed the man wasn't referring to actual kissing. Dex joined her at the other end. Mr. Hilbert eyed them both before heaving an exasperated sigh.

"For the interview tomorrow, let's try sitting closer together and putting out a vibe that you like one another. Clearly, you two know how to do that or we wouldn't be in this predicament."

She opened her mouth to note that Dex had started their kiss—both times—but quickly thought better of it. With the photo as evidence, it was hard to argue she wasn't a willing participant. Instead, she sank lower into the leather cushion and kept her lips tightly sealed. She mentally patted herself on the back. Clearly, she was evolving if she was thinking before she spoke.

"Nancy Miles may be the darling of Milwaukee's morning television, but she is a thorough reporter." Mr. Hilbert aimed a pointed look her way. "She's likely already uncovered Dex's issues with ICE. And if she doesn't ask about it tomorrow, it's only a matter of time before the news gets out."

Andi nearly leapt from the couch.

"If that's the case, then everyone will know we are committing a crime." She couldn't help it. She turned and glared at Dex. "This is bad. Very bad."

"Actually, it's not as bad as you think," Mr. Hilbert interjected. "Dex and I have discussed it, and he agrees it's probably best to meet this head on."

"Head on?" Her gaze ricocheted between the two men. Not only was she peeved they'd discussed something so serious without her, but she had a sinking feeling that both men had lost their minds. "What exactly does that mean? 'Meet this head on.'"

"It means that I will confess to my negligence in getting my paperwork renewed." Dex explained. Although his tone suggested he'd rather endure a colonoscopy than admit to anything that would paint him as inept. "But I'll play it off as providing me with the kick in the arse I needed to persuade you, the love of my life, to marry me."

"The love of my life?" She all but snorted before gesturing to her pink hair and second-hand clothing. "Who in their right mind is going to believe that?"

"Hear me out, Andi," Mr. Hilbert tried to placate her. "The media and football fans are chomping at the bit for the story behind your surprise marriage. We have to get ahead of it and give them our version of the story first. Once we do that tomorrow, along with a cutesy photo shoot, they will have nothing else to snoop around for, and all this unwanted attention will go away."

He made it sound so easy. She felt some of her agitation dissipate. But not all of it.

"But isn't it possible that the more we say publicly, the greater the chances someone will figure out we are lying?"

Mr. Hilbert heaved an exasperated sigh. "We are being truthful with the most crucial part. Dex needed to get married to stay in the country. Trust me, that's the only thing Growlers' fans will care about. This team plays in a very tight division. Dex's leg often makes the difference between making the playoffs or not. The fans will worship you for your part in all of this." His voice grew gentler. "And my mother was right. There is no law that says you have to be in love to get married. There really isn't a crime here."

She pondered the agent's arguments. He presented a strong case. She slumped back against the sofa. "So how do we make them believe that someone like me is—" Her mouth was suddenly very dry. "The love of his life?"

"Fortunately, you both have similar charitable interests. We'll say you met through those," Mr. Hilbert explained.

"Charitable interests?" She didn't give to charity. Heck, she was practically a charity case herself.

"I'm referring to your volunteer work at the Barbara Vey Center for Teens." The attorney glanced through his pages of notes. "Is the information correct that you help students apply for grants and financial aid for college?"

"That's not charity," she argued. "That's helping kids who grew up like me to navigate the system."

Mr. Hilbert's face softened. "All the same. It's a very generous thing to do. And it happens to be where Dex volunteers each week."

She turned her attention to her fake husband who was sitting stone-faced on his end of the sofa. The Vey Center was located in one of the toughest neighborhoods in the city. Altruistic celebrities were happy to throw money at the area, but as far as one of them actually stepping a toe in the ward for more than a photo op, that was unheard of.

Except . . .

She jumped up from the sofa and charged toward the chess set. *It had to be.* She whirled back around to face the two men. "Professor McMath. It didn't click when Hal called you that at the casino. You organized a chess club with the kids. And you coach the math team." She didn't bother tempering the amazement in her voice, because, well, she *was* amazed. Dex was practically a folk hero among the youth and the staff at the Vey Center. Her laughter rang with wonder. "Well, that explains why all the girls have a sudden interest in chess."

For his part, he looked a little uncomfortable. "You know I don't like to publicize my work there, Kurt. That's not why I do it."

"We've been over this. It's the only scenario that makes sense," Mr. Hilbert reminded him.

Dex scrubbed a hand down his face. "Fine." He leveled a steely gaze at Andi. "But we keep the details light. Just that we met while doing charity work with Milwaukee's youth. I don't want television cameras in my face the next time I go over to the center."

Since she wanted to protect the privacy of the kids as well, she was fine with keeping the details vague. "Agreed."

Mr. Hilbert pulled a small jewelry box out of his briefcase and gingerly placed it on the table. "Here is the rest of your costume."

Dex drew in a sharp breath. His agent held up his hand, forestalling any discussion.

"I know you said no rings, but that was before this was public. The wife of a professional athlete does not walk around without a significant piece of ice on her finger."

He flipped the lid of the box open, and Andi wasn't surprised they all weren't immediately blinded.

"That's not a piece of ice," she choked out. "That's an actual ice*berg*!" Her heart began to race. "I can't wear that. What if I lose it? I can't pay to replace it."

"Relax," Mr. Hilbert said. "It's insured." He slid the box in her direction. "See if it fits."

Her fingers were shaking when she pulled the gorgeous ring from its velvet cushion. The oval diamond was the size of a freaking lima bean. Surely, it would look ridiculous on her tiny hand. Except it didn't. The ring slid on her finger perfectly, almost as though it was made for her. A soft sigh escaped her lips before she could catch it.

Mr. Hilbert chuckled. "Diamonds have that effect on women." He gathered up his notes as he stood. "I'll just leave you two to work out what details you do want to share. But remember my advice. Keep it simple. I'll be here before the television crew arrives tomorrow."

With a quick wave, he made his way out of the room.

Dex sighed. "I don't suppose we could get lucky enough that a politician will do something stupid tonight and knock us right out of the news cycle?"

She was so enthralled by the ring on her finger, she almost didn't hear him. "We can always hope."

The chess pieces suddenly went flying, startling Andi. She looked over to see the cat smugly sweeping its tail over the now empty chessboard.

He scolded the animal in an unfamiliar language. "Ignore her. She's a brat when she's not the center of attention."

"She's beautiful."

As if to refute the statement, the cat lifted her hind leg and began licking herself.

"She's a sassy witch," Dex replied.

"Does she have a name?"

"Morag. It's Gaelic for great."

At the sound of her name, the cat sat majestically, waiting to be adored.

Well then. The feline obviously felt the need to live up to her pretentious moniker.

"It's very nice to meet you, Morag." She reached over to pet her.

"Don't!" he warned.

Too late. Andi let out a yelp of pain when Morag slashed her hand, breaking the skin. Dex was on his feet and beside her in one fluid motion. He swatted the air in front of the cat with a violent curse. Morag let out her own yowl of displeasure before strutting away as if she were walking a fashion runway, her tail held high in a mocking salute.

"Let me see," he demanded, taking her hand in his.

She tried to pull free. "It's fine." A total lie. It actually hurt like hell, but she'd learned long ago to never let anyone see her pain.

"Damn it, lass. It's not fine. You're bleeding." He adjusted his grip so he could tug her out of the room. "Marlene keeps a first-aid kit in the kitchen."

"Great. I'll have her help me out then." The less he touched her, the better. The skin beneath his fingers burned more than the stupid scratch by his not-so-friendly feline.

He led her into the kitchen adjacent to the great room. Decked out with professional stainless-steel appliances and concrete counters over dark wood cabinets, the room should have looked cold and foreboding. But the copper pots hanging from a ceiling rack along with an overgrown fern brightened the place up. A plate of home-made cookies sitting beneath a glass cover added that extra homey touch.

"Marlene has already gone home."

"Home? You mean she doesn't live here?"

He shoved her hand beneath the faucet and, with a tap to the chrome, water began to bath her injured skin. "Of course not. She lives with her husband downstairs."

Andi swallowed a gulp. Her presumed buffer was nowhere to be found, and Dex had his hands on her. *Again.* Ever so gently, he caressed the skin Morag had slashed open. The warm water and his gentle probing had her nerve endings dancing with desire. She bit back a contented sigh.

You fool!

It certainly didn't take long for her worst-case scenario to come true. Any moment now, she'd be a puddle on the kitchen floor. She yanked her hand from his in a desperate attempt to regain her long-lost composure.

"I've got this." The words came out with a little more force than was necessary.

He seemed to come to his senses at the same time, putting some distance between them as he searched the cabinets for the first-aid kit.

"Morag must put a damper on your social life if she attacks every woman you bring home."

"You're the only woman she's ever scratched."

Of course. Andi couldn't halt the slump of her shoulders. The fickle feline likely bonded with other catty beauties possessing brightly manicured claws and significant thigh gaps who paraded in and out of Dex's penthouse. A pink alley cat with questionable lineage? Not so much. She dried her hands slowly with a paper towel, ignoring the glitter of the ring on her finger, flashing like a warning beacon telling her to get away as quickly as possible.

"She hasn't been given the opportunity because I've never brought a woman here."

Shocked by his admission, she spun around to face him. His face was averted, however, as he rummaged through the kit, presumably for a bandage.

"As you've already surmised," he continued. "I value my privacy."

He handed her a tube of antibacterial ointment. She slathered a small dollop on the scratch.

"The women I've been with understand the game plan upfront."

His softly uttered words sounded eerily like a warning. A shiver danced down her spine. He peeled open one of the bandages and dangled it between his fingers for her to take. When she struggled to adhere it to the wound one-handed, he took over. He smoothed the bandage with his thumb, keeping his gaze fixed on her hand. His fingers lingered as well for several long heart beats before he lifted her hand to his mouth and brushed his lips over the bandage. Andi's stomach bottomed out as she tried, and failed, to swallow a gasp. At the sound, he lifted his gaze. The passion simmering within his stormy eyes stole her breath. But it was the sorrow lurking within them that had her head spinning.

"You have to know I'm attracted to you, lass. But I can't act on it. *We* can't act on it. Because in six months, this is over. Happy ever after will never be for me. So don't go setting your heart on it. I'm not a good gamble. Not for someone like you. Ye ken?" He dropped her hand. "Get some sleep, lass. We've a busy day of pretend ahead of us tomorrow."

EIGHT

ONE OF THE perks Dex enjoyed most about playing for a professional sports team was the round-the-clock access to private, state-of-the-art training facilities. While he would have much preferred an early morning run out of doors—the weather was perfect for it—the thought of the paparazzi pursuing him along the shores of the lake forced him to enact plan B. As he expected, the Growlers' gym was a veritable ghost town. The players and staff had been given the weekend off before the season opener the following week, leaving him alone with his thoughts while his feet pounded the rubber of a treadmill.

Too bad his thoughts weren't as quiet as the room around him.

He was married. To a stranger, no less. A very alluring, spellbinding, unique stranger. One he had no business being attracted to.

Except he was.

He needed to figure out a way to maintain his sanity over the next six months. Otherwise they'd never be able to pull off this damn charade. *She's not your type,* he kept reminding himself. So why then did his libido go from zero to sixty every time they were in the same room?

He adjusted the speed on the treadmill, kicking his pace up a notch. But he still couldn't outrun his thoughts. *Marrying a stranger in haste was a piss poor idea.* He should have listened to Andi and reached out to one of the actresses who'd used him as an opportunity for more media coverage. Any one of them would have jumped at the publicity a fake marriage to him would provide. Not only that, those women would have approached it as a role, and every time his phony spouse cast a seductive glance his way, he would know she was acting.

Not so with his current fake wife. Those luminous blue eyes of hers were like a window to her soul. Her emotions were on display for everyone to see. And whenever Dex looked into them, he saw desire.

And loneliness.

He forced his feet to move faster. Seeing passion reflected in a woman's eyes wasn't novel for Dex. Most women saw him as a sexy meal ticket in cleats. He felt no real shame knowing that he'd used that to his advantage on multiple occasions. But he couldn't in this case. Despite her pragmatism, there was still an aura of innocence around Andi. Even after all the hard knocks life had thrown at her, she was still bright and shiny, and full of optimism.

So much like Niall, it hurt.

But it was her lonesomeness that would likely doom him. Last night, when he'd rejected her again, the pain in her eyes triggered something within him. He damn near spilled his guts to her. Revealing his darkest secret just to push her away. To protect her. From him.

Swearing violently, he pounded his feet harder on the treadmill.

"For someone on his honeymoon, you sure have a lot of stamina."

Heath Gibson's words nearly had Dex tripping over his own feet. He punched the button to lower his speed to avoid wiping out in front of the Growler's new head coach. Grabbing a towel, he scrubbed it down his face trying to regain some of his legendary composure. So much for a secluded, quiet place to think. He'd been so engrossed in his chaotic thoughts he hadn't noticed the other man's approach.

A former league-leading tailback, Heath Gibson was the ultimate player's coach. It helped that the man, who was barely forty, was still in prime physical shape to keep up with his players. He didn't ask them to do anything he couldn't do and the team respected him for it. Having spent the past three years as the offensive coordinator for the reigning champion Baltimore Blaze, it was no surprise he'd landed the top job with one of the league's other premier teams.

Coach rested a shoulder against one of the weight decks, studying Dex with a bemused grin. "Don't tell me you're in the doghouse so soon after tying the knot?"

Dex draped the towel around his neck while he tried to come up with a likely excuse for being at the practice facility at an hour when he should be in bed with his new wife. "No," he hedged. "Not in trouble. I was just getting a workout in while she gets all glamorous for an interview that we have scheduled for noon today."

"Say no more." Coach shot him a commiserating look. "Been there, done that. Except now, I have to entertain the kids while Merrit gets ready. Then she wonders why I'm always late." The corners of his mouth turned up and he was silent for a long moment, presumably absorbed with his own internal thoughts at the mention of his wife and family. "They're worth it, though. Definitely worth it," he murmured.

The conversation had taken a turn toward the uncomfortable. Dex didn't want to discuss the details of his own marriage. Coach Gibson was obviously besotted with his lovely wife and their two young children. Dex needed to make a gracious exit before the other man began brandishing advice about potty-training.

He glanced at his watch hoping the universal signal would

send the right message to his coach. "I'd better hit the showers so I get back in time or I will end up in the doghouse."

He started to take a step toward the locker room, but the coach's words stopped him in his tracks. "Congratulations, by the way, Fletcher. I'm looking forward to meeting your bride."

Dex swallowed a groan. He didn't want anyone meeting Andi. The more people invested in their marriage, the more awkward it would be when the sham ended. But he couldn't tell his coach that. "She's a wee bit shy," he fibbed. "And all of this being married to a celebrity can be a touch overwhelming for someone like her." When his coach didn't respond, Dex capitulated. "I'm sure she'd enjoy it if you said hi after one of the games, though. Maybe later in the season once she's had a chance to adjust."

A confused look settled on the coach's face. "I was thinking more like at the picnic tomorrow."

Bloody hell!

He'd forgotten all about the annual family picnic the team held every Labor Day. He needed to figure a way out of that and quickly.

"And don't think of using your honeymoon as an excuse to get out of showing up," the coach said as if reading his mind. "Your secret marriage is hot news. No doubt you'll want to get all the ribbing out of the way before we return to practice next week." He pinned Dex with a hard stare. "I'd rather keep the distractions to a minimum so we can concentrate on getting ready for opening day. Besides, Merrit hasn't met a lot of the other wives yet. I'm sure she'd be grateful for another newbie to pal around with. Even one who's 'a wee bit shy.'"

Coach Gibson disappeared in the direction of the commissary, leaving Dex alone again in the gym. This was exactly what he'd hoped to avoid. Keeping up their charade in front of the people who knew him best. He walked over to one of the punching bags and jabbed it with a mean right hook. The stinging in his hand did nothing to lessen his frustration, so he headed for the showers to cool off instead.

When he stepped out of the icy spray fifteen minutes later, he was annoyed to discover he was no longer alone in the locker room. Dex glanced in the direction of his locker and groaned. It had been vandalized with a dozen inflated condoms and the ridiculous ball and chain the players traditionally decorated a teammate's locker with when he got married. He growled at the culprits, Van Horn and Kessler. The two men ignored him. They were tossing a ball between them while having a conversation as if Dex wasn't standing right there.

"Why do you suppose a guy with hot new wife would come and shower in an empty locker room?" Van Horn asked as he chucked the ball at his wide receiver.

"Beats me." Kessler flipped the ball back. "Maybe she got a peek beneath his kilt and ran away in terror."

For his part, Dex was still trying to make sense of the sharp anger coiling through him at Van Horn categorizing his new wife as "hot."

Van Horn spun the ball on his fingertip. "Or maybe this is all just a publicity stunt."

One of the things Dex admired most about Van Horn was his keen intellect. The guy would have likely been awarded a scholarship to Stanford without his rocket arm. The Growlers' quarterback also possessed the uncanny ability to read the defense. It was one of the reasons he'd been named league MVP last season. Right now, however, Dex wished his friend hadn't honed that talent so perfectly. Van Horn tossed the ball back to Kessler and leveled a glare at Dex that was known to make three-hundred-pound linemen squirm.

Trying to appear unfazed by his friends' assumptions, Dex sauntered over to his locker and began pulling on his clothes. "Don't you two morons have something better to do?"

Kessler smirked. "Hmm. He doesn't sound like a man who just spent the weekend getting lucky, either. In fact, he sounds a *wee bit testy.*"

Dex attempted to divert the conversation away from himself.

"If I'm *testy*, it's because you both are standing here goofing off instead of out on the practice field working on crossing routes. Kessler's been dropping a lot of balls that have been thrown right into the bread basket."

The wide-receiver bristled, his ever-present *aw-shucks* grin fading into a scowl. "Screw you and the kilt you rode in on, Fletcher. I haven't had a drop since the second game of last season."

Van Horn held up a hand to calm his favorite receiver. "*The first quarter* of the second game of last season, in fact. But he's just trying to throw us off our game plan, Kessler. For some reason, he's not interested in discussing his love life with us."

Damn straight. Dex shoved his sweaty clothes into his gym bag.

"Well, I still like my theory that he won his pink-haired wife in a poker game. And, dude, who knew you even played professional poker?" Kessler's voice was filled with awe. "It's always the quiet types you've got to watch."

Dex pinched the bridge of his nose. "Look, I'm sorry you both have your jockstraps in a twist, but it's not like I didn't invite you to my bachelor party. There wasn't one."

"Because you never told us you were getting married and we couldn't plan one," Kessler accused.

"About that, Fletcher," Van Horn added. "I've played on the same team with you for seven years. I thought we were friends. The kind of friend who would know when his buddy planned to hightail it off to Vegas to get married."

Dex looked between the two men. His teammates were genuinely miffed at being left out of his wedding. The knowledge should have made him feel good about their friendship. Instead, it had him feeling like a bigger dick than he felt before. Because he had to mislead them, too. If he thought lying to his family was painful, this was just as bad. Hell, his teammates *were* his family.

He blew out a breath. Now was as good a time as any to try out the schtick they had come up with for this afternoon's interview.

Perhaps if his friends bought the story, he'd be more comfortable selling it in front of the TV cameras.

"The wedding wasn't exactly planned," he explained.

Both men shot him identical *no-shit* looks.

"I had to rush into things to avoid being deported."

His unexpected admission quickly wiped the smug looks from both their faces.

"Say what?" Kessler demanded.

Van Horn was more circumspect in his reaction. "Go on."

"There was a mix-up with my paperwork." Dex shrugged. "I had only three days to fix it or I'd have to leave the country and miss the season."

Van Horn crossed his arms in front of him, tucking his long fingers beneath his armpits. "So, what, you up and married a stranger to keep your green card?"

Kessler eyed his quarterback incredulously. "Forget the green card. He did it to stay in uniform. Hell, I would have married him to keep him on the team! He's the best damn kicker in the league."

The quarterback rolled his eyes, but he didn't let Dex off the hook.

"It was the most expedient option." Despite everything his agent had told Andi last night, there was still the potential ICE would sniff out the truth. And he had no doubt the authorities wouldn't hesitate to make an example of a celebrity circumventing the rules. Therefore, it was critical everyone believe he and Andi were a couple before their rushed wedding. Especially his parents, who would be crushed to learn otherwise. "And she isn't a stranger."

Van Horn studied him as if he was analyzing a critical segment of game film. "Funny you never once mentioned her."

Dex mentally kicked himself for not sorting out the pertinent details of their fake relationship with Andi last night. Now he'd have to wing it. He'd just be sure to fill her in before their interview. *Including the part about her being painfully shy.*

"We only met a few months ago."

"Define a few months," Van Horn demanded.

His teammate was starting to piss him off. "I don't know exactly, counselor. The beginning of the summer sometime."

"Dude," Kessler interjected. "Why are you getting all up in his grill? Fletcher did what he had to do to stay on the team. That's really all that matters."

"Because we roomed together for three weeks during training camp and he never once mentioned this woman," Van Horn argued. "Or talk to her on the phone. Or invite her to one of the open practices. I'm calling bullshit, Fletcher." He gestured to the ball and chain. "You're the first one to swear you'd never see that thing chained to your locker. Ever. And now this?"

Dex wiped the sweat from the back of his neck. This was more stressful than lining up for a game winning kick. But he needed his friends to buy his story and back off. For all their sakes. He stared Van Horn down and shrugged.

"What can I say? People change."

Van Horn returned the stare for a long beat, his gaze unwavering until he uttered a noise sounding more like a snort than a sigh and looked away. "She must be someone pretty special to take you down."

"She is."

The words slipped out of Dex's mouth without conscious thought, surprising all three men. That bead of sweat threatened to turn into a river. He was getting carried away with this conversation. He needed to be careful not to lay it on too thick. Except, he wasn't exaggerating about Andi being special. He admired her perseverance and her integrity. The fact she also starred in his X-rated dreams the past two nights had nothing to do with anything.

"Wow." Kessler slapped Dex on the back. "You're a sly one, Fletcher. But I'm glad you found someone to make you happy. Congratulations."

Van Horn shook his head, a sliver of doubt still lingering in his eyes. "I can't wait to chat with this special woman. She must have some sort of mystical powers if she can make a leopard change his spots."

"Or make a Highlander change his plaid," Kessler joked.

Bloody hell. Now Van Horn wanted a one-on-one with Andi. Navigating a meeting with coach would be bad enough, but the quarterback would easily sniff out the truth. And then there was Van Horn's remark about her being "hot." No way he wanted his friend around his wife. But Van Horn would only see the excuse of Andi being a "wee bit shy" as a challenge. Dex was pretty sure the guy was smooth enough to talk the habit off a nun. A more desperate deterrent was needed. He blurted out the first thing that came to mind.

"She stutters."

Both his teammates eyed him circumspectly. With those two words, the hole he was digging for himself became a crater. He silently cursed his decision to come to the training center for a workout. He'd been better off trying to outrun the paparazzi. But, as his Gran would say, in for a penny, in for a pound.

"She's uncomfortable with *chatting* or any type of small talk."

"But she does speak," Kessler asked, no trace of amusement in his voice.

"Aye," Dex snapped.

With that, he snatched up his gym bag and stormed out of the locker before he made things any worse than he already had.

ANDI EYED THE sophisticated woman staring back at her in the mirror, watching as Clive clipped a string of pearls around her neck. There was no denying the linen sheath dress made her look reserved. It also made her look matronly.

"I know I said I wanted to look respectable for Dex's fans." She gestured to her reflection in the mirror. "But isn't PTA president a bit over the top?"

"Nonsense." Clive tutted as he straightened the pearls. "This look is timeless and chic. I striped it from the mannequin at H&M, so don't even try to tell me it's not hip."

"And the pearls are perfect with it," Mrs. Hilbert agreed. The older woman insisted upon tagging along with Clive and Daniel for Andi's makeover, bringing with her a treasure trove of jewelry as if she'd looted a Brighton boutique just for the occasion. "Besides, you needed a something borrowed."

Something borrowed.

The way the three of them were fussing over her, she almost felt like a bride. Except for the fact most brides didn't go into their marriage with a set expiration date. At least that's the way the fairy tale was supposed to work. Happily ever after and all that.

Happy ever after will never be for me. So don't go setting your heart on it. I'm not a good gamble. Not for someone like you. Ye ken?

Oh, she 'ken'd' all right. The story was always the same, no matter the accent. She wasn't happily ever after material. Heck, she wasn't even good enough for a desperate jock who'd do anything to avoid going home to his family. He'd certainly drummed that message into her head enough times throughout their short acquaintance. As if that wasn't enough, he admitted to being attracted to her. Then he'd turned it into a backhanded compliment by issuing a very clear warning that he was never going to act on that desire. The sting of his words kept her tossing and turning most of the night.

Yet, when she replayed the conversation in her head for what had to be the nine-hundredth time, she couldn't help but hear the anguish in his voice. To witness the pain in his eyes. Almost as if he was protecting her from something.

From himself.

Andi nearly laughed. She was used to not being good enough. To having everyone abandon her. Did he expect her to fall to pieces when this farce was over in six months? Hardly.

Sure, he was sexy as hell. Sure, her body nearly self-combusted every time he touched her. Sure, it would be nice to enjoy the fantasy of being more than just pretend for however long it lasted. But while she didn't have the multiple college degrees her fake husband did, she certainly wasn't stupid enough to give anyone else the power to hurt her ever again. Her heart was well and truly fortified. And she'd thrown away the key, thank you very much.

He could think what he wanted. But for the remainder of the season, she'd have no problem playing the role of Declan Fletcher's cool, confident wife. She'd show him he didn't have the power to hurt her.

She lifted a hand to finger the messy knot at the base of her skull where Clive managed to hide her pink strands.

"Will you stop trying to booger up your hair," he scolded, batting her hand away. "The pewter color of this dress brings out the blue of your eyes so perfectly, no one will notice the pink."

"Never mind that you might put your eye out with that rock on your hand." Daniel looked over from where he was seated on the bed. The traitor was stroking the back of a loudly purring Morag. The cat narrowed her eyes at Andi, swishing her tail as if to say *I was here first and I'll still be here when you're gone.*

Stupid cat had the right of it.

"Be sure not to wave that thing in front of the camera," Daniel continued to tease. "You don't want to shatter all those television screens."

The others laughed, but Andi was having trouble finding the humor. She glanced down at the ring on her finger. Her stomach lurched. Despite its beauty, it felt like an ostentatious signal announcing their lie to the world. Her stomach lurched for another reason when she spied her husband's angry face reflected in the mirror.

"What have you done with my wife?"

Dex's thunderous tone had Morag scrambling for cover. Daniel let out a yelp when the cat left behind a fresh set of scratch marks on his arm. For her part, Andi had to stifle a shiver at the possessive way Dex barked the word "wife." Clive, his skin thick thanks to years of bullying and even more therapy, was unfazed, however.

He turned to face Dex with the casual boyish charm he doled out to all his clients.

"We've polished her up for the television cameras." He gave Dex a long look, scrutinizing him from head to toe. Wherever her husband had been hiding the past few hours, it hadn't involved prepping for their interview. And, damn him, even dressed in ratty sweatpants and a faded Growlers T-shirt stretched tight over his muscled chest, he didn't need any additional polish. The self-confidence and sex appeal he exuded were as blinding as her new ring.

Apparently, Clive wasn't picking up the same vibe.

"I'm happy to assist you, too. Were you planning on shaving? Or are we going for the scruffy look today?" He reached a hand toward Dex. "Maybe a little gel to tame those curls."

Dex growled low in his chest, the sound doing crazy things to Andi's stomach—not to mention points south. Clive snatched his fingers back, hastily tucking them into his pockets.

"I donae need to be *Queer-Eyed* by ya, laddie."

And to think, Andi once thought the arrogant asshole's brogue was sexy.

"Hey!" Stepping between the two men, she shot a frosty glare at the idiot she was pretending to be married to. "What gives you the right to storm in here and insult my friends?"

Dex's expression went from stunned to stony in less than ten seconds. "How about the fact that I own *this bloody flat!*"

Well, hell. The man had a valid point. Still, she refused to be the first one to look away.

"Umm, kids," Mr. Hilbert entered her now crowded bedroom and clapped his hands for attention. "The film crew is in the lobby. What do you say we take this discussion down a few notches and return to neutral corners so that we don't blow this thing before we even get started, hmm?"

When no one moved, the lawyer lost his cool. "Everybody, out!"

"Mind your temper, Kurt," Mrs. Hilbert chastised her son while she stuffed her jewelry into a bag. "Have you eaten anything today? He always gets hangry when he skips breakfast," she explained to the room.

"He's not the only one. How about we get some brunch, Mrs. H," Daniel, ever the diplomat, suggested. He took the older lady by the elbow and steered her toward the door.

"I never turn down a free meal with a much younger man." Mrs. Hilbert glared smugly at her son before swatting Dex on the ass as she made her way out the door.

"Mother!" Mr. Hilbert charged after her, stopping briefly next to Dex. "You have two minutes before they walk through that door. Get your head in the game, Fletcher."

If Dex heard the man, he didn't bother acknowledging him. He was too busy staring down Andi. It appeared they were engaged in a test of wills. One that she intended on winning.

"Suit yourself," his agent grumbled. "It's your ass that will be shipped back to Scotland."

That did it. Dex swore violently before spinning on his heel and following his agent out of her bedroom. It was only after a door slammed down the hall that Andi expelled a breath. Clive's gentle touch on her shoulder did nothing to calm the anger rising inside her. It didn't matter if the *flat* was his, he still wasn't going to speak to her friends that way. He could cast off his own family and never see them again, but as long as she was playing the part of his wife, her friends were to be treated like the family they were to her.

"I shouldn't have been so cavalier," Clive said.

"No. He is the one who should be apologizing," she snapped. "His comment was inappropriate. And I'm going to let him know. Right now."

"Andi!" Clive called after her, but it was too late. She was already striding down the hall. If they were going to make this work, they needed some ground rules. He'd given her his stupid rules. Well, now he'd have to listen to a few of hers. And rule number one was to be respectful of her family of friends.

Not trusting that she wouldn't lose her nerve, she didn't bother knocking. Instead, she threw open the door and hurried across the threshold, only to stop short at the sight that greeted her. Dex was peeling off his sweatpants and, wonder of wonders, there was nothing but the smooth skin of a very toned ass beneath them.

Oh. My! The Man with the Million Dollar Legs had an ass that was equally fine. Forget *Magic Mike*. She was pretty sure her fake husband's booty could star in its own movie. It would certainly be starring in her dreams tonight.

Shamelessly, she quickly glanced toward the mirror hoping for a peek at the rest of his spectacular anatomy before forcing her eyes to the carpet. She was *not* here to ogle him, she scolded herself. Spectacular ass aside, he'd been rude to Clive. She opened her mouth to call him out on it, but all that slipped out was a sigh.

His eyes collided with hers in the mirror. "Jayus, Mary, and Joseph!"

Thanks to remarkable athleticism, he was able to frog jump into his walk-in closet without injuring himself. Had she any breath left in her lungs she might have laughed.

"In case you didnae know, lass, that big wooden thing is called a door. It's meant to keep people oot," he shouted from within the closet's depth, his accent again becoming more pronounced.

"Oh, will you cool it with the 'Bob's your uncle' routine," she responded testily.

Silence greeted her from within before he emerged a minute later wearing dark gray pants and a puzzled look. His chest was still bare, however. She attempted to avert her gaze because she was not going to let his annoyingly sexy body distract her from her objective. But her unruly eyes immediately zeroed in on the happy trail of dark hair leading from his chest down to where his fingers fiddled with the buttons at his waist. Her stupid thoughts immediately began to ponder whether he was commando beneath them. With a huff of frustration most definitely fueled by arousal, she crossed her arms over her suddenly tight nipples.

He arched an eyebrow at her. "Bob's your uncle?"

"You know. Your accent. Brogue. Whatever it's called. You use it to distract me."

He shook his head softly like he didn't know what she was talking about, but she could swear the corners of his lips had turned up into a near smile before he looked away.

"You were rude to my friend," she said.

"Aye."

"Clive doesn't deserve to be treated like that just because of his lifesty—wait. What did you say?"

"I said I know. I was wrong."

Well, that was unexpected.

Dex heaved a sigh before dragging his fingers through his hair. "Look, Andi, this is a lot more complicated than it sounded in Kurt's office the other day. There seem to be landmines everywhere I step."

"Tell me about it." She licked her lips at the landmine that was his beautiful body.

"Should I go fetch your friend to help me pick out a shirt? Or is that something you can handle?"

Common sense said it would be better to "fetch" Clive. Not because she couldn't pick out a shirt, but doing so felt . . . intimate somehow. It was something a real wife would do for her husband.

None of this was real, she reminded herself. And hadn't she just given herself a pep talk five minutes earlier about how she wasn't going to let any of this affect her? She would play the part to perfection and then walk away unscathed.

And Bob's your uncle, her subconscious whispered.

"I'd be happy to pick something out."

Chin high, she strutted past him and entered the closet. Except she hadn't stepped into a closet. At least not like any she'd ever seen in her lifetime. The room was almost as large as the adjacent bedroom, lit by two skylights in the ceiling. Its walls were lined with mahogany shelves, drawers, and hundreds of cubbies for shoes. A tufted ottoman, the size of a kitchen table, took up the center of the space. The space was a woman's fantasy even without the naked Highlander who inhabited it.

"This flat was once owned by a pro basketball player. He was passionate about his clothing and footwear," Dex explained a bit sheepishly.

"Ah." She gestured to the rows of athletic shoes lining half of one wall. "What's your excuse?"

"Most of those are freebies." He shrugged unapologetically. "Companies send them hoping I'll agree to endorse them."

"Ah," she repeated, because really, could his life be any sweeter? She had less than ten pairs of shoes to her name. Yet, he had over a hundred pair that would likely never be worn. If she needed another reminder of how different they both were, this was it.

Wandering over to a row of dress shirts hanging on a rod, she plucked off the first one she came to, a soft blue shirt with darker blue pinstripes. With his coloring, the shirt would pop in front of the television cameras. Not that she cared. She just needed him to cover up all of that tantalizing skin so she could think clearly. "This will do."

He pulled the shirt over his shoulders. "Look, Andi," he began.

"No, you look," she interrupted him with a finger jab in the direction of his now covered chest. "You already dictated your rules for this relationship. Now it's time I lay out a few of mine."

He paused in the act of buttoning up his shirt, his eyebrow cocked arrogantly once again. "I seem to recall you already proclaiming one. It had something to do with bacon."

The corners of his mouth were definitely twitching now. The sight stoked her annoyance.

"You will be nice to my friends. At all times. Period."

He nodded once. "Understood. Anything else?"

Well, damn, his ready agreement took a lot of the bluster out of her sails. "Um . . ."

His dimple practically winked at her as a full-on smile threatened. The rat was enjoying this much more than he should. His amusement added to her irritation.

"As a matter of fact, yes. There will be no more of . . . this." She waved her fingers in the vicinity of his still unbuttoned shirt.

Both eyebrows were cocked now. "This?"

Her cheeks were on fire, but no way was she backing down after coming this far. "This! Meaning your nakedness. Keep yourself covered up when I'm around. This isn't a damn locker room."

He had the audacity to laugh at her. A full belly laugh that actually had him wiping his eyes.

"It's not funny." She barely stifled the urge to stomp her foot. "Finish getting dressed and compose yourself so we can get this stupid interview over with."

She stalked in the direction of the door.

"Andi," he called after her.

His eyes were still shining with mirth, but at least he was finishing buttoning up his shirt.

"I don't suppose you'd consider stuttering during the interview?"

What. The. Ever-loving. Hell? Was he serious right now?

"I-I . . . wh-what?" *Damn it.* Him just mentioning it had her stammering.

He laughed again, and this time she did stomp her foot.

"Argh! Why are men such children." Spinning on her heel, she stormed out of his bedroom.

NINE

"I'M SO GLAD you finally let my viewers inside your stunning penthouse, Declan," Nancy What's-her-name gushed. She glanced knowingly at Andi, who was sitting ram-rod straight beside him on the leather sofa looking as if she'd been called to the headmaster's office for cheating.

"I've been begging him for years to grant me a one-on-one interview," the other woman explained. "Growler fans want to know the man behind the million-dollar leg. But up until now, he's been so reclusive."

Damn right. It was bad enough he had to suffer through the mandatory post-game pressers—especially after a game winning kick that went wide-right. But his personal life was just that, personal. He hated revealing any part of it for the rest of the world to dissect. These days, fans—not to mention the rest of the general public—thought they had the right to critique a celebrity's every decision or action. Dex hadn't signed up for any of that bullshit. Just the thought of how his so-called fans would react if they got wind of his biggest mistake had him breaking out in a cold sweat.

"I guess we all owe you a debt of thanks, Andi, for snaring one of Milwaukee's most eligible bachelors so we could get a peek inside his lair," Nancy continued. "Although it will probably take the broken-hearted women of this town a while to forgive you for taking him off the market."

The brittle smile Andi wore wavered slightly. As if the false pregnancy rumors weren't enough, now she had to worry about getting the cold shoulder from the entire female population of Wisconsin. The women of Milwaukee had another thing coming, though. As evidenced by her earlier defense of her friends, Little Orphan Andi didn't back down from anything. Truth be told, he was a wee bit awed by her strength of character. Which made what he was about to do even more nauseating.

"You two certainly pulled off the surprise of the year," Nancy stated. "How were you able to keep your relationship under wraps for so long?"

Dex glanced behind the camera to where Kurt looked on. His agent nodded stoically. They'd agreed to offer as many non-answers to the interviewer's questions as possible, but it would be hard to evade them all. It was bad enough Andi had decided to present herself to the world as a buttoned-up debutante. If people were going to believe their marriage was for real, he needed to let the viewers—and his teammates—know he found her sexy. Not that it was a stretch. He found her sexy as hell. But he was about to let the world know just how sexy. He just hoped she didn't hand him his balls on a paper plate after this was over.

He smiled at Andi before picking up her hand and brushing a kiss over her knuckles. "Well, Nancy, that was easy." He laid her palm against his thigh, placing his hand over top of hers. "We were too busy unwrapping each other that we didn't have time to go public."

For fuck's sake. The line Kurt fed him sounded idiotic coming out of Dex's mouth.

There was an audible gasp somewhere in the room. Mrs. Hilbert, most likely. Dex bit back a wince at the nails currently digging into his thigh as if to say "in your dreams, asshole." He might have overplayed his hand with such a flagrantly suggestive comment, but Kurt was right, it had to be done. To her credit, Andi barely reacted to Dex's change in course.

Nancy, however, was having a bit more difficulty hiding the fact she was flustered.

"Oh, my." She fanned herself with her list of questions. "Perhaps you'd like to tell our viewers how you two met?"

He opened his mouth to answer with the lie they'd concocted the night before about crossing paths at the Vey Center, but Andi beat him to the punch.

"That's another easy one," she replied. "I work at Shear Envy salon. We met when Dex came in to get waxed." Andi smiled smugly, all the while viciously patting his thigh as though she'd seen a spider crawl up his leg.

This time the sound coming from somewhere in the room was an agonized groan. He suspected Kurt was the culprit. His agent was either enjoying Andi's pluck or he was suffering a stroke.

For his part, Dex smothered a snort of surprised laughter. He'd suspected his wife was gritty and determined, but he underestimated her ability to fight dirty. Of course, his idiotic comment to her friend earlier and the suggestion that she stutter during the interview were likely largely responsible for her claws. Still, he had to add her feistiness to the growing list of things he admired about her.

"Waxed?" Seasoned journalist that she was, Nancy was not going to let Andi's statement go without a follow-up.

"Oh yes, twice a month. Like clockwork." Andi leaned forward conspiratorially. "Dude has a back so hairy it's practically a hair shirt."

"You don't say?" The other woman glanced over at him for confirmation.

The only response he could manage was a pained smirk. No doubt he was going to catch hell from his teammates for Andi's lie. Pleased with her counterattack, she settled back against the sofa. He reached an arm around her shoulders, pulling her in tight against his body. She was still stiff as a board, so he massaged his fingers into her shoulder. His movement was greeted with a sharp thumbnail moving dangerously close to his groin.

"Um, so you two bonded over . . . back waxes?"

"Oh, no," he interjected, trying to formulate a comeback while ignoring the impending damage to his manhood. "Andi doesn't fall for just any pretty face. I won her over with my brilliant intellect. You see, she's finishing up business school and was struggling a wee bit with her studies. I offered to tutor her with her classwork and well, you know, one thing led to another from there."

As impossible as it seemed, Andi stiffened even more. No doubt she was annoyed at the sexual innuendoes he was bandying about like a randy lad. She was also a proud woman, though. He suspected she wouldn't enjoy being made to look vulnerable in any aspect of her life, particularly her studies. But she'd met him head on with the back waxing and hair shirt quips, so the game was on. He found himself actually looking forward to whatever she'd come up with next.

"And I won Declan over with my bath soaps," she retaliated.

"Bath soaps?" Nancy donned a "what in the hell" look as her head twisted back and forth between them.

"I make organic bath soaps, lotions, and shampoos. Dex here loves a long soak in a good bubble bath." She turned to him with an insipid smile and clear "bite me" expression in her eyes.

This woman never, ever, did what he expected. There was no calculating the probability of any response from her. And damn if he didn't enjoy trying to figure her out. A smattering of pride bubbled up in his chest at the way she took him on.

Not only that, but he was beginning to realize that his attraction to her was so much more than just a sexual one. He actually liked her. A lot. And maybe he could come away from this fake marriage with something unexpected—a friend.

Of course, given the past five minutes, he might have pooched that opportunity. He needed to get them out of the mess of an interview before it was too late. He reached up and gently toyed with a strand of her hair that had come loose from her uptight hairdo. The simple gesture had her sucking in a ragged breath.

"She does make the most incredible soaps. Andi is very talented with scents." He glanced away from his stunned wife to look at the reporter, grateful Kurt had finally filled him in on her business venture. He hoped Andi would see his declaration as the apology it was meant to be. "We'll send you a basket of some of her best work. You won't be disappointed. Neither will the women of Milwaukee."

He knew the instant Andi realized the interview had gone from a contest of one-upmanship to something else. Her blue eyes softened and the death grip she had on his thigh became more of a gentle caress. The agitated edge was gone from her voice when she spoke.

"And I'm not the only one Dex shares his *brilliant intellect* with. He's very generous with the children of Milwaukee. Especially those who don't have someone to give them that extra push with their school work. Yes, his brain is sexy, but his kindness is definitely his most attractive feature."

Their eyes locked for a long moment. They were both pouring it on thick, but something in her look told him she meant some of what she said. He wasn't sure why her acceptance meant so much to him, but it did. It felt almost as good as kicking the game winning field goal. He nearly forgot they were in the middle of an interview until Nancy spoke.

"Well, I think most of the women in Milwaukee would say that Dex's legs are his most attractive feature."

Andi's mouth turned up into a wicked smile. "That's only because they haven't seen all of him."

Mrs. Hilbert cackled in the background while Dex's adorable, feisty, unpredictable fake wife turned and winked at the damn camera.

HOURS LATER, DEX was nursing a glass of scotch in the quiet of his dimly lit study, mentally preparing himself for the fallout that would likely ensue once the interview aired the following morning. He could only imagine the pranks Kessler would have up his sleeve. So much for Coach Gibson's plan to keep the team focused on their opponent this week. If there was one thing Dex knew about the Growlers' players, they would come together all right, but they'd be unified in torturing him.

Kurt was ridiculously pleased with the spectacle. "You two couldn't be more perfect for each other if your relationship actually was real," he'd claimed, slapping Dex on the back. "The folks at Immigration and your fans will totally buy into your marriage after that performance."

Satisfied his job was done, Kurt took off to Lake Geneva for the remainder of the weekend. His agent's meddling mother, meanwhile, absconded with Andi to parts unknown, leaving Dex to his own devices for the remainder of the day. A week ago, he wouldn't have been bothered by the solitude. It had been his cross to bear for nearly a decade. But for some reason, the isolation felt a little heavier tonight.

Morag hissed from her perch atop the bookshelf, suddenly prancing out of the room in a huff.

"Even the bloody cat has better plans," he murmured as he took another swallow from his glass.

"I think it's more that she doesn't want to be in the same room with me."

He nearly choked on his scotch when Andi's voice drifted in from the shadows. "Where have you been?"

The question came out of his mouth a bit more harshly than he intended. He blamed it on the burn from the alcohol. Andi made her way further into the room. She looked more like his Andi dressed in a pair of skinny jeans and a plain white T-shirt.

His Andi? Where the hell had that come from? She wasn't his. Not now. Not ever.

"Wow." She sat down on the sofa, picking up a pillow and

putting it on her lap as if to use it as a shield. "And here I thought we had one of those open marriages where we didn't have to be in each other's pockets. Next you'll be wanting to add me to your Find My Friends list. Or worse, barefoot and cooking dinner."

He snorted. She was right, of course. Under the agreement, they were supposed to be living separate lives. So why then did her mention of open marriages have his teeth on edge? How had he become so bloody possessive all of a sudden? He needed to focus on the game plan. It was the only way to survive having her in his orbit and not in his bed.

"Let's not go too crazy," he quipped. "Just leave your schedule on the icebox door so I know where to find you the next time I need my back waxed."

Her posture relaxed noticeably. She tossed the pillow to the side and tucked her feet beneath her. "Oh, don't think Clive is going to let you get any free services."

The air suddenly grew charged, along with parts of his body, as he considered all the "free services" he wouldn't be getting. He took another healthy sip from his drink. "Well played on the back wax, by the way." He saluted her with his glass. "For what it's worth, it was Kurt's idea to go in that direction with the interview."

What's an agent for if not to throw under the bus?

Andi shrugged. "Mrs. Hilbert admitted as much. I just wish you boys had clued me in *before* the interview."

"Kurt was worried if we did, you'd bolt."

Her sigh sounded annoyed. "I told you before that my word and my name are the only things in my life I control. And they mean something. I committed to this and I don't plan on letting you or Mr. Hilbert down. You can stop worrying that I'm going flake out over every little thing before the divorce is filed."

Guilt licked at his belly as he studied her over the rim of his glass. She hadn't let him down. Not once. Even when he'd let her off the hook about the marriage, she'd stepped up when most people in her position would have taken the free money and run.

But Andi Larsen was not most people. And he was beginning to appreciate the rare gift she was.

"I can promise you won't be subjected to any more tortuous personal interviews. Today was a one and done."

"Wait." She looked at him in disbelief. "You mean Nancy Miles was telling the truth? This really was your first interview?"

"I do the required press conferences after games, but nothing more."

"But you're a professional athlete. A celebrity. Isn't there something in your DNA that requires you to continually boast about your good fortune?"

Nothing in his DNA had prepared him to be a professional athlete, much less a celebrity. That role had been reserved for Niall. "I'd much rather endure a root canal."

"Why? Because you turn into a Neanderthal jock who has to boast about his sex life when the camera lights go on?"

He deserved that one. "Touché."

It didn't surprise him when she didn't revel in her win. "Seriously, why?"

Because he felt guilty. Guilty for his fame and success when all of that was meant for someone else. He didn't deserve to be feted or idolized. Not after what he'd done.

"My private life is nobody else's damn business," he said instead.

With a heavy sigh, she stood up from the chair. "Yeah, yeah. I get it. You've got the brooding Highlander role down to perfection. My life is an open book, while your secrets will remain just that, secrets. Good thing this isn't a real marriage." She started for the door. "I'll leave you to it then. Night."

Damn. She was right. He was a Neanderthal. But as much as he wanted to apologize and spend the rest of the evening bantering with her, he needed to keep her at arm's length. It would be safer that way. For both of them. Except he also needed to tell her about the picnic.

"Andi, hold up."

Just when he thought she wouldn't, she halted. When she turned toward him, her normally easy to read expression was lost in the shadows. He cleared his throat.

"We have another mandatory appearance tomorrow." He rushed on over her exasperated sigh. "It's a little family picnic the team throws every year. Nothing major."

Her shoulders slumped. "I can see we are going to have to post a schedule on the 'icebox.' Keep in mind I have classes and reading to get done. I wasted most of my study time this afternoon putting together the baskets of soaps and lotions for Nancy and her crew that *you* promised."

So that's where she'd run off to. "Are you complaining about free-advertising, lass?"

"Not at all. Thank you, by the way."

"Anything for you, my queen."

She laughed, the sound making his own lips twitch.

"I'm sure I can handle something as simple as a picnic."

"That's the spirit, lass. It will be simple. You'll see."

TEN

PROFESSIONAL ATHLETES DID NOT picnic like normal people. That was Andi's first observation when she and Dex arrived at the Growler's practice facility the following afternoon. Her second observation? She was incredibly underdressed.

Beneath the massive tent looming over the outdoor field, waitstaff decked out as referees passed through the crowd, handing out drinks and food. The guests themselves looked as if they'd just stepped from the pages of *Town & Country* magazine. Even the kids, their faces painted with big green G's, looked like poster children for Abercrombie Kids.

As they drew closer to the giant tent, she began to drag her feet. Dex took two giant steps before noticing. He turned to her with a quizzical expression on his face.

"What's wrong?"

"You told me this was a 'simple little picnic.'" She glanced around them trying to quiet the panic whirling within her. *Holy hell.* Was that an actual pony those children were riding? She'd felt out of her league since this whole charade began, but this? This was an alternate universe.

He closed the distance between them, his body shielding her from anyone who happened to look their way. "I did tell you it was a picnic. Because that's what this is. A picnic."

"Noooo." The word came out as a near hysterical wheeze. "A picnic is a grill, some burgers, beer, and brats, with maybe a frisbee for fun and a blanket for . . . whatever."

His eyes darkened and his nostrils flared. "Well, as much as I'd like to discuss *whatever* the blanket is for, you're right. This is not that type of picnic. Because it's hosted by the team's owner who likes to show off." He had the nerve to grin. "And, as for frisbees, we don't allow them any longer. Not since Kessler spoiled it for everyone by being too competitive and knocking our former head coach's wife in the head. The sight of the caps from her two front teeth flying through the air is still fresh in everyone's mind. It's worrisome enough they continue to let him around the kiddos with their sparklers."

"Just sparklers? I'm surprised they all don't get their own light sabers." She brought her hands up to her face. Her nerves had her breakfast threatening an instant replay any moment now.

He moved in closer. The amazing scent of his skin had her stomach churning for very different reasons suddenly.

"What is this really about, Andi?" he asked gently.

"Me!" She gestured to her worn white chucks, her cutoff jean shorts, and the Growlers T-shirt she'd bought the night before at a convenience store, before ending with her pink-dipped hair pulled to each side of her head in pig tails. "The people in there look like they're attending a garden party with royalty while I look like . . . this!"

His eyes slowly tracked down her body from head to toe and back up again before he shrugged.

"What's wrong with the way you look? I think it's cute."

Cute?! Cute was not going to allow her to fit in with these people. Not even close. And the next few hours would be another painful reminder of how she never would fit in. She hadn't realized she was clutching her belly until Dex wrapped his arm around her and spun her back in the direction of his Jaguar.

"That's it. I'm taking you home because if you keep holding yourself like that, people are going to wonder if you really are pregnant."

Her stomach pitched even harder. But before they could even take a step, there was a male voice at her shoulder.

"Hold up there, Fletcher," he said. "You've had all weekend with this young lady. It's time you share her with the rest of us."

Dex uttered something obscene sounding beneath his breath. Tightening his arm around her shoulders, he turned her back toward the tent.

"Actually, Coach Gibson, Andi's not feeling all that well."

Sympathetic green eyes carefully surveyed her before coming to some unknown conclusion. The other man's appraisal was followed by a slow, unapologetic grin that had likely melted hearts —not to mention panties—for years. But she was more captivated by the young girl he held in his arms.

She was adorably dressed in a Lily Pulitzer dress with pink sandals. Her shoulder length hair was thick and so black in color, it was almost blue. But not as blue as her wide eyes. As soon as Andi looked her way, the child burrowed her head into the man's shoulder.

"I can empathize." The coach tickled the little girl's chubby thigh. "This one suffers from shyness as well. She didn't want to come at all, today. Even with the promise of pony rides. But when she saw the two of you on television, she changed her mind."

The little girl peeked through her long, inky lashes at them.

"This is my daughter, Harper," he explained. He gestured to the stuffed pink-haired troll doll his daughter had clutched to her side. "As you can see, she's quite taken with people who have pink hair."

Harper's lips trembled slightly before the corners turned up in an impish smile. Just like that, the terror that had seized Andi evaporated.

"Daddy's can be so silly sometimes, right Harper?" Andi said, returning the little girl's smile. "Everyone knows Poppy isn't a person. She's a troll. She also happens to be the star of one of my favorite movies."

Harper's answering giggle renewed Andi's confidence. She could do this. She would not let Dex down. Even if she only ended up making friends with a small child, that was enough. *She* was enough.

Coach Gibson pretended to look chastised. "Well, what does silly old dad know." He kissed his daughter on the tip of her nose. "Can you and Poppy take our new friend over to meet Mommy?" Harper scampered down and the coach locked eyes with Andi. "Our son lost his battle with a tumbler of fruit punch and she's getting him changed. As I told Dex yesterday, my wife, Merrit, is eager to meet you. She'll introduce you around and get you sorted out with all the WAG's activities."

Confused, she looked from one man to the other. "Wags?"

Coach Gibson chuckled. "Wives and girlfriends. I'm not really sure how the acronym came about, but you're one of their club now."

"And they have a club? And . . . *activities?*"

No one had mentioned anything about her participating in activities with the other wives. Or girlfriends for that matter. Her nerves rumbled back into her stomach with speed. She looked over at Dex, who was strategically avoiding her gaze. Before she could call him out, Harper slipped her hand into Andi's and tugged her toward the tent. With a glance over her shoulder that clearly said they'd be discussing this later, Andi moved to follow.

"Andi," he called after them.

He stilled her with a hand on her shoulder. "Are you sure about this?" he murmured.

He was giving her an out. Not that she was surprised. Aside from the ridiculous persona he'd adopted for yesterday's interview, he'd been nothing but chivalrous to her. It was heartening to know he wouldn't ever take advantage of their situation.

Even when she sometimes wished he would.

"I'm good."

He looked like he wanted to object, but he remained silent. Instead, he leaned in and pressed his lips next to her ear. "We'll only stay as long as is politically necessary," he whispered. "But if you need to go before then, all you have to do is say the word."

The urge to sink into him nearly swept her off her feet. He must have felt the same way, because he sucked in a strained breath before squeezing her shoulder and stepping back. Determined not to fail at her role, she pasted on her game face and allowed Harper to lead her into the fray.

"DAMN, FLETCHER, WHAT did you say to make that new wife of yours all squinty-eyed at you?" Trayvon Dawes, the three-hundred-pound leader of the Growlers' offensive line, asked as he handed Dex a can of cold beer.

Dawes and several other linemen quickly moved to form a circle around him while Coach Gibson and his little daughter led Andi away. Despite her reassurance she was fine, Andi looked as if she was being led on a perp walk instead of into a lavish party.

"Yeah, you're doing it all wrong if your lady is miffed at you like that already," Rolando Harris, the team's most veteran player, added. The nose guard wasn't shy about offering sage advice on any subject from which tape was better to protect your fingers during a game to which restaurants served the largest portions in every city.

Too bad Dex wasn't in the mood to hear from Harris or any of his other teammates. He should have ignored Coach and taken Andi home.

"I didn't say anything wrong," he snapped.

The men surrounding him snorted like a bunch of bulls in a pasture.

Oh, for fuck's sake. "I complimented her, damn it."

Trayvon jerked his trio of chins up. "Complimented her how?"

Were these idiots serious? "What's with the twenty questions? I told her she looked cute." And she did. Unlike most of the other women here today, she was actually the only one who looked ...*real.*

A chorus of groans echoed in his ears.

Trayvon slapped a meaty hand against his big head. "Dude, didn't nobody teach you anything about women? Ladies over the age of thirteen don't want to be 'cute.' They want to be *hot.*"

"Man, you went wide right on that kick," Rolando added with a shake of his head. "It's a good thing that your married teammates are here to help a brother out."

Dex bit back a groan. Help from these goons was the last thing he wanted. He had no need for marriage advice because his situation was temporary and one that won't ever be repeated. Not that he could tell his teammates that. He glanced around for an out, but the guys had already closed the circle around him.

Steve Jacobs, one of the Growlers wide-receivers who was married to his high school sweetheart and together had not one, but two sets of twins, sidled up closer. Dex had always made it a point to give Jacobs a wide berth for fear that the other man's happy domesticity—not to mention his fertility—was contagious.

"Women speak a different language than we do, Fletcher," Jacobs explained. "The sooner you understand it, the happier your wife will be. And you know what they say, happy wife, happy life." He slapped Dex on the shoulder.

Dex scanned the crowd, growing more desperate for an escape route. His gaze landed on Andi. She was surrounded by the wives of several of the men currently holding him captive. She looked about as miserable as he felt.

"For instance, when she asks you if her clothes look good on her," Jacobs was saying.

"Or 'Does this outfit makes my butt look big?'" Trayvon interjected with a shrill voice in a ridiculous attempt to imitate a woman.

"The answer is always no," his teammates chorused.

"Never ask 'Are you gonna eat that?'" someone said, eliciting a few groans and shuffled feet from the guys. "And she can take anything she wants off your plate, but you better not touch her plate."

"Yeah, never eat the last cookie, man." Trayvon shuddered.

Another one of his teammates piped up. "And if there's ever a disagreement between her momma and her, always side with your wife."

"But don't make my mistake," one of the guys added. "Don't go trash talking her mother or her sister or her girlfriends. Only she can do that. Your best bet is to nod and say 'sure, baby' every freaking time."

"Trust us, 'sure baby' or 'yes dear' will keep you out of a lot of trouble, my friend." Trayvon slapped Dex on the back.

"And," Rolando announced. "Whenever you ask her what's wrong and she says 'nothing,' something is *always* wrong."

The men surrounding him all nodded solemnly.

"Or if she says 'I'm fine'..." Jacobs added.

"She's not fine!" the guys chorused.

Did they take him for a fool? Out of the corner of his eye, he watched as Van Horn sauntered up to Andi, swiftly culling her from the herd of wives and pulling her aside. Dex wanted to be grateful to his friend for her rescue, but the muscles at the back of his neck tightened painfully for no reason. Reminding himself that jealousy had no place in their fake marriage, he willed himself to relax and participate in the conversation.

"Give me some credit, lads. I've been around a woman or two before."

"Yeah, but never for more than a week at a time," Trayvon remarked. "None of them ever stuck before this one. I gotta wonder if you might have driven a few of the ladies off with your surly, Highlander demeanor."

"Nah. I'm guessing it was his skirt that sent all those other women running." Kessler made his way into the circle carrying a watermelon beneath each arm.

Dex's teammates were really starting to piss him off. And if Kessler had come to toss in his two-cents with this bunch of henpecked buffoons, one of those watermelons was headed straight up his arse.

His friend must have sensed his agitation because he promptly steered the conversation in a different direction. "But enough about the newlyweds, fellas. You can school him on the best topics for pillow-talk later. It's time to see who can long-snap a watermelon the farthest. The winner gets the pot donated to his favorite charity. Palmer's taking bets, so you'd better hurry or you'll be left out."

To Dex's relief, his teammates took the bait and all scattered.

"You're welcome." Kessler tossed one of the watermelons at him.

"Aye. Thanks for the rescue. But I don't have time for any of your games today. I need to find my wife." He tried to shove the watermelon back to his friend, but the asshole wouldn't take it.

"Your mistake for leaving her alone. Don't worry, though. Van Horn took her under his wing. Last time I checked she was mooning over his high cheek bones." He juggled the watermelon between his agile hands.

Dex snapped his head around to where Andi and Van Horn were standing a moment ago. They were no longer there. *Damn it.* He nearly dropped the watermelon in agitation.

Kessler laughed. "Relax, asshole. She's not Van Horn's type. Of course, I wouldn't have guessed she was your type, either. I still say you won her in that poker game."

"Go play with your melons, Kessler." Dex chucked the watermelon at the wide-receiver, his annoyance growing when his friend deftly caught it with one hand.

"Huh. I would have bet the odds of you being smitten with a woman were a million to one. I missed a windfall not offering a bet on that one." Kessler shook his head as he walked away.

"Like I keep sayin', it's always the quiet ones you have to watch."

Dex didn't have time to debate the word "smitten" with the twit. He needed to find Andi. No doubt Van Horn had lured her off somewhere to interrogate her. The quarterback hadn't bothered to disguise the fact he didn't believe Dex's explanation about their relationship. He hated being wrong more than he hated throwing a pick-six. Van Horn's arrogance was just what was needed on the field, not so much away from it. Andi was already uncomfortable enough. The last thing she needed was to be grilled by the team's quarterback just so the cocky arse could prove he was right. He charged toward the tent to find his wife, telling himself his concern was driven by the fear she might compromise their situation, not by any sort of jealousy.

What he hadn't counted on was the number of people wanting to congratulate him on his marriage and wish him well. It seemed everyone had tuned into the morning show that day. As Kurt predicted, no one had any lingering doubts about Dex and Andi's marriage. No one except Van Horn, that is.

Where the hell could they be? He quickly worked the tent from one side to the other, not finding either his wife or Van Horn.

"Such a lovely young woman," the wife of the team owner commented as she pumped his hand. "I loved the sizzle between you two this morning."

Sizzle? He bit back a groan. "You haven't seen my wife around lately, have you, Mrs. Ciaciura?"

"Last I saw, the coach's wife was spiriting her off toward the offices inside," the woman replied. "But when you find her, do bring her over to chat in person. I'd love for her to join us in the owner's box at a game sometime this season."

He didn't bother trying to explain the relief he felt that Andi was no longer with Van Horn. "I'm sure she'd be thrilled to join you in your box for the game. I'll just go find her and bring her over to say hello. Then you two can sort out all of the arrangements."

With a peck on Mrs. Ciaciura's cheek, he headed in the direction of the training facility.

"That's not a good idea," Van Horn said as he fell into step beside him.

Dex jerked to a stop. "What the hell are you talking about? And what did you do with my wife?"

"I saved her from the she-wolves." Van Horn kept on walking. "Coach's wife turned around for a minute to deal with her son and they circled around her like a pod of sharks."

"I can relate," Dex mumbled as he resumed his march toward the building. "The guys weren't much better."

"Except 'the guys' will do anything to protect your Scottish ass, not to mention your million-dollar leg." He gestured back to the crowded tent. "Some of those women are hell bent on tearing other women down. Especially one as innocent as your—" He made quotation marks with his fingers. "*Wife.*"

Once again Dex jerked to a stop, this time glancing around to make sure no one was in hearing distance. The two men stood equal distance between the party tent and the training center.

"She is my *wife*," he growled. "Do I have to show you the bloody marriage license for you to believe me?"

Van Horn waved him off. "I believe you, Fletcher. But don't feed me that bullshit that you would have married her anyway. Not after you spent years swearing off anything close to love. I'll admit, Andi is a sweetheart, but even she isn't enough to melt that frigid heart of yours. You forget who you're talking to. We're on the same page of the playbook where love and serious relationships are concerned."

He opened his mouth to object, but Van Horn held up his hand.

"Look, I don't care how this all went down. And I'm with Kessler. You do what you have to do to stay on the team. Winning is the most important thing. Period." Van Horn crossed his arms over his chest. "But don't think you're going to use that woman as a prop and leave her to her own defenses. I'm not gonna let that happen."

Not gonna let that happen? Who the bloody hell did he think he was? It was all Dex could do not to deck the man who'd been something of a best friend to him for the past seven years. Not to mention the thought of Andi being defenseless against him was laughable.

"You obviously didn't see our interview this morning." He managed to grind the words out through his tight jaw.

Van Horn had the nerve to laugh. "Oh, I saw it. Props to her for the whole woolly mammoth portrait she painted of you. And isn't it a miracle how she overcame her stutter so quickly."

Dex flipped him off.

"But it's not you she needs to worry about," Van Horn continued. "You'd never hurt her purposely. Anyone who knows you knows that." He glanced back toward the tent. "It's them you need to worry about. She's an innocent when it comes to the circus that surrounds us. Suddenly she's thrust into the position of a superstar player's wife. There will be haters. And don't expect the sorority of WAGs to jump to her defense."

Dex felt a knot form in his chest as the quarterback's words sunk in. "The whole purpose of doing the bloody interview was to shut down any further talk."

Van Horn nodded. "It may have worked for the fans and some media, but Andi's sudden fame as the Growler's most interesting wife didn't sit well with the WAGs. It's bad enough the new coach's wife has declared herself Andi's bestie. But now an invitation to the owner's box? I can't remember the last time Mrs. Ciaciura singled out a player's wife. Can you?"

Dex dragged his fingers through his hair. He never paid attention to those things. But Van Horn was always on, always surveying the playing field, whether it was during an actual game or in real life. If his friend was concerned, he had reason to be.

"Fletcher, if the plan was to keep people from questioning your sudden marriage to Andi, it may have backfired."

Fuck.

ELEVEN

HARPER HOPPED FROM one foot to the other.

"Do you need to go potty?" her mother asked quietly.

The little girl nodded before grabbing Andi's fingers and tugging her toward a two-story building on the other side of the tent.

Merrit Gibson lunged after them. "Honey, wait. Mommy will take you. Andi doesn't want to leave the party."

Oh, but she did. She really, really did. Outside of the coach's wife and their precious daughter, every other female in attendance had given her a chilly reception. Andi could think of nothing better than escaping to the ladies' room.

"I'm happy to take her," she said. "I'm just not sure where I'm going."

Merrit glanced over to her husband who had their son, Max, propped on his shoulders. Husband and wife exchanged a look seeming to encompass an entire conversation, concluding with a warm smile on both their faces. Andi felt a bit like a voyeur witnessing a silent communication born from years of intimacy. A feeling of sorrow washed over her. *What would it be like to know someone that well?*

Harper trotted toward the building, her tiny bladder making her steps quicken.

"I appreciate you being so sweet to her," Merrit said as she pulled open the big glass door. "She's usually very shy with strangers."

"I wasn't sure what this picnic would be like," Andi admitted. "I'll take all the friends I can get."

They raced down a long, carpeted hallway. A glass wall lined one side of the hall. Behind the glass was an impressive display of trophies of all sizes and shapes, footballs, and jerseys.

"Oh, trust me," Merrit said as she pushed open the door to the lounge outside the ladies' room. "I can relate to being the new girl in town. Actually, I should thank you for marrying Declan when you did. I'm no longer their favorite target."

"Wow. Good to know they're this welcoming to everyone."

Merrit put her fingers to her lips, ducking to check beneath all of the stall doors to make sure they were empty and no one could overhear them before disappearing into one with her daughter.

"I probably shouldn't have said that," she called through the door. "I'm sure they are always wary of the new head coach's wife. Especially one who was never a WAG before."

"Your husband didn't play before he became a coach?" Andi wasn't all that familiar with the game of football, but she assumed most coaches were former players.

Harper and Merrit emerged from the stall. Merrit lifted her daughter at the waist so Harper could lean in and wash her hands. The little girl made a production of soaping her hands and blowing bubbles toward her troll doll on the counter.

"We weren't together during Heath's playing days."

Judging by the melancholy in Merrit's voice, there was a story to be told, but Andi wasn't comfortable asking about it. She wasn't going to risk pushing away her only friend among the WAGs by being nosy.

Merrit guided Harper's hands beneath the faucet. "It's hard, too, when you have a child who's special." She leaned down to kiss the top of her daughter's head. The little girl's hair was exactly the same color as her mother's. Andi felt another kick in the belly at the intimacy. She didn't even remember the color of her own mother's hair.

"Harper is special." Andi smiled at her little friend in the mirror.

"Most people don't believe us when we tell them she's a total chatterbox at home." Merrit handed Harper a paper towel. "She just doesn't speak around anyone else. The pediatrician said she'll grow out of it. But other parents can be so *judgy*."

Andi sank down to be eye level with Harper. "You're just saving up all your pretty words and opinions for those who appreciate them, aren't you?"

Harper grabbed her troll from the counter and hugged it to her chest, before nodding.

"Atta girl." She brushed a strand of hair out of the little girl's eye. "Be true to yourself. Don't ever forget that."

Andi stood and brushed her hands on her shorts before looking up to see Merrit studying her with a warm grin.

"You've got nothing to worry about with the other WAGs," Merrit said. "You're a lot stronger than you look."

"I'm used to not fitting in most places."

They headed out through the lounge, Merrit carrying the troll doll while Harper skipped between them, each of her hands in one of theirs.

"Oh, I don't think their attitude today had anything to do with you fitting in, Andi. I'm pretty sure they were all just a little bit jealous after that interview."

"Jealous? Whatever for?"

Merrit laughed. "Girl, they were all wishing their significant other looked at them the way Dex was looking at you." She fanned herself with the troll doll. "Given his reputation of stoicism, I really didn't think he had it in him. But he's got it bad for you. Anyone watching could see that."

Andi nearly tripped over her own feet. There had certainly been a moment during the interview when they each weren't trying to skewer the other one, a moment when she'd felt a connection with Dex. But as far as "having it bad" for her, no way. He had made it very clear that he would have no trouble ignoring the sexual attraction between them. She'd already discovered that he was a skilled actor. Especially when he had a lot to lose. He'd just given his fans, and the authorities, everything they wanted. Nothing more.

"So, tell me about your soap business," Merrit asked once they'd left the building. "That sounds like an interesting and creative endeavor. How did you get into it?"

Glad for the change of subject, Andi lifted Harper's arm and gave her a little swing. "Well, like a certain little girl I know, I was special too when I was little. I was born with a very discerning sense of smell. When I lived with my grandmother, she had terrible arthritis and she'd use all those creams to help ease her pain. The smell would be so intense for me that I'd go outside and find other natural scents to camouflage the stench. Soon I was making little sachets to hide around the house. When I moved into foster care, I kept it up. Mostly so I could have something to remember her by."

"Mmm. Better sachets than a tube of Ben Gay."

They both lifted Harper into another swing.

"For sure. One of my foster moms was a science teacher. She liked the idea of having organic soap to use, so she filled in the gaps in my chemistry and the rest was history."

"That's amazing. I have a lot of respect for women entrepreneurs." The genuine awe in Merrit's voice made Andi's shoulders square with pride. "What's the name of your company?"

"Oh, I don't have one yet. A name or a company. I'm pulling together a business plan now in one of my classes," she explained. "I've been slowly working and getting my business degree at night. I hope to finish this semester."

"Good for you. Never let anyone stand in the way of your dreams." Merrit lifted her daughter up and Andi followed suit. Harper let out a soft giggle when the two women swung her between them. "You hear that, little one. You are in the presence of some awesome girl power."

Andi grimaced. "It will only be awesome if I pass managerial accounting this fall. I'm more of a creative than a numbers person."

Merrit halted beside her. "Well, then, Andi Fletcher, today is definitely your lucky day."

She was so shaken by the sound of the name that shouldn't be hers and wouldn't be for long that it took her a moment for the rest of Merrit's statement to register. "How so?"

"Because, I just happen to be a CPA. One who specialized in managerial accounting." Merrit smiled proudly. "If you have questions on anything, I'm your girl."

She stared at Merrit, dumbfounded. *Was she actually offering to help?* The other woman beamed back as if that was exactly what she was offering.

"You don't have to do that," she said before she could stop herself. She was used to doing things herself, getting by on her own. Since she'd crossed paths with Declan Fletcher, however, her luck had changed. She was no longer saddled with a mountain of debt. And now, a woman she'd known for barely an hour was offering to help her pass the one class she'd dreaded her entire college career.

"Of course, I don't *have* to," Merrit countered. "I *want* to. Honestly, you'll be doing me the favor. I haven't done anything to keep my skills sharp since Harper arrived. It'll be fun."

Andi chuckled. "'Fun' is not a word I would use to describe accounting, but if you say so."

Harper tugged on their hands, silently demanding they swing her again. Both women grinned as they once again made their way in the direction of the tent.

"I promise to make it painless," Merrit said. "How does that sound? When do classes start, anyway?"

"This week. Accounting is on Thursday night."

"Oh my gosh!" a woman behind them exclaimed. "I'm in professor Hart's class, too. We can be study buddies."

Andi froze. *Please no. Don't let it be her.*

Harper and Merrit stopped and looked at Andi questioningly. Her first instinct was to yell 'run' but it was too late. Jade Hathaway, last year's Wisconsin Butter Queen and self-anointed social media influencer, blocked their path, her perfect pearly white teeth bared in what was likely intended to be a smile. Except she knew from personal experience that Jade's smiles packed a vicious bite.

So much for luck.

"Hi." The beauty queen extended her perfectly manicured hand to Merrit. "I'm Jade Hathaway, Trey Van Horn's girlfriend."

Figures. Trey was one of the few people who had been nice to her this afternoon. Turns out, he was just another one of those suckers for long legs and big hair.

"I've been dying to meet you, Mrs. Gibson," Jade gushed. "I'm looking forward to working with you on some of the WAGs outreach and community activities. Particularly the gala for the children's hospital. My father is the U.S. attorney for this district," she bragged. "And my mother is one of the patrons of the hospital, so I know the event well. And since Trey is the face of this team, I know it's important that I lend my talents and connections to the efforts."

Andi threw up a little in her throat.

For her part, the coach's wife donned a poised smile. "We appreciate the talents and connections of everyone, no matter what their significant others' position is on the team."

Jade bristled slightly at the diplomatic rebuke, but it didn't deter her. "I'm happy to take the lead on anything."

Andi almost snorted. *Not everything.* When Jade had been assigned to a group project with Andi and two other students in their small business marketing class, Jade wasn't interested in "taking the lead" or any other role, for that matter.

As if reading her mind, Jade shifted her man-eating grin in

Andi's direction. "And it will be so much fun working with Andi again."

"I take it you two know one another?" Merrit glanced between the two of them, a bemused expression on her face.

"We had a class together once," Andi commented, shocked Jade even remembered her name. She left out the part about it being pure torture. Jade had had a mix-up in her schedule and was forced into taking a night class. She'd spent the entire semester complaining about how she was missing *The Bachelor* and could the professor *please, please, please,* dismiss the class early so she could get back to her apartment in time to see the rose ceremony. Not that she wasn't already watching the show on her phone.

"Oh, it was more than that," Jade added. "I wouldn't have survived the class without Andi."

Truth.

"And I'm so glad she'll be in managerial accounting with me. Andi is smart, but I have a feeling we'll both appreciate your help."

Andi doubted Jade originally intended to take the course at night. The professor teaching that section had a reputation for being tough. More likely, she'd seen an opportunity to further her agenda and was taking it.

Merrit looked slightly uncomfortable now, but she, too, had a lot at stake with the WAGs. Alienating the star quarterback's girl-friend just wouldn't do. She shot Andi a pained look. "It would be my pleasure." Except they both knew it wouldn't be a pleasure at all.

DEX SHOVED SEVERAL manscaping tool kits into his gym bag. The kits, along with bottles of depilatory and wax products continued to appear at his locker since the interview earlier in the week. His teammates were having a lot of fun with Andi's version of their meeting. He knew enough to take their shenanigans in stride. Once the season started this weekend, the Growlers would hopefully have something else to think about.

It was Thursday evening and the air was crisp coming off the lake as most of the players made their way out of the locker room. Van Horn was like the Pied Piper leading his offensive line and receiving corps to a steak dinner at the Pack House, his treat. The defense was headed for pizza with their families. Dex glanced over to Palmer standing at his locker with his phone pressed to his ear. As the two members of the kicking corps, he should offer to take the rookie out for dinner or a drink. The kid was likely nervous about his first regular season pro game.

He had just started over in Palmer's direction when the punter let out a loud whoop.

"Everything okay?" he asked.

"Better than okay." Palmer slapped him on the back. "Shaina surprised me and she's coming into town for the game this weekend."

"Shaina?"

"My girl." Palmer whooped again. "I wasn't sure she could get out of a sorority retreat, but she managed to. I've got to get to the airport and pick her up. We've got some catching up to do." With a wink and another whoop, he was gone.

"Sorority retreat," one of the trainers muttered from across the locker room. "We probably should assign someone to check that girl's ID at the game."

The rest of the training staff laughed.

"We should probably check Palmer's ID," Dex added, bringing about another round of laughter.

With a shake of his head, he strode out toward the parking lot. How long it had been since he'd been that happy to see someone? A woman? He doubted he'd ever been as immature as Palmer. Well, except for that once . . .

"Headed home to the missus?" the Growlers media relations director called across the parking lot, interrupting Dex's thoughts before they got dark. "Happy one-week anniversary."

Say what?

Had it been only a week since his life had been turned upside down? Not that he'd seen his pretend wife in three days. When Andi wasn't at work or in class, she was off studying somewhere. Either she was the hardest working woman in Milwaukee, or she was going to extremes to avoid him.

Smart lass.

He shouldn't care. Her absence practically guaranteed him the privacy he craved. Despite their charade, his life would remain pretty much the same. He ought to be relieved. But he couldn't help but wonder what she did all day. She was supposed to be playing the part of doting wife instead of a game of hide and seek.

Dex glanced at the hair removal products jammed into his workout bag. Perhaps there was a way to kill two birds with one stone. He'd just drive by the salon and drop all this shit off. It was a shame to waste them. While he was there, he could check on Andi and remind her that she needed to be at the game on Sunday.

The Shear Envy salon was in an upscale neighborhood just outside of downtown. Despite it being dinner time, the place was still crowded with men and women who'd scheduled their appointments after work. The only person who wasn't there, however, was the pink-haired receptionist. In fact, the front desk was deserted. Dex drummed his fingers on the counter waiting for someone to notice him. Except no one did.

Taking matters into his own hands, he dumped the hair removal products on the counter and stalked into the salon in search of her. He felt the eyes of every client and stylist following him as he made his way back to where Andi's friend—Clive, he thought he remembered his name being—was blow-drying a woman's hair. The woman's eyes grew wide when she caught a glimpse of Dex in the mirror, but Clive ignored him. Taking his time, the stylist fluffed and picked at the woman's hair for several moments before whipping off her cape with a flourish.

"That color looks spectacular on you, as usual." Clive gave his client's shoulder a squeeze. "Why don't you change out of the smock and I'll meet you up front."

The woman gave Dex a shy smile and disappeared. Ignoring Dex, Clive grabbed a broom and began sweeping around his chair. He grudgingly admitted he deserved the cold shoulder after the way he'd treated the man the other day, but his need to make sure Andi was okay stoked his frustration.

"Where's my wife?" he demanded, realizing too late they had an audience and he sounded like the Neanderthal Andi accused him of being.

Clive mumbled something under his breath and put the broom away. He motioned for Dex to follow him to a small office in the back.

"If this is another publicity stunt to get people to buy into your marriage, I'm going to have to ask you to keep the theatrics out of my salon," Clive said once they were away from prying ears. "As much as I'd love the publicity, Andi doesn't need the drama."

His accusation quashed some of Dex's anger. *He thought this was a publicity stunt?* Of course, he did. Their marriage wasn't real, he reminded himself.

He sighed as he ran his fingers through his hair. "I haven't seen her since Monday," he explained quietly. "We both have crazy schedules."

"She has class tonight." Clive didn't come out and call him a mumpty, but his tone implied it.

"Aye. I know that. But the schedule she left me said the class didn't start until seven. It's just half past five."

The other man scrutinized him carefully before answering. "She usually leaves here at five. The bus can be erratic during rush hour. She likes to get to campus early so she can prepare."

"And eat dinner. She'd have time to eat then, right?"

Dex was making a bloody arse out of himself. Of course she ate dinner. Andi wasn't in primary school. She could take care of herself. The woman had been doing it for years before they met. He waved a hand at Clive.

"Forget it. I'm sure she's fine."

Amusement flashed in the other man's eyes. "She took a sandwich with her. And an apple which I assume was not for the teacher. But it is Andi, so you never know."

Feeling like an even bigger fool, Dex nodded. "Thanks." He turned to leave.

"Wait." Clive pulled a sheet of paper from a pile on his desk and handed it to Dex. "Obviously, you need this more than I do."

It was a copy of her schedule for the fall term, complete with professor names and the location of her classes.

"Thanks." He took two steps before turning around again. "I owe you an apology."

Clive crossed his arms over his chest. An arched eyebrow was his only reply.

"What I said the other day was totally inappropriate," he continued. "I'm not that guy. It's just that my world is messed up right now, but that's no excuse for me to take it out on you. My apologies."

The moment stretched and just when he thought Clive wouldn't respond, he did.

"Apology accepted. I have thick skin. I can take it." His eyes narrowed. "But, despite how much she pretends, Andi's skin isn't as thick. Not only that, she has a big heart. A heart that still has hope no matter how many times it's been kicked around. Hear this loud and clear, Declan Fletcher, if you do anything to so much as nick that heart of hers, I will hurt you. You can count on that."

He studied the man before him. Clive's build was slight, his hands delicate. He'd be hard pressed to outlast Dex in a fight.

Clive snorted. "Dude. I'm a master with a pair of scissors."

"Point taken," Dex said with a laugh.

It wasn't until he'd left the salon that the remainder of Clive's threat sank in. Dex laughed out loud. Andi's heart was safe with him. It was the rest of her body that was causing him all kinds of problems.

TWELVE

"HOW DID YOU do it?" Jade demanded.

Andi pinched the bridge of her nose. It had been a long week and the rumors about Professor Hart being tough were not exaggerated. While she'd been able to correctly complete all the practice problems he'd assigned in class tonight, she knew she'd have to stay on top of her game to keep pace as the semester progressed. If she had to spoon-feed the beauty queen the entire time, the course would be doubly hard.

Sighing in resignation, Andi pulled out the notes she'd just shoved into her backpack. "The problems are easier if you break them down."

"No. Not that." Jade waved the paper away. "I'm not talking about this class. I'm talking about you. And Dex. How did someone like you get a superstar athlete to actually marry you?"

The chatter among the rest of the students making their way out of the classroom faded away so that the only thing Andi could hear was the familiar refrain, "someone like you." The paper shook in her fingers. Or maybe it was her hands shaking. It didn't matter.

She was getting sick and tired of always being pushed aside. Of being less than.

The assumption by the media and Growler fans that she, Andi Larsen, was somehow lacking the charisma, aptitude, or sex appeal to land a man like Declan Fletcher hurt. Deeply. But she'd be damned if she'd let some woman who'd had everything in life handed to her on a silver platter by virtue of her looks and her family get to her.

True, her marriage was a sham. But she hadn't tricked him into marrying her like Jade and practically everyone else suspected. In fact, he had the most to lose if anyone found out the truth behind their relationship. And he certainly didn't need his teammate's girl-friend digging around for dirt. While their marriage might not be what everyone expected, she and Dex were still a couple. A couple that had promised to keep each other's secrets. So, if it was gossip Jade wanted, Andi would give it to her, just to throw her off track.

With steadier hands, she carefully tucked the papers back into her backpack and lifted it over her shoulder. She tossed her hair back and responded with the first thing that came into her head.

"Well, Jade, it's really very simple. I'm great in bed."

A choked gasp escaped Jade's mouth. But that was nothing compared to the throat clearing coming from the front of the room. Andi snapped her head around. Professor Hart stood in front of the white board wearing a bemused expression.

Holy hell. That was not the first impression she wanted to make. This is what came of not thinking before she spoke. She dashed out of the room in embarrassment.

Unfortunately, Jade was at her heels. "I don't believe you."

"Seriously?" Andi huffed in annoyance as she hurried down the stairs trying to put some distance between the two of them. "Why do you even care?"

Jade had the advantage of longer legs. "The man dates super-stars and models. There's no way someone like you would end up on his radar."

There it was again. *Someone like you.* Andi was barely able to contain her fury. But rather than embarrass herself in front of strangers again, she kept her mouth shut, her head down, and headed for the doors leading out of the business school.

"It doesn't make sense," Jade called after her. "I know you're up to something. Whatever it is, it better not hurt the team! I'm warning you!"

Several bystanders eyed Andi suspiciously. Tears stung her eyes as she sprung through the doors into the now dark evening. She wasn't even more important than a damn football team.

"I'm going to keep my eye on you."

Jade's taunts followed her as she wound her way through the crowded sidewalk on the way to the bus stop.

"Andi."

The familiar voice was so out of place she nearly lost her step when she heard him. The sidewalk cleared and there was Dex leaning nonchalantly against his Jaguar, his feet crossed at the ankles, his palms resting on the car, looking every bit like the white knight she was beginning to believe him to be.

"How was class?" he asked.

She didn't bother with words. Instead, she launched herself at him without conscious thought, wrapping her arms around his neck and burying her face in his neck. He hesitated briefly before his arms closed around her. They were both silent for several long moments, the familiar scent of him calming Andi's frantic pulse.

"That bad, huh?" His palms began to make slow circles on her back.

When she nodded against his chest, she felt his muscles contract in a sigh beneath her cheek.

"It's okay," he murmured. "I've got you."

I've got you.

She nearly melted at the words. The feeling of having someone in her corner, a protector, someone to pick her up when she fell, was a novel one. It was one she could definitely get used to.

"Isn't this just too cute?" Jade's voice pierced their intimate bubble.

Andi stiffened with anger. Anger at herself as much as at Jade The Obnoxious. *This isn't real*, she reminded herself for what felt like the millionth time. Dex isn't a white knight. He's playing a role. They were standing on a street corner in downtown Milwaukee, for crying out loud. She was the fool who jumped into his arms. He had no choice but to play the scene out.

No one was going to take care of Andi. She took care of herself. Period.

"What's going on, Andi?" he asked quietly.

What was going on was she let some beauty queen get under her skin. Girls like that had been irritating Andi her whole life. She'd learned how to handle them. And she knew exactly how to shut Jade up.

"Sorry, but I've got to break your rule." She rose up on her toes and kissed him before he had time to realize what she was up to.

It was meant to be a simple kiss, a ploy to shut Jade up, but within seconds Andi realized her mistake. As with all the other times they'd kissed, things got out of hand real fast. Despite his prohibition on kissing, he hesitated only briefly before meeting her kiss with an eager one of his own.

His hands shifted lower on her back, drawing her body in closer contact so that she was plastered against him from the hard muscles of his thighs to the even harder muscles of his chest. And everything hard in between. A wave of restless desire washed over her and, instead of pulling away like she should have—*they were on a damn street corner*—she nipped at his bottom lip. He growled possessively in response before slanting his mouth over hers and using his tongue to plunder deeper.

Andi grew warm all over. Suddenly, their kiss wasn't enough. She threaded her greedy fingers through his hair, digging her nails along his skull, urging him closer. His teeth scraped against hers. One of them moaned, she wasn't really sure which one. It didn't matter. The sound reverberated through her body sparking a firestorm deep in her belly. Only to have it quickly doused seconds later. She let out a shaky breath when he suddenly tore his lips away. The sound of catcalls behind them quickly drew Andi out of her sensual fog.

Holy hell.

She buried her face in his chest. His heart hammered beneath her palm. He was just as affected as she was, but, obviously, he possessed a greater amount of self-control.

"We should go home," he said. But he made no move to let her go.

"Is she gone?"

"Who?"

"Your quarterback's girlfriend." His body tensed. "She's not buying our happily ever after. Hence my little display."

Dex swore softly. "I don't see her anywhere."

She avoided his eyes as she untangled herself from his embrace. "Good. Mission accomplished. But I think I missed my bus. Would you mind giving me a ride home?"

He huffed. "Aye, lass. What do you think I'm doing here?" He pulled the passenger door open with a bit more force than was necessary.

Guilt nipped at her as she got in to the car. He'd come to campus to pick her up. It was unexpected. And sweet.

"I'll arrange for a car to take you to and from campus," he announced when he got behind the wheel. "No wife of mine will be riding a public bus."

Not sweet, then.

When would she ever learn? He'd come for the optics. The wife of a multi-million-dollar athlete certainly would never ride public transportation. With a resigned sigh, Andi rested her head against the leather headrest. At least she would save money on the bus fare.

"TELL YOUR DAMN girlfriend to back off, Van Horn," Dex barked at the quarterback the following day.

The other man slowly turned from his locker, eyeing him sharply. "Or what? You're going to spray me with some of that Nair?"

Laughter echoed from all corners of the locker room.

With a growl, Dex tossed the new hair removal products lining the shelf in his locker into the trash can. "Joke's over, you twats!" he shouted at his teammates. "You had your fun. Now let's focus on our game this weekend, you ken?"

A few low guffaws followed, but the laughter died down. They were less than forty-eight hours to opening day and every player knew he needed to concentrate on the game.

"Do we have a problem, Fletcher?" Van Horn sat on the chair in front of his locker and carefully laced up his cleats.

"Aye, we do." Dex kept his voice low. He didn't need anyone else butting into his business. "Your girlfriend is harassing my wife."

Van Horn's fingers stilled on his shoelaces. "For the record, Jade is not my girlfriend. We date off and on, but nothing exclusive."

Dex snorted. "You might want to tell her you're just using her for her father's political connections."

The quarterback ignored him. "I warned you about the WAGs."

"Yeah, well this particular WAG, the one who is *not* your girlfriend, is asking questions about my marriage. Very direct questions."

Sighing heavily, Van Horn stood. "If you're implying that I asked her to, you're wrong. I told you the other day, I don't care. Your marriage is your business."

"You also told me not to hurt Andi," Dex argued. "I'm not. But your arm candy is."

The two men squared off.

"Hold up, you two knuckleheads." Kessler jumped between them. "If there's going to be fisticuffs, I need to run a pool among the guys to see who they think will be the last man standing. I had planned a wager on whether or not Palmer can get his leg up high enough to punt the ball after all the sex he claims he had last night." Kessler smirked at both of them. "But this one might be more interesting."

"Fuck off," Dex and Van Horn said at the same time.

"Jinx." Kessler laughed before adopting a rare, serious tone. "Let's take out our frustrations on the field, gentlemen. You both know better than to let a woman come between you."

Van Horn snapped up his helmet before nodding curtly at Dex. "I'll speak with Jade." He slid past Kessler and made his way out to the practice field.

"That's two you owe me, Fletcher. You can thank me later." Kessler slapped him on the back. "Come on. Let's go see how Palmer is faring."

When Dex pulled into the parking garage beneath the building housing his flat four hours later, Van Horn was leaning a hip against his neighbor's Acura sedan. If the owner only knew he nearly had a Heisman Trophy winner as a hood ornament, he'd likely never wash the car again.

"How were the mathletes?" Van Horn asked casually, any trace of his earlier annoyance long gone.

"Chatty." Dex headed toward the private elevator to the penthouse. Van Horn fell into step beside him.

"Let me guess, they were all wildly curious about your back hair?"

"Will you forget the damn back hair?" He punched the button for the penthouse.

He wasn't about to admit there had been some snickers among the kids about that particular topic. None of them dared bring it up out loud, however. Instead, they'd interrogated him about his new bride. The moony-eyed girls wanting to know every last detail about the wedding ceremony. The lads, too, for that matter, although they were more interested in the Star Wars aspect, with most of them in awe of the fact he'd found a woman who would agree to such an unorthodox wedding. Who would have guessed his crazy predicament would give his tribe of nerds hope for their future selves. He shook his head in amazement.

"I spoke with Jade," his friend announced when the elevator doors opened and both men stepped inside.

"Did you set her straight?"

Van Horn scoffed. "Jade has her own agenda. She doesn't take direction from anyone, including me. But she assured me she had nothing against Andi. In fact, she claims they are—" the quarterback made air quotes. "—study buddies. And, get this, Coach's wife is their tutor."

Jaysus. Just what he'd been trying so hard to avoid. He didn't want Andi getting close to the coach's wife. Hell, he didn't want her getting close to anyone in his orbit. It would only make things more complicated when their marriage came to its preordained conclusion.

The elevator doors opened to a frazzled looking Marlene on the other side.

"Did anyone see you come up?" she demanded.

Dex exchanged a confused look with Van Horn. "Not that I know of," he said. "What's amiss, Marlene?"

"That man was back."

The back of his neck itched. Van Horn stiffened beside him.

"What man?" Dex asked.

"Agent Figueroa."

Shit.

"He was here? In my flat?"

Marlene nodded. "He said he was doing a spontaneous home check."

"Can they fucking do that?" Van Horn asked.

"Hell if I know." Dex pulled out his phone. "Where is he now, Marlene?"

"I told him you weren't home. And neither was Mrs. Fletcher. He said he'd wait in the lobby until one or both of you got home."

"You didn't tell him about the private elevator?"

Marlene cocked her chin indignantly. "Of course not."

"Good lass." Dex gave her shoulder a squeeze. "Why don't you go fix yourself a cup of tea while we figure this out."

He hit the button on his phone for his agent. Kurt picked up on the second ring.

"Damn it, Kurt, I thought you said ICE would give us a formal notification when they were going to interview us."

"They are required to," Kurt said. "What's going on?"

"Agent Figueroa is snooping around my flat, asking to come inside."

Kurt swore. "That's not an adjustment interview. That's a damn bed check."

"A bed check? What the hell is that?"

Beside him, Van Horn's eyes grew wide.

"They perform bed checks when they suspect the marriage isn't real," Kurt explained. "They usually show up early in the morning to see who answers the door. Then they check the bed to see if the couple is sleeping together. They've been known to check the bathroom, too."

"The bathroom?"

"Yeah. Dex, listen to me." Kurt's tone became urgent. "You need to move some of Andi's things as quickly as possible. Make it look like you and she are sharing your room just in case this guy comes back. I'm in my car. I'll be there in five minutes."

Dex was already moving down the hallway, Van Horn on his heels. He threw open the door to Andi's room. Morag was snoozing in the center of the bed, depositing cat hair all over the comforter. The cat startled when Dex loudly yanked open the dresser drawers.

"Leave those," Van Horn said. "I doubt he'll look in the drawers. He'll check for her toothbrush and toiletries in your bathroom, though."

"Good thinking."

They nearly collided with one another trying to fit through the bathroom door at the same time.

"Grab the stuff off her nightstand," Dex ordered. "I'll get this."

It felt like the ultimate invasion of privacy rifling through Andi's most personal possessions. But it had to be done. He grabbed her toothbrush, toothpaste, and the bar of face soap next to the basin. The intoxicating scent of the soap stopped him in his tracks. He couldn't help but breathe it in, his body suddenly hardening remembering the feel of her pressed up against him the previous evening. She'd been so damn passionate, so open. He was a randy teenager the last time he took a woman in his car, but he was willing to do it again last night. Right up until she revealed it was all a ruse. A ploy to keep Jade from discovering the truth. Andi had certainly fooled them both.

"For fuck's sake, Fletcher. You need to move faster if we're going to pull this off." Mumbling something about the kicker being the inferior position on the team, Van Horn reached into one of the bathroom drawers and grabbed a fistful of hair products.

Dex followed him down the hall into his own bathroom. He hung Andi's toothbrush next to his and tossed the soap into the walk-in shower. Both men raced back and began snatching up what remained in Andi's bathroom. Each of them froze with their hand hovering over an open box of tampons when Dex heard a noise from the front of the flat that sounded a lot like the murmur of voices.

"You take it," he insisted, his hands full of more soap and an assortment of make-up.

Van Horn gestured to the razors and shaving cream in his hands. "My hands are full. Unless you want me to ditch these so you can share your Nair with her."

"Fuck off," Dex hissed. He was definitely hearing voices. A cold sweat broke out at the back of his neck. They needed to hurry. He tossed the box to Van Horn. The quarterback batted it back to Dex, who kneed the box in the air. Van Horn head butted the box in Dex's direction. Before he could reach it, the box fell to the floor, the contents scattering around the room like pick-up sticks.

Both men swore violently.

"Marlene, can you please tell me why two professional football players are in my bathroom playing hot potato with a box of tampons?"

Relief washed over him. He turned to see a very peeved looking Andi standing in the bathroom doorway.

"Actually, it's only one professional football player." Van Horn shoved his items into her hands. "I'm out of here. You two kids have fun."

She glanced at Van Horn's retreating back before narrowing her eyes at Dex. "What is going on?"

He gestured to Marlene who nodded as she bent to clean up the mess on the floor. "You're moving. That's what's going on." He nudged her with her shoulder toward the hallway.

"I'm not going anywhere until you tell me what's happening."

Of course she wasn't. He kept forgetting the fact his wife wasn't a pushover.

"There's an immigration officer downstairs," he explained as he herded her in the direction of his room. "He's here to do a bed check."

The color drained from her face. "Bed check? That better not mean what I think it means."

He couldn't decide if he should laugh at her apparent horror or be insulted.

"It means you both need to share the same room for the time being." Kurt strode into the room. "Figueroa wasn't in the lobby, but that doesn't mean he won't decide to drop in at seven in the morning. I should have known they'd perform every step in the damn handbook. You're a celebrity. This is a high-profile case for them."

"Hold on," Andi objected. "Are you suggesting that we not only share the same room but the same bed?"

"Relax." Kurt gestured to the California king bed. "There's enough room for a family of five on that mattress. If you each keep to a side, it'll be like you're sleeping in different rooms. By the way, do you have some sexy negligee?"

"Excuse me?" The blood had returned to her face, now nearly

as pink as the tips of her hair. Marlene stepped in and wrapped a protective arm around Andi as she leveled a stern look at Kurt.

"For crying out loud, Kurt," Dex exclaimed.

"Not to wear. You can dress in a snowsuit for bed for all I care." Kurt pinched the bridge of his nose. "The sexy lingerie is to leave out as a prop. A pair of thong panties carelessly strewn about the room would work just as well."

Andi blinked a few times. "Maybe a few condom wrappers scattered about for that extra touch?"

Kurt snapped his fingers. "That's brilliant."

Dex groaned while Andi threw her hands up in disgust and stalked out of the room. Marlene tsked at both men before following her out.

"What's wrong with them?" Kurt appeared genuinely baffled.

"Jaysus, Kurt. You have as much tact as a bloody bull in a china shop," Dex replied.

"I'm not asking the woman to consummate the damn marriage. But she does need to do whatever it takes to make things look real. All of our reputations are on the line. Not to mention that we are straddling legality here."

"Aye. Andi is well aware of that. And she's done everything we've asked of her. She'll do this, too. It would help if you employed a wee bit more finesse with her feelings, that's all."

"Well then, I'll leave it to you. Based on the rumors, you're an expert at charming women into your bed." He patted Dex on the back and quit the room.

Dex heaved a frustrated sigh. Kurt wasn't lying. He was very skilled at charming women into bed. And all those women left very satisfied, thank you very much. But this situation was different. For one, he'd never allowed a woman in *this* bed. His flat was his sanctuary. A place to retreat to when the women he'd charmed into bed starting looking for more than just a tumble between the sheets. Sharing his flat with Andi was already pushing his resolve to its limit. Sharing a bed with her would be pure torture.

He glanced at the framed photo on his nightstand. A smiling

Niall stared back him, that familiar cheeky challenge in his eyes. Dex walked over and placed the photo facedown into the nightstand drawer. The way he saw it, he had two choices. Charm his fake wife into his bed and endure the agony of not being able to touch her. Or return home to face his greatest screw up. Squaring his shoulders, he chose the lesser of two evils and went in search of Andi.

THIRTEEN

AS IT TURNED out, all it took to get Andi into Dex's bed was a bottle of wine. She'd always been a lightweight when it came to alcohol. A personality flaw that didn't help her reckless tendencies. Case in point, after two sips of champagne she'd followed Dex into a Vegas wedding chapel and said "I do." Well, the seventy thousand dollars he'd gifted her might have been an added incentive, but she felt less like a hypocrite if she blamed the champagne.

There was no getting around his agent's plan. She'd made a vow to do whatever was necessary to make this marriage appear real. And she stuck to her word. But that didn't mean she had to like it. That's why rather than face him to discuss the logistics, she'd holed up in her former bedroom, downing a bottle of rosé. It was childish of her, she knew, but it was the only way to get up the nerve to do what she had to.

Sporting a warm buzz, she crawled between the sheets of Dex's massive bed. Of course, the warm buzz might be aided by all the clothes she was wearing. Normally she donned a pair of sleep shorts and a cami to sleep in. Not tonight. While she hadn't gone so far as to follow Mr. Hilbert's ridiculous suggestion that she wear a snowsuit, she had pulled on a pair of leggings, a sports bra and a long-sleeved T-shirt. Given that Dex was her Kryptonite, she needed all the armor she could muster to prevent herself from doing anything reckless.

Like jump his bones.

She could hear Marlene in the hallway lecturing Dex about propriety. Andi snickered softly. The woman needn't worry about her employer. He had stated repeatedly that he had no intention of consummating their marriage, even though he claimed to be attracted to her. Since there wasn't an audience for him to play to tonight, Andi was quite safe.

Her body sagged in disappointment. The wine was a bad idea. Not only was the bed spinning, but her girl parts were wailing for action they weren't going to see. It was going to take everything she had to match Dex's level of restraint.

A door slammed in the distance before the object of her desire strode into the room. Lucky for her, he was just as overdressed for bed as she was, wearing a pair of dark sweatpants and a Growlers' Henley that fit snugly, showcasing his landscape of sculpted muscles. Andi gulped down a lusty sigh at the sight. She could have sworn he growled as he stalked past her into the bathroom only to storm back out seconds later.

"This is not how you're supposed to squeeze a tube of toothpaste!" He clenched her tube of toothpaste in his hand.

Yep. Definitely growling.

Throwing back the sheets, she jumped out of the bed and grabbed the toothpaste from him. "First of all, that's *my* toothpaste you're holding. And I'll squeeze it any way I want."

His eyes roamed her body, settling in the vicinity of her chest when his expression grew harder. "What in the bloody hell are you wearing?!"

She jabbed the toothpaste in his direction. "If you were expecting a negligee, you can forget about it, buster."

His nostrils flared at the mention of a negligee before he blustered on. "Is that a bloody Viking on your shirt?"

She dropped her arms in confusion. The wine was obviously doing something to her head because he wasn't making much sense. She glanced down at the T-shirt she'd bought at a second-hand store. It featured a floating Viking head. The whimsical graphic, along with the bright purple color, had attracted her right away. She notched her chin up and nodded. "Do you have a problem with Vikings?"

This time his growl was more like a roar. "Yes! Especially when they are our rival team and Sunday's opponent."

"Oh." She felt like the biggest fool. Maybe she should have listened when Clive and Daniel were lecturing her about football the other night. Still, Dex didn't need to be such a tyrant about it. It was an innocent mistake. "Well, being Scandinavian, I'm partial to the team wearing horned helmets like my forefathers."

"For your information, lass, the bloody heathens you claim as your forefathers never wore horned helmets. That's all a bunch of jabby invented by artists in the nineteenth century."

"Jabby?"

"Aye, jabby. It means bullshit, lass!"

To her surprise the distance between them had narrowed and they were now standing inches apart. Her eyes honed in on the muscles of his chest heaving in and out as if he'd just run a four-minute mile. Her fingers twitched. It was all she could do not to reach out and stroke one of his pecs. The warm buzz she'd enjoyed a few moments ago had morphed into an inferno deep in her belly. The musky smell radiating off him only served to fuel the flames.

"Um. Then Mrs. Hall in fifth grade social studies had it all wrong, I guess?" The words sounded raspy for some reason.

"Aye," he murmured softly.

His breath fanned her forehead but she didn't dare look up.

"Did you know the Norsemen were afraid of the Scots?" His quiet question was followed by a soft sigh as he seemed to inhale her.

This Norsewoman might be afraid of a certain Scot right now.

Closing her eyes to shut out the virile image in front of her, she threw caution to the wind. "My Viking forefathers afraid of men in skirts? I think not."

She felt more than heard his low chuckle as he pressed his body in closer. His fingers brushed along her hips and her nipples were suddenly excruciatingly hard. He chuckled again when a gasp snuck past her lips.

"Those Norsemen were constantly trying to take our island."

She shuddered when his fingers made their way beneath her T-shirt. They left a trail of heat and want in their wake as he began to ever so softly trace them along her skin.

"What would they want with your silly island when they had beautiful ones of their own?" Andi managed to grind out.

She had no idea why they were engaged in such a ridiculous conversation. But suddenly she didn't want it to end. Unless it ended with the two of them in bed.

"They wanted our fertile land." His lips brushed her ear. "And our fertile women."

Andi shivered at his words. When his fingers fisted in the fabric of her T-shirt and began to slowly shove the fabric up her body, she finally dared to look at him. His hungry gaze made her panties grow damp.

"Wh-what are you doing?"

He swallowed roughly. "That should be obvious, lass."

Her knees nearly buckled when he slowly drew the shirt over her head. Was he serious this time? Was there a crack in his carefully controlled resolve? Not that she was complaining. Truth be told, she'd been dreaming of this for the past week. Her entire body was practically quivering with need at the idea her fantasy might actually become a reality.

That he might actually desire her.

Dex wadded her T-shirt into a tight ball and tossed it into the trash can near the door. His eyes never left her, however, all the while seeming to drink her in. She was unsuccessful at taming her shiver when he slowly lifted a finger to the silver cross dangling above her breasts. The pad of his thumb brushed along her skin and her core practically ignited.

"Was this your ma's?" His voice was rough, but his tone had softened.

She shook her head. "My grandmother's." Her body was so tense, it hurt to speak. "She regretted not giving it to my mother before she was deployed. She always thought it would have kept her safe somehow."

His eyes jerked up to lock with hers. Something in his gaze told her that little tidbit of her life's story surprised him.

"And your da?"

"Gone before I was born. Cancer."

She was grateful for his silence. Most people gushed with platitudes of pity when they discovered the nature of her parent's deaths. The truth was, Andi couldn't miss a man she'd never known. Her mother had been a fleeting figure in her early years, but not someone Andi remembered well, either. Mostly, it was the idea of parents—of belonging to a family—that she mourned, not the actual people who conceived her. She doubted most people would understand.

But Declan Fletcher wasn't most people. He nodded slowly, but kept his opinions to himself. Just when it looked like he might touch her again, he took a step back. Then another one before turning to the bureau and pulling something out of one of the drawers. Andi sucked in a breath, her body thrumming so loudly with desire, she wouldn't be surprised if Marlene heard in her apartment downstairs.

"The Norsemen never stood a chance." He tossed a T-shirt at her. She caught it with less than steady hands. "We defeated them easily at the Battle of Largs."

Andi let out a confused sigh. *What had just happened?*

"It's a Growlers T-shirt, lass. Put it on." His game face was firmly back in place. "First rule of being the wife of a professional athlete, never wear the opponent's insignia." He turned on his heel and disappeared into the bathroom.

AFTER TWENTY MINUTES standing under the icy spray of the shower, Dex felt he was collected enough to venture back into the bedroom. With luck, Andi would already be asleep. Or at the very least, buried beneath the comforter where her body would no longer be a distraction. He stared at his reflection in the mirror and swore violently. The woman wasn't a fairy, she was a bloody siren. One who'd cast a hex on him.

He was losing his effing grip. It had taken every ounce of composure he had to not toss her on the bed and act on what had been simmering between them the past week. Given the way her body responded every time he touched her, she would not have objected. And it would have been bloody explosive.

But he couldn't. *They* couldn't. If they did, it would muck-up their cockamamie marriage even more than it was already. It was bad enough she'd invaded his private domain. Her scent and her smile tormented him at every turn, stirring up a need he'd long buried. A need for a deeper connection with another human being. A need for a soul-deep intimacy. He'd managed to suppress that need in his relationships with other women. But something about Andi unleashed those cravings. And deep down, he knew if he had sex with her, he'd never be able to rein in that craving again. No way was he giving her any more power to wear down the shield he'd secured around his heart. His penance for his sins was never to have the things he took from Niall.

Dex needed to keep reminding himself his marriage had an expiration date, that's all. His feelings for her were likely more a case of wanting something he couldn't have. If he kept that reasoning in mind, he could get through this.

The room was dark when he quietly slipped into his bedroom, but he could just make out a lump curled up on the far side of the bed. Kurt was right; the mattress was its own island. Dex could likely crawl onto his side and Andi would never know he was there. But he would know *she* was there. Even with his pep talk in the loo, he didn't trust his baser instincts not to overpower his chivalry.

Gently, so as not to jostle the bed and wake her, he grabbed his pillow, the thick quilt his gran made for him when he was a boy, and headed for the floor in front of his closet. Just when he thought he'd made a clean getaway, the light snapped on. He nearly jumped out of his skin.

"Where are you going?" Andi demanded.

The glow of the lamplight cast her in eerie shadows, but not enough to conceal her tear-stained cheeks. *Bloody hell.* He'd done that to her with his boorish behavior.

"I'm letting you have the bed. I'll take the floor."

"Isn't the purpose of this little show for us to be sharing a bed in case the immigration agent returns for a bed check?"

He laid out the quilt on the thankfully plush carpet. "Relax, lass. The doorman knows to ring me if the agent shows up. I'll have plenty of time to muss up the sheets before he gets here."

"Then I'll sleep on the floor. It's your bed." she insisted, just as he knew she would.

"Stay right where you are. I won't have any woman who's a guest in my home sleep on the floor. And that's final." The truth was he didn't think he could resist her if she came close again even if she was dressed head-to-toe in Viking gear.

With a resounding huff, she flopped back against the pillow and snapped off the light. Dex spread out on the quilt, his body immediately objecting to what was going to be a long night.

"If your leg is sore and you can't kick the ball on Sunday, I'm not taking the heat for this with the fans."

That made him laugh. "Never fear, lass. Tomorrow night I'll have a bed to myself in a posh hotel."

"I thought this week's game was at home."

"Aye, it is." He adjusted the pillow in a futile attempt to get comfortable. "The team stays in a hotel the night before every game."

"Really? What an incredible waste of money."

He laughed again. Leave it to practical Andi to see it that way. "It's meant to keep the team focused on the game. It's not like one of those all-night slumber parties you had as a teenager."

She was quiet for a long moment. "I never went to a slumber party."

His chest squeezed tightly. His sister Annis had been the queen of slumber parties. He suddenly felt guilty for all the things he and his sister had growing up. Not just the things, but the comfort and stability he'd certainly taken for granted.

"I find it hard to believe there's no shenanigans at the hotel the night before a game," she said. "Knowing Jade, she loves spending the night at a 'posh hotel' each week."

"No girls allowed."

"For real?" Her laugh had an evil edge to it. "I'm sure Jade isn't happy about that."

"I thought you two were friends?"

Andi snorted. "Puh-leeze. The only friend Jade has is herself. And your quarterback, who seemed like he had a lot more sense when I met him. Guess I misjudged him."

Dex smiled into the darkness. Van Horn had a boatload of sense. He also had a tactical game plan for every element of his life. One he never wavered from. But something inside of him liked the fact she wasn't swooning after the quarterback. "To each his own."

A peaceful quiet settled over the room. Just when he thought he could relax, Andi broke the silence.

"Are you sure—"

"I'm not trading places with you, lass. Now stop your jibber jabbering and let me get to sleep. I have an early morning at the center tomorrow."

"Shouldn't you be practicing your punting or tackling?"

He sighed. She claimed not to know much about football, but he sensed she was baiting him now. "I don't do either of those things. I score points. A lot of them."

"Brag much?"

"Stating the facts isn't bragging."

"I hope you're not as cocky with your mathletes."

"Athletes always play to win, even mathletes."

She snorted again. "You're supposed to be mentoring them."

"I am. I'm mentoring them in winning."

The room grew quiet again. He thought she might have drifted off until she spoke softly.

"Whatever you're doing, it's working," she admitted. "The kids all adore you."

Her unexpected compliment made his face warm. Suddenly he wanted her with him at tomorrow morning's tryouts. Despite what she believed, she was a good judge of character and would likely be a big help selecting new team members as well as consoling those kids who didn't make the cut. Something told him she'd enjoy the morning as much as anyone else. He was surprised at how much he wanted to make Andi happy. To make her feel a part of something.

"And I have a hunch you adore being with those kids, too," she added. "You're a natural."

"It's what I enjoy most. Teaching kids to relish math as much as I do was the only thing I ever wanted to do."

He wasn't sure why he shared that with her. Few people knew that about him. That dream was part of his past. The life he'd left behind after he'd screwed everything up.

"How did you go from wanting to be a math teacher to becoming a super-star professional athlete?"

The answer to that question was complicated and ugly. So ugly, he'd never even shared it with his family. He certainly couldn't share it with his pretend wife. Not if he still wanted her to keep up the charade.

"Fate," he eventually answered.

It wasn't a lie. It just wasn't the whole truth.

She blew out an aggravated sounding breath. "Do you ever answer a question without a cryptic answer?"

"Not if I can help it."

He heard her huff and roll over. Several long minutes passed while something that felt an awful lot like guilt settled into his gut. He was being a jackass. Had been since he walked into the bedroom earlier. She deserved at least part of the story if they were going to spend the next six months pretending to be married.

"I came to the States on a math fellowship," he admitted into the darkness. "I was a graduate assistant at the University of Wisconsin where I earned my Master's. One night, one of my mates in the house I shared dared me to try out for the football team. It seemed they were in desperate need of a kicker. This guy had seen me play intramural football—soccer is what you'd call it." He waited for her to make some snarky comment about American football. When she didn't, he continued his tale. "It turns out, I have pretty good aim. I kicked the winning field goal in the Rose Bowl that year. The rest is history. Kurt persuaded me that I could get my PhD and still have a pro career. So that's what I did."

Silence descended again. Here he'd finally revealed something of himself and the bloody lass was asleep. He punched at his pillow, trying to find a comfortable position when he heard her softly uttered question.

"Do you miss it?"

Did he miss what? College football? "Miss what, lass?"

"Scotland."

That familiar ache settled in the vicinity of his chest, just as it always did when someone mentioned home. "Aye," he uttered before he thought better of it.

When he didn't bother to elaborate, she huffed once more. "Well, at least you're consistent with your cryptic answers. Goodnight, Dex."

He'd hurt her again. *It's for the best.* A physical attraction he could withstand. *Mostly.* But if her heart became involved, it would break him.

FOURTEEN

"YOU'RE WEARING THAT?"

Clive's question greeted Andi when she slipped into the back-seat of Daniel's car. Her friends were season ticket holders for Growlers' games. Since Dex would be traveling to the stadium with the team, she'd hitched a ride to Sunday's game with them.

"It's not my first choice." Andi ran her palm along the thigh of her buff-colored linen pants, willing them not to wrinkle. She'd spent an agonizing hour—not to mention half a month's rent--in a high-end clothing store yesterday looking for clothes that would be worthy of a professional athlete's wife. "But the WAGs dress to impress. You should have seen what they wore to the team picnic."

She'd paired the pants with a sleeveless tank, the clingy fabric nearly the exact color of the team's green uniforms. There was no way the other women could look down on her wardrobe choice today.

"But I think this is the first time I've seen pumps at a football game," Clive said.

"I had to improvise at the last minute. That nasty cat mistook my flats for her litter box."

Daniel laughed. "I'm pretty sure there was no mistaking about it. She's jealous you're making the moves on her man."

She snorted. Nothing could be further from the truth. Not that she didn't want to make the moves on Dex. But she'd sobered up since the other night. Besides, he had been the one making the moves. At least that's how she'd interpreted it in her inebriated state. And then he'd turned off the heat just as quickly. Again. She was getting whiplash from his mixed signals.

"You boys keep forgetting it's not that kind of marriage," she reminded them.

This time Clive snorted. "Please. When you two are together you put off enough sexual energy to light up the entire city of Milwaukee."

"Nobody said it couldn't be that kind of marriage if you want it to be," Daniel added.

Except somebody had said it. Dex. He'd said it repeatedly. And no amount of wanting on her part was going to change that. She turned to look out the window so her friends wouldn't see how much his rejection stung.

"Besides," Daniel continued. "With you two sharing a bed, it's only a matter of time before you both explode."

"We're not sharing a bed. He sleeps on the floor."

Daniel coughed out a laugh.

"Damn. He sounds like one of those guys who thinks sex will mess with his athletic ability," Clive muttered. "Look, honey, don't take his actions as a mark against you. From what I've seen from Dex this week, I get the impression he's a genuine guy. A guy who cares about your well-being. He probably doesn't want to complicate your relationship any more than it already is with sex. And I agree. If you're going to come out of this fauxmance unscathed, you should just keep the status-quo. Let him stay on the floor."

"Don't listen to this party-pooper, Andi." Daniel steered the car toward the stadium entrance. "He's sleeping on the floor because he doesn't trust himself around you. You just need to let him know you're a big girl who can certainly keep her heart out of the game. There's no reason you two can't enjoy all the benefits of marriage these next six months."

Andi stared at the fans making their way toward the stadium as she pondered both men's words. Could it be that simple? She agreed with Clive that Dex was a stand-up guy. And she suspected he did care about her. Of course, he also cared about his mathletes. And Marlene. And his teammates. And, most importantly, the family he refuses to return to.

But what about this crazy desire constantly simmering between them? Could they survive the remainder of their fake marriage without acting on it? Was Daniel right? Should she take the lead?

"This is the VIP entrance." Clive's announcement interrupted her crazy thoughts. "At least you won't be walking too far in those ridiculous shoes."

Andi was inclined to agree, but she wouldn't give her friend the satisfaction. It was bad enough she wobbled slightly when she stepped onto the sidewalk. Clive shook his head in exasperation. She squared her shoulders. "I'm not embarrassing myself in front of those women again."

"Atta girl," Daniel called from the driver's seat. "And win or lose, your man is going to need to let off some steam after the game, so think about what I said."

Clive shot his partner a disgusted look. "If it gets too intense with the WAGs, come find us in our seats." He gestured to her shoes. "If you can walk that far."

The guard at the entrance gave her a jovial smile when he saw her VIP pass. "Congratulations and welcome to the Growlers, Mrs. Fletcher."

"Thank you," she replied, ignoring the squeezing in her stomach the sound of her new name always seemed to bring on. "Um, can you tell me how I get to the suite reserved for the families?"

"Sure thing." He indicated an elevator on the other side of the concrete hallway. "Justin will take you upstairs and point you in the right direction."

The elevator operator waved her on board. "Most of the other ladies have been here for a while. I hope they saved you some lunch."

Andi's stomach sank as the elevator climbed. The game started in thirty minutes. If anything, she thought she was early. Apparently not.

The doors to the suite were manned by a woman in a green Growlers jacket. "Hi there, Mrs. Fletcher," she said cheerfully. "We were getting worried you wouldn't make it."

When she swung open the door to admit Andi, the women and children inside all seemed to turn and look at once. Andi scanned the room, open to the field below. A buffet was set up to her left, crammed with food and drink while a trio of waiters stood behind it ready to serve. Tables were scattered throughout the space where the women congregated, many with children in their laps. Nearly all of them were dressed in a Growler's jersey.

So much for not embarrassing herself among the WAGs.

"Andi. You're finally here," Jade drawled. "I guess the only thing you're not fashionably late for is class." She made a show of studying Andi from head to toe. "Did you just come from a fancy brunch?"

If she could manage it in her stupid stiletto heels, she would march away from the WAGs in search of Clive and Daniel. But something seemed to be holding her in place. Or someone, rather. She looked down into the eyes of Harper Gibson, who had her one arm wrapped around Andi's leg, her other arm holding her ever present troll doll. The little girl must have sensed Andi's desire to flee because her eyes were pleading with her to stay.

Pushing out a cleansing breath, she patted the child on the head. "Hello Harper. Hello Poppy. I'm sorry I'm late."

"You're not late." Merrit Gibson moved in beside them. "I shouldn't have assumed Jade would give you the details on what goes on during home games."

Jade managed a sheepish look. "My bad. Did I forget to fill you in?"

Some of the other WAGs tittered in the background. Merrit squeezed Andi's elbow as she led her into the room. A young woman sporting a Growler's jersey that had been bedazzled to within an inch of its life jumped in front of them.

"Oh my gosh, am I glad to see you." Her long blonde hair bobbed as she talked. "I'm Shaina, Kane Palmer's girlfriend." She extended her hand and looked at Andi expectantly.

Andi must not have done a good job hiding her confusion because the other girl's smile dimmed.

"The punter," she amended.

Ahh. She quickly apologized as she shook Shaina's hand. "You'll have to excuse me. I don't know all the player's names yet."

Shaina blew out a relieved breath. "We're the only two WAGs from the kicking unit. Since Kane's a rookie, I don't really know anyone here, either." She glanced around the room shyly. "I figured maybe we could stick together."

Shaina looked like one of the many coeds Andi had endured for the past nearly seven years—eager to be appear more worldly than they actually were. Socially accepted and privileged enough that she could be carefree with her college years. Andi had nothing in common with those girls.

But there was a slight tremor to Shaina's lip that belied her earnest expression. She was just as much out of her element as Andi was. And Andi couldn't afford to turn down any offer of friendship among the WAGs.

She smiled at the younger woman. "I'd like that. Especially since you seem to know more about what's going on than I do."

Shaina's shoulders relaxed. Harper carefully eyed the other woman's jersey.

"Isn't it lovely, Harper?" Andi said. "Did you do it yourself?"

A proud smile formed on the other woman's lips. "I did. I'm a design major so I get a kick out of this kind of stuff." She glanced around the room and lowered her voice. "I think it might be a bit over the top for some of the other ladies."

"Nonsense," Merrit interjected. "It's lovely. Don't let anyone dampen your spirit."

Shaina beamed, her brown eyes sparkling. "Thank you, ma'am."

Merrit laughed. "Please. You don't have to ma'am me. It makes me feel old. Now that you two are settled, I'm going to check on Max." She held out a hand to her daughter but the little girl stubbornly held her ground between Andi and Shaina.

Andi took the little girl's hand. "We'll keep an eye on her."

As Merrit walked away, Jade clapped her hands at the center of the suite to get everyone's attention.

"Ladies! Now that we are all here." She leveled another disapproving glance in Andi's direction. "It's time to begin handing out assignments for next month's charity gala for the children's hospital."

Shaina practically bounced on her toes. "Oh, a ball. That sounds so much cooler than a sorority formal, doesn't it?"

Andi didn't bother pointing out that she had as much experience with sorority formals as she did balls. Or galas. Or whatever the heck the event they were talking about was. She was too busy tamping down on the bitterness that Jade always seemed to conjure up within her. A wide-eyed Harper wiggled between the two women to get a better view.

"For those of you who don't know." Jade sent another pointed look in their direction. "This is Joan Zell, the Growler's community relations director. She is coordinating the team's efforts to raise funds through the ball. Since my parents have long been patrons with the hospital, I've volunteered to act as a liaison between the hospital and the team in organizing the ball."

Jade paused here, presumably waiting for applause. Andi was infinitely grateful when there was none.

"And we thank you for your help, Jade," Joan added with a

smile. "We have lots of opportunities for the rest of you all to help out."

"Ooo." Shaina's hand shot into the air. "I'd love to help with anything design related. I interned for the Oklahoma rodeo circuit this summer doing their print media."

Her announcement was met with an awkward silence.

"Oh, honey." Of course it would have to be Jade who spoke up. "I think we should assign the tasks to wives and girlfriends who are in Milwaukee full-time. It will just be easier that way."

Several of the women in the room nodded in agreement.

Joan donned a pitying look. "That's probably best, dear."

She deflated beside Andi. Harper leveled a belligerent stare at Jade while slipping her small hand into Shaina's.

"Oh . . . yeah. Of course," Shaina stammered. "That makes sense."

Except it didn't make sense and they all knew it. Jade was just being a bully. And for some reason everyone in the suite was willing to let her get away with it. Everyone except Andi.

"I don't think it's best," she said.

"Andi," Shaina whispered. "It's okay."

"No. It's not," Andi repeated. She glanced around the room. Several of the ladies donned curious expressions. One of the wives she'd met at the picnic, the one with all the kids, Nicole, nodded at her to go on. "If we're going to draw lines here, why shouldn't we exclude all the girlfriends. After all, there's no guarantee they'll be around when the ball actually takes place."

A buzz rose up within the suite. Jade's eyes narrowed to slits. Suddenly, Andi had the power in this dynamic. And it was a pretty heady feeling.

"Andi's right," Nicole called out from across the suite. "I don't think we should exclude anyone."

"And the design work is done by computer anyway," one of the other wives added. "She doesn't have to be in town to do that. I worked on the programs last year and they were pretty basic. They could use some sprucing up for someone who knows what they're doing."

Joan looked a little flustered as she traded a glance with Merrit.

"We should use our talent the best way we can," the coach's wife said.

"It's settled then," Joan said with a bit more confidence. She nodded at Shaina. "You're on the program committee. I'll just leave the signup sheets here for the rest of you." She spread several papers on one of the tables.

Jade jumped in. "Since we're using our in-house talent so to speak, Andi perhaps you'd like to contribute some of those lovely bath soaps and lotions you make to the gift bags for our guests?"

The other women shifted their gazes between Jade to Andi as if they were watching a tennis match. And Jade was grinning as though she'd just served up an ace. But Andi saw right through her. She could certainly manage the time to create a few signature lotions and soaps for some guest bags. In fact, it would be better than serving on a committee because she could work at her own pace. Jade didn't know it, but she'd just served up Andi the match.

"It would be my pleasure," she replied.

This time, there was applause.

"That's wonderful," Joan said as she joined in on the applause. "We usually stuff them with Growlers swag, but I'm sure the ladies will love something just for them. We fill the bags the week before. You'll have no problem getting us five hundred pieces by then, will you?"

Andi wobbled on her heels. *Five hundred pieces? Holy hell!* She didn't have the manufacturing capability to make that much product in four weeks. Not to mention the money to buy the supplies. What had she just gotten herself into?

Jade eyed her with a wily look. The rest of the room wore varying expressions of expectation. Harper slipped her hand into hers and gave it an encouraging squeeze. When she glanced down at the little girl's trusting face, she felt a burst of energy surge through her. There was no way Andi was letting Jade win. She winked at Harper.

"Nope," she responded. "No problem at all."

DEX DRESSED QUICKLY after the game. The team was subdued as they milled around the locker room chatting with reporters and each other. The Growlers had managed a win, but it was an ugly one. Trayvon went down with a knee injury that looked to be season ending. His replacement had allowed the other team's linemen to sack Van Horn not once, but twice. Van Horn wasn't too fond of having his face planted in the turf, and he didn't mince words letting his teammates know it. The faster Dex could get out of the locker room, the better.

Grabbing his bag, he weaved through the sea of bodies between him and the door. A crowd of reporters was camped out in front of Palmer's locker. Not surprising. Palmer shanked a punt in the fourth quarter giving their opponent the ball in the red zone. Fortunately, the defense held them to only three points on the drive. The Growlers held onto the lead and won the game. The media, however, was out for blood.

Dex muttered an expletive. As much as the kid annoyed him, Palmer didn't deserve to be vilified after his first game. Rookies should be allowed a mistake here and there, especially when they don't affect the outcome of the game. Palmer was beginning to look a little harried by the ridiculous questions being hurled at him. Dex glanced around for the special teams' coach, Bill Kelly, to intervene, but, of course, the guy was nowhere to be found.

With another murmured curse—there was nothing he hated more than the nosey media—he stepped into the fray.

"Nice game, Palmer," he said loud enough for his voice to carry throughout the locker room. "I missed two extra points my first game in the pros. Yet, I'm still here. You'll do better next week and each week after that."

"Good game, rookie," Kessler called out.

Several other players followed suit.

"That's your cue to hit the showers." Dex nodded in the direction of the back of the locker room where the media were not permitted.

Palmer squared his shoulders as his cocky smile fell back into place. "See y'all next week."

With no one left to torment, the reporters turned on Dex, blocking his path.

"Only two points today, Declan," one of them called out. "You didn't even post in the top five of the fantasy leagues. Do you think you have it in you this year to lead the league in scoring?"

It was stupid questions like that that made him dislike the media so much. It was the first game of the bloody season and some clown was already asking a ridiculous question like that one. He'd only scored two points because the offense only got in the end zone twice, he wanted to shout. But that would only piss off his teammates. Now *that* would fuel the headlines and the click-bait. The media loved animosity among players. Dex and his teammates, however, did not. They were careful to settle whatever irked them behind closed doors.

"It's a long season," he responded, inching his way toward the door.

"But this is your first season as a married man," another reporter commented. "Do you think marriage will impact your game?"

What a bunch of bloody morons. His marriage had nothing to do with his kicking game. He wasn't some lovesick swine mooning over his wife.

Except he had been dreaming of her repeatedly since they'd first met. And every time he touched her . . .

"Well, I guess that answers our question," one of the female reporters interjected. "The look on his face says it all."

What look on his face? There wasn't any look, for fuck's sake. He was clenching his teeth so hard he was surprised they hadn't turned to sawdust. Trying to compose his features into a sublime expression, he managed to push out an answer.

"Half the men on this team are married and it doesn't affect their game one bit."

The woman had the nerve to smile seductively at him. "We'll have to see, won't we?"

"Can I get a word with you, Fletcher?" Coach Kelly called out from behind the reporters.

It was about bloody time the special teams' coach made an appearance. Ignoring the rest of the questions being peppered at him, he followed the coach to the office area where media were barred from entering.

"What the hell was that about?" Coach Kelly asked.

"Fuck if I know. That's the last time I jump in to save Palmer's ass. From now on, that's your job."

The coach chuckled. "Palmer is going to have to learn to face the music after both good and bad games. But I appreciate what you did for him in there. He's still young. Much younger than you when you started in this league. It's a nice thing you're doing, taking him under your wing."

"I'm not taking that man-child under my wing," Dex argued. "That's what I'm telling you. And I'm done talking to those morons."

He turned on his heel and headed toward the exit leading to the family area of the stadium. The coach chuckled behind him.

"Your sudden marriage is going to be the hot topic for most of the season. Especially with your wife front and center among the other wives."

His words stopped Dex in his tracks. "What does that mean?" he demanded, although he was slightly afraid of the answer.

The coach gestured with his cellphone. "My wife texted me earlier that your young bride put the rest of the WAGs in their place."

Bloody hell. Andi wasn't supposed to get tight with the WAGs, much less put anyone in their place. What has she done? What had *he* done? This charade of a marriage was becoming more complicated by the minute.

"My wife and some of the more senior WAGs were very impressed," Coach Kelly continued. "Be nice to that one, Declan. She's a keeper."

Dex's stomach churned as he made his way to the area of the stadium where the player's families waited after the games. Having never had anyone waiting for him before, he usually avoided the chaotic scene. Something flickered in his chest at the sight of kids racing along the concrete hallways, most wearing their father's jersey. Kessler frolicked among them, tossing out footballs, like a big kid himself. Van Horn's pretentious girlfriend stood preening, her politically connected father in tow, waiting for the quarterback to emerge from his press briefing. As usual, the only face he couldn't seem to locate was his wife's.

"I owe you one." Palmer stepped into his path, a pretty blonde wearing a tricked-out version of his jersey smiling beside him. "Thanks for saving my ass back there."

"You're going to have to learn to not let it show when they get to you," Dex advised. "They're like sharks when they sense any vulnerability."

Palmer grinned. "Got it, bro. Shaina, this is the guy I've been telling you about. Dex, this is my girl, Shaina."

"I'm so glad to finally meet you," Shaina gushed. "Kane talks about you all the time. You wouldn't believe how excited he was to have you to help ease him into the pros."

Oh, for the love of Christ. It was not Dex's job to molly coddle the rookie.

Palmer's cheeks held a tinge of pink. "Don't give him anymore fuel for his ego, Shaina."

Shaina's eyes danced. "Well, wait until you see what I do to your jersey for next week!"

"You're not wearing his jersey!" Palmer exclaimed.

"I'm not wearing a jersey like that on the field," Dex said at the same time.

"No, sillies." Shaina laughed. "For your wife. Andi looked amazing today, but I think she'd feel more relaxed wearing a jersey like everyone else."

Dex's belly was twisting itself in knots again, but this time for a different reason. He searched the area for Andi, but he still couldn't find her. Had she felt dressed inappropriately again? And what was it with women and their bloody clothes? Hopefully, the other women hadn't made her feel out of place. As much as he didn't want her to become too entrenched in the WAGs so when she wasn't around next year, few would notice, he didn't want them to hurt her.

"Have you seen Andi?" he asked Shaina.

"She was with the owner's wife a minute ago, but I lost them. I have to find her before we leave for the airport."

Palmer slapped him on the shoulder. "Our girls have bonded. The only thing that would make them closer was if they were in the same sorority."

Dex stifled a groan. He didn't want Andi bonding with Palmer's girlfriend or with Mrs. Ciaciura. This was getting way out of hand.

"There she is!" Shaina squealed before dashing off into the throng.

The crowd parted and, sure enough, there was his pink-haired wife, laughing at something Mrs. Ciaciura said. Shaina was right, Andi did look amazing, if not a tad overdressed. He was relieved to see her clothing choice wasn't bothering her like it had at the picnic.

He and Palmer made their way in her direction. Shaina was already there, pulling Andi into a tight hug.

"Study buddies Saturday night while the boys are at the hotel," Shaina said. "I'll bring the mock-ups for the program designs and we'll work on your branding assignment."

"I'll bring the wine," Andi replied.

Dex pinned her with a look. It hadn't escaped his attention that she'd been soused the other night. Her lips twitched when her eyes met his.

"There's nothing in the rule book that says you boys should have all the fun the night before a game," she said.

"You had me at wine." Mrs. Ciaciura wrapped an arm around Shaina and Andi.

Dex nearly choked. When exactly had he lost control of this situation?

"Although studying doesn't sound that interesting to me," Mrs. Ciaciura added. "Perhaps it's best if I catch up with you two at the game. And you're both invited to watch from our box next week."

Shaina could hardly contain her excitement. "That would be so cool. I can make you a jersey just like this one, too."

The older woman's eyes widened before she donned an affectionate grin. "You know, I think I'd quite like one of those."

Shaina beamed.

"You gentlemen take care of these two," Mrs. Ciaciura. "Both of them have added a much-needed spark to the Growler family."

He swallowed a groan of defeat while Andi wore a smug smile as she arched an eyebrow at him. Mrs. Ciaciura let out a surprised gasp when Shaina abruptly hugged her.

"Thank you for including me in the Growler family." Shaina wrapped her arms around Andi next. "Thank you for sticking up for me. You are totally amazing."

He glanced at his wife with a questioning gaze. Andi just shook her head before Shaina's arms were suddenly around his neck.

"It was so great to meet you," she whispered. "Thanks for taking care of Kane."

Palmer chuckled as he pulled his girlfriend away. "I've got to get this pretty girl to the airport before she misses her flight. The girls can plan a double-date for Friday night."

Before Dex could roar a protest—because he was never *ever* going on a fucking double date with Palmer and his underage sorority girlfriend—Andi was beside him, linking her arm through his.

"Definitely." She gave his arm a firm squeeze. "We'll talk this week."

Palmer's girlfriend bounced again like a rabbit on steroids before the punter led her to the exit.

"What in the hell—"

She silenced him with a soft kiss. "Careful. We're in public," she murmured against his lips.

He was grateful for the reminder because the moment her lips touched his everyone else faded away. It was that way every bloody time.

"Let's go home," he heard himself say when she pulled away.

Her eyes widened and her breath hitched momentarily before she nodded. He threaded his fingers through hers and headed for the car park.

"Oh, if it isn't the couple de jour."

Unfortunately, Van Horn and the increasingly annoying woman who was supposedly not his girlfriend stood in their way.

"Aren't they cute, babe?" Jade wrapped herself around Van Horn like a boa constrictor. "So lovely dovey."

"Adorable," Van Horn drawled.

Dex had the sudden urge to punch his friend in the mouth. Andi gave his hand a squeeze.

"We were just leaving," he practically growled.

"Oh, not before you've met, Daddy." Jade waved her father over. "I know he wants to offer up his congratulations on your . . . marriage."

Andi's grip became a lot harder. She'd likely been navigating hostile territory all day and she was worn out. He didn't blame her. He gave her hand a reassuring squeeze back and readied himself for a quick exit. He didn't need to suck up to Jade Whatshername's district attorney daddy. Politics was Van Horn's game. He needed to get Andi out of there.

"Mr. and Mrs. Fletcher, I presume?" The man stuck his hand in Dex's direction.

Dex didn't want to extract his fingers from Andi's to shake the other man's hand, but the manners his ma had drummed into him when he was young forced him to.

"Congratulations." The DA pumped Dex's hand before eyeing Andi openly.

Something ugly churned in Dex's belly. He quickly snatched her hand back and drew her in closer to his body. No man should look at another man's wife that way. "Thank you, but we were just leaving."

Van Horn narrowed his eyes at him. Well, his friend could just sod off if he thought Dex was being rude.

"So soon? I was hoping we could all grab dinner," the other man said. "I'd enjoy chatting with your lovely new wife. And hearing about how you two met."

When hell freezes over.

"We've got plans," Dex responded tersely. "Newlyweds, you know."

He shot a heated look—one that wasn't entirely an act—at Andi before tugging her hand. She didn't hesitate in following him. Jade's father chuckled in the background. Van Horn gaped at them as a few whistles and cat calls followed them out of the stadium and into the night.

FIFTEEN

AS SOON AS they were safely in Dex's car, Andi peeled off her shoes and began massaging her feet.

"My dogs are eternally grateful you parked close."

The Jaguar's engine purred to life. "One of the perks of leaving my car here early this morning. I get the nearest spot."

"Don't the other guys bring their cars over, too?"

"They have their wives or girlfriends do it for them."

She sighed. "Of course they do."

Dex glanced over at her. "I'm sorry. I'm so used to doing things on my own, I just didn't think about it." His gaze roamed over her. "I never paid attention to what the WAGs wear to the games, either. And I didn't think to ask someone. I should have, though. That's on me." He dragged his fingers through his hair. "I don't mean for you to feel out of place, Andi. That's not my intention at all."

The sincerity of his apology warmed her. The streetlight shining through the windshield illuminated his face. He was genuinely distressed. She placed her hand on top of his hand resting on the gear shift. "I know that."

Her act of reassurance did more than that. Just touching him stoked the fire constantly simmering between them. Their eyes met, and before she knew what was happening, he was leaning in for a kiss. He kissed her long and slow, as if they had all the time in the world. Her hand left his to trail along the stubble lining his jaw. He stroked his tongue over hers, prying a sigh from deep in her belly. His hand found her thigh, dragging her closer to him. Following his lead, she shifted in the seat, the interior of the car suddenly too small and too warm.

A loud banging on the window had her nearly hitting her head on the roof when she jumped away.

"Get a room, you two," Van Horn called from outside.

Dex swore violently and put the car in drive. "He better not be anywhere near because I might run the bastard over."

"I take it we're not double-dating with them?" Andi was surprised how quickly she'd recovered her composure.

He laughed. "Not on your life." He risked a glance at her before pulling out onto the main road. "You needn't worry about Jade, lass. Given Van Horn's track record, she won't be around long."

"Does she know that? Because I'm pretty sure she's already picked out her ring."

"Van Horn isn't the marrying type."

She rolled her eyes, but his gaze was firmly on the road ahead of them. "They said that about you."

They stopped for a stoplight and he looked over at her. "He doesn't have deportation hanging over his head."

If Andi needed another reminder that their relationship wasn't real, his quietly uttered words were it. But the kiss they'd just shared had been real. Very real. Sure, he'd kissed her because he knew his teammates were likely watching, but Daniel was right. Why shouldn't they enjoy the perks of being married and the close proximity they were forced to endure? They both knew what the eventual outcome was. They'd be walking away from each other in six months. But in the meantime, there wasn't anything preventing them from enjoying each other's company.

"Jade likes to think she's in charge because she's dating the QB, I take it?" he asked, interrupting her internal debate.

"Something like that. And stupid me fell right into her trap."

He stopped the car to wait for the gate to the apartment's garage to open. "How so?"

She sighed. She'd been a fool to rise to the other woman's bait. But she'd wanted so badly to be accepted by the other WAGs, she would have promised anything at that point.

"It's all your fault," she declared. "I was just trying to play the role everyone expects your wife to play. And you're the one who mentioned my soaps during that interview."

He pulled the car into its assigned space and killed the engine. "Aye. And let's not forget I gave your friend Clive some free advertising, too. What exactly did Jade trick you into?"

She slumped against the seatback. "Apparently there's this gala every year the team puts on for the children's hospital."

"Aye. It's held at the Milwaukee Art Museum."

Envy, hot and ugly, rolled in her stomach. Of course Dex had been to the gala. The entire team was expected to attend. She tried to block out the images of all the women he'd walked the red carpet with before.

"Then you also must know they give out swag bags to all the attendees each year."

He waved a hand. "They do at all those types of events. I give mine to Marlene."

"Well, this year she'll get some of my soaps and lotions in her bag."

"Really?" His dimple winked at her when he grinned. "But that's a good thing. You can't ask for better advertising than that."

Andi put her hands to her face. "Not if I can't mass produce five hundred items. That could take me weeks. Not to mention the cost. And it's not like I have a lot of free time."

Dex was quiet beside her. She peeked at him through her fingers before he reached over and began to gently peel them away from her face.

"First of all, you keep forgetting you're not alone in this. Not anymore." He took one of her hands in his. "I'll pay for any supplies you need."

She opened her mouth to object, but he held up a finger and continued.

"You wouldn't be incurring those costs if it wasn't for me. And as for producing the necessary number of items, I'll help. Marlene and her husband will, too. Hell, since Palmer seems to be attached to my hip, he can lend a hand. Just tell us what you need and it will get done."

The car was growing warm again, but for an entirely different reason. *You're not alone in this.* That's twice now he'd said that to her. She wanted so much to sink into the feeling of someone being her partner, her teammate. But she didn't dare let herself get too used to the idea. Not when this marriage had an expiration date. She'd be on her own again soon enough.

He reached up and fingered a piece of her hair. "You're awfully quiet, lass."

"I don't know what to say." It was the truth.

"I find it's always best to start with thank you when someone offers to help." He leaned in and brushed a kiss over her lips.

She rubbed her fingertips over her lips when he pulled back. "Why did you do that? No one is here to see."

His eyes darkened with what she was beginning to recognize as desire.

"Because I wanted to, Andi," he murmured. "Sometimes it's all I can think about doing."

Her stomach fluttered at his unexpected admission. "Take me inside, Dex," she whispered before she could stop herself.

"Don't move," he commanded. Coming around to her side of the car, he opened her door and lifted her into his arms.

"What are you doing?"

"That should be obvious, lass. My queen's feet hurt, so I'm carrying her inside."

Embarrassed not only by his chivalrous display but his earlier words, Andi buried her face into his neck. She breathed in his unique scent with a sigh. His fingers traced the curve of her bottom. Andi responded by trailing her lips along his neck. He growled when the elevator doors to the penthouse didn't open fast enough.

Heat began to build deep within her core and drawing in enough air became a bit more difficult. When the doors finally opened, Dex bypassed the living areas and strode with determination down the long hall to his bedroom—*their* bedroom. He kicked the door closed behind them. Both were silent for a long moment when he stopped in front of the big bed.

Unable to stand it any longer, she whispered his name, the single word sounding more like a plea when it left her lips. He gently released her legs, letting them trail down his body so she was flush with his. She quickly discovered she wasn't the only one aroused. He kept his arms wrapped tightly around her waist so that her tender feet barely brushed the carpet.

She draped her arms over his shoulders and lifted her chin to meet his heated gaze. "I don't want you to sleep on the floor tonight."

He shuddered against her. "You don't know what you're asking. I slept on the floor because ya tempt me fiercely, lass. I dinnae want ta take advantage of ya."

The raw honesty of his words had her nerve endings dancing with restless desire. The fact that his brogue was creeping into the conversation told her he wasn't as in control as he wanted to be. The knowledge emboldened her. She blew out a shaky breath.

"It's not taking advantage if I want it, too."

He growled again. "I can't give you everything ya want, Andi. Ya ken?"

The longing building inside her snuffed out the warning coming from her brain. "What if all I want is sex? I'm a big girl who can separate a physical act from happily ever after. I just want you for your body, Declan Fletcher. Is that too much to ask?"

His chest rumbled again with a low, possessive groan. Then his lips were on hers. The kiss he gave her was so thorough and hot, the room began a lazy spin. Andi fisted her hands in his shirt to keep from falling. His mouth ate at hers while his fingers gathered up the hem of her blouse. The cool air washed over her hot skin when he lifted the fabric higher. Andi writhed against him, eliciting another one of those low growls from deep within him.

Breaking the kiss, he quickly stripped the blouse from her body. She struggled to keep her balance. They were both panting for air. His hands anchored her waist yet again, but he kept their bodies a forearm's length apart. Andi embarrassed herself by whimpering as she tried to close the distance between them. He barked a harsh laugh but held her steady.

"You're very greedy, lass." His gravelly voice brought goosebumps to her feverish skin. "We've got all night. And I aim to use up every moment giving you pleasure."

His promise had her legs turning to Jell-O, but his warm fingers dug into her waist, holding her upright. He took his time studying her before slowly dropping to his knees. Andi's whole body quaked when his lips found the sensitive skin around her belly button. Gripping his muscled shoulders, she thrust her hips toward him with a frustrated sigh. She felt him chuckle against her belly.

"You are nae what I expected, lass," he murmured before his tongue delved into her belly button sending shockwaves throughout her body.

"Dex," she moaned. "I want—"

"I ken what you want," he said right before his fingers tore at the fastenings to her pants. "And I'm going to give it to you until you scream for mercy."

Holy hell.

A breath later, her pants were around her ankles. Andi was frantic to step out of them, but he was too busy burying his face into her panties. His talented fingers slid beneath the fabric, cupping her bottom. The slide of the silk over her core was making her ache in parts of her body she didn't know existed.

"You always smell so good," he murmured. "So bloody good. I can only imagine how you'll taste."

She was wet in an instant. "Damn it, Dex."

With one fluid motion, her pants and panties were on the floor and he was on his feet. He eased her onto the bed, her legs dangling over the edge before he stepped back. She watched as he shed his clothes with the ease and speed of a man who'd had a lot of practice at stripping before a woman. But Andi didn't let her mind go there. Not when her body was throbbing for release and he was looming over her.

Reaching behind her, she undid her bra. He stilled, his nostrils flaring as he watched her. She smiled slyly, taking her time revealing herself to him. When she finally flung the bra off the bed, she watched as his gaze drank her in like an alcoholic eyeing a glass of whiskey. Feeling brazen, she leaned back on her elbows, naked except for her grandmother's cross dangling between her breasts. With another one of those growls that made her core contract, he fell on top of her. His hands wandered her torso, teasing her pebbled nipples until she begged for his mouth to replace them.

"What will ya have me do next?" He teased her breast with his tongue.

Unable to form a cohesive response, she thrashed her head from side-to-side with a frustrated moan.

"Poor lass." His fingers found the juncture of her thighs. "Does this make it better?"

She would have bucked off the bed had his body not been holding her down. "Yessss." It came out of her mouth more as a sigh, but he seemed to understand because he murmured against her skin before sliding another thick finger inside her. He wound her body so tight, tears of frustration burned the backs of her eyes.

"Shh," he soothed as he slid his body lower. "I'm going to take care of you."

Her body tensed even more in anticipation of the relief he promised. She eased her hips higher as his weight shifted lower. Her breath sawed through her lungs frantically and she worried she might perish before she climaxed.

"I'm here, lass." His words blew against her most sensitive skin.

A deep, keening moan sailed past her lips when his mouth found her. He stoked the fire within her impossibly higher before his tongue stilled.

"No!" She pounded her fists into his shoulders.

His very talented mouth went to work on her again taking her right back up to the crest. When he retreated again, she threaded her fingers through his thick curls to keep him where she wanted him.

"Please," she wailed.

This time, he didn't relent, working his magic until she was flying over the edge with reckless abandon.

ANDI SHATTERING BENEATH him was a sight to behold. Dex took great pride in the fact that he succeeded in pleasuring the women he took to bed, but this felt different somehow. An unfamiliar sensation was bubbling up inside of him and he couldn't explain it. To be honest, he wasn't sure he wanted to quantify it. Not right now, anyway.

He kissed his way up her limp, sated body. She smiled serenely when he got to her lips.

"You weren't kidding when you said I'd beg for mercy," she whispered, her eyelids fluttering in an attempt to stay open.

He cocked an eyebrow. "It's an integral part of my skill set."

She breathed a shallow laugh and flailed a hand in the direction of his arm, but it was clear she was too spent to even spar with him. He slipped his hands beneath her and lifted her to the center of the bed.

"Up you go, lass."

A few sounds of protest came from her lips when he crawled to one side of the bed. He rummaged around the drawer in his nightstand until his fingers met with foil. When he turned back to the bed, she was sitting up, her eyes wide, her lip quivering.

"Dex?"

Jaysus. The poor lass thought he was leaving her. His chest squeezed uncomfortably. How many times must one be abandoned before one expects it every time?

"I'm not going anywhere," he reassured her as he stalked back toward the bed. He held his hand open so she could see the condoms. "Just fetching my protection."

She nodded, ducking her face, but not quick enough that he didn't see the moisture shimmering in her eyes. Dropping the condoms on the mattress, he dragged her chin up with his finger.

"I'm here, Andi."

He leaned in and took her mouth in a slow, patient kiss, trying to convey with his lips what she needed to feel—desired. She responded with a greedy thrust of her tongue, and just like that, they were a tangle of naked, slick limbs. He let her have her way with her mouth and hands on his body for several long, intoxicating moments, before his own pent-up desire roared to life again.

Breaking their kiss, he grabbed several pillows and rolled her onto her belly on top of them. He stroked his hands along the sweet globes of her ass. She arched her back with a sigh and his already hard body turned to granite. His hands trembled slightly when he rolled the condom over his erection. Andi glanced over her shoulder at him, a wicked smile aimed his way.

He was over her in an instant, filling her with one thrust. Her erotic moan bouncing off the walls excited him more. She curled into him greeting each one of his thrusts with an exhaled *yes*. Dex was lost. His heart hammered against his chest while the heady feeling of being inside Andi threatened to overwhelm him. He wanted to make things last, to make her come again, but he was so bloody close to the edge.

They were moving as one, each breath they took coming in unison. Dex reached a hand around to caress her breast, but Andi had other ideas. She dragged his fingers to her clit and pressed them where she wanted them. A moan of pure ecstasy reverberated around the room when he began to knead the swollen nub. Seconds later, her muscles convulsed around him tightly. He came in a rush so powerful, it had him roaring her name like a rallying cry.

They collapsed as one on their sides, him still inside her quivering body. Both of them gasping for air. His heart pounded in his chest so hard, he was sure she could feel it against her back. A lock of her hair was stuck to the stubble on his face, but he ignored it. He doubted he could move his arm anyway. Andi, on the other hand, managed to wriggle her very fine ass against him as she snuggled back against him.

"Have mercy, lass, will ya?"

"Now who's the one begging?"

He nipped at her shoulder. "The night is still young. You may regret yer taunt."

She shivered and he wrapped his arms more tightly around her midsection, letting one of his hands palm a breast. A contented sigh filled the air. It took Dex a minute to realize it had come from him. A lick of panic walked up his spine. So much for getting Andi out of his system. He had a niggling suspicion that he might never get enough of the woman in his arms. And that should have scared the bloody hell out of him.

Yet it didn't. Andi wasn't like those wily women trying to trick a rich athlete into putting a ring on it. Hell, he'd had to practically trick her to marry him. And she was as honest as they come. She knew the score. And they were married after all. Why not enjoy the marriage bed while they were legally bond?

"I imagine if Agent Figueroa and his friends from ICE popped in now, they'd be satisfied about our case."

She stiffened beside him. "I'd prefer they'd not 'pop in' at all. Especially when I'm naked."

Dex nuzzled her neck. "We have a problem then, lass, because I plan on keeping you naked every time we're in this bed."

He was surprised at how much he meant it.

SIXTEEN

THE SALON WAS CLOSED on Mondays, making it Andi's favorite day to work. She usually spent the day restocking, confirming appointments, and ordering supplies. Today, however, she was finding it hard to concentrate. Her mind continually drifted to the night before. Dex's boast about giving her pleasure all night long hadn't been a boast at all. The man certainly had the stamina and conditioning of a prime athlete performing at his peak.

Not that she was complaining. Her body was tight as a bow just thinking about how he'd brought her to ecstasy over and over. She fanned her warm face with the list of supplies she'd been creating.

"Jeez, Andi, are you glowing?"

She nearly jumped out of her chair at the sound of Clive's voice.

"What are you doing here?" Flustered, she gathered up all her papers and stacked them into a neat pile.

Stepping into his office, the one she normally commandeered on Mondays, he leaned a hip against one of the file cabinets while studying her with a speculative eye.

"Last time I checked I owned the place, which means I can come here whenever I want."

She ground her teeth. "I meant, what are you doing here on your day off?"

He set down a brown paper bag on the corner of his desk. "Daniel thought you might want some catnip to help tame Fletcher's wee beasty."

"Oh." Because what else could she say. He was just trying to be sweet and here she was biting his head off.

"Your turn." He crossed his arms over his chest, tucking his hands beneath his armpits. "Why are you glowing?"

She avoided his gaze. "I'm not glowing. It's just warm in here."

He made a sound of disbelief. "Oh, for crying out loud. You slept with him, didn't you?"

"I—I . . ." She didn't want to lie to her friend, but she didn't want him knowing the truth either, as if talking about it would burst the bubble of bliss. Clive was sure to bring up the ticking clock that measured the lifespan of her marriage, and she wasn't ready to deal in realities just yet.

"Never mind. I don't want to know." He snatched the folder from the desk. "I just hope you know what you're doing, Andi."

She did. Or, at least, she thought she did.

"Clive," she called after him. "Is it okay if I order some supplies under your account?"

She normally ordered what she needed for her soaps and lotions using the salon account to take advantage of the discount and free-shipping. But this order was going to be sizable given what she needed for the swag bags. She didn't feel right not running it by her friend first.

"I thought you weren't going to need anything new until your branding project at the end of the semester?"

"Change in plans." She was equal parts excited and overwhelmed by the opportunity she was given. It likely showed in her expression because he wandered back into the office, a concerned look in his eyes.

"Meaning what, exactly?"

"My soaps are going in the swag bags for the Growlers' ball. They're expecting five hundred guests."

He whistled. "That's incredible."

"I know. I just hope I can get it done in time."

"You will. You're Andi Larsen, remember?"

She swallowed roughly at the use of her maiden name. "Actually, legally I'm Andi Fletcher now. I had to change my name for the time being. You know, to make things look . . . real. Mr. Hilbert even got me a passport. Crazy, huh?"

He gave his head an annoyed shake. "Whatever. I'm happy to front you the money, if that's what you're asking. Daniel and I know you're good for it."

"Actually, it's okay." She plucked the Platinum card Dex had handed her earlier this morning from the pile on the desk. "I've got it covered."

His eyes grew wide. "Please don't tell me you slept with him for his damn credit card?"

She recoiled as if he'd actually struck her. It took her a moment to push words past the disgust squeezing her throat. "It's not like that!"

"It certainly looks like that from where I stand," he shouted. "Andi you signed a contract. Whatever this is you two are playing at, it's over in six months. Hell, with his track record, he'll be on to someone else days later."

Her chest burned with every breath she drew. It didn't help that her friend was right. Still, she wasn't going to give him the satisfaction of admitting that at the moment.

"Never mind," she snapped. "I'm sure Dex won't mind me charging the extra shipping. I'm sure I can make it worth his while tonight."

Turning her back on him, she sat back down and opened her laptop. She stared at the screen until his retreating footsteps faded. She wanted to thrash him for turning what was a lovely experience with Dex into something tawdry and disgusting. Unfortunately, if the truth came out, the rest of the world would see things the exact same way.

Andi buried her face in her hands. She'd been reckless to sleep with him. But at the same time, she didn't regret it. She'd spent most of her life feeling alone, expendable, and not worthy. Last night, Dex made her feel like the center of the universe. So what if she had to give all that up in six months. Until then, she was going to be greedy and take what she could. Especially since it would likely have to last her the rest of her life. Squaring her shoulders, she pulled up the list of items she needed to order.

"I'm sorry."

Once again, Clive's words had her jumping out of her seat.

"I had no right to say what I did," he continued. "I've known you for practically all my life and you've never judged me the way I just judged you."

She didn't trust her words to come out as anything more than a sob, so she simply nodded.

"How can I help?"

Andi threw herself at him. He wrapped his arms around her, gently rocking her from side to side. They stood like that for several long moments.

"Is that a serious offer?" she murmured against his shoulder.

"I love you Andi Lar—Fletcher. And I'm always in your corner. Now what can I do?"

"How would you like to host a soap-making party Friday night?"

He groaned.

But he didn't say no.

OF ALL THE things Dex imagined himself doing on a Friday night, making soap in someone's garage was nowhere on that list. Especially if the evening included the Growler's goofball punter and his "super-excited" girlfriend.

"Isn't this fun?" Andi smiled up at him.

"Yes," he said, surprising himself. Of course, he suspected he'd enjoy himself actually getting his back waxed if she was with him. He leaned down and brushed a kiss over her nose.

"Enough of that," her friend Daniel called from the other end of the garage. "You two are here to make soap, not whoopie."

Marlene's husband laughed. "You kids are still calling it that nowadays?"

"No, but that's the only euphemism Daniel can use in polite company," Clive replied.

Everyone laughed. Andi moved to the center of the garage.

"We need to get started. In order to get enough soap to make five hundred bars, we're going to need to repeat the process twice." She gestured to the four workstations set up in each corner. "We'll work in groups of two. All the ingredients and tools you'll need are at each station. I'm going to guide you through the process step-by-step."

Palmer pulled on a pair of rubber gloves and safety glasses. "Cool. This is gonna be a lot like high school chemistry."

"I hope not," Shaina said. "I seem to remember you setting your lab table on fire with a Bunsen burner."

Andi shot a worried look at Dex. "Maybe we should have someone supervise him?" she whispered.

Not if it meant Dex couldn't work with Andi. As usual, both their schedules had been crazy all week. Their only time together between the sheets or in the shower. He was reluctant to give up another moment with her. Especially not for the annoying punter who'd been dogging him since Sunday.

"Get serious, rookie," Dex commanded. "We're here to work."

Palmer gave him a jaunty salute.

Andi sighed. "Besides your stainless-steel mixing bowl, you should all have a few spoons, a thermometer, and an immersion blender."

"Hey. Is this one from our kitchen?" Clive asked.

"You said you'd do anything to help me." Andi batted her eyes at him. "Consider it a donation to the cause."

"You're buying me a new one, Fletcher."

"Add it to my back-wax tab."

Another round of laughter erupted within the garage. Dex suddenly couldn't remember the last time he'd enjoyed himself like this.

"The ingredients need to be measured precisely," Andi continued. "We only have one scale, so I need someone with a good eye and a good head for numbers to handle this part."

"That's me," Daniel and Dex said at the same time.

"Fine," Andi said. "It doesn't hurt to have two sets of eyes."

A lot of trash talking between he and Daniel followed, each one claiming to have a better head for numbers. It didn't take them long to get everything measured and dispersed to each couple. By the time they were done with the task, Dex had recruited Daniel to work with his mathletes on the curriculum involving calculating financial ratios.

"When do we get to the good part," Palmer complained. "I want to wear my mask."

"In a minute," Andi replied. "First we mix the oils. For our carrier oils we are using coconut and jojoba oils. Go ahead and pour that into your bowl. Then we'll add the essential oils. Each station has a different scent. One has tea tree, one has eucalyptus, one has lemongrass, and Dex and I have citrus. Carefully add those to the oils and mix them together with your spoon."

Dex mixed the two oils into the bowl. Andi picked up the spoon and began to blend them together. The smell of both oils combined to make the irresistible scent of Andi. He wrapped his arms around her as she stirred.

"Lass, you have no idea what that scent does to me," he murmured against her ear.

"Actually, I think I do." She wiggled her ass against the erection straining his jeans.

Dex groaned.

"Can we get to the good part, now?" Palmer complained.

"Yeah, can we?" Dex whispered.

Chuckling softly, Andi pushed his arms away and stepped back into the middle of the room.

"Apparently not all of us," Dex mumbled.

Before he knew it, they were all donning masks and safety gear. Daniel moved to open the garage door for better ventilation.

"I hope none of the nosy media following you drives by," he quipped. "Lord knows what they think we're doing."

They carefully mixed the lye with the distilled water.

"That's it?" Palmer's disappointment echoed throughout the garage. "I thought there was going to be a lot more smoke or something."

"Only if you did it wrong," Clive said. "Now we take a cocktail break while the water cools to a hundred degrees, right boss?"

"Not too many cocktails," Andi warned. "We still have more work to do."

When she moved to follow the rest inside, Dex wrapped his arms around her waist and pulled her out into the cool night.

"How long does this part take?" He grazed his lips along her jaw.

"Mmm. It depends. Twenty, thirty minutes."

"I can think of a lot of things we can be doing during that time."

Her fingers wandered to the fly of his blue jeans. "Perhaps you can show me."

They made it to his car without anyone noticing. He pulled her on top of him in the passenger suit, dragging her face down for a fierce kiss. Straddling him, she pressed up and down against his erection.

Jaysus. He'd had this woman multiple times a day, multiple ways for a week now and he still couldn't get enough. He nipped at her bottom lip.

"I wanted to take you just like this the other night on campus," he told her. "You have no idea how bad I burned for it."

She pulled the lever beside him, pressing the seatback down so he was nearly horizontal. As she nibbled way along his chest, she slid lower until she was crouched on the floorboard, her mouth lined up with the part that wanted her the most. He bucked when she palmed the inside of his thighs, the denim abrading the sensitive skin there.

Realizing what she was up to, he groaned harshly. "Andi."

She ignored his warning. Her hands brushed against his belly as she pulled the button on his fly free. The sound of the zipper lowering was like the referee's whistle to his body. He let out a pained breath when his john sprung free. As much as he wanted her to climb on top of him now, there was no way he could make himself say the words. He was mesmerized watching her.

Her eyelids slid shut when her fingers wrapped around him. He thrust into her palm, willing her to move. A laugh that sounded more like a pleasured sigh passed from her lips as she began to stroke him up and down.

Slowly.

Too slowly.

"Lass," he groaned.

"Mmhmm." She leaned over and blew on the tip.

Dex thought he was going to die before she finally put him out of his misery and drew him into her mouth. Unable to keep still, he threw his head back. All sorts of unintelligible noises roared from his chest as the pleasure built. He fisted his hands in her hair, guiding her hot, wet mouth over him. When her fingers reached into his jeans and found his balls it was all over. He came so fiercely he was sure the car would roll.

When he was finally able to open his eyes again, there was his Andi, her hair tangled from his fingers, her cheeks glowing and a generous smile on her face. She kissed him on the corner of his mouth before silently slipping out of the car.

It was at that moment that Dex decided he rather liked making soap.

THE FOLLOWING NIGHT, Dex was holed up in the hotel room he shared with Van Horn. Their pre-game rituals were dramatically different. Both attended the evening meal and team meeting, but afterwards, Van Horn retreated to the offensive coordinator's suite to go over game film one last time. Dex, on the other hand, enjoyed a game of chess with the team's equipment manager. He was surprised, therefore, to find Van Horn back in their room long before curfew.

"You wouldn't believe the tales Palmer is spreading," Van Horn led with.

Dex blew out an annoyed breath. He could only imagine the stories the rookie was regaling his teammates with. Most likely about their little soap making party the night before.

"Feeling slighted?" Dex asked, deciding to simply take the bull by the horns. "Your non-girlfriend doesn't look like the type to enjoy getting dirty, so we left you off the invite list."

Van Horn snorted. "Jade can get quite dirty when she thinks there's something in it for her. But you're right. I doubt something as domestic as making soap would appeal."

"There you have it then." He stretched out on his bed and picked up the book he'd brought along. Something about his friend's demeanor put him off.

"I don't get it," Van Horn said a few minutes later.

Dex snapped the book shut. "Don't. Get. What?"

"A week ago, you were sleeping in separate rooms. Now you two are disappearing for long chunks of time to do the wild thing in your car. What gives?"

Damn Palmer. Dex leaped off the bed. He was going to rip the punter's tongue out of his mouth. Andi and his absence had been obvious, but there was no way anyone saw them. The asshole rookie was just spreading tales. True tales, but no one had to know that.

"I donnae appreciate my teammates gossiping like a bunch of hens about what I do with me wife!"

Kessler chose that moment to pop his head in the room. "Hey, Fletcher, Maryland is putting a hurt on Wisconsin. Your Badgers need some of your juju. You wanna come watch?" He glanced between Dex and Van Horn before stepping into the room and closing the door. "What the hell has gotten into you two lately? You look like you're ready to rip off each other's head."

"The only head I'm looking for right now is bloody Palmer's," Dex ground out.

"You don't have to worry about Palmer," Van Horn replied. "I sent him to his room without dessert."

He glared at the quarterback. The asshole was enjoying this.

"Great. Then why don't you guys come watch the game with the rest of us?" Kessler asked, attempting to do what the receiver always did, diffuse a contentious situation. The rest of the Growlers may not have noticed, but Dex saw right through Kessler. The guy was a veritable Pollyanna in pads. The crazy dares or wagers were his way of conflict avoidance. Kessler liked his view of the world to be rose colored, his glass more than half full. The only conflict the guy put up with was on the playing field with the opposing team. And even then, he was the first one there with a hand out when a player from the other team was ass down on the turf.

There was a story there for sure, but right now Dex didn't have the patience to suss it out of his friend. He was too busy keeping his own secrets intact.

Van Horn powered up his laptop and reached for his noise-cancelling headphones. "Nah, I'm going to give this film one more look."

Dex picked up his book again. "I'll check the score in a minute. I'm just gonna read to clear my head."

Kessler shrugged. "Suit yourselves." He pinned them both with a hard look before slipping out the door.

A tentative silence settled over the room. Dex should have known it wouldn't last.

"I warned you about hurting her," Van Horn said, matter-of-factly. "Andi may have gone into this thinking she could handle a pretend relationship. But once you start having sex, it's no longer pretend, dude."

Dex jumped back off the bed and let loose a string of expletives that should have had his roommate cowering. Except it didn't.

"What happened to my marriage being none of your business?"

Van Horn kept his gaze on the computer's screen. "She's a sweet girl, Declan. She's taken some hard knocks in her life, but that doesn't mean she can handle the heartache coming her way when the game is over."

"Worry about your own bloody girlfriend, asshole."

The quarterback had the nerve to laugh. "I doubt Jade has a heart. She's like us." Van Horn did look up at him now. "We don't need another person for anything more to satisfy our needs or advance our career. All Jade wants out of life is her own satisfaction. And her standards are freakishly high."

Jaysus. Was that how people saw him? That's not who Dex was. Van Horn was wrong. It wasn't that he didn't want someone to love. It was that he *couldn't* have that. Not after what he'd done. There was a big difference.

And as for hurting Andi, that was the last thing he would ever intentionally do. His friend didn't know her like he did. She was much stronger than she looked. Besides, her heart wasn't in play. She'd said so herself. Not that he was going to share that tidbit with his idiot roommate. The guy would just twist things around.

He threw his book onto the bed and stormed to the door. Watching his Badgers get beat up by some namby pamby turtles was better than listening to this shit.

SEVENTEEN

ANDI CAREFULLY TRANSFERRED THE GROWLERS' logo onto the last few bars of soap. Squeezed into the salon's back room beside her, Mrs. Hilbert wrapped each bar in cellophane before tying them with a piece of green ribbon.

"These are gorgeous, Andi. And they smell lovely, too." She waved a bar beneath her nose. "I'm going to insist that Kurt buy me a ticket to the gala just so I can have one for myself."

Andi smiled at the woman's finagling. "I'm sure we'll have a few extras, Mrs. H. I'll put one aside for you as a thank you for all your help."

"A football bath bomb, too?"

"I think I can probably get you one of those, yes."

Mrs. Hilbert smiled. "Once these are out in the real world, you won't need any investors. People are going to gobble them up. Although I still believe Kurt should get you on *Shark Tank* even if it's just for the free advertising." She winked at Andi. "They all do that, you know."

Andi's laugh was a bit shaky. "Honestly, it's all happening so fast. I haven't even worked out how I'm going to produce more orders. My intention was just to have a little storefront with a shop in the back where we did specialty orders for spas, boutique hotels, and maybe a bride here and there. Nothing too big. But this . . ." She sighed heavily.

"You'll figure things out," the older woman reassured her. "And if you encounter any roadblocks, I'm sure that hunky husband of yours will help you out."

Mrs. Hilbert was right. Her "hunky husband" had turned out to be quite the partner. Not only was he willing to help her out of her clothes every opportunity he got, he'd been true to his word about helping her with the swag for the gala. Last night, she'd returned from class to find him carefully sorting the cured bars of soap into stacks so she could more quickly transport them to the salon. He'd also gone to bat with the team licensing department to allow her to use the Growler logo, something she never would have thought to do.

He was thoughtful in other ways, as well. The car and driver he'd promised turned out to be a godsend. Not only that, but on the nights when she had class, he made sure Marlene prepared dinner for her, often sitting with her while she ate, the whole time peppering her with questions about her day and her coursework. The other evenings, she spent curled up on one of the sofas in his study, doing homework while he read or worked out drills for his mathletes. He'd even started to teach her to play chess. She was pretty sure he even let her win a time or two.

She knew that once they became involved physically, walking away from him after their contract expired would be difficult. But she hadn't counted on the other countless ways he'd become a part of her life. While she'd certainly miss their physical connection, she was beginning to suspect it was his companionship outside of the bedroom she'd miss a whole lot more when they parted.

"I knew you two would make a great couple. You may have started out as a business arrangement, but that look on your face says it all."

Mrs. Hilbert's words refocused Andi's thoughts back to the

here and now, thankfully. She couldn't afford to dwell on the what-if scenario. She glanced around making sure the room was still empty. "It's still a business arrangement," she said, lowering her voice. "Nothing has changed."

"Oh, poppycock. My neighbor Peggy has that same look on her face whenever she's got herself some." Mrs. Hilbert tied the ribbon with a little more force. "Now she's going after Fred Baker, the little hussy. She won't be happy until she has every man in the entire retirement community in her bed. Well, she's got another thing coming. I saw Fred first. And I don't like losing."

Andi stared at the other woman, unsure how to even respond.

"Oh, don't look at me that way, missy," Mrs. Hilbert added. "Just because I carry an AARP card doesn't mean I don't have needs."

Clive stuck his head in the door just in time to save Andi from answering. "You've got mail." He handed her an envelope addressed with her name, care of the salon. "I didn't know you were here today, Mrs. H."

"I came to help Andi put the finishing touches on everything. But I also wanted to ask you something. How do you think I'd look as a redhead?"

Clive risked a glance at Andi who just shrugged.

"You're a beautiful mature woman," he replied, diplomatically. "I think you'd look good in whatever color hair you choose."

The other woman pondered his response. "Hmm. I'll have to think a bit more about it. The other day at dinner, Fred happened to mention he was partial to redheads. I might just give it a go if it will get his attention."

"Oh, now, Mrs. H, never go changing up who you are for the sake of another person. Love yourself first," Clive advised. "And if this Fred guy doesn't see what a wonderful catch you are, then he's not the one you want."

She rose up on her toes and kissed him on the cheek. "You're right. I think I'll just go see if I can get a bikini wax instead."

The color drained from Clive's face. He sank down into the

chair Mrs. Hilbert had just vacated. "Damn. That's an image I'll never be able to scrub from my mind."

Andi chuckled. "I so want to be her when I grow up."

She studied the envelope he'd handed her. There was no return address, but it was postmarked from Las Vegas. The handwriting was also very familiar.

"Kenny?" he asked.

"Yep." She tore open the envelope. As soon as the news broke about her marriage to Dex, the idiot began blowing up her phone until she'd blocked him. "Unless there's a check inside for seventy thousand dollars, I'm not interested in what he has to say."

Of course Kenny would want to make nice now that she had connections to the Growlers. He was a huge fan of the team. Next, he'd be angling for a seat in the owner's suite.

"I still think you should prosecute him."

"Mr. Hilbert thinks it would draw too much attention back to our marriage. Besides, I don't need the money for the loans any longer. And, I changed all the passwords to my accounts. He can't hurt me anymore." She peeked inside. "No check. Just a note. And I don't really want to read another one of his fake apologies. Not today."

She shoved the letter inside her backpack.

"Is it okay if I clean this up first thing in the morning? I need to get this stuff over to the training center before I meet Dex. The team is leaving early tomorrow for their game in L.A. They're staying on the west coast all week to ensure they're not jetlagged for their Thursday night game in Seattle. Dex said he had something special planned for tonight."

Clive nodded. "I'll bet he's just glad he doesn't have to spend another Friday night making soap. I know I am."

She ducked her head so her friend wouldn't see the fiery blush on her face. "Making soap" had become one of Dex's favorite Friday night activities.

"I'm done for the day if you'd like an extra pair of hands carting those boxes across town," he offered.

"That would be awesome."

Forty minutes later, Clive, Andi, and her driver lugged the boxes into one of the conference rooms the Growlers staff had designated for filling the swag bags the following day. Joan Zell, the team's community relations director, greeted them at the door.

"Oh, I'm so excited for these." She directed them to place the boxes on the center table. "It will be nice to have something unique and different in the bags this year. Are those football shaped bath bombs?"

"They are." Andi handed her one. "I infused some with sandalwood and others with peppermint. I'm really pleased with how they turned out."

Clive draped an arm over her shoulders. "The Growlers are lucky to have this girl on their team."

Joan beamed back at them. "I agree. We can't thank you enough, Mrs. Fletcher. People will be talking about these for weeks."

"I guess that's better than them remembering you for your pink hair, isn't it, *Mrs. Fletcher*?" Jade announced as she strutted into the room, her presence immediately killing Andi's buzz of pride.

Clive's hand tightened on her shoulder. He was always poised for a fight when someone disparaged his work. Little did he know, Jade wasn't worth it. Andi's best course of action was to get him out of the building quickly. In her haste, however, she spilled her backpack. Her calculator, books, and paper scraps she used to scribble notes on went flying across the floor and beneath the table like a blanket of snow. Joan dropped to her knees beside Andi, scooping up the scattered papers.

"Let me help you with that, Mrs. Fletcher," she said.

She smiled at Joan. "Please, call me Andi. And I'm so glad I could contribute in this small way. We have a few extras soaps and bath bombs at the salon, so let me know if you need anything else."

Jade let out an annoyed huff as she kicked a pen across the floor with the toe of her Tory Burch flat. Andi hastily shoved her stuff back in her bag before springing to her feet so she could get out of there before doing anything else to look dumb in front of Jade. Securing her backpack over her shoulder, she motioned Clive toward the door, unaware that one of her notes remained beneath a chair.

Unfortunately, Jade wasn't done with her yet. "Before you go, we are giving the media a list of the designers each of the WAGs will be wearing at the gala next weekend. Did you give your info to Joan already?"

Holy hell. She was supposed to wear a designer gown to this thing? How much would that run her? And how exactly did one go about finding a designer gown? Andi's plan was to troll the aisles of Nordstrom Rack on Sunday and see what they had that would fit her—and her credit limit.

"Tori Holmes," Clive answered for her. "With jewelry provided by Suttons. Her footwear will be Christian Louboutin." He smiled generously at Joan. "Have a nice weekend, ladies," he said before dragging a stunned Andi from the room.

"What have you done?" she hissed at him once they'd reached the entrance to the facility. "I've never heard of the first two, but I do know those shoes cost more than a month's rent."

"Actually, they cost nearly double the rent in your old place," he said blithely.

"If that's the case, maybe I'll just get two pair!"

"Sure." He continued toward the parking lot.

She stopped in her tracks, fear and something else that felt a lot like misery gnawing at her. "You know, it's going to be really embarrassing next Friday when I show up on the red-carpet wearing pumps from Payless!"

He halted and turned to face her, a steely look on his face. "You will be wearing everything I told them. And you'll look like the damn princess that you are, Andi Larsen Fletcher. Do you hear me?"

She'd never seen her friend like this before. "H-how? Why?"

"Because bitches like that one—" he pointed toward the building. "They've been pushing people like you and me around for too long. You aren't the only one who's been rubbing noses with the rich and famous, sister. I'm going to call in a few favors. Next week, you will shine ten times brighter than her or any other WAG associated with this team, you got that?"

She bobbed her chin up and down, but she still wasn't sure what had just happened.

"Good." He turned to the door. "Let's go. You have a date with your husband tonight, remember?"

"YO, PROFESSOR MCMATH," Eugene called out around a mouthful of pizza. "If we win again next week, how about a tour of the stadium."

The twelve teens who comprised Dex's Math Bowl team all nodded in unison. They were crowded into a neighborhood pizza parlor where he was treating them to dinner after their first victory of the school year.

"Ooo, and can we meet Trey Van Horn?" Angela asked with a sigh.

"I'm not bringing any of you lasses within ten feet of that man," Dex replied. "He breaks young women's hearts as a hobby. I can't have him ruining the top team of mathletes in the city of Milwaukee."

He risked a look at Andi beside him. She winked at him before turning to the teens. "You girls are definitely too smart for him."

Dex couldn't tame his broad smile. Obviously, he didn't have to worry about Andi mooning over the quarterback. Good thing she didn't know Van Horn had become her staunchest defender. He considered the quarterback to be one of his closest friends—at least as close as Dex let anyone get to him. It irked him that Van Horn continued to question his motives with regard to Andi. Contrary to what his friend thought, there would be no broken hearts when their marriage reached its forgone conclusion. Because neither one of their hearts was engaged.

A painful stabbing sensation emanated from the vicinity of his chest. He told himself it was indigestion from the pepperoni.

Andi laughed at something one of the kids said, refocusing his attention back to the present. He doubted any other woman he'd been with would be comfortable hanging out with a group of nerdy teens, eating cheap pizza on a Friday night. But there she was, looking as if she belonged. Making each one of the kids feel like *they* belonged.

Out of the corner of his eye, he saw two of the boys gawking at her with moon-eyed expressions. Dex couldn't blame them. She wasn't like any other woman they were likely to meet.

"Rehema has a date for homecoming," one of the boys teased.

Across the table, the girl blushed.

"He asked her in orchestra, playing a song he'd written just for her," Angela supplied.

The boys around the room made gagging noises.

"How sweet," Andi said. "Ignore them. Is the dance formal?"

"No tuxes, but some of the girls go all out," Angela replied with air quotes around the word some of the girls.

She meant the girls who could afford it. The team of mathletes was comprised of kids from the center. They all went to different schools, some of them more prosperous than others. But the kids on his team could barely afford the blazers they competed in, much less fancy formal clothes for a dance.

Andi pulled something out of her backpack and handed it across the table. "Call me at this number on Monday. We'll set up an appointment to get your hair done the day of the dance."

Rehema blanched. There was no way she could afford that. Dex opened his mouth to intervene, but Andi beat him to it.

"It's okay," she told them. "Clive and I used to hang out at the Vey Center when we were in high school, too. This will be on us."

There was that tightness in his chest again. Rehema's eyes were shining and the other kids at the table looked at Andi with nothing but worship in their eyes. At that moment, he knew exactly how they felt.

Andi rummaged through her backpack again, her brow creased with confusion.

"Something amiss, lass?"

"I thought I'd stuck something in here earlier." A flicker of worry shadowed her eyes. "It must have fallen out somewhere."

Rehema leaned forward in her chair. "Was it important?"

The hint of concern in Rehema's question further softened his heart. These kids already had accepted Andi as a friend. If she answered "yes", they'd be searching the streets for whatever it was she'd lost.

Andi gave her head a little shake, almost as if she was trying to erase away her worries. She smiled brightly at the kids. "Nope. It wasn't important at all."

Her gaze collided with his. He arched an eyebrow in question. She shook her head with more enthusiasm this time. Her shoulders relaxed. Whatever had troubled her was seemingly forgotten.

The waitress appeared at Dex's shoulder. "Are we having dessert tonight?"

The table erupted into a chorus of requests for ice cream sundaes. The rest of the meal passed in a flurry of laughter.

"Thank you for coming tonight," he said when they arrived back at his flat later that evening. "I know it wasn't what you might have expected when I said we were doing something special, but they wanted to meet you."

And I wanted you to meet them.

She smiled serenely before closing the distance between them and wrapping her arms around his neck.

"What makes you think I didn't find the evening special?" she asked. "They're awesome kids. I enjoyed spending time with them." She brushed her lips along his. "Especially since it meant I got to spend time with you."

Need, nearly blinding in its urgency, surged through him with the touch of her lips on his. He dug his fingers into her hips and jerked her against him. She let out a shaky breath at the contact. Scooping her up in his arms, he turned toward his bedroom only to encounter Morag sitting directly in the middle of the hallway. The cat had the nerve to hiss at them.

If it wasn't so bloody annoying, he might have laughed at the feline's unnecessary jealousy. But Marlene had told him how the cat had been torturing Andi these past few weeks. And enough was enough.

"Listen up, ya wee beasty," he snarled at the cat. "This stops tonight. Or it's back to the farm with ya. Ya ken?"

Morag didn't move. Not even her tail. He could swear the bloody animal narrowed her eyes at him. He took a menacing step toward her. With a low purr that sounded like a rumble, the cat disappeared in a streak to parts unknown.

"You let me know if she bothers you again," he said.

She pressed her lips against his neck. "You're not going to hurt that cat."

He stared down into her eyes. "If she's a nuisance to you, then I will send her back to where she came from."

"No. She was here first."

Dex paused just inside his bedroom door, the unspoken words weighing heavy in the air all of a sudden.

And she'll be here when I'm gone.

Despite it being the truth, the fact was unsettling for some reason.

"You have a plane to catch in less than twelve hours," Andi whispered before tracing the shell of his ear with her tongue. "Maybe we can forget about the cat for now and move on to other things."

And just like that, he forgot all about his bloody cat and everything else.

Later, Andi lay draped over his chest, her naked body warm and sated. Dex wasn't having as easy a time relaxing. Despite just having her—twice—his body craved more. This insatiable desire was supposed to have died down by now. The shine wore off most of his relationships after a couple weeks. But not this time.

The tension was back in his chest again.

It was their close proximity. That had to be it. He'd never spent this much time with a woman. He certainly never let another woman into his private life like he had Andi. She was in his bloody bed, for crying out loud. Every night. And she was becoming more firmly entrenched in his everyday life. As much as he wanted her to come with him and meet his mathletes tonight, it had been a mistake. She'd charmed them all just as easily as she was casting a spell on him. Hell, she'd even defended his bloody cat. He needed to take control of the situation before things completely spiraled out of hand.

This road trip couldn't have come at a better time. The physical distance would help him to reestablish the emotional distance he needed to maintain with her. By removing the object of his desire, his body's cravings would diminish. It was standard science. When he returned in a week, he'd establish some new ground rules.

She'd need to move back to her former room, for starters. He'd just have to sic Kurt on Agent Figueroa and put an end to this bed check nonsense once and for all. His body protested at the idea, but he knew this was the wisest course of action. Especially since they'd be going their separate ways in less than four months.

Andi let out a sultry sigh as she shifted against him. He traced his fingers through her hair, the pink now tinting just the very edges. She was the wildcard in his plan to reestablish boundaries in their relationship. Sure, she'd been practical about everything up to this point, but he'd had more than one woman fly off the handle when he'd pulled back. The thing was, he hadn't minded walking away from those women. But Andi . . .

"Can't you sleep?"

He glanced down. Barely able to keep her eyes open, she studied him beneath a fringe of lashes.

"Just keyed up about my trip."

"Mmm." She rolled on top of him, resting her chin on top of her hands on his chest.

So much for training his body not to want her. He was barely able to suppress his needy groan.

"A week away from the WAGs." A sly smile played on her lips. "Whatever will you boys do?"

"Won't you miss me?" He told himself he was asking to gauge her reaction for the changes he intended to implement when he returned.

"Oh, every minute." Her response dripped with sarcasm. She leaned in and brushed a kiss along his collar bone. "Try not to take this personally my king, but my week is crazy busy with work, two tests, and helping get those darn swag bags set for the gala to miss you."

Something hitched in his chest. *Relief.* At least that's what he was identifying it as. She was still his practical Andi.

She slid lower on his body. "But I'm happy to give you something to remember me so *you* don't miss *me.*"

A heavy sigh escaped him when she slipped beneath the sheets. Apparently she was made of sterner stuff than he because his body was quaking at the very idea of detoxing her from his system. But he wasn't fool enough to reject what she was offering. He could right the ship when he returned.

EIGHTEEN

"YOU'RE AS PREPARED as you can be for this week's test." Merrit smiled at Andi from across her kitchen table. "Despite what you think, you do have a head for numbers. And now that you understand the formulas, the rest of the course should come easily."

"I hope so." Andi rested her chin on top of Harper's head. The little girl had climbed onto her lap the minute Andi settled into a chair an hour before. "I really can't thank you enough. I wish you'd let me pay you."

Merrit rose and headed to the counter where she opened a bottle of wine. "Nonsense. I told you, I need the brain stimulation. Besides, I'm grateful for the company on a Saturday night." She handed Andi a glass. "I understand Heath's reasoning for staying out west between the games, but the kids are used to away games only being overnight. Seven days without Daddy is a long time." She took a healthy swallow from her own glass. "For Mommy, too. And it's only night one."

"Do you ever travel with the team?"

"With two little kids?" Merrit set a cup of grape juice next to the stack of crayons Harper was using. "Not unless it's the Super Bowl. Well, except for the game in London next month. I'm definitely going to that one."

Andi picked up one of Harper's crayons and began to doodle on her worksheet. The Growlers were playing a game in London? Something hovered on the edge of her memory, but she couldn't quite grasp it. "That's a long trip to make for a football game," she said. "I didn't even know they played American football there."

"They don't. We'll be playing another team from the league. It's meant to showcase our country's version of football to other countries. The game is scheduled so both teams have their bye week either before or after," Merrit explained. "The Growlers are chartering a plane and pretty much all the spouses are going. I'm looking forward to it."

A lick of unease traveled down Andi's spine.

"I'm sure Dex will have all his family there to see him play," Merrit continued. "They must be so thrilled. Have you met any of them yet?"

No. And I'm never going to, either.

Just like that, the memory she was trying to summon surfaced. *"Andi won't be coming to London, Ma,"* he had told his mother the morning after their wedding. *"She's afraid to fly."*

The tip of the crayon snapped off, the noise loud in the quiet room. Harper looked up at her with a forlorn look on her face.

"I'm sorry, sweetie," Andi apologized. With the way this night was going, it was probably Harper's favorite color.

"I'm the one who's sorry," Merrit said. "I didn't realize. Meeting your husband's family after you've married has to be daunting. I didn't mean to stress you out. But, if it's any consolation, we'll be there if you need to get away from them."

Andi swallowed painfully. "Actually, I won't be going."

Merrit stared at her, wide-eyed. "Why not?"

"School," Andi fibbed, sweeping her hand over the textbook on the table. "I can't get away."

The other woman looked as if she was going to argue, but

evidently thought better of it. She cleared her throat. "Well, that's a shame, but I admire your dedication. Hey, I don't feel like cooking tonight. What do you say we order some Chinese food and watch a movie? You've studied enough for one day. Please stay."

Harper bounced up and down in her lap. After what she'd just discovered, Andi doubted she'd have much of an appetite. She understood the reason he'd never mentioned the game in London. He'd been upfront with her from the very start. His family would never meet her. Nothing had changed. But that didn't mean it didn't hurt. Her feelings had become so jumbled, her head was beginning to throb. Some wine and a mindless movie might be just the thing.

"Sure," she replied, even managing a smile.

Merrit responded with a relieved smile of her own. "Great. I'll get the menu."

Two nights later, Andi entered the lobby of Dex's apartment, mentally exhausted after her first exam of the week. She was confident she'd aced it, however, and that gave her a boost going into her accounting exam later this week. Without the added distraction of Dex home, she could study hard the next three nights.

The Growlers lost their game the day before on a last-second field goal by the opposing kicker. Dex surprised her by calling after the game to wish her luck on her test. Despite the loss, he seemed upbeat. She was ashamed to admit she'd dropped several hints about the game in London, but he didn't bite.

Perhaps she shouldn't have given him the impression that she wouldn't miss him while he was gone. It seemed the prudent thing to do, however. She'd agreed to keep things between them light. Her deepening feelings for Dex were something she was still trying to sort out. She didn't want to give him the impression she wanted more than their contracted agreement. Not when she didn't know whether or not he did, too. Although she was encouraged by his reluctance to be away on this road trip and his phone call last night.

The truth was, the big empty penthouse was lonely without him, not to mention his bed. Even worse, despite Dex's threat,

Morag hadn't ceased her taunting. This morning, Andi awoke to discover the cat had torn up several pages of notes Andi left out on the nightstand. Still, the cat was important to Dex, so she wasn't giving up without a fight. She fingered the new box of catnip in her pocket.

"Andi Larsen."

The sound of a male voice calling her by her maiden name jerked her from the merry-go-round of her thoughts. She stopped just short of the elevator taking her to the penthouse. A man dressed sharply in a suit and tie stepped up beside. A shiver of unease raced down her spine. She glanced over to the concierge desk where the doorman and the clerk were both keeping a watchful eye on her.

"Can I help you?"

"I'm Agent Figueroa with ICE." He flashed his credentials at her. "I was wondering if I could have a word with you, Ms. Larsen."

"It's Mrs. Fletcher, which you are aware," she snapped. "And I don't think so."

He donned a bemused expression at the mention of her married name. "This will only take a minute."

"Shouldn't this meeting be taking place someplace official?" she argued. "With my lawyer present?"

She didn't have a lawyer, but it sounded like something she should say. Besides, she was confident Mr. Hilbert would step in if for no other reason than because it would help Dex.

"Yeah, funny thing about that. It seems the powers that be have called off any additional investigation into your marriage. All you have to do is stay married to the guy for another few months and the Man with the Million Dollar Leg will no longer be in danger of being deported."

His statement surprised her. Did that mean the imminent threat of a bed check no longer existed? Had they finally convinced the government they were the real thing? Dex's immigration status was no longer in jeopardy. He would be so relieved.

"And yet, here you are." She scrutinized the agent carefully. "If the case is closed, why is it you want a word with me, as you say?"

"I was curious about a seventy thousand dollar student loan debt that was recently paid in full before the first installment is even due."

Her mouth was suddenly dry.

"A wedding gift perhaps?" he asked quietly.

Her knees shifted beneath her. Or maybe it was the floor. "Something tells me this conversation would be better had with my lawyer present," she managed to say.

Agent Figueroa waved her off. "As I said, the government is no longer interested in your marriage."

"Then what do you want?" Andi's heart was racing. Was she to be robbed again? By a man carrying a badge no less?

"Just doing a good deed. I've seen a few of these cases in my career. They never end well for the U.S. citizen spouse. Particularly, the women."

Andi's spine stiffened.

"Even if you go into it with eyes wide open, he's going to come out of this unscathed. He's the celebrity, after all. You'll be the pariah who took him for his money. The press, the fans, they'll tear you apart. Whatever career you're trying to establish will be ruined. No matter what he's promised you." He stepped closer. "Heed my warning. Whatever you do, don't make the even greater mistake and let your heart get engaged. These types of marriages aren't built for love."

He left without another word. It took Andi several painful heartbeats before she realized the doorman was standing beside her.

"Everything okay, Mrs. Fletcher?"

She nodded weakly. "Fine. I'm fine."

He looked at her like he didn't agree, but he was paid well enough to keep his thoughts to himself. Instead, he punched the code for the elevator to the penthouse. The doors slid open and Andi mindlessly stepped in.

"Thank you," she breathed as the doors slid closed.

Marlene was waiting when she arrived. "How was the test?" One look at Andi's face and the older woman's own face fell. "That bad?"

Andi wasn't sure she could form words to offer up an explanation right now. Agent Figueroa's ugly words clogged up her brain. A shake of her head was all she could muster in response.

"How about a nice grilled cheese sandwich and some tomato soup," Marlene offered. "That always cheers me up."

Tears burned the back of Andi's eyes at the woman's kindness. Apparently she had let herself get attached to Marlene as well. But was Marlene being kind to her because she worked for Dex? That stupid ICE agent had ruined everything.

How had she been so stupid? How had she thought she could walk away from this at the end of her fake marriage?

Her stomach rolled. "Thank you, Marlene, but I think I'm going to take a hot bath and go to bed. It's been a long day."

She made her way down the hall into the bedroom she shared with Dex. Morag sat in the middle of the big bed cleansing herself, her body language screaming "eff you."

"I can't handle you right now," she whispered. Her gaze traveled about the room before landing on his pillow. She knew if she buried her nose in it, his scent still lingered. Her throat burned. "Either of you."

Hurrying down the hall, she slipped into her old bedroom and locked the door behind her.

A THICK FOG shrouded the stadium in an eerie light despite the fact it was only four in the afternoon. Dex and his teammates prowled around the field, assessing the conditions before their game scheduled to kick off an hour later.

"This ought to be fun." Kessler held his gloved hands out. "I can barely see my hands in front of my face. Looks like I'll be blocking all night. There go my fantasy numbers for the week."

Dex paced off the scrimmage lines in front of the goalpost. If his team needed a field goal longer than twenty-five yards, he'd be kicking blind. His heartbeat kicked up a notch at the challenge.

"There you are."

He turned to find Kurt striding down the sideline toward him.

"Looks like Mother Nature has made the game a lot more interesting," Kurt said.

"I didn't know you were coming," Dex replied.

"I'm looking at a kid over at Oregon State on Saturday. I thought I'd come out early and catch your game while I was at it."

Dex snorted. "You just wanted to get out of attending the gala tomorrow night."

Kurt laughed. "I'm not going to deny that didn't factor into my decision. It was cheaper to whisk my wife off to wine country in Oregon for a weekend than what the silent auction at that damn gala usually costs me every year." He glanced up to the sky. "You may be able to dodge the same bullet if this fog holds."

Something kicked in his stomach. He wasn't looking forward to donning a monkey suit and opening his wallet, but he was anxious to get back to Milwaukee. *To Andi.* She'd been hard to pin down with a phone call all week. He normally didn't call her on a game weekend, but he'd been keyed up after Sunday's game and he still had four more days before seeing her again. He was surprised at how much hearing her voice settled him. But since then, his phone calls all went to voicemail. She'd texted saying her schedule was crazy and she'd see him when he got back. He should have been relieved. It was his intention to lessen their connection, after all. But instead, he felt . . . jilted.

Bloody ridiculous.

"Listen, about that thing you wanted me to take care of." Lowering his voice, Kurt steered him to a deserted area of the sideline. "ICE has formally dropped any investigation of your marriage. Your deportation is no longer pending. Your visa will be renewed at the end of your probationary marriage period." His agent smiled broadly. "We pulled it off. You and Andi just need to play things out in public for the next few months. Once we receive the approved visa, we can sign the divorce papers and you two can go your separate ways."

A maelstrom of emotions swirled deep within him. He didn't have to return home to Scotland. He didn't have to remain married. His life could continue just as he wanted it.

So why wasn't he happy?

You two can go your separate ways.

The words were ringing in his ears.

"Declan, did you hear me?" Kurt asked. "Catastrophe avoided."

"Aye, I heard ya." He slapped his agent on the back. "Thanks for everything."

"That's what you pay me for. Have a good game tonight. Be careful in this fog," his agent warned before the mist seemed to swallow him up.

That annoying ache was back in his chest again. Dex pulled out his phone and dialed Andi's number. It rang four times before going to voicemail. He swore violently. Her voice came on the line inviting him to leave a message, except he wasn't sure what he wanted to say or why he'd even rung her.

"Hey there, lass. I just wanted to wish you luck on your exam tonight." He hesitated. "I know you don't need it though. The game will end late your time, but our flight should get in before you're off to work in the morning. Maybe we can grab a coffee. I'll see ya then."

He shoved his phone back into the pocket of his warmups and trotted to the locker room to get dressed for the game.

As it turned out, it was closer to noon when he arrived back at his penthouse, exhausted and frustrated. The Growlers eked out a win over Seattle by one point—the difference maker an extra point Dex managed to get through the uprights despite the visibility being less than fifty feet. Afterwards, the fog kept them stranded on the tarmac in Seattle for seven long hours. He'd spent the morning playing phone tag again with Andi. She'd gone to work early to accommodate all the added appointments brought on by tonight's gala. Her plan was to meet him at the museum that night, claiming she needed to sort out a situation with the swag bags beforehand. Dex had been relegated to riding with Palmer and Shaina.

This was good, he reminded himself. He didn't want her to be one of those needy, clingy women. Not if he was weaning his body off her. He'd been right. This road trip was the best thing that could have happened.

"I'd suggest coffee, but you look like you need some sleep first," Marlene said.

"Aye, Harris kept the whole back of the plane awake with his bloody snoring."

Marlene nodded. "Your tuxedo and the rest of your clothes for this evening are already set out in your closet."

He kissed her on the cheek. "You're a gem."

She responded with a stiff smile.

"Is something amiss?" he asked.

Just when she looked like she was going to speak, she shook her head. Dex scrutinized her for a long moment, but she offered up nothing else. He shrugged.

"Don't let me sleep too long," he warned her before striding down to his bedroom.

Morag jumped off the bed when he entered the room. The cat chorused a few welcoming meows while weaving her way between his feet.

"Well, there's my sweet girl. You seem to have taken my warning to heart." He reached down and stroked the cat's back. Morag purred loudly, butting his hand with her head. "I'm happy to see the women in my home finally living peacefully together."

Toeing off his shoes, he shucked his shirt before cruising into the bathroom. He stopped abruptly once he passed over the threshold, however. A cold shiver of dread ran up his spine. Something wasn't right. He glanced at the sink. His toothbrush stood solo in its holder. The hairbrushes and makeup that had slowly encroached on his counter space these past several weeks were nowhere to be seen. He grabbed a towel and sniffed it. Even her scent was gone.

What the hell? He stormed out of the room and over to the bed, yanking up her pillow and inhaling. Nothing. Her hand cream and note cards were no longer littering up her nightstand. The back of his neck was contracting so tightly, it threatened to cut off his breath.

"Marlene!" he bellowed as he jogged toward the guest bedroom and threw the door open. The familiar scent that belonged only to Andi wafted beneath his nose and he gulped in a relieved breath. Her note cards were strewn on the dresser. He fingered a hair tie on the bedside table. In the bathroom, her toothbrush hung alone.

He turned to find Marlene standing in the doorway to the bedroom, a closed look on her face.

"What in the bloody hell is going on?" he demanded.

She shrugged. He narrowed his eyes at his employee. Her shoulders sagged.

"Honestly, Declan, I really don't know."

"How long?" He pushed the words out around the boulder in his throat. "How long has she been in here?"

"A few days."

He drew in a harsh breath. *This is what you wanted,* he reminded himself. He didn't have to do anything about their relationship because Andi had already done it for him. He should be dancing a jig. She hadn't missed him. She hadn't bloody missed him at all.

"If there's nothing else you need, I'm going out to run some errands," Marlene was saying.

Dex waved her off. When he heard the front door close, he sank down on the bed. He traced his fingers along her pillow before pulling it up to his face and breathing it in. Damn, he was tired. He blamed his exhaustion for the fact that he wasn't elated by this latest turn of events. Forcing his weary limbs to move, he tucked the pillow beneath his head before stretching out on the mattress. He closed his eyes, telling himself it was only for a moment, as he tried not to dwell on the fact that she hadn't missed him as much as he'd missed her.

NINETEEN

ANDI TOOK MERRIT'S credit card and swiped it through the machine.

"I am so glad you introduced me to Clive." She turned her head from side-to-side, admiring her up-do in the mirror above the salon's reception desk. "Now I've just got to make sure my kids keep their sticky fingers out of it for the next four hours."

"I'm glad you like him. Your hair looks amazing." Andi handed her back her card. "It's the least I could do for all your help with my accounting class."

"I'm glad the test went well last night." Merrit's face softened. "But you still look stressed. Is everything okay?"

No. Everything wasn't okay. Not by a long shot. After all her efforts to keep her heart safe and protected from her fake husband, she feared she was beginning to fall for the man. And of all the mistakes she'd made in her life, that one would be the most reckless.

These types of marriages aren't built for love.

Agent Figueroa's words haunted her all week. But they were exactly the wake-up call she needed. Apparently, she wasn't exactly the big girl she claimed to be with regard to no-strings-attached sex. So, she'd have to take sex off the table. She nearly chuckled at the thought because, well, there had been a few times when they hadn't quite made it to his bed and a table or wall had been their next best option.

"I'm just a little strung-out from the hectic week, that's all," she eventually responded.

Merrit gave her a knowing smile. "And missing your husband, I'll bet. That darn fog. They got in long after you left for work this morning." She patted Andi's hand. "But the team has the entire weekend off, so you'll have plenty of opportunities to make up for lost time. And, lucky for you, there will be no kids to interrupt, er, whatever it is you both will be doing."

Fortunately for Andi, Clive walked up to the desk, saving her from having to answer.

"Okay. Cinderella, it's your turn to get glamorous for the gala." He draped an arm over her shoulders. "Behold the before, Merrit, because you will be dazzled by the after."

"She deserves to be pampered," Merrit commented. "Enjoy. I'll see you tonight."

He handed her a robe as he steered to the back of the salon. "Your throne awaits. When I get through with you, you're going to rule this gala like the beauty queen you were born to be."

Queen.

His word choice stoked up memories of her quirky wedding and suddenly she was having trouble swallowing. As silly as their ceremony was, Andi had made a promise. She'd signed a contract to portray Dex's wife, but in that ridiculous wedding chapel, she'd promised to love him. She staggered slightly at the thought.

"When was the last time you ate something?" Clive demanded as he guided her into the styling chair.

Andi wasn't hungry. She hadn't been for days. Apparently, she was love-sick.

"This morning." *Maybe.*

Abruptly he began rattling off orders to the salon staff. Peanut butter crackers and an apple appeared before her.

"Eat," he commanded. "I'm not going through all this trouble playing Fairy Godmother to have you pass out on the red carpet."

She dutifully nibbled at the food while he applied color and foils to her hair. An hour later, while her hair was processing, the salon's esthetician began applying hydrating patches beneath her eyes and on her décolletage. Another woman was polishing her nails. Alone with her ping-ponging thoughts, she considered her options. How could she continue her role as Dex's pretend wife and maintain her sanity? Especially now that she was certain she loved him.

"Andi? Is that you?"

She snapped her eyes open to find Mrs. Hilbert seated in the chair next to her.

"Hi there, Mrs. H. Were you on the books today?" She was certain the woman didn't have an appointment.

"Not with Clive, but Amy Curl had an open slot, so I grabbed it. You're not the only one getting dolled up for the gala."

"Your son was able to get you a ticket?" Tickets for the fundraiser sold for a thousand dollars apiece. In spite of the exorbitant price, the event sold out months ago.

"He *gave* me his tickets. The silly man went to rainy Portland to visit a winery instead." She snorted. "I'm sure his wife talked him into it. Not that I mind. Especially since Fred is a Growlers fan *and* he owns a tux." She winked at Andi. "Best of all, my neighbor will be in such a snit when she sees us stepping out together."

Andi had to laugh. "Well, that sure did work out nicely for you."

"And for you too, deary."

Not exactly.

She hadn't realized she'd spoken the words out loud until Mrs. Hilbert responded. "Nonsense. You outsmarted that fool, Kenny, and you landed a sexy husband to boot."

The manicurist and the esthetician finished and returned to the spa side of the salon. Andi lowered her voice.

"As I keep telling you, my marriage is only temporary," she reminded the other woman. "You know that. It was your crazy idea in the first place."

Mrs. Hilbert huffed. "It's not so crazy if it gets the job done. Your loans are paid off and he wasn't deported."

"But who cares if I end up with a broken heart when it's over!" she blurted out.

"Who says it ever has to be over?"

Andi's frustration mounted. "The contract. There's a firm end-date."

"Oh, for Pete's sake." Mrs. Hilbert waved her hand in the air. "Those are just words on a piece of paper. They can be changed or the contract torn up. It's what's in here that matters most." She tapped her chest. "And you forget, I've seen the way he looks at you. You have the upper hand here."

"The upper hand?"

Mrs. Hilbert shook her head. "What is wrong with young women these days? Why do you continue to believe you have to wait for a man to make the first move? You can chase after him, you know. Take advantage of his obvious desire and see where it leads. Better yet, tell him how you feel. You might be surprised. Perhaps he thinks you're the one who wants things to end when the time comes."

Amy walked up just then. "Mrs. Hilbert, are you sure you want me to weave fairy strands in your hair?"

"Of course, I'm sure." The woman jumped from her seat, gesturing to her hair. "One gold strand on each side of my face. Andi can't be the only princess at the gala, you know." She winked at Andi again. "Oh, and I still want those extra soaps you promised me. They'll be perfect as the ante for my Sunday night poker game. Everyone will be bidding for a bar."

The other stylist shot Andi an amused look before leading Mrs. Hilbert away.

Was it that simple? Could her relationship with Dex outlive its contracted termination date? More importantly, did she have the guts to even try?

Clive came up behind her and peeked beneath the foils. "Oh, wow. The color came out perfectly. It's going to really pop with the dress. Jade is going to shrivel up with jealousy." He gave her shoulders a squeeze. "And your husband is going to be fighting his teammates off with a stick. Let's go finish making you glam."

Take advantage of his obvious desire. Mrs. Hilbert's advice rang out within Andi's ears like a call to action. Agent Figueroa didn't know what he was talking about. And she was going to prove it.

Hours later, she arrived at the Milwaukee Art Museum accompanying Mrs. Hilbert and her charming date, Fred. Dex was likely peeved she'd left him to ride with Kane and Shaina. She'd lied and told him she needed to help with the swag bags. The truth was, she was still working up the courage to tell him how she really felt. She needed a few more minutes of alone time to convince herself to go through with it.

"Did you know, the museum was named one of the sexiest buildings in the world," Mrs. Hilbert recited before giving Fred's arm an amorous squeeze.

Andi didn't doubt it. Located on the shores of Lake Michigan, the futuristic building with its gleaming white suspension bridge, ninety-foot vaulted glass ceiling, and operational cantilevered wings, was as much a work of art as the items displayed inside it. The museum had been the site of several fondly remembered school field trips during her youth. She especially loved the Georgia O'Keefe exhibit and the antique furniture housed there. Both reminded Andi of her grandmother.

"This way." One of the docents escorted them to the staging area where the WAGs were putting the finishing touches on the auction items.

Laughter and the chatter of voices traveled down the hallway. Andi drew in a nervous breath. Her fingers went to the sapphire pendant dangling from her neck, the stone perfectly reflecting the colors of the jewel-toned gown Clive had somehow managed to convince his designer friend to lend her. The dress was daring without being too vulgar. The sheath design hugged her body and the wrap bodice made her appear more endowed than she actually was. Her arms were bare except for a sapphire and diamond tennis bracelet on her left arm. Andi was afraid if she unclenched her fist, the borrowed bracelet would slide off and be lost forever.

"Fred and I are going to wander around before they open the red carpet. Can you believe we get to strut our stuff in front of the media? I hope we make the nine o'clock news. The girls fall asleep before the later newscast and I don't want anyone to miss us."

She smiled at the older woman's attitude. There was a lot to be said for her zest for life. Not to mention her knack for getting what she wanted. It was time Andi adopted the same boldness. Squaring her shoulders, she pushed open the door to the room where the other WAGs were assembled. It was time to put her plan into motion.

"WHAT? NO KILT TONIGHT?" Palmer asked as soon as Dex climbed into the car.

He would have responded with something obscene, but Shaina was also in the car and he found he rather liked Palmer's girlfriend. Her poor taste in men notwithstanding.

"Ignore him," she said. "Kane is just jealous he doesn't own a kilt."

"I certainly have the legs for it," the punter bragged. "They're not hairy and muscle bound like Fletcher's."

A snarl escaped Dex's mouth. He should have walked the ten blocks to the bloody museum. Ever since discovering Andi's retreat to the guest room, he'd been on edge. After waking in her bed, he'd given himself a stern lecture in the shower. He wasn't going to look a gift horse in the mouth. Andi's actions coincided with his plans. Dex just needed to convince certain parts of his body to play along.

"Hey, I know," Palmer continued, apparently unaware that his manhood was at risk. "I'm headed to St. Andrews for the bye week to play golf with my dad. While we are there, you can take me to your favorite shop and help me pick out a kilt of my own. Maybe there's a Palmer plaid or something. Afterwards we can go to your favorite pub and grab a pint. My dad would love that."

Memories of the last time Dex had enjoyed a pint in his favorite pub washed over him painfully. That night had changed his life irrevocably.

"I won't be going to Scotland."

The statement came out more menacing than Dex intended. But he was getting tired of always having to defend his decision not to return to Scotland. His family had stopped asking years ago, but with his marriage to Andi, his mother had recommenced her haranguing about him never coming home.

And then there was Andi. She'd obviously become aware of the upcoming game in London. She'd certainly dropped enough hints the last time they spoke. Was that what prompted her little relocation? Was she miffed? As much as he would enjoy having her by his side when he saw his family in London, he wouldn't do that to her. Or his family. This thing between them would be over soon enough. There was no reason for them to become attached to Andi and vice versa.

Ma would love her. Annis, too.

Andi was straight-forward and unpretentious like them. She cared about the people around her. His father would fall under her spell immediately. Sucked in by her quicksilver smile and her grit. Not to mention her intelligence.

No! They could never meet. He'd already brought enough shame down on his family. He didn't need to add to their pain. It was better they simply hate him.

In the front seat, Palmer exchanged a look with his girlfriend. Dex turned to stare out the window. The museum loomed in front of them, its exterior lit against the dusk. The wings were still open, making it appear like a bird lifting off over Lake Michigan.

He was out of the car before Palmer had time to hand the valet his keys. Andi had finally responded to his texts. She said she would be waiting in a small alcove just outside Windham Hall, the main part of the museum, so they could walk the red carpet together. She may have deserted his bed, but she wasn't shirking her duties per their contract. He expected nothing less of his Andi.

"There he is. The man who saved our game last night."

Mrs. Ciaciura's voice stopped him in his tracks. As much as he wanted to find his bride, it was bad form to ignore the wife of the man who signed his paychecks.

"You look lovely tonight." He leaned in and dropped a kiss on her cheek.

"Not as lovely as that wife of yours," she replied. "Who, by the way, is as much of an asset to this team as you are." She waved a finger at him. "Don't do anything to mess that up."

An uncomfortable sensation settled in his chest. This was the very reason he wasn't taking Andi to London. It was going to be difficult enough explaining things to everyone who had already met her when their marriage ended.

"Speaking of Andi, have you seen her?"

The woman's eyes twinkled. "I have. And if I were you, as soon as I found her, I wouldn't let her out of my sight."

One of the team's community relations' staff appeared at her side. "Excuse me, Mrs. Ciaciura. They're ready to line up for the red carpet. We'd like for you and your husband to lead us off."

"Show time, Declan. Go find your wife."

He weaved through the crowd of his teammates searching for Andi, ignoring the comments asking about his bloody kilt. People began to "ooo" and "ahh" when the brise soleil wings slowly descended, shrouding the pavilion in starlight from the lake beyond. But Dex wasn't paying attention to all that. He'd found her, standing alone beside a suit of armor that would look at home in his grandfather's study.

At least he thought it was his Andi.

Gone was the hair dipped in pink, replaced by a riot of waves that looked as if they were spun from pure gold. Her dress was a sight to behold, its color deepening as the light faded. Simple but stunning, the gown showed off the dainty curve of her hips. A slender leg peeked out of a thigh high slit. He let his eyes slowly travel up her body, stopping briefly on the sensuous mouth he was rapidly dying to taste. She toyed with her bottom lip and the zipper of his trousers was swiftly uncomfortable.

She was nervous. One look into her eyes and he could see her trepidation. It didn't make sense. She'd been playing this charade for more than a month now, each day with more confidence. So what had her spooked this evening?

"Close your mouth, Fletcher, before you get drool all over the red carpet."

Van Horn's acerbic comment snapped Dex back into the here and now.

"Not that anyone here blames you," Van Horn said beside him. "Your wife is stunning. And very creative." The quarterback slapped him on the back. "Which begs the question, how did you ever talk her into marrying you?"

Dex clenched his fists.

"Trey!" Van Horn's non-girlfriend whined. "We're next on the red carpet." The woman had the gall to snap her fingers.

Van Horn stiffened beside him.

"I'd say one of us is luckier than the other," Dex drawled.

His friend sighed heavily. "And it's definitely you, my friend. You found the rare one worth taking a leap with. Don't leave her standing there alone, dumbass."

Dex didn't intend to. But when he took a step in Andi's direction, she drew in a tremulous breath. *Jaysus.* Unease, heavy and unwelcome, settled in his belly. She wasn't nervous about walking the bloody red carpet. She was nervous about being with him.

"Lass," he whispered when he was finally in front of her.

"Hi," she breathed, a burst of cinnamon escaping her mouth. She brought her hand over her lips. "Sorry. Fireball. Would you believe Mrs. Hilbert carries a flask in her purse?"

He would believe anything about that crazy old bat. But Dex was more concerned with his wife's jitters.

"Something's amiss. What is it?"

She drew in another shaky breath before reaching out and taking his hand in hers. "Not anymore." Her lips slowly turned up into a smile, lighting up her face. "I just missed you, that's all."

The dread that had been building evaporated with her touch. She had missed him after all. The relief he felt should have terrified him. He didn't want her missing him. But at this moment, he didn't care. He just wanted her. His Andi.

He tugged her gently toward him. The heels she was wearing brought her nearly eye-to-eye with him. "I missed you, too, lass. I missed you something fierce."

Her pupils dilated before her lips found his in an eager kiss. A groan rumbled from his chest in response. He wrapped his arms around her, letting his fingers skim over her body.

A throat cleared behind them. Andi pulled her lips away with a sigh so aggravated in its sound, Dex nearly laughed.

"Excuse me, Mr. and Mrs. Fletcher," the community affairs staffer said. "But we need you on the red carpet."

Mr. and Mrs. Fletcher.

Long ago, he'd vowed there never would be a Mrs. Fletcher. Not after the mess he'd left behind in Scotland. Not after taking everything away from Niall. Yet here he was about to parade down the red carpet with a wife on his arm. And it felt so perfect, he didn't want dwell on the fact their marriage was a sham. Or that it would be over soon.

He brushed a quick kiss over her lips. "Later," he promised. He wasn't sure if he meant the promise to her or to his conscience screaming at him not to get into this relationship any deeper than he already was. Turning to her, he extended his arm. "Shall we, Mrs. Fletcher?"

She blushed gorgeously. "After you, Mr. Fletcher." Linking her arm through his, they made their way to where the press waited in the Windhover Hall.

TWENTY

ANDI COULDN'T HELP but feel like the Cinderella Clive had turned her into. In all her life, she never dreamed of attending an event like this, much less being the center of attention. It was heady enough to have Dex's hungry gaze following her around all night, but guests kept seeking her out to compliment her on the swag bags.

"Finally, something I want to use." Nicole Jacobs pulled a bar of soap out of her gift bag. "There's only so many Growler's can koozies and luggage tags a girl needs, you know what I mean? I was thinking that some personalized bath bombs would make the perfect party favors for my sister's baby shower next month. Is that something you can do?"

"As long as you aren't inviting five hundred people," Andi replied with a grin. "I'm not sure my nerves can handle that a second time."

Nicole laughed. "Honey, I love my baby sister something fierce, but she can be a trip. I'm probably going to have to pay my own family to attend this shower. That's why I want the favors to be special. I'll be in touch next week." She surprised Andi by leaning in for a hug.

Another of the WAGs came up right behind her. "I just googled your dress designer. Her stuff is amazing. She's quite the rising star among the fashion scene. I'd love to see if she'd be interested in designing a dress I can wear to a charity event over the holidays. Do you think you could put me in touch with her?"

"Sure." Clive would be happy to throw some business his friend's way.

Shaina squealed beside her. "Oh, Andi. Isn't this so exciting? I've never met so many famous people before. Can you believe as the wife of a Growler, you'll get to do this every year?"

A kaleidoscope of butterflies swarmed through Andi's stomach. She risked a glance at Dex. Fortunately, he was regaling a fan with the play-by-play from the winning point after the night before. Shaina couldn't have been more wrong. According to the contract she'd signed, her marriage would be over in a few months and she wouldn't be around for any future galas. But she wanted to renegotiate that contract. Specifically, for one with a longer term.

As in forever.

Until she saw him earlier, she wasn't sure her plan was more than a pipedream. But something in the way he'd looked at her gave her courage. There was more than just simple desire in his eyes. There had been genuine concern, too. He cared for her. Over the past weeks, he'd demonstrated that in countless ways. But tonight, she felt that caring all the way in her soul.

They'd gone about their marriage in the opposite order of how it was supposed to occur. But did it matter how they got there as long as they were here now? She needed to bite the bullet and follow Mrs. Hilbert's advice. She needed to tell him how she felt. And she needed to tell him sooner rather than later so as not to lose her nerve.

Catching his eye, she tilted her head toward the exhibit room at the back of the pavilion. His nostrils flared in answer. She threaded her way through the crowd, confident he was behind her. Once she reached the open floor, his big hand was on her back steering her toward the alcove where she'd waited for him earlier. Without a word, he led her behind the knight standing sentry and he pressed her up against the wall with his hips. His mouth was on hers in an instant.

"How long before we can leave without being rude?" she murmured when his lips moved to her neck several minutes later.

"Just long enough for me to leave a check and call an Uber."

"I need to grab my things from the conference room. I'll meet you in the lobby in ten minutes?"

He teased her lips with his own. "Don't be late, Mrs. Fletcher. I've been dreaming of unwrapping that dress from your body since the moment I walked in."

Dex using her married name buoyed her confidence even further. They could make this work. Joy surged through her. She could barely contain her smile as she made her way to where she'd left her things.

"Oh, you might be smiling now."

Andi nearly collided with Jade on her way out of the conference room.

The other woman's gorgeous clothes, hair and makeup did nothing to detract from the ugly sneer on her face. "You might have conned everyone into believing you are the belle of the ball tonight, but like my Gammy likes to say, you can't make a silk purse out of a sow's ear."

Ignoring her, Andi kept her steps light as she dodged past. Not even Jade was going to spoil her mood.

"Look at you," Jade continued, following her down the corridor. "In a borrowed dress from a no-name designer. But then you've been wearing borrowed clothes for most of your life, haven't you? I'm surprised they even let you walk around with that necklace without an armed escort making sure you don't pocket it."

Before, the other woman's words might have made Andi feel inferior, just as she intended them to. But not tonight. Jade was jealous. Pure and simple. And that jealousy only fueled Andi's confidence even more.

"What do you want?"

Jade took a step closer. "Soon enough, I'll be the new wife on this team. The wife of the Growler's most notable player. Their team's leader. And then, little orphan Andi, you're going to wish our paths never crossed because I know exactly what you're hiding. And I can't wait to out you and your sham of a marriage."

A shiver ran down Andi's spine before she quashed it. The other woman was bluffing. Grasping at straws. Whatever "proof" she spoke of was a figment of envy. She refused to endure Jade's jealousy any longer.

Before she could challenge the other woman's claim, however, Trey Van Horn emerged from the shadows.

"Jade."

Jade drew in a startled breath. "There you are, babe. I was just telling Andi here what a great job she did with her contribution to the swag bags. They've been the talk of the party."

The quarterback's expression was inscrutable in the face of Jade's lie. Andi was fairly certain he'd overhead everything. She waited for him to make excuses for his girlfriend or simply ignore her behavior.

A slow, chagrined smile broke out on his face instead. He stepped past Jade and reached for Andi's hand. "I was looking for her to tell her the very same thing." His eyes softened. "I'm very glad Dex convinced you to marry him, Andi. If I haven't said it already, welcome to the Growler family."

Jade bristled when her boyfriend leaned in and kissed Andi on the cheek.

"He's pacing the front lobby for you." Van Horn gave her hand a squeeze before releasing it. "You better go find him before he goes all Highlander on us."

"Thank you." She returned his warm smile with one of her own. "Goodnight."

"Maybe we should make an early night of it, too," Jade suggested.

"That's an excellent idea," Andi heard Van Horn respond as she made her way down the corridor. "I believe I will head home. Alone."

"I told you Van Horn wouldn't keep her around long," Dex said when they arrived back at the penthouse fifteen minutes later. "I'm only sorry he didn't do it weeks ago so you wouldn't have had to endure her torture for as long as you did."

There it was again. That concern for her well-being. Her happiness. It had to mean something. She sincerely hoped it did, especially since she was about to open up her heart and tell him how she felt.

She draped her arms around his neck. "I'm only sorry I didn't have you in my life years ago to look out for me."

He placed his fingers on her waist and pulled her forward so they were nearly nose-to-nose. "Do you want to explain to me why you moved out of our room?"

"Agent Figueroa stopped by the other night."

His grip grew tight. "What did he want?"

She drew in a deep breath. "To tell us that his investigation into our marriage had been dropped." She omitted the part of their conversation that included his warning.

The news left Dex looking equal parts relieved and peeved. "And that made you scamper back down the hall?"

She shrugged. "I assumed that with the threat of a bed-check gone, you'd want me to move back to the guest room."

Andi felt as well as heard the low groan coming from his chest when he dragged her body in contact with his. "You assumed wrong, lass."

"Are you sure, Dex? I don't want to be in your bed because you need someone to pretend to be your wife. I want to be there because you want me. Because you want this relationship. For more than just pretend."

A war of emotions played out on his face. His body went so still, she feared he'd stopped breathing. Just when she thought she might faint from the shame of putting herself out there, he responded.

"Aye," he whispered. "I want this."

Their mouths fused in a searing kiss. Before she knew it, they'd made it as far as his study and he was tugging at the fabric of her dress with wild abandon.

"Wait," she laughed. "You have to be careful with it. It's not mine. The designer wants it back."

He huffed with impatience. "Take it off then. I want to take you wearing nothing but that bloody necklace, and those heels."

Her stomach pinched at his demand. She reached around to tug on the zipper only to have it get stuck. She swore in frustration. "It won't budge."

"Here, let me." He spun her around, his fingers bringing goose bumps to her fevered skin.

"Jaysus. The bloody thing is well and truly jammed. I'm going to have to get the kitchen shears to cut it out."

"You can't!" she protested. "The designer is using it in a show next week."

"If she's that good with a needle she can bloody well sew a zipper back in. Don't. Move."

Panicked, she pulled open his desk drawers, rifling through them looking for something less destructive than kitchen shears. Her hand abruptly stilled when she spied a packet of letters addressed to her. Her feelings of guilt for snooping were quickly snuffed out by curiosity. Sitting back in the leather desk chair, she fingered the expensive stationary. The letters were postmarked from Scotland. All four of them bearing her name. The return address listed Annis Fletcher as the sender. The warm glow she'd been enjoying all evening abruptly fizzled. A cold numbness settled over her in its place.

"Andi."

She looked up to see Dex standing in the doorway, a grim expression on his face.

"Your sister has been writing to me?" It was more a statement than a question, but she was so confused why he hadn't given them to her that everything running through her mind was a question.

"No," he had the nerve to say.

"My name is right here." She waved the envelopes at him.

He was across the room in three strides. "Give them to me."

She jumped up, putting the big leather chair between them. "No!"

He moved to grab the envelopes from her. She clutched the letters to her chest.

"Lass." He uttered the word with a threatening undertone.

"Don't you dare 'lass' me, Declan Fletcher! I want to know why you withheld these letters from me."

"You know why."

"No. I don't!" she cried.

"I told you from the beginning you and my family are never going to cross paths," he bellowed.

Clearly, she wasn't numb enough because a painful ache was beginning to unfurl in her chest. "I don't understand. Not more than five minutes ago you said you wanted me. You wanted everything." Her voice scraped painfully against the back of her throat. "With me. But apparently I'm not good enough to be . . . family?" She was ashamed when she choked over the last word.

He clenched and unclenched his fists at his sides. "That's not how it is."

"Then how is it?" she demanded. "Explain it to me!"

"I can't!"

The harshly spoken words nearly knocked her to her knees. She gripped at the chair like a lifeline.

"Can't? Or won't?" The words were raw with anguish as they slipped out of her mouth.

He stood a few feet away, his face hard and his eyes unreadable. His mouth unmoving. His silence telling her everything she needed to know.

The breath continued to saw through her lungs. She was still upright. Andi counted both as small blessings. She'd had a lifetime of not being enough. Of not being worthy of unconditional love. By now it shouldn't hurt as much as it did.

She quickly righted herself on the stupid heels Clive insisted she wear and began a slow march toward the door, going the long way around the room to avoid Dex. So much for Cinderella. At least she was able to make her escape from the ball with her dignity intact.

"Andi—" He moved to block her path.

"Don't!" She slipped past him to the threshold of the room. When she glanced back at him, she could have sworn there was anguish reflected in his eyes before he shuttered them. "You can keep your family to yourself, Declan. I've managed as a party of one just fine all these years. I don't see that changing anytime soon."

With a grace she didn't realize she possessed, she navigated the walk to the guest room without falling to pieces. But only just barely. Behind her locked door, she let the tatters of her heart fall along with her tears.

SEVERAL HOURS AND two-thirds of a bottle of scotch later, Dex realized Andi had taken the letters with her. Truth be told, she took a lot more from him than those letters. He unleashed a string of vulgarities as he tried, and failed, to get up from the sofa. From somewhere in the study, Morag scolded him with a baleful meow.

"Not you, too." He wadded up his bowtie and tossed it in the direction of the cat's caterwauling. "Keep out of this, ya wee beastie."

The bloody cat had the nerve to move within his field of vision. She was wise enough to stay out of reach, however, sitting on the chess table and staring him down with a look of cold disdain that looked eerily similar to the one his ma used on him when he was a wild youth.

"Aye, cat, I ken. I've mucked things up royally."

Morag responded with a condescending meow. He arched an eyebrow at the bloody cat. At least, he tried to. He couldn't really feel his face at the moment, so he wasn't sure what his expression looked like. Giving in to gravity, he rested his spinning head back down against the cushion.

"The thing is, for a wee moment tonight, I really did think I could have it all, ya ken?"

He'd known exactly what she'd been asking when she told him she wanted it all. All the things the contract stipulated she would not have. And damned if at that moment, he didn't want the same thing. *The happily ever after.* A lifetime of waking up next to Andi, seeing her smile, keeping her safe. A future.

All the things he'd taken away from Niall.

No, it was good she'd found the letters, he told himself. It was better that she hated him. Besides, she could never hate him as much as he hated himself.

Morag continued to lecture him with a series of loud meows.

"Aw, pipe down. I know I hurt her. But I warned the lass upfront. I can't give her what she wants. Ever."

The dull ache in his chest he'd been trying to numb with scotch persisted. He took another swallow from the bottle dangling from his fingertips. "Once she knows the truth, she won't want me any longer anyways."

The cat made a frustrated sound.

"Argue with me all ye want, silly cat. But it's true. Sweet Andi won't want anything to do with me once she finds out I killed my best friend."

TWENTY-ONE

ANDI TRIED TO ignore the murmured conversation between Clive, Daniel, and Mrs. Hilbert. But since the trio was standing no more than six feet away from the salon's receptionist desk, it was nearly impossible to tune out their concerned whispers.

"She looks so sad," Mrs. Hilbert said. "There must be something we can do."

"I think you've done enough, Mrs. H," Daniel accused.

"Don't blame this on me." Mrs. Hilbert huffed. "It's that skirt-wearing husband of hers who messed everything up."

"Yeah, well, I warned him not to hurt her." Clive began viciously snipping his scissors. "I told him I'd come after his million-dollar legs if he did. And don't think I won't."

"You'd do more damage if you aimed a little higher. That would fix him." Mrs. Hilbert laughed.

"The only person we need to fix is Andi," Daniel said.

"You do know I'm standing right here and I can hear you, right?" Andi lashed out when she'd had enough. "And no one is going after Dex. This is nobody's fault but mine." She paused. If she wanted to fool her friends into thinking she was okay, she needed to keep her voice steady. "Mrs. Hilbert may have come up with the idea of our marriage, but I was the one who agreed to it. Even after Dex told me I didn't have to."

Stupid her for having a conscience. She should have taken the money and run. But the truth was, she was a sucker. A sucker who kept putting herself out there, only to have her heart trampled again and again. But this time she was going to embrace the lesson the universe was trying so very hard to teach her. The simple truth was, she wasn't meant to be a part of a couple or a family. Just like she'd told her fake husband a week earlier, she was a party of one.

So be it. She had well-meaning, if not maddening, friends. And she'd survived worse things in life.

Her friends stared at her mutely, each of them looking as if they were bursting to say something more. Andi held up her hand, forestalling any further discussion.

"I'm fine," she reassured them for the forty-secondth time this week. "Really."

In an effort to put an end to the conversation—for the time being, at least—she walked over to the salon door and turned the lock to admit the Saturday customers already waiting outside. Her ring sparkled in the sunlight reminding her she was still tied to Dex for at least a few more months, no matter what she wanted.

At least she didn't have to see him every day.

The morning after the gala, she'd packed a few things and moved into the guest room in Clive and Daniel's house. Thanks to Agent Figueroa's visit, she knew the government wasn't watching her as closely. She could live wherever she wanted. Just as long as she didn't sign a lease, Mr. Hilbert had advised when he came storming into the salon several days ago.

"You still have a contract to fulfill. That means several more months of playing Mrs. Declan Fletcher in public," he'd very vehemently reminded her. "Just because ICE has backed-off bed checks doesn't mean they aren't still watching you both. You leasing a new place would be a glaring red flag."

Andi wasn't sure which hurt more, the fact that Dex's agent

thought she was an imbecile or Mr. Hilbert's lack of any attempt to get her to change her mind and move back into Dex's penthouse. Clearly, Dex hadn't send his agent as an emissary, but rather an enforcer to make sure she didn't renege on their contract. As she'd told both him and his agent numerous times, she wouldn't go back on her word. She had over seventy thousand reasons why she couldn't. Not to mention her pride.

"Good morning, Andi." The mail carrier greeted her with a friendly smile as she set the mail on the reception desk. "Tell that gorgeous Highlander husband of yours to kick the tar out of those Bears this week, you hear?"

Andi offered the woman a noncommittal smile before sorting through the pile of envelopes into junk mail and invoices. She hadn't spoken to Dex in over a week and she didn't plan to today. She'd attend the game the next day, but only to finalize Nicole's orders for bath bombs. After she and Dex split, she was certain the WAGs wouldn't want anything to do with her. Tomorrow, she would just slip in and slip out of the stadium without ever having to come in contact with her fake husband.

Among the stack of mail was another letter addressed to her. Her heart sank when she recognized the handwriting on the envelop as belonging to Kenny. The postmark still Las Vegas.

"Is it a love letter?" Mrs. Hilbert asked as Andi tore it open. "Dex has seen the error of his ways and is writing sonnets to win you back?"

"Hardly."

She peeked inside the envelope hoping for a check. Of course, there wasn't one. Her luck didn't run that way. Whatever was possessing Kenny to write to her, she didn't have enough emotional energy left in her tank to find out. Besides, he was the real villain here. Clive and Mrs. Hilbert could blame Dex all they wanted, but Andi wouldn't have been in this mess had it not for her deadbeat ex. Crumbling up the envelope, the letter still inside, she tossed it into the trash. She'd never found the one he'd sent her earlier. Not that she cared. With luck, it had been washed down a sewer drain.

Mrs. Hilbert wrapped her arms around Andi, stifling her search. "Men are fools."

"That's no way to talk about the superior gender."

At the sound of Trey Van Horn's voice, Mrs. Hilbert dropped her arms.

"Well, that fine body of yours may be prime, but I wouldn't go so far as to say you or any man is superior." Mrs. Hilbert responded.

Trey laughed at the older woman.

Mrs. Hilbert turned to Andi. "I don't want to leave you alone with the enemy, but Fred is taking me to the farmer's market, and I need to drop by the drugstore to—" she dropped her voice to a stage-whisper. "Pick up some lube for later, just in case Fred lives up to his nickname of Frisky Freddie." She leveled a last stern look at the quarterback before scooting out the door.

Trey grimaced. "Please tell me she was talking about Ben Gay."

Andi bit back a smile. She didn't want to chat with Dex's friend, much less enjoy it.

"Do you have an appointment?" she asked.

One corner of his mouth cocked up in his trademark smile that likely earned him millions each year in endorsements. "Do I need an appointment to speak with you for a few minutes?"

"'Fraid so. It's a Saturday. Our busiest day."

"Not even if I volunteer for one of those back waxes? I've always admired Dex's silky smooth skin."

Her lips twitched again at his obvious teasing. She did not want to like this man. He dated Jade, for crying out loud. Although, the tabloids had confirmed what she'd overheard the weekend before. Jade eagerly gave her version of events—which were not surprisingly vastly different from what actually went down—making Van Horn look like an arrogant tool. She had to give him props for being the bigger person and not refuting her account with the truth.

"Most men spend their waxing sessions crying for their mamas, not carrying on polite conversation."

This time she got the full smile and, holy hell, it was potent. She sighed.

"I really am busy right now—"

"I just wanted to apologize," he interrupted. "For Jade. And the things she said. I should have shut her down when Dex first told me she was bothering you."

"Dex told you that?" Why wasn't she surprised?

He nodded. "Threatened me with all kinds of bodily harm if I didn't make her stop. I accepted her word over his. Big mistake. And way too late to prevent her from insulting you. And for that, I'm sorry."

The unfairness of it all had the tears she'd been keeping at bay for days pressing against the back of her eyes. Dex cared for her enough to defend her, just not enough for her to be family.

"He really is a good guy," he said quietly. "Whatever he's done to wreck your relationship, I'm sure he didn't do it out of malice."

"What makes you think there is anything wrong with our marriage?" she snapped. She didn't need anyone else speculating on the status of their relationship.

His laugh was humorless. "The fact that he's been a boar to be around for the past week, gnashing his teeth whenever anyone speaks to him. At practice he's kicking the ball so hard, it's halfway to Canada before the equipment manager can retrieve it." He studied her face. "And, frankly, you don't look any happier than he does."

She wasn't having this conversation. Not with Trey Van Horn. Even though she suspected he knew the secret behind their marriage.

"If you want a back wax, I can book you an appointment for Thursday."

"I'll be in London Thursday."

Of course he would. The team and their spouses were leaving

Tuesday night on a chartered flight. They'd all be there. Everyone but her.

"Look, Andi. What I really came here to say is that I never realized how happy you made Fletcher until, well, he was an asshole again."

His words were the last straw. She pushed past him and fled out the door for some much-needed air. Unfortunately, he was right behind her.

"Sit," he commanded.

He pulled out a chair to one of the outdoor tables at the coffee shop next door. She should walk away. Protect her battered heart. Instead she did what he asked and sat.

"I come from a family that has elevated the practice of serial matrimony to an artform," he began, his unexpected statement surprising her.

"Serial matrimony?"

He nodded. "My mother's been married three times. In his quest to constantly one-up her, my dad is on marriage number four."

"Wow." Because really, how does one respond to that?

"Yeah. Given their excellent example, I've taken a solemn vow never to marry."

"Never?"

He shrugged. "I have aspirations beyond football. If an advantageous match presents itself, I might act on it."

"That's very—"

"Mercenary of me?" He interrupted.

"I was thinking of another word, but that fits, too."

"I didn't come here to analyze my hang-ups." He waved a hand. "I stopped by because I wanted you to know that all this time, I thought Dex saw the hypocrisy of love and happy ever after and all that bullshit the same as I did. But this week I realized it isn't bitterness that turned him off all that. It's sadness. A bone-deep melancholy that I suspect is why he doesn't go home to Scotland. Yet, somehow it mellowed when you came along. You brought him out of the shadows he was hiding in, Andi."

She rubbed her hands over her jean clad thighs, willing herself not to care about what the quarterback was saying. Her heart was being held together with silly string. She needed to do whatever she could to keep it in one piece.

He sighed when she didn't respond. "Anyway. I came here today to ask you not to give up on him. Beneath that brooding, stoic veneer is a guy with a vulnerable heart. From what I gather, marriage—or any long-term relationship—requires work. You strike me as a woman who doesn't back down from a challenge. I hope you won't back down from this one."

Dex was the one who gave up on their marriage, she wanted to shout. Except that wouldn't be the truth. He'd been upfront since the beginning. The only one pining for a happily ever after was Andi. She'd broken her own rule by putting her heart in play. Now she was paying the price.

Trey leaned over and planted a quick kiss on her cheek. "I hope I'll see you around."

He'd walked a few steps before turning back toward her.

"You said you would use another word besides mercenary to describe my theory on relationships," he said. "What was it?"

"Short-sighted," she responded without hesitation. "As someone who has been alone all my life, it's difficult to understand how another person would willingly choose that path."

He seemed to ponder her words before nodding curtly and disappearing around the corner. Ignoring the doubt beginning to niggle deep inside her, she headed back into the salon. The more she immersed herself in work, the less time she had to dwell on the fake marriage she wished was real.

For most of the day, she did a really good job at it. Right up until Dex's mathletes showed up in the salon at closing time. The teens burst through the door nearly as one unit, their faces lit with broad smiles. The large shiny trophy Rehema was holding explained their boisterous mood.

Andi couldn't help but get swept up in their joy. "Oh, my gosh! You won!"

"We kicked some butt," Louis said proudly.

"Crushed 'em is more like it," Eugene added. "They've been the city champs for three years straight, but not today. Professor McMath is the boss!"

Her heart leapt to her throat as she scanned the room for Dex. She wasn't ready to face him again. Not yet.

"He had to go to the team meeting and then the hotel." Rehema eyed her shrewdly. "We told him not to tell you because we wanted to surprise you with the news."

"I'm so glad you did," Andi replied after breathing a relieved sigh. "I'm sure he is very proud of you. So am I."

"We're getting our tour of the stadium on Tuesday," Angela announced.

Several of their faces dimmed.

"Um," Angela continued. "We were wondering if you can come, too. That way maybe Professor McMath will be in a better mood."

Oh no. Not the mathletes, too.

"I'd love too, but unfortunately I have to work that day," Andi hedged. "And I'm sure Dex wasn't in a bad mood. He's just stressed about tomorrow's game. They need to win to stay ahead in their division."

If you'd asked her three months ago if she would know, much less care, about the Growlers' record, she would have laughed. Oh how times had changed.

Eugene snorted. "He never stresses over a game. He's like a machine."

"And I didn't say he was in a bad mood. He was just distract-ed." Angela added.

"Yeah. And sad," Rehema said.

The group of teens nodded solemnly. Andi glanced around the salon for some reinforcements, but Clive and the rest of the staff were cleaning up their stations.

"I'm sure he'll be in a better mood for your tour," she tried to reassure them.

"Yeah, if you kiss and make up," Angela insisted.

"I'm sorry?" Surely Mr. I-Am-An-Island hadn't shared details about their personal life with a group of teenagers.

"We're not stupid," Rehema explained. "We have parents. Most of us even have both parents living in the same house. We have eyes, you know."

Andi was speechless.

"Look," Eugene said. "We could win state this year. We need Professor McMath to bring his A-game. We can't have him moping during practice and going through the motions."

Rehema glared at her teammate. "It's not just about winning. We want the happy Professor McMath back. The one that showed up after he married you." She gave Andi a sympathetic smile. "You two are really cute together."

The teen picked up the trophy and gestured to the door with her chin. Her teammates silently filed out.

"What was that about?" Clive asked.

Once again, she had to work to steady her voice. "They wanted to let me know they'd won today. That's all."

"Daniel is making his famous mojitos for happy hour. Some friends are going to stop over." He draped his arm over her shoulder and hugged her close. "Maybe we'll even break out the Karaoke machine."

The last thing she wanted was to keep up her happy façade in front of Clive and Daniel's friends. It was bad enough she had to pretend to be okay in front of her own friends. But she couldn't very well hide out in their guest room studying with a party going on.

"Actually, I was going to head back over to the penthouse tonight." She wasn't sure where the idea came from, but it was a good one. "Dex will be at the team hotel so I'll have the place to myself. I can study and grab some more of my things." The more she talked, the more sense her plan made. Especially if Marlene had made some Snickerdoodles.

"You do realize you're choosing your fake husband's surly cat over your friends?"

She rested her head on his shoulder. "It's not that. I'm just not feeling very festive tonight and I don't want to be a Debbie Downer at your party. Besides, Morag will probably shriek with glee when she sees me carrying more of my stuff out of the penthouse."

He pressed his lips to the top of her head. "Suit yourself. My money is on you anyway. It always is."

Thirty minutes later, Andi entered the penthouse. Marlene had already left for the evening, leaving Andi alone in the quiet. She snatched a few cookies from the plate Dex's assistant always left in the kitchen and wandered down the hall. Maybe it was Trey Van Horn's or Rehema's words, but Andi felt something a lot like grief hovering in the air. It was as if the life had been sucked out of the place.

"Don't let them get to you," she murmured to herself. "Dex is fine. He made his own choices."

Her suite was just as she left it. She set her backpack on the table in front of the gas fireplace and glanced up at the beautiful landscape. Even it had an eerie quality to it. Tamping down on her silly emotions, she quickly changed into some leggings and a T-shirt and forced herself to get down to studying.

She'd just settled into the big chair in front of the fireplace when something soft brushed against her ankles, startling her.

"Morag."

She steeled herself for the retaliatory scratch that was sure to follow from the meddlesome cat. But none came. Instead, Morag plopped down, cocked her head and stared up at her before releasing a soft, plaintive meow.

"What kind of game are you playing?" she asked, suspiciously.

Morag responded with a swish of her tail and another pleading meow.

"Do you actually want me to pet you?"

Before she knew what was happening, the cat was in her lap, purring loudly before curling up in a ball and closing her eyes. Andi kept herself still, unsure how to respond. Morag's contented purrs reverberated against Andi's stomach. Gently, she brushed her fingers along the cat's silky fur. Morag arched into her touch, much to her delight.

They sat like that for several long moments until the cat went limp with sleep. Andi tried to finish the chapter she was reading for accounting, but her thoughts kept drifting. She gazed down at Dex's cat, slumbering in her lap. Morag had come to her for reassurance. For comfort.

You brought him out of the shadows he was hiding in, Andi. Don't give up on him. Trey Van Horn's earlier words echoed inside her head, Rehema's plea chasing behind it. *We want the happy Professor McMath back. The one that showed up after he married you.*

Was the cat trying to tell her the same thing? The breath got stuck in her lungs. Was Dex really as down as everyone was claiming? Because of her? Something else Van Horn said floated to the top of her memory.

A bone-deep melancholy that I suspect is why he doesn't go home to Scotland.

Could it be that he wasn't ashamed of her? That he didn't want her to meet his family for some other reason?

Suddenly, her breath was moving more freely again, but now it was coming so fast and furious she was panting. *The letters.*

Maybe there was some clue in the letters Dex's sister had sent. Andi carefully scooped up the cat, earning her a sleepy side-eye but thankfully no scratch, and headed into the bedroom. Something had kept her from opening the letters the other night. A mix of pride and shame. If he didn't want her to know his family, then she wasn't going to torture herself by reading his sister's missives. Worse, she suspected she couldn't have handled it if the letters contained even more rejection.

But that didn't matter now. She needed answers. And she was hopeful she'd find them within the pages of Annis' elegant stationary.

Settling Morag beside her on the bed, she opened the night-stand where she stashed the letters and pulled them out. She arranged them in order according to their postmarks and cautiously slid her finger against the seal to open the first one.

"Here goes nothing."

Morag swished her tail against Andi's thigh in encouragement.

By the time she'd read the fourth letter, she was a mass of conflicting emotions. Frustration and sadness tugging at her chest painfully, while another, more powerful feeling bubbled up inside her.

Hope.

She fingered her grandmother's cross for courage. Because now that she had the answers, it was time to enact a plan.

"Come on, Morag." Andi jumped up from the bed. "We've got a lot of work to do tonight."

TWENTY-TWO

DEX GRABBED HIS carryon and followed his teammates off the bus, his mother's text still aggravating him. She'd made dinner reservations for tomorrow night and the night after, totally disregarding his request they keep things low-key since most of his time in London needed to be spent practicing with his team. Most likely, she'd seen right through his ploy, and she was aware how little a place-kicker actually trained before a game. His ma was diabolical that way.

At least she'd stopped bothering him about traveling home to St. Andrews for the bye week. He'd given her and his family another line about wanting to return home to Andi. His gut twisted just thinking about the lie.

Except it wasn't a lie.

He did want to return home to Andi, but his fake wife was now only a part of his life as a name on a piece of paper. *It's better this way,* he told himself for the millionth time in the past ten days. Too bad the rest of his body refused to get the bloody message.

Darkness had just fallen when the Growlers walked across the tarmac to the private plane the team had chartered for the trip.

Dex hoped and prayed that his teammates were smart enough to sleep during the eight-and-a-half-hour flight. He wasn't in the mood for a party in the cabin.

Things weren't starting off well, however. A queue of players formed at the bottom of the steps where Rolando Harris was carrying on board a jumbo pack of toilet paper, of all things.

"Who brings a damn twenty-four-pack of TP on a plane?" one of his teammates shouted.

"Hey!" Harris bellowed in return. "You'll be begging me for a roll of this stuff when we get to London. Those Limeys over there only use cheap one-ply. Try wiping yourself with that, man."

Harris spied Dex in the line. "Oh, sorry, Fletcher. Didn't mean to offend you with my Limey remark."

Dex shook his head. "None taken." He wasn't in the mood for a history lesson today, so he didn't bother pointing out he wasn't British.

Palmer jogged up to cut the line. "Hey, Fletcher. I want you to meet my dad." The punter gestured to a man further back behind them. "Dad, come on."

He didn't want to meet Palmer's da. Hell, the two words he'd just spoken to Harris were the extent of the polite conversation he'd been able to muster in the past ten days. He just wanted to board the bloody plane, find a seat away from everyone so he could brood in silence.

"What an honor." Palmer's da pumped Dex's hand. "Kane says you're from St. Andrews. I'm sure he told you we are heading there after the game. I'd love it if I can pick your brain for some recommendations while we are there."

"I haven't been there in over a decade." Not a lie. "Can't help ya," he replied, his tone chilly by Arctic standards judging by the way Palmer's da flinched.

Bloody hell.

Palmer looked as if someone had kicked his dog.

"My family will be in London," he heard himself saying. "I'm sure my da would be a better resource. Why don't you two join us for dinner tomorrow night." If nothing else, he'd just given himself a buffer from the interrogation his parents no doubt planned.

The punter's face lit up. He slapped his da on the back. "Told ya, Dad. My best friend won't let us down."

Dex bit back a grimace at the *best friend* reference. With a beleaguered sigh, he waved the two Palmers ahead of him in line.

"Should I tell the rookie you aren't interested in any friends?" Van Horn murmured behind him.

"You're just jealous that the cub is taking your place."

Van Horn snorted as they climbed the steps up to the cabin. One of the Growlers' community relations staff was waiting at the top handing out hats for the game.

"Welcome aboard!"

A bow wave of chatter slammed into Dex. So much for a quiet flight. The party atmosphere was going to be inescapable. The front of the plane was already filled with families of players and staff, all of them seeming to talk at once.

Guilt washed over him. Andi should be here. The ache in his chest ratcheted up seeing all the other WAGs laughing and enjoying themselves. She would have loved this, too. And he would have loved watching her soak up the experience.

He really needed to stop thinking about her if he was going to survive this trip. Ducking his head so he didn't have to make any more conversation, he made a beeline for the back of the plane. His heart stopped when a shock of pink hair caught his eye. Glancing to his left, he locked eyes with Coach's adorable cherub. She smiled shyly at him, her pink-haired troll doll clutched to her chest. He let out a breath he didn't realize he was holding and returned the little girl's grin with one of his own.

The first real one he'd managed in days.

Taking another step, he nodded to the woman seated beside the child only to stop short once again. His mouth dropped to his chin when his wife arched an eyebrow at him. The little girl donned a mulish look as she clutched at Andi's arm.

"I promised Harper I'd sit with her," Andi said matter-of-factly, as if it was the most normal thing in the world for her to be on the plane.

"Wise choice." Van Horn's voice came from behind him. Good thing, since Dex couldn't seem to find his own. "Kessler instigated a burrito eating contest at lunch today. It's going to be a gas chamber back there. Odds are that TP won't make it as far as London."

She smiled gorgeously at the quarterback. "Well, I'll leave you guys to all the excitement then. We ladies are going to learn to braid hair."

A roaring began in his ears, its potency matching the burning in his chest. *What the bloody hell was going on?* Andi couldn't be on this plane. She could *not* go to London with them. His family was in London. His worst nightmare was coming true.

He tried to draw a breath or form a coherent sentence, but neither was happening at the moment. Her smile wavered, concern lacing her expression. She glanced back at Van Horn, a question in her eyes.

"You're holding up the line, Fletcher," Van Horn murmured. "Let's go."

Dex's hand balled into a fist at the obvious silent communication between his now former best friend and his wife.

"Donnae tell me what to do," he snarled.

"Dex." Her voice was soft, but steely. "Go take your seat. I'll come back and sit with you once Harper falls asleep."

"No. We'll talk now. On the tarmac."

The little girl's lip began to quiver as the chatter around them seemed to quiet. He was making a scene, but he didn't care. If he had to tear the bloody plane apart, she was getting off. He couldn't risk her finding out his darkest secret. He could live with her anger. But he wouldn't survive if she learned the truth and loathed him, too.

Her gaze collided with his and the unexpected compassion he saw reflected there nearly took him out at the knees.

"Please," she uttered quietly.

The simple word was like a knife to his heart.

"Fletcher!" Coach's voice boomed over the plane's intercom. "Get moving. You're messing up our flight plan."

Andi nodded slightly as if to encourage him to move. Van Horn let out an exasperated sigh behind him.

"Am I going to have to fucking carry you?" The quarterback's hands hovered over Dex's shoulders.

Dex shrugged him away. With one last look at his wife, he headed for the back of the plane, tossing his stuff into the window seat of the rear row.

"I'm not sure we want to be this close to the lavatory, but you're driving this crazy train." Van Horn dropped into the seat next to him.

"Fuck off," Dex said. "Go find someone else to bother."

Van Horn shook his head. "No can do. Somebody has got to keep you from making an . . . *arse* of yourself."

"What the bloody hell is that supposed to mean?"

His friend had the nerve to chuckle. "It means that people in love do stupid shit. And you've obviously already done something incredibly stupid. I'm doing you the favor of not letting you compound it."

Love? Van Horn didn't know how close he was to being strung up by his balls of the back of a 737. Dex was not in love with Andi.

Except he was.

The uncomfortable realization settled heavily over him like a weighted blanket. Truth be told, he'd been besotted since their first meeting in Kurt's office when she hadn't sucked up to him for his fame or fortune. Even more so when she agreed to marry him because she believed it was the right thing to do. He'd fallen a little more in love with her each day he'd been lucky enough to be around her. So much so that pushing her away was leaving a gaping hole in his chest.

Beside him, Van Horn waggled his eyebrows. With a smug grin, he gestured to Dex's seatbelt. "Buckle up, buttercup. There's nothing you can do about it now."

And that's the part that scared the living shit out of him. In just over eight hours, Andi would meet his family and know the truth about him. And then she'd want nothing to do with him. The cabin lights dimmed. Minutes later they were screaming down the runway. He closed his eyes and tried to wrestle his racing heart into submission.

ANDI WAS SURPRISED Dex hadn't sought her out the moment the captain shut off the seatbelt sign. Either Trey had tied him to his seat or he'd seen the wisdom of not making a scene in front of his teammates. After all, his visa still wasn't guaranteed. And now that she knew the reason behind his dogged determination not to return home, she understood why his immigration situation was so important to him. But that still didn't explain why he had to wall himself off from everyone. From his family. From her. Or why he was so emphatic that she and his family should never meet.

She glanced down at the sleeping child on her lap. As gently as she could, she placed a pillow under Harper's head and left her in the seat she'd just vacated. Merrit mouthed thank you to Andi as she passed. Max was sprawled out across the other woman's chest, little bubbles forming between his lips as he slept.

Her heart squeezed at the sight. She wanted children. Dex's children. But if she couldn't unlock whatever was holding him back, they didn't have a chance.

Don't give up on him.

Dex's sister echoed Van Horn's challenge when Andi spoke with her two days earlier. She drew strength in the knowledge that his family and friends cared for him enough to want him to be happy. She just hoped she could make him see she was the right woman to do that. Sighing with determination, she headed for the back of the plane.

She only made it halfway back before she was practically

tackled in the dark aisleway. Breathing in the familiar scent of her husband, she forced herself to relax against his urgent hold. Behind them, Van Horn met her eyes with his own and shrugged as if to say "I tried." She gave him a reassuring smile and he disappeared back to his seat.

"You're coming with me," Dex commanded, half dragging, half carrying her to the back of the plane.

"I hope you're not considering tossing me out the emergency exit," she joked in an effort to lighten his mood.

He didn't bother responding. Kane Palmer was just making his way toward the lavatory when Dex nearly bowled him over, shoving her in the tiny compartment first. She could hear Kane chuckle, murmuring something about the mile-high club when Dex joined her, closing the door in the punter's face. The light came on when he slid the lock home. With their bodies pressed up against one another, she could feel his ragged breathing. But it was the desperation etched on his face that had her own breath catching.

"Oh, Dex." She drew her arms up between them and looped them around his neck. "It's okay."

The plane dipped and his grip on her waist tightened.

"It's okay," she repeated as he buried his face in her neck. "I know about Niall."

His body sagged against her. She dragged her fingers through the curls at the back of his neck trying to sooth him.

"I know how hard it is to lose people," she continued. "He was your best friend. Practically your brother. I can't imagine the pain you still carry around at losing him. But it was an accident, Dex. At some point you're going to have to go home to face the memories."

He stiffened beneath her touch. She sucked in a breath. Had she ruined her chance already by saying the wrong thing? He tried to pull away, but there was nowhere to go in the close confines of the small bathroom. He restlessly dragged his fingers through his hair.

"Naill is dead because I killed him."

The harshly uttered statement hung in the air between them.

"No." Bewildered, she tried to recall the story his sister told her. "He died in a car accident. Alone." She swallowed, worried about speaking ill of the dead and offending Dex. "He was driving drunk."

Dex gripped her arms and shook her. "Aye. Because I let him down. I let everyone down."

He wasn't making sense. Her confusion must have been apparent because he continued.

"I knew he was drinking heavily, but I left him at the pub anyway." A shamed expression lined his face. "I left with a woman. I don't even know the bloody chit's name."

A bubble of jealousy formed in her chest.

"If I had stayed . . ." He shook his head in disgust.

"If you had stayed, there is no reason to believe he wouldn't have been behind the wheel anyway and you both would be dead." Her heart stuttered at the thought.

"But I didn't stay! You ken? I followed my bloody dick and Niall paid the price. Because. Of. Me!"

Understanding suddenly dawned. "This is why you keep yourself so walled off from everyone. Why you don't go home. Dex, you're punishing yourself for something that's not your fault. You're punishing your family. And you're punishing me." Aggravation at him threatened to choke her. "You won't accept my love because of some stupid misguided guilt." She punctuated the last words with her fists pounding on his chest.

He grabbed her wrists. "How can you claim to love me after what I've just told you?"

She groaned in frustration. "How can someone so smart be so stupid? I love you, Declan Fletcher and that's not going to change. Believe me, I've spent the last week trying." She pressed her lips against his jaw. "I've loved you since our first plane ride together when you put aside your own discomfort to make sure I was okay. You've been my White Knight ever since."

His arms wrapped around her. "I don't deserve you," he whispered.

A loud banging startled them both.

"Hey, can you two newlyweds knock it off in there. We've got a crisis situation out here."

He sighed heavily before reaching behind him and unlocking the door. He wrapped his fingers around her wrist and led her past the row of his teammates casting them knowing looks. Grabbing the blanket off Van Horn's lap, he gestured for the quarterback to give up his seat. Trey winked at her before traipsing up the aisle. Dex pulled her into the seat beside him and tented the blanket over their heads. His lips found hers in the dark, and pure unadulterated joy swept through Andi at his touch. After all these years, she had found her home.

"I'VE MISSED YA, lass. More than I thought possible."

Dex felt her smile against his neck. "Mmm. You won't have to suffer without me again, because you're stuck with me now."

He swore his chest swelled at her words.

"I can't wait to meet your family. To see your home."

Just like that, his happiness dissipated.

"I can't take you home, lass."

She tensed in his arms. "Not this again. There's no reason you can't go home to Scotland. No one blames you for Niall's death."

"Colleen does."

"Colleen? Niall's wife?"

"Aye."

She shifted so she was at his side. "Tell me why you think that."

He leaned his head on her shoulder. Despite the darkness beneath the blanket, it was difficult telling this tale face-to-face. Memories he'd relived in his dreams for so many years came to him unbidden. Colleen, inconsolable after Niall's funeral.

You promised me you wouldn't let him get drunk, she had accused. *You know his dark moods as well as anyone.*

"Niall was destined for greatness. He was so talented with the sticks on the course. It was fun to watch him outsmart the game." He drew in breath. "But the better he got at his golf game, the more unhappy he became. It was almost as if he left all his joy out on the green."

Andi found his hand and laced her fingers through his. She gave his fingers a squeeze in encouragement.

"That night he was especially glum. It's was Colleen's idea for me to take him out for a pint."

She made a little sound of disapproval. He brought their joined hands up and brushed his lips against hers.

"Don't go getting your knickers in a wad. Colleen was at home with a baby. She couldn't handle two at once. And Niall and I were one in the same. We understood each other."

He felt her nod.

"But with me at university and him on the European tour, we understood each other less and less, it seemed. I wasn't as tolerant of Niall's blues as I should have been that night. He must have sensed it because he encouraged me to go off with the redhead. He said one of us should have some fun." His laugh was humorless. "He promised he was headed home after he finished his ale."

"Except he didn't."

"Nah. The bloody bartender let him drink five more pints."

"I'm still not seeing a reason for Colleen to blame you," Andi insisted.

Niall was my soulmate. And now he's gone. How am I supposed to live without him? How am I supposed to look at you again? Whenever I do, I see him. I see you letting us both down.

"I was responsible for him that night." He swallowed roughly. "It was easier to blame me than Niall."

"But that's not fair!"

"With Niall gone, his endorsements and tour money were gone, too. Colleen had an infant to care for. She needed her family and the people she'd known all her life to care for her. She couldn't go off and start a new life away from the memories. But I could."

"Again. Not fair."

"Life isn't fair. If it was, Niall would still be here. With Colleen and their son."

She heaved a frustrated sigh. He wrapped her in his arms and pulled her back onto his lap and kissed her deeply. She melted against him and soon he was close to losing his mind and taking her on a crowded airplane.

He tore his mouth away. "What am I to do with you, lass?"

"Don't shut me out," she whispered against his mouth. "Love me."

"Aye," he replied, surprising himself with the intensity of his response. "Your wish is my command, my queen."

TWENTY-THREE

ANDI TWISTED A strand of her hair around her finger before hastily tucking it back behind her ear.

"Are you sure my outfit is okay? Should I have not worn jeans? Maybe I should have worn a dress? Or at least a skirt?"

"Relax." Draping an arm across her shoulders, Dex pulled her closer to his side of the seat they shared in the back of a cab. "My family will adore you even if you were dressed in a paper bag." He brushed his lips along her forehead.

Easy for him to say. The people they were about to meet had gifted him with unconditional love for thirty years. *What did that even feel like?* She shivered slightly.

He rubbed his palm up and down her arm. Even through the barrier of the leather jacket she'd thrown over a cashmere sweater, his touch made her skin tingle. It boggled her mind that despite an afternoon with his body wrapped around hers, she still ached for him. Even when he was sitting right beside her. She snuggled in closer, hoping to soak up some of his confidence in her. At least if they rejected her, she'd still have him by her side.

Hopefully.

"Have you been fretting about this all day?"

"No. Of course not," she lied.

They had arrived in London earlier that morning. After clearing immigration, the team and its entourage were shuttled off to a sprawling resort north of London. Despite being a long cab ride from the stadium downtown, the location was chosen because there was a rugby field on the grounds where the team could practice. The posh hotel rooms and Michelin-rated restaurants were an added bonus.

Most of the WAGS hurried to take advantage of the spa while the team ran through a light workout and drills once they'd settled in. Pleading jet lag, Andi headed to their suite for some rest, but she'd been too jumpy to sleep. She'd been texting or emailing with Dex's sister and mother for days now. Both women could not have been more enthusiastic and excited about meeting her.

But what if they were just being polite? Being nice because they were desperate to spend time with Dex? What if they don't accept me?

As much as she tried to stifle the doubts, they refused to be quiet. It was the story of her life, after all. Even grateful and awed by his love as she was, Andi was ashamed to admit she selfishly wanted more. Waiting for her at a London restaurant was the one thing she'd given up hoping for some time ago. *A family.* One she could call hers. She crossed her fingers in her lap.

"I just don't want to embarrass you." *Or to give them any reason to reject me.*

He placed a finger beneath her chin and lifted her eyes to meet his twinkling gray ones. "Lass, it's more likely my family will do the embarrassing. They are a raucous and wild clan when you get them all in one place. You might find yourself sorry you wished so hard for a family."

"I doubt they are that bad."

He laughed. "Ya ken? All right, then don't stand too close to Aunt Janna. The woman spits like a rainstorm when she talks. Aunt

Claire has six kids and so many grands, I've lost count. Be careful she doesn't back you into a corner and monopolize you with endless photos. Oh, and avoid Uncle Reginald, too. He has a fondness for Old Spice which wouldn't be so bad if he still had his sense of smell."

Andi laughed when he wrinkled his nose and waved a hand in front of his face. She appreciated his attempt at calming her racing nerves. By the time they pulled up to the restaurant, her mood was lighter.

"I've got you, lass," he murmured against her ear when he helped her out of the cab. "Never forget that."

If a heart could smile, hers most definitely would.

The hostess led them to a back room crowded with people all seeming to be talking at once. Dex hadn't exaggerated when he'd called his family raucous. Her stomach did a little nervous flip as she hesitated in the doorway. Beside her, Dex let out a loud whistle and the room quieted instantly as each and every one of the occupants turned in their direction. Her heart was beating so loudly, she was sure the entire Fletcher clan heard it.

With a soft cry, a woman emerged from the center of the room. His mother. *My mother-in-law.* Andi's stomach fluttered again as she shifted out of the way to give the other woman access to her son. She was stunned, however, when Rose Fletcher wrapped her arms around her instead.

Just as suddenly, there was a throng of people lining up to envelope Andi in welcoming hugs. Names were thrown out, none of which she would be able to remember, but she didn't care. She was too busy soaking up the love being showered upon her. Beside her, Dex was enduring some good-natured ribbing and congratulations on their hasty wedding. Their gazes locked and he arched an eyebrow as if to say "see what I mean?"

"Look, they're already sharing secret looks." Annis' announcement was followed by more teasing and laughter.

Her new sister-in-law threaded her arm through Andi's and guided her to one of the tables. Annis was even more beautiful than her photos. She had the same dimple as her older brother, only on her it looked mischievous.

"You have no idea how happy I am to have a sister," the younger woman gushed. "I've been waiting all my life for you, Andi."

Sister. Not ever sister-in-law. Annis' declaration had tears of joy forming at the back of Andi's eyes.

"I'm so glad you and Declan found each other. I've worried about him being alone over there in America." The younger woman donned a bemused smile as she peeked back at her brother. "But now he has you. And I can tell by just looking at him, you make him happy. I don't think I've seen him this relaxed . . . well, ever." Her smile brightened, if that was even possible, when she turned her attention back to Andi. "And now, he can spend his time being over-protective of you instead of me."

She threw in a saucy wink that had Andi grinning widely.

"Ah, so my job is to run interference?"

"Something like that." Annis sobered up. "In all seriousness, I'm really looking forward to getting to know you better. Anyone who can capture Declan's heart has to be pretty special."

"Your brother is kind of special himself."

"Oh, don't I know it? But don't you dare tell him I said so!"

The two broke out in another round of laughter just as the tinkling of a glass sounded throughout the room.

"Everyone, please take your places. Dinner is served," her father-in-law announced.

Dex made his way between them, wrapping an arm around each of their waists. "Something tells me I may have to keep my eye on my two favorite lasses," he murmured. His sister jabbed him playfully with her elbow.

"A toast!" Doug Fletcher lifted his glass into the air. "Congratulations Declan and Andi. May all your days be happy ones! Great health and every good blessing to ya." He shifted his gaze to focus on her. "Andi, my love. Welcome to the Fletcher clan. We have a saying in Scotland that goes like this: The strength of a family is in the loyalty to each other. You are one of us now, lass. You will never be alone. *Slàinte mhath!*"

Everyone in the room echoed Douglas Fletcher's toast. Andi swallowed roughly before taking a sip from her glass. The joy she felt bubbled up every nerve ending. Dex held her closer. When she looked up at him, he touched his forehead to hers.

"I told you they'd love you, lass."

Annis laughed beside them. "I ken they love her a wee bit more than you, big brother."

"That will change when the check comes around," he joked.

Dinner was filled with laughter and stories. Andi hardly recalled if she even ate anything. Her mouth was too busy smiling to swallow any food. All the times she'd imagined having a family —*a clan*—she'd never imagined the depth of joy she'd feel knowing she was a part of something bigger than her. *You will never be alone.* She let the words wash over her again and again until at last, they sunk in.

The party broke up a few hours later with plans made for Andi to have lunch with the Fletcher women the next day followed by a tour of London and dinner with the entire group again.

"Is it the goal of everyone in this bloody family to monopolize my wife's time all week?" Dex complained halfheartedly when they were alone with his parents and Annis in the hotel room he'd booked for them downtown.

"You've had her all to yourself for nearly three months now," his mother argued while patting Andi's hand. "It won't kill you to share her with the rest of her family."

"Besides, we don't want her spending too much time with you, brother," Annis teased. "We can't have her changing her mind."

Douglas Fletcher chuckled as he handed his wife a cup of tea. "Give it up, Declan. The balance of power in our family has shifted. It's now three against two."

Dex shot her a pained look. One that almost had Andi feeling sorry for him. Except that she was too busy enjoying the moment of her dreams. "I'm looking forward to spending more time with everyone. Especially since it will likely take me a few days to learn all their names."

"And this isn't even everyone in the family," Annis added. "Just wait until you get to Scotland next week. Half the town is practically related somehow."

Dex went still beside her. His mother shot an anxious look at her husband. In all the texts and phone calls she'd exchanged with his family these past few days, there had never been any discussion of them traveling to Scotland after the game. Andi had certainly hoped they would, but that was before his revelations aboard the plane last night.

His family didn't understand the depth of his guilt like she did. As much as she believed his blame was unfounded, he needed to do this on his own terms. Even it meant disappointing his parents.

She found his hand beside her and laced her fingers with his, silently communicating her support. "Unfortunately, we have to head back to Wisconsin after the game. I can't miss another week of classes." She hated lying to his parents, but she'd do what she had to in order to shield Dex from any more pain than he already carried.

Rose Fletcher's sigh sounded a lot like a sob caught in her throat. Dex jerked at the sound.

"But what about the blessing of the rings ceremony Ma has planned?" Annis said, her eyes wide with concern.

Andi watched as Dex exchanged a look with his father. There was no censure in Douglas Fletcher's eyes. Instead, he seemed to be pleading with his son.

Tell them. She gave his hand an encouraging squeeze. The air around them crackled with tension. A long moment later, Dex sighed heavily. He returned the hand squeeze.

"Didn't you say your professors would be willing to let you sit in on your classes online if we could work it out?" he surprised the heck out of her by asking.

Andi was sure of it now. Her heart was *definitely* smiling.

"Aye, Highlander," she replied. "And I'm sure we can work that out."

DEX WASN'T SURE which he found more satisfying, kicking the game winning field goal in Wembley Stadium with his parents, extended family, and friends cheering him on, or watching his beautiful wife get swallowed up in the bosom of his family. The Fletcher clan embraced her as one of their own from the moment they laid eyes on her.

How could they not? he thought to himself happily. His wife was perfect.

And she was his.

Every so often he'd catch his mother smiling adoringly at her. Then Ma would look over at him and grin gloriously. His sister Annis declared it a miracle that any woman would commit to spending the rest of her life with her stodgy old brother. Dex thought it pretty miraculous himself, not that he admitted anything of the sort to his sister.

Somehow, arrangements were made for them to return to Scotland for the bye week. Palmer and his da, along with Coach and his family, were already headed that way. It didn't take him long to convince his buddies Van Horn and Kessler to tag along. The festivities began as soon as they landed, capped off by the parish priest's blessing of their marriage in front of over a hundred guests and a reception afterwards. He could only marvel at his mother's efforts.

"You didn't expect your ma to not throw a party celebrating your marriage, did ya?" His father asked with a grin.

A week ago, Dex hadn't expected his family to even meet Andi, much less that the two of them would be traveling back home after a decade away. Yet, here they were. Surrounded by everyone he'd ever known, it seemed. And the angst that normally gripped him whenever he contemplated returning to Scotland had faded away.

So, too, the loneliness. Until now, he hadn't realized just how lonely he had been all these years.

And it was all thanks to one extraordinary lass. Her selflessness and steadfast support the other night shattered whatever bindings remained on his heart. He glanced over at his wife, beaming radiantly among the guests lined up to meet her. Thanks to her, he'd never be lonely again. Thanks to her, he'd overcome the painful memories of the past. And thanks to her, he could finally exorcise the rest of his guilt.

She seemed to feel the pull of his gaze because she looked over at him. Dex tilted his head slightly and she nodded.

"Aye, Da. It's a smashing party. As usual, Ma has outdone herself." He slapped his father on the shoulder. "There's something I need to take care. Cover for me, will ya?"

"I ken. I'd best go see about your rowdy teammates. The way Palmer is sashaying around in that kilt, he's likely to flash one of the old ladies from the parish." His father winked at him before heading in the direction of Ma's garden. "And if you're thinking of disappearing with your new wife, don't. Your ma has a cake she'll be wanting the two of you to cut."

Dex nodded. As much as he wanted to sneak off with Andi and have his way with her, there was something he needed to take care of first. His palms grew sweaty as he made his way through the hall to the terrace where guests were taking advantage of the rare sunny late autumn day. He'd seen Colleen head in that direction earlier. It was a surprise to find her in attendance, but he suspected his cagey wife had something to do with it. Yet another thing to be grateful to Andi for.

He would recognize Niall's son anywhere. The boy had the same shock of burnt orange hair and impish smile. Dex stood still for a moment watching him dribble a football around the grass with another man. Memories of two other young boys doing the same flashed before his eyes. He couldn't help but smile.

"Da!" the boy called in an effort to get the man's attention.

Dex flinched.

"He's the only father Patrick has ever known," Colleen said from beside him.

The guilt he thought he'd managed to bury surged to the surface.

"Don't," Colleen admonished him. "Don't feel guilty."

Anger replaced the guilt as he turned to face her. She dared to say that to him now?

"An apology is long overdue." She'd changed over the years. Grown prettier if that was possible. But there was something more, something that hadn't been there when he last saw her. *Peace.*

"Although had you come home once in a while, I might have gotten to this earlier." Her cheeky smile only served to anger him more.

"I didn't come home because I was honoring your bloody wishes," he bit out.

She breathed a forlorn sigh. "I know. I guess I underestimated your thoughtfulness. Most people would have ignored my ultimatum after a few years. But not you. Your stubbornness is legendary."

"This was a bloody mistake." Peeved beyond belief, he turned to head back to the party.

"No." She stayed him with her hand to his arm. "I'm glad for the opportunity for you to finally hear me out." Dragging in a deep breath, she gave his arm a gentle squeeze. "I was wrong to blame you. I was devastated and scared, not to mention young and stupid. And I took it out on you. I shouldn't have."

The tension gripping his shoulders began to ease. He opened his mouth to respond, but she shook her head.

"Let me finish. I knew he was unhappy, but I didn't want to examine things too closely. The truth is, I didn't want to find out if I was the cause of his unhappiness."

"Coll." Dex took her hand in his. "He adored you."

She smiled grimly. "Aye. But did you know he was offered a scholarship to play golf at university in America?"

Her revelation had the tension gripping him all over again.

Niall had never told him that. The knowledge stung. "No. I didnae."

What else had his best friend kept from him?

"I suspect he might have gone had I not gotten pregnant."

There was an ominous tone to her words that had him bracing for another blow.

"I trapped him, Dex. I found out about the scholarship and I got pregnant on purpose. I was so afraid of losing him."

Her eyes glistened with unshed tears. He pulled her into a fierce hug.

"It was immature and desperate. I see that now," she said against his chest. "I blamed you for the accident so I didn't have to blame myself. But I've learned through lots of therapy that I wasn't responsible for Niall's decision that night. And neither were you."

He held her close for several long moments, both of them shedding the weight of guilt that had been dogging them.

"I can't regret getting pregnant either," she eventually said. "Because at least there will always be a piece of him living on through Patrick."

He looked over at the boy, racing with a group of kids across the lawn. "Aye," he consoled her. "That there will be."

Colleen pulled away and swiped at her eyes. "I'd like for you to be a part of his life, Dex. I know Niall would want that, too."

A boulder had formed in his throat, so he simply nodded.

She arched an eyebrow at him. "I hope we won't have to come to the States for that, though."

"Nah. We'll be back."

"I hope so. This is your home. I should never have taken it away from you."

Harper's laughter had him turning toward the doorway. Andi held the little girl in her arms as she swayed to the music drifting from inside. The two bowed their heads together so their foreheads were touching. His chest grew tight just watching them. He couldn't wait for the day when she held their child so joyfully.

"She has the way of him, too."

Colleen's soft words had him turning back to her abruptly.

She smiled knowingly. "Andi has that same effervescence for life that Niall had. I can see why you love her."

There were so many reasons why he loved Andi. But he was glad Colleen thought she was remarkable, too.

"Aye, Coll. She's something special all right."

TWENTY-FOUR

"LOOK AT THAT, Fletcher, my kilt selfie is trending on social media." Kane declared from his seat at the front of the plane. "Guess you're not the only one with million-dollar legs, baby."

The occupants of the private jet headed back from Scotland let out a collective groan at the punter's announcement.

"Jaysus," Dex murmured beside Andi.

"What are the odds he wears that damn kilt to practice this week?" Luke Kessler asked.

Their quarterback shook his head in halfhearted annoyance. "Given that he hasn't taken it off all week, those are odds I'm not going to take. Although I still say we should have gotten him the knee socks."

"Nah," Kessler replied. "His legs are already girlish enough. We don't want to risk someone mistaking him for a parochial school girl."

Dex chuckled. "Just wait until the cold air hits his ballocks. He'll be shimmying back into his bloody skinny jeans in a hot second."

His teammates laughed.

"There are still seven games left in the season, rookie," Coach Gibson called to Kane. "Before you go hiring Lloyds of London to insure those legs of yours, why don't you concentrate on keeping your punting percentage first in the league. After the season you're free to borrow some of Fletcher's wax for your glamour shots."

Luke and Trey laughed even harder.

Merrit shushed her husband, gesturing to their sleeping son. Andi brushed her hand over Harper's head where it rested in her lap. The little girl's stirring ceased. Beside her, Dex shifted in annoyance, mumbling something obscene just under his breath. She patted his thigh.

"Had enough Bro-time, I take it?" Andi quietly asked her husband even though she knew he enjoyed having his friends in Scotland supporting him.

"Aye." His eyes darkened with arousal. "I'm looking forward to getting back to some privacy." He whispered before kissing the tip of her nose. "Not to mention, our own bed."

She snuggled in closer. "I don't know. I kind of enjoyed getting creative so your mother wouldn't hear us."

His fingers dug into her hip. "I'll take you on a proper honeymoon after the Super Bowl."

She had to look away, resting her head on his shoulder before his hot gaze melted her sweater right off.

"Or we could just go back to Scotland after the season."

He sighed. "It that's what you want. But the weather that time of year won't be any better than Wisconsin's."

"That doesn't matter. The important thing is that we'd be home with your family."

Family.

She finally had one. He brushed a kiss over the top of her head, likely because he understood this was about her need to belong as much as it was about his need to reconnect. While she was content to be heading back to the only place she'd ever lived, she felt she'd left her home in Scotland just as much as he had. At least his family would be coming to Milwaukee for the holidays. It wouldn't be too long before they were together again.

Thirty minutes later, after customs had cleared the plane, they were disembarking through the gate at Mitchell airport reserved for private planes and charters. The early morning was cold and raw with rain. Andi shivered.

Dex leaned down to whisper in her ear. "We'll be home soon enough and I will warm you up, love."

But the cold wasn't what had her trembling. Hurrying down the hall, her rolling bag clicking along the tile floor, was none other than Jade. Andi nearly tripped over her own feet when she spied Agent Figueroa striding purposefully beside her. But it was the person reluctantly bringing up the rear that made the room slowly spin.

Kenny.

"Welcome home everyone," Jade sang out cheerfully.

Too bad for her, her enthusiasm wasn't reciprocated.

"What are you doing here, Jade?" Trey demanded, stepping in front of Andi and Dex. Luke did the same, both players' innate instinct to protect their friend on full display. Kane sidled up beside his teammates and adopted a menacing stance—at least as menacing as he could look in a kilt with an oversized University of Oklahoma hoodie draped over it.

Dex didn't seem to notice the human shield his friends had formed. His gaze was locked onto Agent Figueroa. "What the bloody hell is all this?"

. "I'm so glad you asked that, Declan." Jade stepped forward only to have her path blocked by Kane. She cast a disdainful look at his outfit and huffed a breath. "I'm here with my friends to make a citizen's arrest."

Trey snorted. "For fuck's sake, Jade. Whatever vendetta you think you have with Andi and Dex should be with me. Leave them alone."

Jade tossed her hair over her shoulder. "This isn't a vendetta,

Trey. It's a crime. And you need to get over yourself. Not everything is about you."

"I don't have time for this woman's bloody jibber-jabber," Dex exclaimed. "I was under the impression that your investigation into our marriage was completed, Agent Figueroa."

The agent gestured to Jade. "Her father plays racquet ball with my boss. Apparently, the U.S. Attorney wants the case re-opened based on new evidence." He lifted his shoulders in a weary shrug. "I warned you, Andi, this would not end well. The quick pay-off of your student loan debt is a huge red flag."

The ominous feeling that dogged her for most of her life was suddenly back with a vengeance, and it was doing all kinds of painful things to Andi's insides.

"You'll address my wife properly, Figueroa," Dex growled. "And whatever beef you seem to have, discuss it with me."

The agent sighed. "Then perhaps we should discuss you paying a woman you'd never met before to marry you so you wouldn't be deported."

Coach Gibson stepped between Dex and the ICE Agent. "That's a bold statement to make about one of my players," he accused. "You had better have some damn good proof."

Andi cringed. She'd forgotten they had an audience. Their friends were going to be so disappointed when they learned the truth.

"Of course we have proof. Thanks to my brilliant detective work." Jade aimed a smug look at Andi. "While you were pulling one over on everyone across the pond, I made a little trip to Las Vegas where I met poor, jilted Kenny."

The room spun again. Were it not for Dex's arm anchoring her to his body, she might have sunk to the floor and dissolved into a pile of broken dreams.

"Your former lover has been very forthcoming An—Miss Larsen," Agent Figueroa added.

Her stomach rolled at the agent's announcement. She had never loved Kenny the way she loved Dex.

"Mrs. Fletcher." Dex annunciated the two words clearly, but there was no mistaking the threatening tone. "Her legal name is Andrea Faith Fletcher."

The room grew still for a long moment until Jade huffed behind the agent.

"It doesn't matter what her name is," she snapped. "She's lying about knowing you before you were married. And the only reason she agreed to marry you was because you paid her seventy thousand dollars to do so." With a cat-ate-the-canary grin, she gestured at Kenny. "And your friend Kenny here is going to testify to that fact."

Dex and his teammates redirected their intimidating stares to a wide-eyed Kenny.

"I'm not testifying to anything." Kenny crossed his arms over his chest. "I'm here as an uncooperative witness. I'm taking the fifth."

"You can't do that!" Jade whirled on him. "Tell him, Agent Figueroa."

The ICE agent mumbled something under his breath. Despite the fact his own body was stiff with tension, Dex's fingers gently caressed Andi's shoulder letting her know she was not alone. And she wasn't. Not any longer. Her feelings of inadequacy evaporated at his touch. She drew on the strength Dex's love provided her and straightened her spine.

"Why are you here then, Kenny?"

"I only came because I needed to talk to you, Andi." He moved toward her, only to have Kane step into his path. He took a wary step back. "You blocked my texts and my calls. Even after I wrote to you, you blew me off."

Was he kidding?

"You stole my identity and used it to borrow seventy thousand dollars, Kenny. What more did you want from me?"

He dropped his head, but not far enough that she couldn't see the woeful expression in his eyes. Too bad for him that look didn't have the power over her it used to.

"What I did was wrong. I know that now."

"*Now?*" Andi couldn't believe her ears. "You know that *now?*"

"I know you don't believe me, but I was going to pay it back. I swear it." Kenny crossed his heart with his finger. "I still intend to. That's what I wanted to tell you. I have a plan. I laid it out in my letters. I never meant to hurt you, Andi."

The sound of Jade's Stuart Weitzman boot heel loudly connecting with the tile floor had everyone turning their attention her way.

"This is not happening," she ground out through clenched teeth. "People need to learn that U.S. citizenship is not for sale. Marriage fraud is punishable with a two hundred fifty thousand dollar fine and up to five years in prison. And you," she pointed a shaky finger in Andi's direction. "You can face additional time for visa fraud and harboring an alien, not to mention making false statements, to name a few. You're both going to pay the price for this."

Kane scoffed. "Did you look that up yourself? Or did daddy help you?"

The sound coming from Jade's mouth was not the least bit ladylike. She pulled a folded-up piece of paper and envelope from the pocket of her jacket. "We don't need this loser's testimony. I still have his letter." She sneered at Andi. "You should be more protective of your love notes."

The missing letter. Jade must have snared it the day at the Growlers headquarters when she'd accidently dumped her backpack. That explained how she found out about Kenny in the first place. A cold dread settled over her, the weight of it robbing her of breath. She had no idea what information the letter even contained. Would it be enough to prosecute them?

Dex's fingers stilled against her skin. "What's the game here, Figueroa?" he demanded.

"Well—"

The agent never finished his thought. Kenny rushed Jade,

snatched the letter from her fingertips and began tearing it into pieces.

"Nooooo!" she screeched.

Kenny ignored her, shoving pieces of the letter into his mouth. Kane and Luke jumped in, grabbing bits of paper and swallowing them as well. Jade, her face nearly purple with rage, launched herself at Kenny. But Trey was quicker, grabbing her by the waist and holding her against his body until she ceased struggling.

"This ends here and now, Jade," Trey said.

Jade was breathing hard, but the fight seemed to be all out of her.

"I'm taking you home now," he murmured softly to her. "You'll tell your father you were mistaken and we are all going to forget this ever happened."

She gulped in a lungful of air before abruptly shaking off Trey's arms. Turning on her heel, she grabbed her carryon and strutted away, chin high.

Trey blew out an exasperated breath. "I'll make sure she gets home without causing any more trouble."

Coach Gibson nodded. "Good idea."

"Aye. Thanks." Dex exchanged a fist bump with his friend.

"Well." Agent Figueroa pulled his overcoat more tightly around him. "I guess I'll let my superiors know the evidence didn't pan out. Congratulations. You got away with one." He touched his finger to his brow in mock salute before following Jade and Trey out of the gate area.

Andi sagged against Dex in relief. Exhaling heavily, he buried his face in her neck. Kane let out a whoop before coughing up the remains of the paper in his mouth. Coach slapped him on the shoulder.

"That was a bold move," he said his punter. "But if you'd choked and died before the season was over, I would have had to kick your ass."

Luke donned a broad grin. "I knew you weren't lucky enough to convince a woman as lovely as Andi to marry your sorry Scottish arse, Fletcher," he teased. "You *did* win her in a poker game." He winked at Andi. "Didn't he?"

She laughed as Dex's arms tightened around her.

"Aye, something like that," he said. "And I'd do it all again in a heartbeat."

She twisted her head to look at him. Dex's warm smile went a long way toward settling her nerves.

"I don't regret a thing. Marrying you was the best thing that ever happened to me, lass. I never thought I could be as happy as I am right now. With you. I love you, lass. Nothing that happens next is going to change that."

Her lips trembled beneath his when he kissed her softly.

Kenny's throat clearing scattered some of her bliss. For a moment, she'd forgotten he was even there.

"Look, Andi," he began. "I never meant to hurt you. You have to believe me. I love you." At Dex's low growl, his eyes grew wide. "Well, not anymore. I mean . . ." He struggled to find his words. "I'll always love you, Andi, but not in the way you need." His eyes darted to Dex before quickly landing on her again. "You seem happy. I'm really glad you found someone who puts that glow on your face. You deserve it. You really do. That's all I wanted to say to you. That and I'm sorry."

His sincerity had her heart squeezing. As angry as she was at his poor life choices, they still shared a history. Andi had just grown up faster, that was all. Of course, it remained to be seen whether he'd actually grown up at all. Still, he'd come all this way . . .

"Thank you for that, Kenny." She was by no means ready to forgive him, but if she acknowledged he was trying, then perhaps they could both move on.

Dex's fingers began to dance on her shoulder again, their firm pressure reassuring her.

Kenny's face relaxed into a sloppy smile. "I knew you couldn't hate me, Andi." He tried closing the distance between them again.

She arched a warning eyebrow at him and he stopped.

"I meant it when I said I'm going to pay you back. All of it."

Biting her tongue, she didn't bother mentioning that what he intended and what he actually did were often two different things. He seemed to sense her doubt.

"I'm serious." He notched his chin up. "I got a job. At one of those warehouse stores. I even have benefits and the potential for education money in the future. No more relying on someone else. I'm going to make something of myself. Just like you."

Words failed her.

"Stay away from the tables," her husband warned.

Kenny nodded. "I know. I joined gambler's anonymous. My sponsor was the one who helped me get the job."

"That's . . . that's wonderful, Kenny." Because what else could she say?

"Yeah, well, I just wanted you to know. If you're ever back in Vegas, I hope you'll look me up." He lifted his hand in a brief wave before turning to leave.

Andi's breath hitched. "Kenny," she called after him. He glanced back, a hopeful look on his face.

"Good luck," was all she could manage to say.

Dex pulled her in closer.

The smile Kenny gave her was filled with apology. With another wave, he was gone.

"What did I miss?" Merrit emerged from the restroom with Max and Harper. Her gaze darted from one person to the other.

Laughter bubbled up from deep inside Andi, and soon the rest of their entourage was laughing, too.

"What?" Merrit demanded.

Her husband took their sleepy son from her arms. "Long story. I'll tell you in the car." With a wave he steered his family toward the main terminal. "I'll see you boys at practice in the morning."

"I don't know about you, Kessler," Kane said. "But I could really use something to wash that nasty paper down with."

The wide receiver took in the punter's appearance and let out a beleaguered sigh. "I'm just desperate enough to join you even though you're wearing a skirt."

Dex winced at the word "skirt" before exchanging man-hugs with each of his teammates.

"Thank you," Andi said as she kissed them both on the cheek.

"The Growlers are a family," Kessler replied. "And you're one of the family now."

The two men headed toward baggage claim.

Andi hefted her backpack onto her shoulder. "Well, that was . . . fun."

With a weary laugh, Dex draped his arm across her shoulders. "Not quite the fun I had in mind, but we are going to make up for that. Let's go home, Mrs. Fletcher."

"You want to go back to Scotland?"

He turned her so her chest was pressed against his. Gently cradling her chin with his fingers, he pressed his lips to the corners of her mouth. "Scotland was where I was born and where my—*our*—family lives. But my home, my home is wherever you are, Andi. You are my home."

And then he kissed her until her limbs were weak again, but this time for a very different reason.

"Then by all means," she whispered when he eventually dragged his lips away. "Take me home, Mr. Fletcher."

EPILOGUE

"HAPPY CHRISTMAS, LASS."

Andi sighed with contentment as she burrowed deeper beneath the covers, her sated limbs seeking the heat of Dex's warm, naked body. The draperies were open, giving them an unobstructed view of the early morning snow trying, and failing, to blanket the rough surf of Lake Michigan. She snuggled closer, pressing her back against his chest.

"Mmm, I think *happy* may be too tame a word for what I'm feeling right now."

It was true. Even in her wildest longings, she never imagined the bone deep joy she would feel having all her dreams come true. Of course, a lot of that joy had to do with the man whose body was cocooning hers at the moment. He was so much more than she ever dared hope for.

He brushed his lips along her shoulder. "Aye, lass. I can't remember enjoying a Christmas as much as I have this one." His fingers traced lazy circles on her thigh.

"That's because no one ever gave you a Millennium Falcon ornament for your tree," she teased.

His booming laughter had quickly become one of her favorite sounds. Ever since their trip to Scotland, he'd become lighter and less resolute. She'd fallen in love with the old Dex—the white knight who'd let guilt dictate his life. But she adored this version of him so much more. So did her body judging by the way her insides were turning to jelly at his touch.

"All those years as a young lad, I was so eager to jump out of bed Christmas morn and open presents from some old fat guy with a beard." He nibbled on her neck. "What a fool I was. Now, all I want to do is stay beneath these sheets and bury myself in the best present of all. One who is certainly much sexier."

With a laugh, Andi wriggled around so they were facing one another. "You just did that not more than twenty minutes ago." She touched her nose to his. "As much as the idea appeals to me, we have plans for the day. Starting with brunch with your parents. We're hosting, remember?"

His chest rumbled with an annoyed growl while his talented fingers found their way to her breasts. "Sometimes I ken ya love my family more than you do me, lass."

"That's not true." The last word came out as a lusty sigh when his fingers wandered lower on her body.

Stormy gray eyes, dark with passion dared her. "Prove it."

And because she was halfway there already, she did. Twice. It was Christmas after all.

"MERRY CHRISTMAS!" Harper cried as she wrapped her arms around Andi's knees.

The Growlers were hosting a lavish dinner for the team and their families. The final game of the season was in two days. They needed a win to make the playoffs. Despite the pressure, the mood at the party was festive and relaxed.

Just like at the picnic, management had gone all out. When Andi and Dex arrived with his parents, and Annis, it was like stepping into one of those sappy Hallmark Christmas movies with the explosion of decorations, the festive lighting, and children running amok feeding, *holy hell*, live reindeer. There was even a hired troupe of carolers.

"Merry Christmas to you, too." Andi lifted the little girl into her arms. "Did Santa bring you lots of fun toys?"

Harper nodded. She had begun to speak more in public, but she was still a child of few words. Not that Andi minded, because Harper gave great hugs.

"You're a natural with children." Dex's mother grinned eagerly.

Her son groaned.

Annis let out an exasperated sigh. "Ma, you promised."

"Time for us to hit the bar, Rose," Dex's father interceded, linking his arm through his wife's. "I'm pretty sure I see a bowl of hot buttered rum with your name on it."

"Great idea, Da. Because a wee dram is going to quiet her." Dex aimed his sarcastic comment in the direction of his father's retreating back.

"Ooo, there's Luke Kessler." Annis smoothed her hands over the hips of her velvet dress. "I ken I'll just wander over and wish him a happy Christmas."

She was off before Dex could react. But that didn't mean her brother wasn't going to go Highlander at any moment.

"What the bloody—"

Andi wrapped her fingers around his biceps, giving it a gentle squeeze. "Language, Declan." She gestured with her chin to Harper. "Little ears."

With a wide-eyed stare, Harper bit her lip. Dex's body was still tense beneath her hand, but he remained where he was. *Thank heavens for small favors.*

"There's no need to make a scene. They flirted a little in Scotland. It was harmless." Probably the wrong choice of words on her part because Dex's nostrils were now beginning to flare. Andi couldn't help it. She laughed. Harper joined in.

"She's not old enough to be flirting," he bit out.

"This is the twenty-first century, Highlander," Andi countered. "Twenty-three is now considered old enough to flirt."

His pained expression had the mirth bubbling up inside her again. Rather than laugh at him, she leaned in and brushed a kiss over his lips.

"Relax," she murmured.

Harper mimicked her actions, leaning in and planting a hand on his cheek. "Relax," she repeated.

Dex's eyes narrowed and he curled his lip at the child. A moment later he'd snatched her from Andi's arms and was tossing her high in the air. Harper's peals of delight filled the room. They were followed by Dex's own belly laugh. Andi's throat grew tight at the scene playing out in front of her.

Their relationship had come about in such an unorthodox way, they'd never discussed kids. Motherhood had never been something she'd let herself dream of. Not the way her life had been going. The goal was always to graduate and get her business off the ground.

But that was before fate intervened.

She was married to a man who loved her. And two weeks ago, she'd proudly donned a cap and gown to celebrate the awarding of her business degree. As wonderful as the achievement was, the ceremony was made all the more sweeter knowing Dex, his family, and so many of her friends—old and new—were in the auditorium cheering her on. She'd gone from a party of one to a party of many.

And why shouldn't that party include children? Given the adoring way Dex was gazing down at Harper, she was pretty sure he'd agree.

"You're a little minx." Dex tickled Harper beneath her chin, resulting in a new round of giggles. He planted a sloppy kiss on the little girl's forehead just as Merrit and Coach Gibson arrived.

"Are you trying to tickle my daughter to death, Fletcher?" Wearing an adoring smile, the coach rescued his daughter from Dex's arms.

"Aye." Dex tweaked the girl's cheek. "She started it."

Coach Gibson snorted. "Coach Kelly and I have something we want to run by you. Can I steal him away, Andi?"

Merrit arched an eyebrow. "You promised to leave the game planning back in your office."

The coach donned the same impish smile as his daughter's. "It's a recruiting question. And it will only take a minute." He dropped kiss on his wife's lips. "We'll be right back."

"Something tells me Santa isn't responsible for the fabulous bath soaps and lotions in the WAG's gift bags," Merrit commented as they watched their husbands walk away.

Andi couldn't keep the smile off her face. "Mrs. Ciaciura commissioned them. She even helped pick out the scents. And, she put me in touch with a venture capitalist group that supports female owned companies. I have a meeting with them after the first of the year."

"That's fantastic." Merrit hugged her. "And good for you for following your dream."

"It is fantastic." Daniel was already negotiating a lease for a small store front around the corner from Shear Envy. Shaina was graduating early and would come on board as the marketing director. "Everything is falling into place."

"Uh, oh. That sounds a little ominous." Trey Van Horn strolled up beside Andi. "What are you two lovely ladies plotting?"

Merrit laughed. "If we told you, where would the surprise be?" Her eyes grew wide before she make a mad dash across the room. "Max! No!"

Trey and Andi watched as the coach's young son tossed a football into one of the ice sculptures, nearly sending it toppling to the floor.

"Kid has potential," he said with a trace of awe punctuating his words.

Andi studied the quarterback, recalling the conversation they'd had weeks before. It was a shame he was so determined not to marry.

"You know, just because your parents set such a bad example doesn't mean you can't have a successful relationship," she couldn't help saying. "No one wants to be alone."

Something looking a lot like regret settled into his eyes before he quickly chased it away. His lips turned up into the artificial grin he reserved for press conferences and photo shoots. "Who says I'm alone, Andi?"

She scoffed. "If you keep picking man-eaters like Jade, you're destined for unhappiness."

He laughed. "I can't help it if the good ones are already taken." He placed a soft kiss on her cheek. "And as for Jade, she landed on her feet. Apparently, her wish has come true. She's going to be a contestant on *The Bachelor*."

Andi was stunned into silence.

"How many times do I have to tell you to keep your bloody paws off my wife?" Dex speared his friend with a scathing look while wrapping his arm around her waist.

Trey held up his hands. "Technically, it was only my lips. And she protested the entire time." He had the nerve to wink at her.

"Argh. See that it doesn't happen again," Dex commanded.

"I make no promises," Trey teased. "But before you take me apart bodily, I have shoes for you. My sponsors went a little overboard with the gifts this year. I've got twenty new pairs of sneakers you can have."

"Excellent," Dex replied. "Kessler and Jacobs donated several pairs each."

Andi huffed. "I don't understand why you keep encouraging Kenny."

For some reason, Dex had tracked down the weasel, then made it his pet project to ensure his success in life. Starting with giving him the athletic shoes Dex and his teammates were gifted from companies hoping to sign them to a sponsorship deal. Kenny's eBay business had never been more robust.

"I'm not encouraging him, lass. He's working for me. Kenny sells the shoes, keeps a small percentage for himself, and donates the rest of the profits to the Vey Center." He turned her in his arms and leaned his forehead down, gently resting it against hers. "Think of it as community service. He stole seventy thousand dollars from you. Now he's paying it back."

She fiddled with the lapels of his suit jacket. "I just don't get why he's so important to you."

"Don't you, lass?" he asked softly. He lifted her chin with his finger, guiding her gaze up to his. "Without Kenny, I wouldnae have the love of my life."

Her heart stuttered in her chest.

"And while he dinnae know it, lass, twas the best gift ever."

The back of her eyes burned at his words. Stretching up on her toes, she brought her lips to his. Their kiss was modest and sweet, but it held the promise of more. *So much more.*

I HOPE YOU enjoyed Andi and Dex's story. Look for more Milwaukee Growler books soon. In the meantime, check out my Out of Bounds series featuring the Baltimore Blaze football team where you can read Heath and Merrit's story, A NUMBER'S GAME for free.

Out of Bounds

A NUMBERS GAME (novella)

GAME ON

FOOLISH GAMES

RISKY GAME

SLEEPING WITH THE ENEMY

Second Chances

BACK TO BEFORE

ALL THEY EVER WANTED

Firefighters of Montana

SMOLDER

***

Men of the Secret Service

RECIPE FOR DISASTER

SHOT IN THE DARK

BETWEEN LOVE AND HONOR

***

Magnolia Bay

HOLIDAY AT MAGNOLIA BAY

For all the news on upcoming books, and some fun giveaways,

Don't forget to get social!

Website: https://www.tracysolheim.com/

Facebook: https://www.facebook.com/TracySolheimBooks

Twitter: https://twitter.com/TracyKSolheim

Instagram: https://www.instagram.com/tracyksolheim/?hl=en

Pinterest: https://www.pinterest.com/solheim0062/

Goodreads: https://www.goodreads.com/author/show/6519003.Tracy_Solheim

BoobBub: https://www.bookbub.com/authors/tracy-solheim

ABOUT THE AUTHOR

After years of writing reports and testimony for Congress, **Tracy Solheim** decided to put her creative talents to better use. A two-time finalist for the Maggie Award for Excellence and recipient of the 2020 Georgia Author of the Year Award, she's the *USA Today* best-selling author of contemporary sports romance, romantic suspense, and small-town second chance novels. Tracy lives in the heart of SEC country, also known as the suburbs of Atlanta, with her husband, two adult children who frequently show up at dinner time, and a neurotic Labrador retriever who keeps her company while she writes. See what she's up to at TracySolheim.com.